BALANCE OF FATE
BY
SAMUEL PETER

Chapter 1

"I wonder what spell could possibly be cast that would allow an ordinary person to
mimic your skills. Watching you is almost beyond belief."
Ryson Acumen shook his head and replied with a laugh. "This said by a wizard that is
right now flying over my head."
Indeed, Enin was quite literally flying just above the tree tops, but the delver's
response was lost on the wizard. Swooping and gliding through the air, Enin continued to
peer through the leafless branches as he studied the delver from nearly every angle.
Trying to categorize Ryson's movements and match them to a potential spell, however,
proved much more difficult than flying and even more elusive than the cold wind that
blew through the clear blues skies of this day. Watching the delver closely, the wizard
marveled at how Ryson could leap, run, twist and turn—basically dance without rest or
pause through, over and under the myriad of obstacles the forest presented.
As he often did, Enin began to speak out loud, more to himself than anyone else, as he
considered the purpose of his desire.
"So many different aspects, even animal tendencies, I see perfect qualities of nature
within you. You move with the grace of so many different animals at once, it would be
almost impossible for me to try and match your powers with any spell, or even series of
spells, that might match the particular skills of a single animal. I mean really, you move
like a cat but without the predatory aim. You dart about like a fish in the sea, but without
the haphazard defensive response."
"Sounds like a catfish," Ryson offered playfully.
The wizard ignored him. "And it's not just simulating the advantages of different
animals, it goes well beyond that. There's definitely an instinctive quality in the way you
move, instinctive like a horse that gallops effortlessly just because it can. And it goes
beyond animal instinct, you have the very essence of nature within you. You have a
quality of the wind about you. Your   you can change
directions with ease. The problem i   a wind definition would
be very difficult. No, wind movement   y. The problem is
compounded by the fact that you crea   ..azes me to this moment,

so I wouldn't even begin to know how to add an element of fire for lift. The power that
allows you to move the way you do seems to be beyond the normal elements of nature."

Enin willed himself forward at a greater pace. He was having a difficult time keeping
up with the delver at these speeds even though his path was clear of all obstacles while
Ryson faced a continuous barrage of trees and underbrush that filled this section of Dark
Spruce Forest. Still, Enin remained focused on his spell considerations and his desire to
match Ryson's speed forced him forward at a faster pace.

"There are so many different facets to magical energies—wind, fire, water, air,
shadow, illusion, light—I find it amazing to see so many close connections with your
abilities, yet I still can't define with accuracy even one component. I believe there is
definitely an inherent connection to the land, but it's even harder for me to pinpoint that
one. Some science-loving egghead once told me about magnetism and how it might help
explain the magical energies. Well, this man's ramblings went on and on with no clear
point but—."

"Not like yours of course," Ryson chuckled to himself.

Enin ignored the implication. "The point is he just didn't want to admit that magic existed, which kind of threw his whole perspective out of balance. I mean really, how can you deny that magic exists when you are staring into the face of a mountain shag or a river rogue? While his overall theory was truly absurd, he did have some interesting points. I always have to keep in mind that the physical world does intertwine with the magical energies. It wouldn't surprise me if somehow or other the idea of magnetism is somehow linked with your powers. The land has its own magical properties and they seem to be present in you as well."

Ryson did not stop moving, but he did call out louder this time with the obvious intention of being heard. He found this consideration interesting and didn't want the wizard to dismiss his question. "You've said that word before when you analyzed me, 'powers'. Sounds to me as if you think I'm using magic like you do. Is that what you think?"

"Like me?" the wizard sounded almost baffled at first. "No, no, no—not like me at all." With that said, the wizard floated down into the trees and closer to ground level so that he could carry on this new conversation more personally. He continued to fly as it was the best way he could keep up with the delver, but he felt the discussion at hand was now more sensitive and he felt the need to be closer to Ryson before he spoke. "One of the most amazing things about the magic is how different it affects each one of us as well as each race. You know what is most amazing about the delvers?"

"Enlighten me."

"You don't use the magic, you are the magic."

Ryson raised an eyebrow at the wizard. "Come again? I am the magic. I have no idea what that means." The delver continued moving, albeit at a much slower pace to accommodate the wizard that now had to navigate through the trees as well. Ryson didn't want to move too far away from Enin mostly because he wanted to hear this explanation.

The wizard heaved a heavy breath as he tried to place his words in a context that Ryson could understand. He didn't feel he had to speak down to the delver, but there was a lack of equal reference points. He understood magic in ways almost no one else in the land could. For him to speak of magic to another, it was almost like explaining music to someone totally tone deaf. He grabbed on the story of legend that ended up being so consequential to Ryson and the return of magic to Uton.

"When Ingar made that sphere of his," Enin began, "it was supposed to remove all the

magical energy in the land. It did, but only that energy that was free. It could not remove
energy that was kept internally. That's why magic casters were afraid to cast spells after
the sphere was created. Once they let it out of their being, it was free to be absorbed by
the sphere. Magic that is held to, or stored within, was safe from the sphere as long as it is
not cast free. You follow this logic, yes?"

"Yes."

"Very good. Keeping with that thought, you should be able to follow that magic is
absorbed in different ways by different creatures. Some can store great quantities, some
are incapable of storing any at all. Some are very susceptible to spells, and others are very
resistant. These qualities can vary greatly in degree. For whatever reason, I was given the
gift to do more that just store and use magical energy. I have a very deep and personal
connection to it. I can store vast amounts internally and I can draw energies from various
sources from great distances."

"Won't argue that," Ryson allowed. "Doesn't answer the question, though, which is
what does that have to do with me?"

"Not just you, all delvers. You don't store the magic to use it. You don't absorb it
from the land, sea and air. Well, I shouldn't say that, that's not exactly true. You have the
ability to be a magic caster, I've told you that before. You could use the magic in spells,
but that's not what I'm talking about. I'm talking about the abilities that make you a
delver, those qualities that set you apart from other races. Didn't you ever really stop to
think about how you can do the things you do? It's magical power, but you don't cast it.
You are born with it. The magic is a very part of you, like your skin."

"You're kidding right?"

"How else would you explain the way you move, how you can travel so far so fast and
without tiring the way no one else in the land can?"

"Elves can move pretty quickly," Ryson offered.

"You and I both know an elf is no match for a delver in what we're talking about."

"But elves are quicker than dwarves and humans."

"Indeed they are, and the magic affects them differently as well." Enin shook his head
as if flustered. He was not making his point as well as he wished. "To a degree, you are
right. Elves are also born with the magic within them. That is why elves can do the things
they do. They move lightly and quickly, see for great distances, so yes, you are right. I
shouldn't have been so quick to dismiss that. Elves are born with the magic, but not quite
like delvers, not to the same extent, that's what I meant. Delvers are born with a great
deal of magical energy inherent in their bodies. It doesn't have to be used as spells, but it
gives you certain powers—ah abilities."

Ryson frowned for a moment as he continued through his own path in the forest. "If
all this is true, then why didn't the sphere wipe out the elves and the delvers when it was
created by Ingar? I'm not talking about the poison that was killing the elves. I'm talking
about making the magic disappear. Dark creatures disappeared. Magic-casters
disappeared. Why didn't the delvers and the elves all cease to exist when the sphere
captured all the magic and was buried in Sanctum?"

"It's like I said," Enin answered, "the sphere could only capture free magic and it
captured every shred of free magic it could. The magic that is within delvers, and to a
lesser extent within elves, is never free. It is created at your birth and stays within you at
all times. Dark creatures need free magic in the air to remain in this realm. Magic-casters
need to capture and absorb magic to continue casting spells. Delvers and elves don't need

magic free across the land to exist in this realm, but that doesn't mean the magic isn't part
of them."

"So you're saying I'm a magical being."

"That is exactly what I'm saying and exactly why I'm trying to determine if I could
cast a spell that would allow a non-delver to move as a delver."

"You want to duplicate me?"

"Not you," Enin explained, "just your powers. Now where was I?" The wizard floated
back up to a higher level to watch the delver move from a different perspective without
having to worry about crashing into a tree. He began speaking about spells again as if he
never departed from his earlier thoughts. "You flow like water, but even that's not a fair
assessment. Water is fluid and thus its movements tend to be loose in scope and direction.
Still, when you splash water, droplets can dart in well defined paths. If I were to include

water qualities in the spell, it would have to be that of a well defined stream as opposed
to a massive wave. Perhaps more ice than water."

Enin suddenly grumbled with frustration. "This is most perplexing. I believe I can
easily simulate part of the things you do with one spell, but that would represent only a
small portion of your delver qualities. I could give someone speed, and maybe stamina,
but not the same grace. I could give balance and athleticism but not the same awareness
of the surroundings. No, to duplicate your abilities with any degree of accuracy, it would
require a series of spells and most likely they would have the affect of canceling each
other out."

"I guess if you need the skills of a delver, you'll just have to call on me. Just won't be
able to conjure one up by waving your hand over some bug or something. Shame."

"It is indeed a shame. Your movements are quite extraordinary. To duplicate them
would allow for transportation methods that might be unheard of. Imagine if we could
give a team of horses the movement capabilities of a delver. Think of it."

"I think I'd rather fly," Ryson responded.

Enin shook his head strenuously. "Horses flying? No, that would not be a good thing."

"Not the horses, me. I've watched you cast that flying spell and I've always been
envious."

"The way you move and you are envious of me?" the wizard asked revealing a great
deal of surprise.

"You can fly, so yes I am. I always wondered why you don't cast that spell on others.
You know, allow some of the guard at Burbon to fly around on patrol. They could scout
the area better."

"I can't cast it on someone else. It's purely a matter of control. The spell is almost
constantly and instantaneously altered with my own thoughts and movements. It has to
be. If I cast it on someone else, the results would be disastrous. Now I can make you
float, and I can move you from one area to another by levitating you, as long as you don't
resist me, but I can't give you the same power of flight that I have right now. As I said,
the spell requires constant and instantaneous updating. The moment you wanted to move
in a new direction and the spell wasn't corrected properly for that desire, you'd probably
end up rocketing beyond the horizon."

"That would be bad."

"Indeed, like horses flying," Enin added.

Ryson shrugged. "Ok, so I can't fly, doesn't mean I don't want to."

"But you can fly." The wizard offered without a hint of doubt. "Not with a flying spell

like I do, but if you want to experience the sensation of flying, that can be done under
your own power."

Ryson pulled to a slow stop. "Explain that one to me. You're telling me I can fly?
Like a bird?"

"Almost exactly like a bird, and I can show you as long as you understand you must
adjust your perception."

"Once more, explain please."

Enin looked about the landscape over the trees. He quickly spotted an area that suited
his purpose. He pointed in that direction as he called down to the delver.

"Ok, I need to move you to open ground. There is a nice area over to the Southwest.
Do you want to run there or should I levitate you there?"

"I'll get there myself," Ryson stated with certainty. "When you levitate me, I always feel like I'm about to be dropped on my head."

"Hmmph. I would only drop you if you resist me. I could transport a hundred people or more at once if I had to, as long as they just allowed me to move them. Nobody likes being moved, though, and they always complain. They start fighting it and then they start falling. It's not me, it's them."

"I'll meet you there," Ryson stated with a degree of finality.

"Fine."

Ryson took off in a blur and stopped in the middle of a clearing. He looked over the level ground that extended on a wide path beyond the edge of a nearby stream. He realized it was a flood plain which would explain the lack of trees in this localized area. The ground was hard, mostly frozen from the colder night temperatures. A few areas thawed slightly from the midday sun, but even these patches remained firm. For the most part, the ground was comprised of matted down, dormant high grass. Several rocks littered the area, but not enough to worry about.

Enin flew into the clearing and down closer to the delver as there were no longer any trees to impede his path. "Now first, you have to remove all expectations of what you think flying will be like. Can you do that?"

"I can try."

"Well, try hard. Next, survey the surroundings so you have a good idea of what you are going to be running over."

"I thought I was going to be flying, not running."

Enin sighed in exasperation. "You're not trying very hard."

"Oh, sorry. Anyway, I already gave the ground a once over. Looks clear to me."

"Excellent. Now, I need you to set yourself up at one end of the clearing so you have the entire expanse available for one straight run. Move over to the far northern border of this clearing and face south."

The delver complied with a blur of motion and within a heartbeat stood at the far northern end of the clearing, facing south toward its full expanse.

Enin shouted even though the delver's keen hearing would have allowed him to hear Enin whisper from even this greater distance. "I'm going to cast a wind spell, a small one. It will only create a constant rush of air that will flow into your face. I'm doing that not to give you extra lift or anything like that, so don't try to float on the breeze. I just want to make sure you have the sensation of wind in your face. After I cast the spell, I want you to run into the wind, but not like a delver. I want you to run with long bounding strides that send you as much upward as they do forward. I want you to run with timing

as well, one…two…three… at that pace. It has to be slow, smooth and steady. Do you
understand?"

Ryson nodded.

"While you run, I want you to put your arms out to the side. Don't flap them or
anything silly like that. You're not a bird, so don't act like one. Simply hold them up, but
beyond that, keep them relaxed as possible. Ready?"

Ryson nodded again.

With that, Enin flicked his wrists and two perfect circles of white energy appeared at
his palms. He whispered a few inaudible words and pressed his hands outward. The two

circles of energy flowed out toward the delver, collapsing into the air as a stiff breeze
now pushed forward in their place.

When Ryson felt the flow of air, he did as the wizard asked. He ran due south directly
into the wind. His legs pressed him both forward and upward in what appeared to be a
slow dash of one leap after another. He stretched his arms out to his sides, but kept his
muscles relaxed. As he continued through the clearing, he waited to be lifted high up into
the air. To his disappointment, he never left the ground. When he reached the boundary
of trees at the far end of the clearing, he turned back to Enin.

"What went wrong?"

"Nothing went wrong, that is to say, nothing beyond your perception of what was to
happen. You expected to be soaring above the trees like a bird, yes?"

"Yes."

"I didn't say you had the power to soar above the trees, I said you had the power
within you to realize the sensation of flying. If you consider what you just did, and what a
bird does, you'd realize that you felt what it's like for a bird to fly. A bird must flap its
wings to gain lift and momentum. As it lifts in the air, it can soar for distances without
flapping its wings, but it still must work to some extent to remain airborne for any length
of time. Instead of flapping wings, you propelled yourself with your legs. You left the
ground and remained in the air until you came back to the ground and propelled yourself
up once more. It's the same concept as flying only in shorter bursts and lower to the
ground."

"Well, that's disappointing to say the least," Ryson stated with a dissatisfied tone.

"Disappointing? Nonsense. As far as sensation goes, it is all the same. Perception,
that's all that's different, but you can change your perception. With the wind in your face
and your legs pressing you forward, you feel what the bird feels. As that same wind
rushes past your ears, you hear what the bird hears. As you look to your left and right and
see the landscape pass you by, you see what the bird sees. If instead of the clearing you
ran through the trees, you would know what its like for a bird to soar through branches.
Perception! Focus on it. Understand that what you are doing is no different then what the
bird is doing. The bird is simply lighter so it can stay off the ground longer. It can beat its
wings against the air while you must press your feet against the ground, but in those
moments that your feet have propelled you off the ground and into the air, you are truly
in flight. It may only be for scant moments, but for those moments, as brief as they are,

you are as the bird. Perception."

Ryson frowned.

Enin, however, would not give up. "Give it a try one more time and free your mind of
your expectations as I first asked of you. Feel the wind in your face and look about you
all at once. When you leave the ground, focus on that very instant—not on what will
happen next, not on the fact that you will eventually land, but on that instant that you are
in midair. When you think too far in the future, even a mere instant in the future, you
know you will fall to the ground. If, however, you can focus on a single instant in the
present, then you will not care about what will happen next. You will only know what is
happening now. You are in the air, you are moving, thus you are flying!"

"Alright, I'll give it a try. It's just not what I expected." With that Ryson turned and
took off once more. He concentrated on the moments he was in the air. He felt the wind
in his face and across his outstretched arms. At the very moment he was at the peak of his

elevation off the ground, he finally began to realize what Enin was saying. He was
airborne. He was moving forward. He was, in a fashion, flying.

Enin smiled from a distance and cast another quick spell. This time the air did not
move, but the space around the delver shimmered ever so slightly. The delver appeared to
be caught in suspended animation, but only for a moment. The shimmering effect quickly
dissolved and Ryson again was moving as normal.

"Whoa!" the delver shouted. "What did you just do?"

The wizard smiled broadly. "Let's see, how would I describe it? It was kind of a
floating dimension spell, no, actually more like I suspended time around you. Well, that's
not really it either, because time always marches on. However, you know when an
important event is about to happen and everything sort of slows down around you? Well,
that's what I did for you. That way you could really appreciate that moment you were
gliding across the air, flying if you will."

"Seemed like I was flying forever there for a moment," Ryson replied almost gleefully
as he turned and raced back toward the wizard.

"Barely a few moments, actually, but in your mind those moments were extended.
You were able to think and react and even move as if everything else around you was
placed in a state of slower motion."

"Thank you very much, that was more of what I expected. It really did feel like I was
flying."

"Only because you allowed yourself to perceive beyond what you thought you knew.
When I saw that, I knew you were ready to experience the sensation."

With those words, Ryson suddenly stopped in his tracks. He stood stone still as his
eyes narrowed and his chin lifted slightly into the air.

The delver's reaction was not lost upon the wizard and Enin immediately tried to gain
Ryson's attention. "Can I ask why you are doing that? Well, I know why you're doing
that, you're sensing something. That's obvious, but what is it that you think you're
sensing? Can you describe it?"

At first Ryson appeared to ignore the wizard, he continued to tilt his head from one
side then to the other. His eyes would not fix on anything in the distance and he did not
bother to sniff the wind. Instead, he simply moved his head slowly about as if the skin on
his face could catch something very elusive in the breeze, like a single strand of a spider
web caught on his brow. Finally, he spoke without looking toward Enin, without looking
toward anything at all.

"I don't know… I really don't. It's something magical, that's about all I can say for
sure."

Enin began to question Ryson further, but caught himself and stopped. He grunted
about something inaudibly until he finally spoke with almost guarded words. "I've seen
you like this before over the past few days. The fact that you say it's magical is a serious
consideration. I'm most curious about what you think is the source of this sensation."

"I don't know what to tell you," Ryson offered. "Ever since the sphere was destroyed,
I've always felt the magic. It was new to the land, basically it still is. It seems to be
everywhere and sensing it is a feeling I am getting used to, but this isn't quite the same.
It's powerful, powerful but deceptive. Sometimes I think its hiding, then again I find that
hard to believe. I actually believe that whatever it is, it knows I can sense it right now.

Still, it doesn't care; doesn't try to mask itself beyond whatever it's doing to keep in
secret as it is. I know that doesn't make sense."

"No, that I can understand. Keep going. What else do you feel?"

"Well, what I feel is difficult to put into words. Dry. That's what comes to mind. Not
dry like the desert or dry like thirsty, but still dry. At first I was going to say dread, but
that's not really it. When you dread something, you know it's coming and you hope it
doesn't. Dread is heavy suppressing. This isn't the same. This is more empty than heavy,
but then again empty doesn't quite explain it either. I keep coming back to dry."

"I see." Enin wanted to ask more, but his own attention was quickly pulled in another
direction. With a distinct mutter of dissatisfaction, he quickly turned and peered with
great intent to the Northeast. He lifted his left hand above his shoulder and flicked his
fingers in an odd fashion. Immediately, two snow white circles again danced about his
left hand. They slipped off his fingers into midair, crashed together in an almost powdery
explosion, and disappeared leaving behind a small distortion in the air. Enin focused
deeply into this fist-sized mass of twisted, blurry air.

"Sazar!" he said bluntly. "Must be. Too many creatures to be anyone else this close.
Goblins, a good many of them, a river rogue, a couple of shags, maybe even more than
two, hard to say, a hook hawk, even a rock beetle. Has to be Sazar."

Ryson spoke out with an even but commanding tone. He wanted to be heard by the
wizard and he wanted an immediate answer.

"Where?"

"Pinesway."

"You're sure?"

"Without a doubt. I've cast several web spells near areas that might give us advanced
warning of any movement that might affect Burbon. Pinesway always offered itself as a
staging area for some unpleasant creatures. That's why most of the people abandoned it.
One of the web spells I cast there just sent me a warning. I just cast a sight spell to
connect to it and other web spells I placed in the area. I can see the creatures I described
to you. They are swarming over the town."

A vision of the monsters raiding Pinesway crashed into Ryson's thoughts. He didn't
like what he envisioned. "Can we help?"

"We'd never reach the few that are left in time. The town is mostly deserted, thank
Godson. Those that remain will either escape safely or meet their fate. There's nothing
we can do."

"Nothing at all?"

Enin grimaced. "No. I'm sorry."

Ryson's hands fell to his sides in clenched fists. "I'm really beginning to hate that serp."

Enin heaved another heavy sigh as the bubble of distortion faded before him. "I think we should get back to Burbon. I need to tell Sy what I've seen. I doubt it will be a threat to us at this instant, but he needs to know. I must ask that you allow me to move us both together. If you wanted to, you can run faster than I can fly, but I'm not just going to levitate. I'm going to—hmmmm, how should I say it? The egghead that liked science might state that I was bending space. If that helps you understand, then I'll leave it at that. In essence, I'm going to reduce the distance we have to travel, but we have to move together."

"Whatever you have to do," Ryson allowed.

Chapter 2

Intermittent screams of fear and pain echoed through the shadowed alleys of
Pinesway. Tall grass and abandoned carts muffled the sounds in spots, but there was little
else to cover the sporadic sounds of panic. There was no alarm, no shouts of militia, no
bark of guard dogs—no sound of any organized resistance whatsoever. It was during
broad daylight, yet there were no markets full of suddenly panicked shoppers, no offices
filled with curious clerks, and no stalls busy with concerned laborers. As the few but
unmistakable sounds of sheer terror initially blistered through the streets, a light breeze
scattered dust across the empty roads, very little of anything else stirred.

The bulk of Pinesway's residents abandoned the town immediately after the very first
goblin raid. Those that remained after the initial raid quickly realized that their lack of
numbers now made them an even greater target. When a river rogue staked a territorial
claim at the town's northwestern edge and shags started making frequent appearances to
the south, even the hardy homesteaders that needed little to scratch a living decided to
leave as well. When the dormant season took hold of the small town, the resident
population was mostly made up of vagrants, petty bandits, opportunistic thieves,
homeless wanderers, and a handful of stubborn citizens that refused to leave their homes
for any reason.

Joel Portsmith was a citizen of the latter. He was considered an old cantankerous man
by his neighbors before the magic returned to Uton. He didn't care. He didn't particularly
like people. He worked his whole life at the docks of towns along the western shores. He
saved his money, found a woman that could stand him enough to marry him, and the two
of them eventually moved inland, away from the ocean he never truly cared for. He built
his house with his own hands, and then served as a volunteer in the town's militia as a
way to defend his home. His woman was killed in that first goblin raid. He buried her in
his backyard when others loaded their carts to run for Connel or some other larger city.
He wouldn't run—he would stay, no matter what.

Joel let the exterior of his own home appear to be as abandoned as those around it. He
broke boards with nails in them and scattered them around the porch. He didn't plan to sit
out there as a target for a goblin arrow, so why should he care if the new decorations
made the porch more of a hazard than a pleasant place to relax. He broke the front gate in

a locked position so it was near impossible to move. Only he knew that the section of
fence two posts down to the left could swing open for easy entry. He let the weeds and
grass grow long, nailed shut the windows, and threw broken glass about the front walk.
He pulled the shutters closed and nailed them in place. He left the front door barred from
the inside and out. A walk-down basement door was sufficient for his use, so the loss of
the front entrance was inconsequential.

From the street, his house looked dark, decaying and long devoid of any real care, as if
it had been the town eyesore even before the other residents abandoned their homes. And
that was exactly what he wanted. A clean, well-kept looking house was an invitation to
other less desirable visitors to this town, visitors he had no desire to entertain. Let the
vagrants and bandits choose another home to camp in.

Inside, however, the house was clean and simply organized. He had everything he
needed to survive—warm clothes, utensils, blankets, comfortable places to sit and sleep,

as well as a few diversions such as books, wood carving tools, and a spy glass to keep an
eye on the surrounding streets. Those supplies he would run out of over time—food,
water, and wood for a fire in a small stove that he would only burn at night—these items
he could collect easily from other abandoned buildings in town or from the nearby forest.
Since he didn't mind being alone, he was content to stay and live with the threat of river
rouges, shags, and goblin raids.

It was from inside his house that he heard the first indications of the current unrest. He
immediately knew that something very odd was going on outside. He had grown aware of
certain sounds, learned to listen for hints of dark creatures and how these noises differed
from a brigand fight or the mugging of a hapless wanderer. The current commotion
clearly indicated a goblin attack even though the sun was now shining bright and goblins
usually used the cover of darkness. This in itself perplexed Joel, but more ominous was
the combination of additional noises that indicated something much more than a goblin
raid was occurring outside his door.

The shrieking caw of a hook hawk flying overhead could not be dismissed at any time
of day. The fact that it mixed in with the guttural rants of goblins nearby made Joel
cringe. During previous days to pass the time, he had watched hook hawks from afar. He
learned that these flying nightmares particularly enjoyed snacking on goblins, thus
goblins usually scattered when one was nearby. For whatever reason, they were not
scattering now.

The sounds he could currently make out from the goblins in the distance were not the
fearful squeals of disorganized panic as he would expect, but more of war shouts, and
these sounded as if they extended all around the town. That also confused Joel. Goblins
usually ran in, quickly took what they deemed important, and then ran out. They didn't
take time to whoop and holler. Mixed in with these indiscernible ravings, Joel could
make out the screams of humans. It almost sounded as if the goblins were actually
targeting the thieves that nested in this otherwise deserted place. Shrieks from these
hunted victims continued to grow and Joel began to wonder just what he was up against
this time.

Through past experience, he knew enough when to sit tight and when to move out. It
all depended on the situation and the enemy. Human bandits and thieves that entered the
town with the intent to stir up trouble wouldn't go house to house looking for valuables,

they were too lazy. They normally appraised targets from the outside. They looked for
sizable warehouses or fancy large houses with grand ornamentation, thus his home was
always ignored. Goblins, however, weren't as picky.

With goblins, Joel could never be completely sure of their intentions. He watched
them in darkness on several different occasions to assess their tactics. For the most part,
he could predict their movements once he figured out what they really wanted. If they
were just eyeing some finished wood or a cart, they would just take what they wanted and
leave. If they were in search of weapons or tools, they would seek larger buildings, enter,
and ransack the place. Every now and then, however, they would also enter ordinary
residences and come out with blankets, clothes, and even drawers full of useless junk—as
if the piles of worthless scrap actually held some true value. These particular raids were
the most worrisome for Joel, because if Goblins simply wanted to collect odds and ends,
they might enter his house if they happened to turn up his street. These were the times
Joel would not allow himself to be caught trapped inside with no way of escape.

The problem Joel now faced was that he simply could not fathom exactly what was going on outside from the confusing sounds he was hearing. People were dying, of that he was sure. That disturbed him as he never encountered the goblins actively hunting down the remaining residents of Pinesway. Shags and the river rogue did their share of hunting, but not when a hook hawk was screeching above in the day-lit sky.

Joel peered out a broken slit in an upstairs shutter with his spyscope hoping to gain a better perspective of what was going on outside. He saw little that made him happy.

"Blasted goblins are moving in coordinated patterns," he grumbled to himself. "OK, they're not raiding the area, they're securing it. What the blazes are they up to? And a shag standing right next to them with a hook hawk overhead! Not good."

Joel didn't need to see anymore. This was not the time to risk sticking it out in his home, it was better to be on the move. With a decision made, he did what he always does before he opts for different ground. He hid his most important supplies under loose boards in a dark corner of an empty bedroom and more behind a fake wall of the back closet. He surveyed the area making sure that nothing of any value appeared in sight. He threw a dusty, old, moth-eaten blanket over one chair and tipped another one over on its side. He scattered some broken glass he kept in a jar across the floor and table top and quickly climbed down the stairs into the cellar.

When he reached the large tin door that opened upward to the back yard, he realized he was now in a bit of uncharted territory. He never made this type of move in daylight before. Streaks of sunlight broke through the edges of the door and made long glowing lines on the floor.

"Blasted bright out there," he grunted lightly to himself. "Ok, how to do this without being seen?"

He knew where he wanted to go first, and he went over the path he would take in his mind. He believed there would be sufficient cover of overgrown hedges that would block sight of him from street level. The goblins would probably not see him. The hook hawk, however, presented another problem. If the bird decided to circle back in his direction, there were not enough trees to cover his position and the trees that were there were devoid of all leaves.

"Ok, not much choice," he muttered.

With that, he opened the door. A breath of cold air crashed into his face as he crept outside making one quick swooping glance of the skies overhead. Thankfully, the hawk

was not in the area. Immediately but as silently as possible, he moved to his left and his
first objective, an abandoned house two doors down that looked as bad as his own home
from the outside. He crawled through a hole in the wall that he himself had cut with an
axe. He had placed that same axe, as well as a long dagger, swords of various weights
and lengths, and a crossbow with plenty of bolts in a hidden cache in this house's
basement.
   Now in the cover of the interior of the house, Joel moved with more speed as he
bounded across the bare floor to the basement door and down the creaky stairs. He turned
at the bottom and scrambled noiselessly over to a cobweb covered corner. What the eye
could not see was a shallow pit because he had covered it with splintered boards. A few
large, hairy spiders darted across the planks as he began to disturb the slightly rotted
wood. He was never afraid of such insignificant creatures and brushed them away as if
they were nothing more than lifeless dust balls. Carefully and quietly, he moved the

boards off to the side revealing several sacks and blanket-wrapped mounds. Along with the weapons, the pit contained several other useful supplies such as torches, flints, oils, and armor of different types.

Joel, almost without thinking, picked up one of his more useful inventions. It was a spiked forearm brace. Made of leather, he could bind it around the lower part of his forearm, covering the entire area from the lower elbow all the way down past the wrist just to the bottom of his palm. The brace was covered with small razor sharp spikes that nestled themselves in rows and jutted out in various directions. He designed and produced the arm covering himself as a way to deal with what he previously viewed as the greatest threat to his safety. That threat was in the shape of human thieves that might fall on him when he was on a supply run. He had witnessed several attacks occurring throughout the town when the bandits first showed up to take advantage of the fact that lawlessness was now the rule.

With his spyscope, he watched muggings and beatings from his house. The thieves would jump an isolated wanderer rummaging through debris in back alleys. As they outnumbered their target, two or more of the robbers would always grab for the victim's arms while the one in charge took advantage of the situation. Beatings were often vicious and Joel vowed never to be victimized by such a ploy. He created this armband as a first line of defense.

More than once when he had ventured out of his house for supplies, he had been set upon by brigands that meant to separate him from any useful equipment. As they did to their other targets, they encircled him and rushed him from the sides. Once upon him, they always tried to grab him by the arms. When they did, they were not happy.

Joel would begin to twist and pull his arms with the makeshift leather sleeves bound around each forearm, apparently trying to wrest his hands free. Nothing was further from the truth. He wanted the moronic bandits to grab even tighter, which they often did when he began his struggle. This in turn only aggravated their inevitable injuries. The spikes would jab into the palms of their hand. Then, when Joel twisted his own arm, the metal would slice large gouges into their skin. Eventually, they would realize what was happening and let go, but by then it was too late as their hands appeared more like raw, battered meat. While they stood gaping at their own wounds, Joel showed no such hesitation and used the same armored forearm to smash them in the face.

With the underlings out of the fight, it was then a match between Joel and the lead thug, the one that always waited for the others to move in first, the one that enjoyed beating a helpless victim. While Joel was usually much older than any such bandit leader, he was also always more in control and better trained. Joel rarely showed mercy.

On this day, however, Joel wasn't facing a group of thieves. He was facing goblins and he hoped none would get close enough to get a hold of him. Still, he wrapped one brace around his right arm, but decided to leave his left arm open for a sleeve that would hold additional bolts for his crossbow. He also tied a belt around his waist with another two holds on each of his sides for even more crossbow ammo. From what he saw at his window, this was an enemy he wanted to fight from a distance. A sword or dagger was not going to help him and the extra weight would only slow him down.

#

Sazar stood at the outskirts of Pinesway. A gigantic shag crouched uneasily at the
serp's side, but it made no attempt to join the carnage or kill the goblin that stumbled
dazedly toward them.

Sazar did not wait for a report, he already knew what had transpired. In essence, he
was seeing it now from the thoughts of his minions that he controlled and had ordered to
attack this inviting target. He spoke an order to the apparently confused goblin with a
hypnotizing tone.

"Now that we have made our presence known, secure that large building to my right,
the one just past the main road's entrance into the town. Do you see the one I mean?"

The goblin looked almost bewildered at the serp.

Sazar glared into the goblin's glassy eyes.

"Point to the building," the serp commanded.

The goblin did so and pointed to the correct structure.

With that, Sazar nodded. "Very good. Now go."

The serp took several steps in different directions as he peered across what was left of
Pinesway. He listened carefully to what he could hear and focused on images that flashed
through his mind. These images came from the minds of several goblins. He kept an
active link to their minds throughout this first phase of the battle. His forward assault
force made substantial progress through the town, catching many of the small time
thieves unprepared for the onslaught. The thieves would be killed on sight, their bodies
would eventually be plundered for treasure and weapons once certain strategic points
were secured.

That would occur later, right now he demanded an overwhelming forward movement
by his forces, a blitz that would take a U-shaped form around the edges of the town and
eventually swing around the back end. When this was accomplished, he would have
Pinesway encircled and escape cut off.

As Sazar contemplated the initial progress of his assault, he grinned with appreciation.
The screams he heard in the distant matched the bloody images that flashed through his
mind. His goblins moved forward unopposed, not that Sazar expected any opposition. His
hook hawk scouted the town for many days before this assault. He knew Pinesway held
little more than riffraff and thieves—the dregs of human society that would not stand and
fight but rather flee from a superior enemy. The ensuing panic that now gripped this town
confirmed his assumptions. These thieves posed no real threat to him or his minions.

These same humans, however, collected the spoils of looting escapades over many weeks, and Sazar knew the value of obtaining this treasure. This is why he targeted this abandoned town in the first place. The human bandits did the work for him, pillaging empty houses, plundering town stores, attacking wayward travelers that stumbled unaware into this place and relieving them of their valuables. Sazar now coveted these valuables. They could be sold and traded to other unscrupulous humans for the tools and weapons his minions lacked the talent to create for themselves. He could buy food that would entice other dark creatures to his side, close enough for him to weave his mind controlling spell over them and increase the size and power of his army.

Mostly, however, he wanted Pinesway for his own. The buildings would serve as suitable quarters for a multitude of goblins that he could keep close by. If he could keep the goblins fed and near his presence, then he could maintain control over them. It was when they were scattered, when his minions ventured too far in the distance, that was

when his hold was least tenable and when he lost most of his troops. By utilizing
Pinesway as a headquarters, he could keep this from occurring. Goblins by the hundreds
would flock to his town for free food and shelter and ultimately to serve him. That is why
he now stood at the entrance of this place that the humans abandoned.

"All goes well," the serp snickered. "The humans panic and they run for cover. They
stupidly run for the sanctuary of their own hidden shelters. They will lead us to the
supplies they looted for themselves. In the very chaos I create, I will obtain all that I
want."

He snickered again as he moved toward the building he ordered the goblin scout to
secure. He motioned for the massive shag to follow as he inhaled the smell of blood and
terror in the air.

Sazar found the chaos invigorating. He didn't need order to control his minions—just
the opposite. Unfettered chaos held great advantages for him. The pandemonium kept
those under his control from ever clearing their minds, not that the minds of goblins,
shags or the other monsters under his control could ever be accused of being complex.
Still, simplicity led to simple desires as well as simple fears. Desires offered one stimulus
and fear another. Chaos kept these dark creatures from seeing a clear path to their own
needs, kept them from wiping away the confusion that cluttered their dark, twisted minds,
and it fed the fear that made them easier to control.

The human targets of his raids also felt the fear of chaos. With shouts and cries ringing
from every corner, with screams of terror filling the air just as the smoke from
surrounding fires, few of the remaining humans in this town would organize into a
dangerous party. Instead, they would cower in dark corners or run in panic, and thus
create more confusion and feed the frenzy.

The only real difficulty with such turmoil was keeping the hook hawk from grabbing
goblins as prey. Hook hawks with their gnarled talons and bent necks flew more like
swirling boomerangs in a tornado. Their curved bodies allowed them to circle and swerve
with razor quickness and they easily snatched that which moved in the same type of
haphazard frenzied direction. Those that ran in straight paths could often avoid a hook
hawk, but goblins tended to run in mindless patterns and were thus the perfect prey.

Still, it was good to get a high overview of any skirmish, and Sazar could see what his
minions saw. The loss of a few goblins here and there was small enough sacrifice. The

hook hawk circling above gave him the perfect perspective for ascertaining the overall
movements and progress of his ground born forces.

Far better than the hook hawk, however, was the perception he gained from the rock
beetle under his control. Now here was a creature that Sazar truly appreciated. The rock
beetle did not rely on sight as it spent most of its time just under the surface of the
ground. Rock beetles utilized their other senses. They could pick up a scent that
originated from a great distance even when it had to be absorbed through layers of soil.
And smell was not the only sense that was heightened to compensate for the beetle's dark
underground world. They could isolate and distinguish sounds that most other animals
could not even perceive. When linked with a rock beetle, Sazar could hear well beyond
even what a hook hawk could see.

A rock beetle, however, did more than just hear sounds. It felt vibrations, felt them
like a spider feels a victim trapped in its web. The beetle could sense movement in all
directions and at distances almost too far to believe. The ability to seize upon this

incredible sense allowed Sazar to actually physically experience the battle as it occurred,
and this was beyond invigorating.

Through the beetle, Sazar felt the forward movements of his own minions as well as
the horrified retreat of those humans still in Pinesway. Beyond that, the beetle's senses
actually allowed Sazar to sense the pulse of the battle. It was more than smelling, hearing
or feeling. It was a deep perception of tremor and vibration. The serp became aware of
the twang of each goblin crossbow, the thundering step of his shags, and every dull thud
of a human body that crumbled to the ground in pain and agony. These palpable
sensations allowed him to actually taste the crippling fear and chaos as he placed these
sensations in context with the images that flashed in his mind.

"This is turning out to be a delightful day," the serp hummed in enjoyment as he
stepped up to the building he had previously pointed out. He stepped inside past two
other goblins that stood guard at the door. These creatures instinctively backed further off
to the sides when the hulking shag tried to enter.

The hairy monster was not meant to enter human sized buildings and it twisted,
turned, crouched and bent in an attempt to fit through the door. The wood of the frame
began to crack and splinter.

"Stay outside," Sazar commanded. "Wait at this spot and do not move from it."

The shag immediately ceased its efforts to obtain entry into the building and stood like
a statue just outside the now somewhat mangled door frame.

"This will serve as my lair until a more appropriate setting is discovered and secured.
For now it will suffice." Sazar then turned to the goblins that waited at the door. "Patrol
the exterior of this building continuously until I tell you otherwise. Do not engage in any
battles or attempt to loot any buildings. Simply circle this building over and over and
watch everything that is in your view. Go."

Sazar quickly mouthed a spell and a gray, misshapen, jagged star of energy appeared
above his head. It crackled with energy and then dissolved, but he now had an even more
direct link with the two goblins that patrolled his new home. His spells were usually weak
and the magical energy he could draw on to cast them was limited, but certain spells
could assist him in maintaining a better level of security. With this new spell, his link
went beyond the fact that he could see what they see. Now, he was linked to their
instincts as well. If they felt threatened, he would feel threatened.

Turning his attention back to the battle, he voiced new commands that he sent

telepathically to his reserve minions waiting at the outskirts of town. He commanded
them to enter the town and reinforce the forward goblins and fall into positions at several
cross roads. He would seal off this section of town in mere moments and press his
goblins further around the edges of Pinesway. It wouldn't be long before he had the town
surrounded with his forces.

                         #

     With a crossbow draped over his back and a leather chest guard snapped securely to
his upper body, Joel took back to the basement stairs and bounded up to the ground floor
of the house that stored his cache of weapons. He quickly moved to the hole in the wall
where he entered the house, but stayed clear of the opening. He pulled out his spy glass
and peered through it.

"Nasty buggers are closing in on me," he mumbled to himself. "Ok, don't want to get caught in here, but need a plan. Blast, need to know what in blazes is going on is what I need. Blasted creatures never attacked like this before."

Through the spyscope he could see groupings of goblins making coordinated movements up several different streets. When they reached a crossroad, they secured each corner and then waved to their flanks. Immediately, another group of goblins would then appear and press forward beyond their position.

He watched with great concern toward the goblin efficiency when he witnessed the goblins force a young human male out of hiding from an old merchant's store. Crossbow fire took out the victim's legs first. When he crumpled to the ground, three ran up to him and took hold of the arrows that stuck out of his thighs. When he tried to pull away, they twisted the arrow rods over, causing apparent agony in their victim. A fourth goblin took hold of the victim's head, mouthed something that Joel could not make out. The victim shook his head. With that, the fourth goblin jabbed a dagger in the young man's throat. With the man gurgling blood in death throws, the four goblins released him and left him to die in the street.

Joel grimaced as he considered his own plight. "Ok, they're cleaning out buildings. They're not taking prisoners and it won't do to be forced out into the open. Can't stay here, and just can't run without knowing what I'm running toward. Ok, one step at a time."

He poked his head out the hole in the wall and looked skyward. He could hear the hook hawk screeching in the distance.

"Other side of town. Good."

Joel did not waste the chance. He extricated himself out of the hole, kept to the side of the house, and rounded the back corner. He then sprinted as fast as his old legs could carry him across the small back yard to a hedge that served as a natural fence. He dove to the ground and rolled deep into the overgrowth of weeds. With the hedges and weeds serving cover, he took out his scope once more.

"Ok, think this thing out," he whispered to himself. "Don't want to get trapped in a building, shags can smell me out if I try to hide. Can't just keep moving in the open, hook hawk will make it back here eventually. I can break for the woods, but no telling how many goblins are waiting in the trees. Blazes, not a good choice to make."

Joel shook his head as he considered his dwindling options. "Not leaving, that's that.

Ok, where to go? Northwest bridge. River rogue there ain't going to be happy if goblins
try to move into its territory, 'specially goblins with a shag in tow. Probably already
ticked off at the hook hawk flying around so close. Might not be happy to see me, so
can't let that happen. Still, it's going to try to fight off any goblins, even the shag. Maybe
the safest place to be. Ok, best I can think of."

He took a moment to take another look overhead. "Now, how do I get there? Tree
lined paths through the old park and then the cemetery, that's a good bet. Seems like
goblins are sticking to the roads, just don't know which roads, sounds like all of them.
Ok, one block at a time. Shortest path to park is that way," and he nodded his head due
north.

As silently as he could, he pressed aside a series of branches that made up the lower
portion of the hedge in front of him. It was not an easy fit, but he made it through. Once
on the other side of the hedge he wasted no time in jumping to his feet and running to the

back of a newer home that was now in front of him. He clung to the wall and with his
back against it, slid his way to the corner.

This house faced a newer street, a wider street, and with no trees lining either side. It
was open ground and he could hear goblin movements in almost every direction. He had
no idea where his enemies might be at the moment.

"Not going to just trust luck," he grumbled. He took the crossbow from his back,
loaded a bolt, and aimed at the back of another home a good distance down the road to
his left. "Have to hope they hear the glass and not the sound of the bow. I guess if they're
close enough to distinguish that, then I'm as good as dead anyway."

Joel pulled the trigger and watched hopefully as the bolt made a long arc through the
air. The window was a large target but it was far in the distance. It almost seemed as if
the bolt was traveling in slow motion. Thankfully, it hit its mark and the glass shattered.
Joel did not pause to watch through his spyscope. He crouched low, and hustled off in the
opposite direction toward the neighboring house to his right. He bounded around the
corner, down the side and front yards, and finally across the street. He almost expected to
feel the stinging pain of arrows piercing his legs, but he made it to the cover of an
overgrown flower bed and dropped to the ground. He looked up and down the street and
saw nothing. He didn't know if his diversion made any difference, but at least it felt
better than simply running and hoping for the best.

He had to make it across several more streets closer to the center of town before he
could make it to the park, but thankfully it was quieter here. He could still hear the
sounds of skirmishes in almost every direction, but the alleys he now traveled remained
still. He kept to the sides of buildings and had to dodge for cover twice when he heard the
hook hawk closing in on his position. Eventually, he made it to the park and turned
westward.

Though it was dormant season, the ground here was free of snow and ice. It had been
dry so far this season and Joel was thankful for this. Still, the ground remained hard and
frozen as the sun hung low in the horizon and direct light could not break the shadows of
the thicker rows of trees. Evergreens allowed for greater cover and Joel used them to his
advantage. He made it through the park in quicker time and stopped to gauge his next
path.

A stone fence separated the park from the cemetery. He would have to jump it. It was
only a few feet high, but his body did not look forward to the task. Right now, he felt

every year of his age. His lungs fought harder for air and his lower back throbbed. An
arthritic knee let him know it wasn't happy either. His hands bled from various scrapes
and cuts, but this wasn't the time for bandages. He stood under a large spruce and gauged
the distance to the stone wall and then the terrain of the ground beyond.

The cemetery would be open ground around the headstones, not the best place to
travel. The stone wall also stood mostly in open space, but there was enough overhang
from trees in the park to give him sufficient cover there. He could travel the wall along
the park border until it turned at the back end of the cemetery. Along this rear border, the
wall changed over to a wrought iron fence. Most of the fence and back paths were as
lined with trees. Unless the goblins had taken position along the fence, Joel believed a
clear path now existed to the northwestern part of town that bordered the river.

With a little luck he could make it to the north bridge and perhaps find a store house to
hide in. It would be dangerous, basically caught between the attackers and the river

rogue, but hopefully they would all be concerned with each other. Enough different
scents in the air and he might be able to conceal himself until nightfall at least. It was a
good as plan as any.

When he made his first step out from under the pine tree, his plan changed drastically.

The ground rumbled before him and dirt shattered up in his face. He could feel his feet
begin to slip under him in loose dirt. Luckily, his foot caught the stability of a large root
near the surface and he avoided falling forward. He leapt back toward the trunk of the
pine he previously used for cover and grabbed its trunk. The ground continued to crack
and crumble and even more dirt flew into the air. In the next instant, a black as pitch
mound rose up from the ground. It was the rounded, humped back of a rock beetle and it
was looking for a meal.

Joel's eyes widened in terror as glistening pinchers covered in hair and filth jutted out
from the front of this disgusting creature. Multiple legs pitched the gigantic insect from
the earth as the rest of its body broke from the surrounding soil. Joel didn't need to see
anymore. He took off back to the other end of the park, hoping he could outrun this thing.

                           #

Sazar saw the image of Joel fleeing flash through his mind. The serp continued his
mental connection with the beetle. The old man, however, was not his main concern at
this point. The beetle was needed to ascertain the position of the river rogue that staked a
territory a bit further north of this point of the town. The rogue was not under Sazar's
control, not yet anyway. Sazar wished to avoid any conflict between the rogue and his
own minions until he had the opportunity to visit the rogue and convince it to join with
them rather than fight. For that, he needed time and more calm surroundings. So, for the
time being, he wanted to pinpoint the exact location of the rogue and isolate it. Perhaps
not totally isolate, as he would throw it a goblin or two for a quick snack and as a gesture
of friendship. With the town now very near his grasp, he would have all the goblins he
needed. Losing one or two to gain a river rogue was well worth the price.

"Forget the human," Sazar hummed as he directed his thoughts to the beetle. When he
made this kind of direct communication with one monster he would often lose links with
others. It was at this time, Sazar risked losing an advantage of battle as the minds of his
other minions he was controlling would go suddenly blank, as if a curtain had been
pulled. The battle in the town, however, moved surprisingly well and far swifter than he

had hoped. He could spare the momentary diversion.

Sazar could sense the beetle's hunger and understood what it wanted. "Go north.
Easier meals will be there waiting for you."

He broke off direct communications with the beetle and established a connection with
two goblins that were very near the cemetery. "Leave the cemetery and go north about
two blocks. Wait there and don't move."

He then broke off that link and reestablished his focus on the assault forces that were
quickly encircling the town.

"It would have been easier to feed the beetle some human remains, but I don't have
time to collect them at the moment," the serp mused to himself. "I haven't lost any
goblins in the strike yet, so I guess if I lose two goblins to the beetle and two to the rogue
I'll hardly notice."

#

Joel didn't stop running until he got back to the center of town. It remained quiet in
this area, but now intermittent shrieks of agony pierced the air in all directions. If he had
any hopes of reaching the north bridge, they died with the appearance of the beetle. With
relative quiet at his current position and his back to the wall of some unknown building,
he knew his options dwindled.

"Ok, I'm not getting out of here. Truth is, I pretty much knew that a long time ago. If I
was going to leave, I would have done that weeks ago. Didn't want to leave then, so why
bother now? Just a matter of where to go."

He looked back toward the direction of his own home.

"If I'm going to die, then it's going to be there."

Chapter 3

Lief Woodson stood patiently in the limbs of a very tall oak tree. His eyes scanned the forest while noting the positions of the elf guards that stationed themselves in surrounding trees. The dormant season made this endeavor slightly more possible. All but the evergreens had dropped their leaves. Most of the elite elf guard managed to conceal their presence well, but those that were forced to reconnoiter wider paths gave away their position with slight movements.

A muffled breeze pulled in colder air from the north, but because elves, for the most part, enjoyed indifference to colder temperatures, Lief felt no true chill. If anything, he welcomed the fresh air that would keep this day crisp and dry. The sun hung low as it was the season of lesser light, but the sky remained a deep blue and even the penetrating grey of the woods could not dampen the sparkle of sunlight when it chanced upon scattered ice trapped within the surrounding branches.

Lief switched his gaze downward upon the members of his camp. For the most part, they busily moved about the forest floor. Nearly all seemed occupied with other tasks— collecting wood, mending clothes, crafting weapons or tools. Only one or two of the camp elders seemed to pay his meeting with Standish Loftber any true mind.

Loftber also stood silently in the very same limbs as Lief, leaning carefully against a stout branch that angled slightly toward him. His gaze was far off, focused on nothing in particular. It was almost as if the deep grey of the forest swallowed his consciousness. He closed his eyes heavily as if garnering his strength. When he opened them, they bore into Lief.

"Petiole has been delivered to the dwarves of Dunop, as you already know," the older Loftber began. "I have no idea whether they will condemn him to death for his crimes or imprison him in their dungeon for what is left of his life, nor do I care." This last was said with near disgust. "I only know he will not be returning and this leaves our camp without a leader."

Loftber paused and bowed his head slightly as he corrected himself.

"Actually, without an elder leader," the Loftber stated almost apologetically.

Lief narrowed his eyes at the camp elder, wondering why Loftber would make such a gesture. It seemed as if the older elf was almost apologizing directly to him for making a simple statement of fact. Their camp had no leader now that Petiole was gone. That much had become painfully obvious in the past few days.

Petiole had been the senior camp elder, the oldest elf on the council of elders with
proper lineage in elflore, and thus the leader of the camp. Petiole, however, was a weak
and foolish elf, an elf that committed the heinous crime of dropping shadow tree seeds on
the underground dwarf town of Dunop. He did this not out of necessity, but out of
resentment, out of ignorance, and out of weakness. Petiole acted out of selfish desires to
prove what was obviously not true, that he was a powerful leader that should be feared or
respected. Now, instead of being revered as he hoped, Petiole was languishing in the vast
underground cave dungeons of the dwarves.

As to the camp being without a leader, that was almost bewildering to Lief Woodson.
Elves lived by tradition, by the guidance of elflore. Such guidance made it clear as to
what should happen next. It was now up to the council of camp elders to rally around

Standish Loftber, the current eldest of elders, and allow him to lead. Something, however, had prevented this.

While the elders met over the past few days, no indication was given that Loftber would take the reigns of leadership. Instead, there had been late discussions—not heated arguments, nor debates of power—just simple deliberations without any clear direction given to the rest of the camp.

In fact, it appeared as if the council was almost as directionless as it had been when Petiole had been in charge, and that was something Lief would not allow again. He had almost said something himself when Loftber called for this private meeting.

It was now Loftber that spoke inquisitively to Lief.

"You look at me with a question on your lips," the elder elf noted with an expectant expression.

"The question is not mine to ask," Lief deferred. "The council must address the issue, as I'm sure it will."

"Address it we have, but at the moment we are in a dilemma. This camp needs a leader. At present, it has none. Well, not a proper leader."

Lief again offered a puzzled expression to the elder elf and Loftber offered a quick explanation

"You wonder why I say we have no leader and then correct myself? This camp does have a leader of sorts, and that leader is you. Please forgive any lack of respect. None was intended."

Lief could not remain quiet. His expression revealed surprise, but his tone betrayed more than a hint of annoyance.

"Lack of respect?" Lief questioned with a near harsh tone. "What are you talking about? I do not lead this camp. I am not an elder. I am not even on the council…"

Loftber cut him off.

"You are right on the last, but no on the first. You are not an elder, thus you are not on the council, but you do lead. The elves of this camp now look to you. You are the one that gives them direction."

Lief would have stepped back in denial had it not meant him falling out of the tree. Instead, he had to hold his ground, but he vehemently shook his head in denial. "No, I do not…"

Again Loftber quickly interrupted. "Please Lief, I am not accusing you of anything other then perhaps denying the truth you do not wish to see. Hold for a moment and let me speak what you eventually will know as the truth."

Lief took a deep breath but acquiesced to the elder and remained silent.

Loftber looked down upon the elves below and nodded to them as he began his
explanation.

"No one, not a single elf believes for a moment that you forced yourself into power,
that you purposefully and deliberately grabbed the role of leadership from the proper
elders. No, you are a victim of circumstance just as this camp is a victim of circumstance.
You are the elf that stood on Sanctum and helped destroy the Sphere of Ingar. Thus, you
are a hero and more. You stood against Yave and helped to stop her. And you were with
Ryson Acumen when he saved Dunop from the shadow trees."

The elder elf turned his attention back to the forest and looked once more to the trees
in the distance and beyond.

"And it was you that stood up to Petiole and his crimes, stopped another elf-dwarf
war, and sent that criminal to justice. Petiole was an elf elder and the leader of this camp.
His word was final on all matters. When he committed his crimes, you put an end to his
lead. You faced the elf guard, you faced the traditions, and you did what was right and
necessary.

"In less than a full cycle of the seasons you acted more heroically than most of the
legendary elves in elflore. You have a place now with Shayed as one of the most
respected elves in all our history. Yes, you did all these things and not out of a sense of
adventure, or out of ambition. You did all of this because you had to, because
circumstances dictated you do it."

At this pause, Lief finally spoke.

"I do not deny anything you say, however, I'm not sure of my place in history, but I'm
sure of my place in this camp. Whatever I did, it does not make me its leader. It was
Mappel that directed me during each moment of our trials with Ingar and his sphere.
When Mappel died on Sanctum and Petiole took over, I looked to Petiole to make
decisions to spare this camp. I never placed myself above him. I pleaded with him to do
what needed to be done and still he did not listen to me, thus I never led at any point."

"You led when it mattered," countered Loftber. "You led at the end. When Petiole
committed his crime, it was you that stood up against him."

"I did so, but not as a leader!" Lief stated harshly as he became visibly frustrated. "I
waited for the council of elders to act. I waited for you to act! It was the responsibility of
the elders to stop Petiole. When you failed, I had to…"

"We failed in many of our responsibilities," Loftber admitted. "I do not flee from that
charge for one single instant. Still, to understand elder leadership is to understand what
keeps us together, what allows us to survive. Certainly there have been poor leaders in
the past, but never one so poor as Petiole that followed one so great as Mappel. We could
not have asked for a worse situation. Mappel was exactly what we needed at the very
time we needed it. Petiole was exactly what we did not need at a point we surely couldn't
afford to have him. As I said, the circumstances dictated what you had to do, and there is
not a moment I don't thank all of elflore for what you have done. That is why what I must
do is so much more painful."

Lief could not hold his tongue and it lashed out with further disbelief in its tone.

"So now you believe me to be the true leader of this camp and you wish to throw that burden upon me?"

Loftber mumbled barely loud enough for Lief to hear him.

"If only it were that simple," Loftber sighed.

The elder elf steadied himself once more and again looked into the face of an elf for which he had the greatest respect and admiration.

"No, I will not ask you to take the role of leader. I had considered it, but it would not solve the problem. The problem is actually very simple; there can not be two leaders, two different spokes of authority. An elf camp has to have one clear direction, one clear voice when the good of the camp is involved. The council of elders serves as advisors, allows for greater communication, ensures stability during times of upheaval, but it is the camp elder that leads. Age, health, commitment and elflore have always been the determining factors in selecting the new camp elder. When a camp elder has passed or becomes too weak to lead, it is a simple process for the camp to select its new leader. The eldest elf serving on the council with proper lineage outlined in elflore becomes the new camp elder as long as he or she is healthy enough to take on the responsibility. Thus, it is always clear to the camp which elf must lead."

Lief jumped on this point.

"It is clear now. You are that elf! The entire camp knows that. It is now your responsibility." Lief softened his tone. "I know you Standish. You are not Petiole. I have no fears of your leadership. I know you will serve us all well."

"And you think that is that?" Loftber shot back quickly. "You will simply retreat into the shadows and allow me to lead?"

The sharp retort took Lief by surprise.

"You think I would stand in your way?"

"You really don't understand do you?" questioned the elf elder. "Leadership is not simply dependent on the leader. It is also very much dependent on the ones that must follow. There must be little doubt in their minds about who has the authority and the responsibility to lead them. How will you make the people of the camp forget you? Will you simply go out and tell them they should ignore you? Go ahead, for all the good it will do. In their hearts and in their minds, you have already taken on a position of power in this camp. If you tell them you will not lead, they will accept that at face value. They will look to me and follow my direction."

"Then what is the problem?" Lief demanded.

"The problem is that they will follow my lead for only as long as they agree with my decisions or as long as we don't face difficult times. The moment and I mean the very instant I make a decision which with some might disagree, they will look for an alternative. They will look to you. That is something we can not have, even you would agree to that. The magic has returned fully to the land, we are using it to our best advantage, but we also face so many dangers that we have never faced before. We have an opportunity for a truly wonderful time or a truly desperate time. We can use the magic to help our camp prosper, but we also face dark creatures returning in force to our home. That means we face difficult decisions at every turn. This camp must act with one voice, one direction, or else we will not survive."

Loftber's expression turned more sympathetic as he tried to explain his own understanding of the dilemma he believed the elf camp faced.

"Again, understand I know it's not your desire and I don't believe you would interfere even if you disagreed with every decision I make, but it's simply not just up to you. The elves of this camp now view you as a legend, as part of elflore. The very mention of your

name is now done in the highest regard. You simply can't brush that away, and in truth, I
wouldn't want you to. It does, however, mean that you hold an important standing in this
camp. You are regarded not just with respect, but as holding authority."

Lief took long moments to consider the situation put before him. He looked once more
at the elf guards that stood nearby. It was their job to protect the camp elder, the leader of
the camp. Certainly, they were there to protect Loftber, but were they also protecting
him? Did he now count more than the other elves of his camp?

"I find it difficult to argue with what you say," Lief allowed. "You are right on many
counts, we do face difficult times and we must have one true leader, one voice that will
direct us all. I suppose for all Petiole's faults he understood that as well. Perhaps that is
why he acted toward me as he did, perhaps I should have done more to help him."

"Petiole would have viewed your help with disdain, would have looked upon it as an
insult to his authority." Loftber interjected.

Lief nodded. "I suppose my help would have simply created greater controversy."

"Indeed, it would have."

"The same type of controversy you talk about now," Lief admitted.

Loftber said nothing, simply looked closely at the younger elf before him.

"So where does that leave us?" Lief wondered aloud. He then stopped and returned
Loftber's gaze. "I asked you before if you were going to put the burden of leadership on
me and you said it would not be that easy. If you can not lead, and I can not lead, where
does this leave us—a problem with no solution?"

"There is a solution," Standish Loftber said with more than a hint of sorrow, "a bitter
one, but a solution none the less. No, you can not lead this camp for you are not the camp
elder. You would face the same challenges I would face. The camp will follow you even
during difficult times, probably much longer than they would follow me, but if times
grew truly dark, their loyalties would eventually be torn between following you and
looking to an elder. Elflore is powerful in its guidance to keep us together. If you were to
assume the role of leadership, it would be in stark contrast to the very essence of elflore.
Eventually, even your leadership would be questioned."

"Then how can there be a solution?"

Loftber answered quickly this time as if he knew he must forge ahead and any delay
would only make it more difficult.

"There can be a solution because it can be possible for an elder to lead. The dilemma
occurs only if you are here. If you were not, there would no longer be a question of
authority. The problem exists only while you are a member of this camp. Do you
understand?"

Lief grimaced as if a sword plunged into his chest, and Loftber continued so as not to
let silence deepen the wound.

"If you leave, this camp survives. If you stay, I and the other elders on the council
believe we will fall into disarray. You will witness the chaos of anarchy as dark creatures
prey on us because we are no longer able to act as one. While it pains me to ask you to
leave, understand that if you stayed you would only witness the destruction of your
camp."

"So I am to be exiled, and the camp will follow you as the camp elder?" Lief
questioned with an edge of anger beginning to grip his voice.

Loftber answered Lief's bitterness with somberness of his own.

"It will be a short tenure of leadership. Once I announce that you are leaving the camp at my request and with your agreement, I will announce that I am leaving as well."

For a brief moment, any trace of Lief's growing resentment was quickly replaced with
bewilderment.

"You're going to relinquish? Then again the camp will have no leader! This is not
making any sense."

"It makes perfect sense," Loftber stated with a steadfast determination. "This camp
will have a leader, one leader, and a leader that can not be blamed for sending away the
legendary Lief Woodson just to accommodate his own weaknesses. I will hand over the
camp elder position to the next in line. Shantree Wispon will take over. She will then be
in position to lead this camp with no bitterness, and no question to her authority. No one

will blame her for your departure, and after you have departed, no one will wonder
whether her decisions meet with your approval. I believe she is well suited to handle the
situation."

"I have no doubts about Shantree's abilities," Lief argued. "But that is not the point.
You are supposed to lead, not her. How can you ask me to leave because it will restrict
your ability to lead, and then turn around and avoid what is required of you?"

"Is that it? You think I am simply surrendering my responsibility? No, that is not the
case at all. It is just the opposite. I am taking full responsibility. I see clearly what I am
doing. First, I am asking you to leave your home, to accept banishment as a reward for
your noble actions. You have done nothing for yourself. Your actions saved this camp,
indeed the entire elf race. And now I stand here and tell you to go. I believe you will
eventually understand why I'm doing this, but that is not nearly enough. If I am to ask
that of you, I must be ready to make the same sacrifice myself.

"Think for a moment, Lief. What I ask of you, I feel I must. I do it because I believe it
is the only way this camp will survive. If I stay, then it appears I did if for myself, to
remove you as a challenge to my authority. I will appear as Petiole, weak and selfish. I
could not live with myself. If, however, I accept banishment as well, I will have acted
purely in the best interests of this camp. No one can second guess my intentions. No one
can for one moment believe that I acted to satisfy my own desires. It is the only way for
the situation to truly be resolved. You accept banishment, I accept banishment. We move
on and allow this camp to survive as it has for generations and will for generations
more."

The elder elf quickly moved to a related matter so as to make his understanding of the
matter as clear as possible.

"There is something else you should know," Loftber continued. "I will also be asking
Holli Brances to leave this camp. For the very same reasons you must leave, she also
must go. Holli is a guard and is looked at in a different light than you. She went to
Sanctum as part of her duty and she assisted against Yave as a trained member of the elf
guard. Still, she now also has her own place in elflore, a legendary standing. If Shantree
faces difficult times, and I believe she will with so many dark creatures appearing in our
midst, then she can not afford to have anyone in this camp that would be viewed as—
what is the best way to put it—an alternative."

A cloud of confusion began to swirl in Lief's thoughts. The bitterness he could almost
taste was growing. It was becoming hard to think and harder still to control his anger. A
sharp question flew from his lips.

"And have you spoken to her of this yet? Have you tried to soften her banishment with
your unselfish decision to leave on your own?"

Loftber paused. He did not like the tone of Lief's voice and liked even less the raging
glare that was glowing in the younger elf's eyes.

"No, but I have no doubt she will agree. I am a camp elder, she is an elf guard. She
knows her duty. She will do what I ask, though I believe it will be a greater burden on her
than on the two of us."

"Duty?" Lief almost laughed at this word. "You wish to speak of duty, the all
encompassing word that will ensure her cooperation? You can say that word to her and
you know she will do as she is told, but you wonder whether or not I will agree?"

"Indeed I do. And that, Lief, is truly an illustration of the problem that exists. If you do not agree, I can not force you. I could order the elf guard to remove you, but I wonder if they would actually follow that order. Only an elf guard might be able to answer that, and I am not ready to put that to the test. The traditions of the elf guard are very strong. I do not wish to be remembered as the elf that destroyed those traditions."

With this, Lief tensed. His glare became almost hateful and Standish Loftber could actually sense the deep anger that boiled in the younger elf. The elder elf did his best to control the situation and sooth the growing tensions between them.

"As you said, I am the camp elder. You ask me to lead, then I will do so. Any wisdom I can draw on tells me that I am doing exactly what must be done, no matter how difficult it is. I take responsibility for resolving the issue before this camp. If you stop me in this— my first order as leader—then you prove my point and allow the dilemma to continue. If you realize that instead I am doing exactly what you want me to do, what this camp needs me to do—to lead, then you will cease your objections. I need you to withdraw from this camp, to strike out on your own. You are now legend and no one will forget you, but your final days in this land must be spent elsewhere. Where you go, I leave that to you. Once you accept this request, I will also withdraw from this camp and will seek refuge elsewhere. The legend will be gone as will the one that asked him to leave. The camp moves on without both. Do you really wish to continue to debate this with me and prove that my leadership means nothing to you and start our spiral to final oblivion? Look upon the elves below us, see how they all now watch us and understand that there is no other way."

Lief, however, ignored the stares from the elves below. He vented his ire directly at the elf before him, the elf that represented the elders of this camp that did nothing when Petiole acted so foolishly.

"Words… words of so-called wisdom." Lief now spoke in a low growl as he tilted his head downward ever so slightly. He brought his glare of sheer anger directly upon Loftber. "How long did it take you and the other elders to put together such an eloquent speech?"

Lief paused only long enough to allow Loftber to open his mouth, but the younger elf pressed forward before a single utterance could be spoken.

"Where were these words when they were needed? You said you didn't want to be remembered as the elf that destroyed the traditions, is that what you are concerned with…

how you will be remembered? Let me tell you how I remember you, as a member of the
camp council that did nothing when we faced our greatest dangers. You now think you
make a grand sacrifice so your name can be placed in elflore? It would be a disgrace to
those that truly belong there if such an attempt was ever made. Here is some truth for you
and the other elders, something for you to contemplate during your self-imposed exile.
You bickered and argued when Petiole led this camp, the lot of you. You showed all the
courage of a yearling deer that bolts at the first snap of a twig. You allowed Petiole to
drop the seeds! Do you hear me Loftber?!! You and the others allowed this to happen.
You knew what was happening and you allowed it! You should all be facing judgment in
Dunop right along with Petiole himself."

Lief could feel the anger that he swallowed for so long during the reign of Petiole
throb and expand in his head. No longer would he swallow his fury, no longer would he
try to be diplomatic. That would end now. The younger elf stepped forward on the tree

branch that held them both. He stepped so near Loftber that he could feel his breath on
his face. His eyes continued to blaze, but now they danced with a true fury and the elder
elf felt great fear.

Loftber tried to step back, but the limb he leaned upon held him in place. Panic took
hold and to anyone watching it was clear he feared for his very life. Still, the elf guards
did not move to his side.

Lief spoke now with guttural hate.

"I want to repeat this so I know you understand. You allowed the shadow seeds to fall.
You could have stopped it… SHOULD have stopped it. You did nothing! How much less
would you have been responsible if there was another elf-dwarf war? You wish to throw
all the responsibility upon Petiole? It does not work that way. You said it yourself only
moments ago. You said that leadership also depends on the ones that follow. Think long
and hard about that during your seasons alone when you want to consider your so-called
heroic gesture. Petiole made the decision, but the camp elders allowed it to happen."

Lief took his eyes off Loftber for just a moment and gazed down upon the other camp
elders that were now frozen, eyes fixed upon them both.

"You are all guilty!" Lief roared.

He then turned his fury back toward Loftber. "I would be within my rights to slay you
here and now. In my mind, you are nothing less than a criminal convicted of the most
heinous crime."

It was at that moment that Holli Brances dropped onto the tree limb.

"Lief!" she spoke in a soft tone, but with no less conviction than if she shouted across
a battlefield. "You must not do this. I cannot let you do this."

Lief at first said nothing. His body shook as his hands remained clenched in tight fists
at his side. Finally, he turned swiftly about away from Loftber, as if the sight of the elder
elf made him sick. He spoke directly to Holli. "You have nothing to worry about. I have
no intention of wasting anymore energy on this pathetic excuse of an elf, or on any other
elder of this camp. In fact, I'm going to do exactly what he wants, but not because of his
reasoning. I do so of my own reckoning and I do so gladly. Good luck to you Holli,
wherever you might end up."

Holli's expression remained stoic and steadfast, but she tilted her head slightly in a
moment of confusion.

"Ask him." Lief waved his hand in backward disgust toward Loftber, and then he
simply leapt away.

Chapter 4

Enin and Ryson landed in the grassy hills just outside Burbon.

"I didn't want to bring us to the center of town because I don't like how this spell affects surrounding space," the wizard explained. "I didn't want to send an innocent passerby into shock if one happened into our path at the wrong moment. It was safer to land here."

"I'll take it," Ryson said while eyeing the sun in the sky. "It's about mid afternoon. Sy should be in his command post. I'll meet you there."

With that, the delver exploded in a blur of motion that almost could not be detected by the wizard's eye. He blazed a trail to a side gate where he stopped stone still just long enough to be identified by a tower guard and the gatekeeper. He then moved with slightly less speed as he darted his way past the wall, through the town streets, and ultimately to the center of town.

Enin floated up into the air and flew just past a guard tower. He waved with an uneasy smile before making his way to Sy's command post by floating above the building rooftops. When he reached his intended goal, he quickly dropped to the ground and landed at the front door. He stepped into the office where he saw Ryson already explaining what he knew to Sy Fenden, Burbon's leader and Captain of the Guard.

Ryson paused to acknowledge the wizard's entrance.

Sy appeared grim as he considered the news brought to him by the delver. Still, he had many questions, and he quickly brought Enin into the conversation.

"Ryson told me what you saw. You used a spell to see Pinesway?"

"Yes," Enin answered simply without going into an extravagant explanation of the components of his spell.

Sy was grateful for the short answer, but pursued the topic further. "Do you think Sazar was aware that you were watching him or his minions?"

"You're worried he thinks we're spying on him?" Enin appeared almost ready to laugh. "There's not much he can do to stop me."

"I'm more concerned that we've alerted him to our own awareness. I'm not sure what he's up to, but it would be nice to know the extent of his own information. What he does, or what we do in response for that matter, depends on a great many things. So, do you think he knows about your spell or not?"

Enin reconsidered the question. "Hmmmm… I'd say it's possible, but not probable. I would guess not. He's not that kind of a spell caster that he would be able to detect the use of magic in that fashion. Those with a higher connection to magical energy can sense

spells. He, however, does not have that kind of connection. That is not where his power
lies."

"But you said it was possible."

"Yes, he might have learned a spell that could act as a, how should I put it, warning
system for any directed magic. Problem with that is I don't think he has the power to cast
such a spell. He could, however, have obtained a magical item that would serve that
purpose for him."

Sy frowned again. "Alright, since it's possible then we should probably assume he
knows we are aware of what he's doing. Tell me exactly what you saw."

Enin described all the creatures he witnessed, their movements, as well as the reaction of the few people he could see.

"Casualties?" Sy asked.

"Yes."

"Can you estimate how many?"

"I only saw a few."

Sy shook his head. "There aren't many people left over there. That's the good news. The bad news is in everything else you just told me. Sazar has a sizable force of creatures from your description. The question now is what do you think he wants?"

Ryson interjected at this point. "Whatever he can get his claws on."

Sy did not totally dismiss the sentiment, but he explained his own considerations. "I'm sure he's taking everything he can, but what's the real purpose of this?" He looked to both Ryson and Enin with expectation as he spelled out the situation. "This can't just be a raid to loot supplies. Doesn't add up. What he can get from Pinesway, he can get in different ways. There is no guard or militia to protect the town. In effect, there really is no town anymore. For the most part, it's just abandoned buildings and a transient population. From what my scouts tell me, thieves have done a good job ransacking the place. Anything worth any value, they've already taken. Actually, the thieves and bandits have pretty much taken the place over, and these people aren't going to risk their lives to fight off goblins for an abandoned town. Sazar knows this, so why does he go in there with a force of that size and actually attack?"

Ryson frowned as he considered the question. "Didn't think of it like that. Maybe his goblins are getting restless and he just wants to pacify them with whatever blood they can draw."

"Maybe," Sy allowed, "but I'm not sure it makes total sense, either. I mean if that was his objective, why not go in at night? Why go in the middle of the day? And why go in the way he did? From what I'm hearing it sounded more of a coordinated attack. Enin, you said they moved in with reserves in the back and they were attacking in organized movements. You didn't see them just running wild through the streets?"

"No, not wild at all." Enin then took a moment to consider his own thoughts of goblins. "It's interesting actually. Over the past season, I've seen some goblins up close, even threw some harmless spells at them just to see how they react. They're certainly not the brightest thing to come over from the dark realm. Actually, in a battle of wits, I'd probably choose a shag over a goblin any day. Goblins can be sneaky if they want to, no doubt about that. They have guile and stealth, but they run scared quite a bit as well. They

can organize, but not like a human militia. They rely on great numbers, but they are
inherently distrusting. While they could become a threat if they amassed into a large
army, I can't imagine the bickering that would take place. From what I saw, they moved
as if directed by a fairly cohesive plan. Yes, I would have to say with little doubt that
Sazar was directing them. That was plain enough for me to see."

Sy followed Enin's analysis with more questions. "This is the part that doesn't add up.
Why would Sazar direct the battle if the goal was to appease the blood lust of a bunch of
goblins? Why not just let them run wild, then reorganize them, take whatever spoils he
could find, and leave? No, I'm not seeing this as just a simple raid one way or the other.
He didn't have to do it in this way to take supplies, and he wouldn't have done it this way
to just let his little monsters go on a killing spree. Something else is up."

"I don't think it's going to be that easy to figure out what a serp really wants," Ryson
acknowledged. He then decided it was time for him to reveal his own intentions. "And
even if we don't know, I want to go to Pinesway."

Sy rubbed his chin as he eyed the delver carefully. "You want to go to Pinesway? I
assume you wish to leave now?"

"Yes, waiting doesn't do any good."

In truth, the captain was not surprised to hear this. He kept his own emotions buried
as he now pressed the delver for an explanation. "Why do you want to do this?"

"A lot of reasons." The delver replied almost too simply.

"Can you give me some of them?" Sy asked.

Ryson nodded and spoke openly of why he needed to go. "First of all, Pinesway may
be abandoned, but it's not completely deserted. We all know there are still people there
that might need help."

Sy kept his tone even, he didn't wish to sound sarcastic in any way, but the delver
needed to be told of obvious flaws in this objective. "Noble, but how can you help a
group of people that are wounded or already dead?"

"I can't help the dead, but if I find wounded, I can get them out of there."

"And if you find a dozen wounded, you're going to treat their wounds and get them to
safety? How are you going to manage that? Are you going to carry them all on your back
at once or one at a time?"

Ryson saw where Sy led him and heaved a heavy sigh. "Ok, maybe there's not much I
can do for the wounded. Maybe I can get them temporarily to a safe place to hide, I can
worry about that when I see what I'm up against. I might also be able to find some that
are neither dead nor wounded, maybe they're just scared and hiding. We can't just leave
them there."

Sy pressed with his pessimism. "While I don't wish to be coldhearted about this, I
could argue that most of those that are now residing in Pinesway are doing so because it
has been abandoned. They are opportunists that knew the risks. They took over
abandoned homes because there was no one there to stop them. An empty town makes a
good hideout for bandits. These people know how to take care of themselves, that's what
they're best at. If they saw a problem coming, they are probably already gone. If not, I
doubt there's anything left of them to save."

"Maybe most of the people that were in Pinesway were the type that would take off at
the first sign of trouble, but not all of them." Ryson noted. "There were a few that just
didn't want to leave their homes, even if it meant living with bandits and transients, and

having to deal with goblin raids. Remember, I've scouted Pinesway on more than one
occasion. There are some people there that just don't want to leave. I don't think they
would argue with any help I could give."

"I can't argue that," Sy offered, "but they also knew the risks. They didn't have to
stay. You have to consider that they are basically now dealing with the inevitable, with
what they knew had to eventually happen. It's not necessarily your job to help people that
didn't want help in the first place. But let's leave that aside for now. I believe there's
more to this, so tell me why else do you want to go."

"To scout the area, to see what Sazar is up to, to get an idea of the size of his new
band of monsters."

"Well, our wizard here has already given us a good idea of that."

Enin jumped into the conversation without much thought to Sy's intentions. "I used a sight spell, but it was connected to the web spell. It doesn't really see the whole town, you know, just bits and pieces. A street here, and an alley there, kind of blurry vision of the whole. It's probably an accurate count only to a degree." The wizard put a finger to his chin as he considered something new. "Now, that's a thought. I wonder if I could cast a clearer sight spell, something that wasn't connected to an object or another spell—a spell that would allow me to see anything at a particular area. It would be my own vision, not transplanting images obtained from something else. I'd have to bend light, that wouldn't be difficult, but I'd have to bend it there and back, kind of a reflection, but what would it reflect?"

"While you think about that, let me continue with the delver's wishes." Sy turned his attention back to the delver "As for scouting, my men scout that area every day. As you just said, I've had you scout it several times yourself. You know the condition of the town before the raid and the lay of the land. As for what Sazar's up to, we just talked about that. We don't have an idea at this point, and let's be honest, he's not going to tell you even if you go right up and ask him. We would still have to guess at that just as we will estimate the size of his forces. Even if Enin hasn't given us an exact count of the number of goblins and shags and whatever else might be involved in this attack, we both know he's given us a good idea of what's out there."

"Yes, but we also know he has a larger force with him now. That in itself is a bit of a surprise and getting a better look might not hurt."

"Actually, I don't think it is a surprise," Sy countered. "Think about it for a moment. We know for a fact that Sazar followed the dwarves into Dunop after they were defeated here. We have to believe he took a great amount of wealth from Dunop before he took off. He could use that to buy food and weapons to keep a fair amount of goblins happy for a while. We also know from Enin that he can control them to a great extent. The more creatures he controls, the more supplies he can steal. The more supplies he gets the more goblins he can entice into his camp. One will keep leading to the other."

Here Ryson spoke with much more certainty. "That's another reason I want to go. I know you can't be happy with what you just said, Sazar growing in strength. I want to see if maybe I can put a dent in that. If he goes in and strips Pinesway clean, he just gets that much stronger. I don't think you want that to happen."

"No I don't," Sy allowed. "I also know that alone you can't really stop the force that
Sazar is controlling."

"True, but I'm not going to stop them, just to irritate them, cause them some problems,
let them know that they just can't waltz anywhere they please without some kind of
resistance. I mean let's really look at this from a hard perspective. Sazar attacked in broad
daylight. Don't you think that's sending some kind of message?"

"I have already considered that, and I'm not happy with it myself." Sy turned about
and looked at the map on the wall with Burbon at its center. The map illustrated several
strategic points in all the surrounding areas. Hand drawn marks indicated contact with
varied monsters, suspected territories of dark creatures, and paths of travel for goblin
raiding parties. The map drew a grim picture, but other factors existed that could not be
illustrated on this chart and Sy spoke of them openly. "Message or not, daylight or dark,
we have to consider the ultimate truth. I do not believe that Burbon is in any danger from
this attack, and that has to be my first concern. Sazar is not going to hit us even with a

force three times the size Enin described. This town is not abandoned. If he attacked, he
would have to deal with our wall and towers, a trained corps of guards that know how to
fight goblins, a purebred delver that also knows how to deal with an assortment of dark
creatures, and let's not forget our wizard here. If Sazar attacked us, he would lose
probably his entire force and gain nothing. He's too smart for that, too calculating, and
that's the shame of it. So, with a fair amount of certainty, I can say that we're not his
primary target now or in the foreseeable future. There are, however, several outposts to
the north, farms on the outskirts of Connel, and small villages to the southeast that would
be a ripe target for him. If he believes he can waltz into Pinesway and just take whatever
he wants in broad daylight, then he's not far from advancing on these other targets as
well."

Sy turned back to Ryson, but remained frowning. "Still, while I understand why you
want to go, I don't know yet what you think you're going to do out there. It's dangerous
and I know you don't like killing things. I can't see you doing any great damage to
Sazar's numbers if you're only going to stir up some kind of frenzy. You put yourself at
great risk and I'd like to know what you think you're going to ultimately accomplish.
This has to have more of a reason."

"Well, I have no intention of doing some kind of frontal assault if that's what you're
worried about."

"What is you intention?"

"First, I do want to do a quick scout. I think we should get a better idea of Sazar's
true force and not just base it on what Enin saw in that spell of his. Second, I want to
create some havoc, knock a few goblins out of the fight. You're right, I have no intention
of killing any, but I can make them run scared, and if they run far enough, they might not
come back. If I stir up enough trouble, I can maybe even cause a shag to lose control. A
shag that takes off after me might also get beyond Sazar's range and that's one less
monster the serp has to control. Third, I want to try and remove some of the supplies they
are stealing, remove or destroy, same thing. I can't carry it away, but I can sabotage a cart
or set it on fire. Finally, I want to send a message right back to Sazar, let him know that I
have my eye on him. Sazar knows me, knows us. You're right, he doesn't attack Burbon,
and I think it's mostly because of our wizard here, but he also knows we are prepared for
him. If I take a quick shot at him while he's trying to make a strike in a neighboring

town, then he also knows we will go beyond the walls of Burbon to keep him at bay. If he wants to send a message by attacking in broad daylight, I want to send one right back to him, one that's says I'm not impressed."

Sy nodded and carefully considered what the delver just offered. He could not help but agree with many of the points. "The truth of the matter is I can't argue with anything you just said. I'm not happy that Pinesway is sitting out there so close to us and abandoned. It serves as an easy target that invites the wrong type of element. Choosing between thieves and dark creatures doesn't make me comfortable. That I do not like. I'd much rather have an empty hillside then what's there now. I also don't like Sazar thinking he can pick off easy victims without risk. He needs to know we're ready to counter anything he might throw at us. He seems to be the biggest threat in our immediate area."

"So you don't have a problem with me going?" Ryson sounded almost amazed.

Sy quickly explained. "I have lots of problems with it. It's risky, I don't want to lose
you, and you're outnumbered. But you're also a delver and I've seen what you can do. If
you keep your mind to your business, I doubt they'll touch you. There are, however,
other considerations."

"Such as?"

"Such as should I send a contingent of guards as well."

"They'd only slow me down."

"It would not be my order to have them accompany you," Sy explained. "As I said,
I've seen what you can do. They wouldn't be able to keep up and would probably just
end up causing you greater risks. I am thinking, however, of sending them to follow up
after you. If you create the kind of havoc I believe you can, they might be able to clean
up after you, take out several goblins that end up fleeing or a shag that gets separated
form the main group. You might have something against killing these creatures, but I
don't. It wouldn't upset me to put a bigger hurt on Sazar."

"Didn't think of that," Ryson admitted.

"Of course, I doubt that will be necessary if Enin decides to go with you. Then he
could probably cause more pain and inflict much more damage then several hundred of
my best men."

Both Ryson and Sy looked to the wizard almost expectantly. Enin had said nothing
since he began to consider his sight spell. They wondered if he had paid any further
attention to the conversation. His reply made it clear he had.

"Me? Go to Pinesway?" The wizard shook his head with a noticeable grimace. "No,
not a good idea. Didn't ever really consider it actually. You both know I don't like
interfering in the decisions of any creature, even dark creatures. There are problems you
have to decide for yourself, work out for yourself, that kind of thing. Kind of hard to
explain really. It's hard for me sometime, you know. I like to help, but I can't interfere. If
I start doing everything, then what is there left for you to do? We all have our place and
our jobs. You have to do what you have to do. If I started taking over everything, where
would it stop? It's really a trap. I don't want that kind of responsibility, and I don't really
think most of the people around here would appreciate it. I guess you must think it almost
lazy of me, but that's not it at all. You do understand, don't you?"

"Enin, the day I understand you is a day I both fear and welcome, and a day that I
think will never appear." Sy then turned back to the delver. "I won't try to stop you from
going, but I will ask you to be careful."

"I will."

"Actually, I need you to be more than careful," Sy added quickly.

"What do you mean?" Ryson turned his head curiously as he waited for an answer.

Sy appeared to take his time in selecting his words. Eventually, he spoke with a greater tone of concern and less the voice of authority that was his normal manner.

"I know you, Ryson. I know you want to help anyone that's trapped in Pinesway, but I also meant what I said before. I know you think everyone is worth your help, and I'm not going to try and argue that. What I will say is that everyone that is now in danger in Pinesway is in that danger of their own choosing. They had ample opportunity to leave, they decided not to. Some came from other towns to stake a claim after most residents abandoned the place. In my mind, that's asking for trouble. Now they have it. You want to do what you can to save them, and I won't condemn you for trying as long as you also

understand that people have to ultimately take responsibility for their own decisions.
There is a line between doing what's needed and going too far. I also wasn't trying to be
obnoxious when I asked how you intended on helping the wounded. It's not only about
getting careless, it's also about realizing that sometimes there's just nothing you can do.
If you don't accept that, bad things will happen. That's a plain truth. I don't want to see
anything happen to you, Enin doesn't want to see anything happen to you—most of all,
Linda doesn't want to see anything happen to you. I know your desire to help is just that,
you're not trying to be a hero. It's a noble thing to do. What I've always worried about is
that one day you might end up being too noble. You want to help, fine, help where you
can, but understand that some risks help no one and can hurt others. We need you back
here."

Ryson exhaled heavily and did the best he could to reassure his friend. "I'll be careful.
You have my word."

Sy offered one more reminder to the delver about the challenges he faced.
"Remember, the people in Pinesway knew raids like this were coming. They still wanted
to stay. Although you might want to, sometimes you can't save people from themselves.
You have to let them be."

Enin suddenly offered his own opinion on the matter. He spoke with a greater weight
to his voice as if he wanted to offer a deeper understanding. "What the captain says is
very true. Do not dismiss it, my friend. You can't save people from themselves, and even
more so, you can't keep people from their fate."

Ryson found the last statement too confusing to ignore. "You're saying that anyone
that dies in this raid was supposed to die."

"I'm saying there are things beyond our control," Enin explained almost sternly,
"things that each individual must face on his own. It isn't always good, but for whatever
reason, it must be faced. We might not like everything that happens, but things happen
for a reason. Keep that in mind. It will serve you well both now and in the future."

"Not sure I understand that, not even sure I want to," Ryson admitted. "Anyway, I
need to leave now. I should hit Pinesway before the sunsets and I'll be back here before
the sun rises. Linda thinks I'm out on a scout with Enin so she won't expect me back
until late tomorrow anyway. She doesn't need to know or worry, so I'd appreciate it if
you didn't tell her where I'm going."

"She won't see me," Enin declared. "I'm returning to my house, there's something I

need to look into myself. I'll be busy for sometime." Enin paused to take a deep look at
the delver. He then took a small jewel from his pocket. "You'll be fine, but if you need
help, really need help, hold this tight in your palm and think of me."

Ryson took the gem and held it loosely in his hand. If felt near weightless and he
couldn't identify it. Its color changed with each passing moment. "Never saw one of
these before. What kind of stone is it? It's not a ruby, diamond, or emerald."

"It's not a natural stone. I made it. If you need me, however, it will tell me. That's all
that's important. Good luck to you." Enin said no more, he simply walked out the door.

Sy looked from the stone to the delver to the door that Enin walked through. "I may
not understand him, but I think I am actually getting used to him. And I know I thank
every day that he's here with us." Sy turned his attention back to the delver. "Anyway,
just so you know, I am going to send men to the outskirts of Pinesway. I'm not going to
order them into town, but they will have orders to strike any group of dark creatures they

can handle safely. Any stray goblins that try to leave or enter are not going to have an
easy time of it. They're also going to warn any travelers and help any stragglers that have
escaped the town that make it to the open roads. Keep that in mind for yourself and
anyone that you meet up with. You won't be completely alone."

Ryson looked once more at the stone in his hand and then deposited it in his own
pocket. "I guess not. Thanks. I'll see you tomorrow."

With that, the delver dashed out of the office.

Chapter 5

"Hello, brother." The voice that greeted Enin filled the air with emotion, and this emotion spanned the spectrum of feelings. It held joy drifting toward anger, happiness betrayed by sadness, enthusiasm cut off by indifference. The inhabitant of this otherwise hollow region made no attempt to temper the tone of his voice. Instead, he allowed the opposing passions of these two simple words to vibrate incessantly around the space of this shadowy realm that he himself created.

Enin firmed himself against the icy shivers that always rode down his spine whenever he entered this place. He could feel the intense emotions biting at his very flesh and this cold tingle reminded him just how much he hated coming here. He spoke quickly in response as if hoping to brush off any lasting echoes or at the very least to quickly diminish the sentiment of the greeting.

"I am not your brother, Baannat."

Enin's tone held no such dueling emotional ambiguity. His words rang quite clearly of caution and distrust.

Baannat, however, was not so easily swayed. Even more emotion spilled out of his words that followed.

"Not brothers? Well, no. Perhaps not in the way lesser creatures see relations, but you have to admit they are rather limited in their understanding of things. Sometimes you have to go beyond the limits, expand your definition. Think of that, brother. We do that all the time, you and I. We constantly expand what we can do, what we can sense, what we understand. In this context, we are more closely related than these inferior things that call themselves siblings. Just because they spilled out of the same mindless creature that bore them, that's enough for them to feel some kind of bond. You wish to ignore the bond we have? You acknowledge it every time you come here. We certainly are brothers. Look at the similarities. It goes far beyond our simple meetings here, it goes to the very breadth of our abilities, abilities that no other can match. We both cast white magic, and we both cast with two perfect circles…"

"That is where the similarities end."

"Perhaps they do, but in that alone we are more alike than any so-called 'relation' of these lesser beings with which you tend to waste so much time."

In truth, Enin could not be exactly sure if there were any further similarities, for while Baannat was eager to be heard, he remained less willing to be seen. He masked his visual presence from Enin with shadow and distortion. Enin never got a good look at his

adversary, thus he could only guess as to what Baannat truly was. Despite this lack of
knowledge, Enin remained resolute in his belief that he had little in common with
Baannat, and they were certainly not brothers.

"We are not alike, we are very much opposite," Enin stated.

Baannat almost allowed a cackle to slip across his tongue, but he held it back in order
to torment his guest further. "Opposites, you've talked about that with me before, haven't
you? Opposing sides and such, it is almost necessary according to your concept of
existence. It is all for the sake of balance. Isn't that what you always say? And balance is
so very important. It explains those things which you can't explain. Perfection is

impossible to obtain because perfection is out of balance. These lesser creatures must
face hardships for the sake of balance."

"That is only part of it," Enin replied stoically.

"And what are the other parts again?"

"You know them as well as I do. Lessons need to be learned. Paths need to be
followed. When the time comes, decisions need to be made. These 'lesser beings' as you
refer to them to must be allowed to make certain choices…"

"But not everything is a choice," Baannat quickly interrupted.

"Choices must be made without prejudice—with balance."

"And is that why you won't act against this serp that is currently making problems for
you and your friends? You're afraid of tipping the balance?"

At the mention of the serp, Enin grew slightly more suspicious of Baannat. He had not
mentioned Sazar as of yet, but in truth, that meant little. Baannat certainly had ways to
see into the land, to know of events as they happened. It was not beyond reason to expect
that Baannat knew of the serp's actions.

"I do not act for many reasons, it's not my time, nor is it my place," Enin declared
with a distinct tone of certainty. "I will not interfere in the workings of grander designs."

"Ahh, when we don't talk about balance we always come back to these thoughts of
destiny and fate. You think we all have some part to play in this grand scheme, it's all
pretty much set in stone."

"No, not set in stone, as I've said to you many times before. The event may be set, but
the choice is not. I've tried to explain it to you, but you just can't grasp it. Is it because
you can't see it?"

"I see everything that is important to see," Baannat growled with more than a hint of
displeasure.

"Your weakness," Enin noted. "You don't like to admit that there are things beyond
your understanding."

"There are many more beyond yours." This time, there existed a great mix of emotion
in these words, and again, Baannat allowed the depth of these opposing feelings to
pulsate freely through the air of his realm.

Enin did his best to brush the vibrations from his being. "Those things I do not
understand, I do not wish to know. It does not benefit me to know why some twisted
individuals gain favor in taking advantage of others. I do not profit from insight of
actions spawned by selfish greed. And I certainly do not grow in spirit from
understanding why some beings, whether they be lesser or greater, would choose to bring
pain and torment to the innocent. You have clearly probed such things, and you

understand them far better than I. With that, there is one clear truth—this knowledge has
not strengthened you in any way shape or form."

"One day you will discover that is not as clear a truth as you would like to believe,"
Baannat growled, holding only the emotion of hate.

"That day shall not come to pass."

Baannat's tone returned to its previous mix of emotions, the hate remaining but mixed
in with so many other trembling sentiments. "And yet again we return to the anchor of
you miscalculated beliefs, your ideas of fate. You think you won't have to face me
because it falls to this delver. You keep on believing that."

Thinking of the delver, Enin allowed his own passions to stir much more upbeat. "And you go right on hoping you won't have to face Ryson Acumen. He senses you." With that said, Enin seized on a new vibration he had not felt before. "You know that, don't you? You are aware the delver can feel your presence, even though you are in hiding, he can actually sense you."

Baannat did not reveal any concern. "He's a delver, he senses lots of things, or maybe I'm just playing with him, or playing with you for that matter. However, my patience is not limitless as you well know. Why are you here?"

Enin made no attempt to mask his intentions. "I am here because of the serp you have already mentioned. I am also here because of the delver. The moment that the serp attacked an abandon town, Ryson Acumen sensed you. I came here to find out if you are in any way connected to the serp's most recent actions or if it is simple coincidence."

"Is that a question?"

"I never intended on asking you directly, because I know I would not be able to trust whatever answer you gave me."

"Then a pointless trip here?"

"Baannat, your power nearly equals mine. You know what I can do, because you know what you can do. Do you really think I need to speak to you to find out if you are involved with this serp's actions?"

"You always get me with your logic."

"It's not logic, it is truth. I came here simply to gauge the echoes of magic. If you were involved, I would feel it, and thus, I would know it. I have been here long enough to see that you do not have a hand in this as of yet. That, Baannat, is quite long enough for me. Hopefully, I will not see you again any time soon."

Before Enin could leave, however, Baannat spoke up to ensure he would be heard.

"You wish to leave before we have had our fun? That is not very nice of you. I'm almost embarrassed to call you brother."

"Must we go through this every time I come here?" Enin asked without masking his tone of annoyance.

Baannat matched Enin's tone with an expression of indignation. "You are the one complaining? You come to my realm unannounced, come here of your own volition and without invitation, and yet you always wish to protest when I ask this small thing of you. It's not like I asked you here and it's not like I put any barriers to prevent you from entering. You come when you like, you leave just as quickly. Is it so much to ask for you to carry out this one little thing for me?"

"It is tiresome and wasteful," Enin replied plainly. "We accomplish nothing, the result
is always the same and yet you insist on this silly game each time I come here."

"Would you rather I spend my time designing ways to prevent you from coming here.
Or perhaps you would rather me focus on finding ways to drop in on you when you are in
your home? Hmmmm, that's an idea. How would you like that, brother? How would you
like it if I just popped in on you without word or notice?"

"I would not like it, nor would I allow it to happen more than once."

"A threat?" Baannat laughed.

"Call it what you like."

Baannat became hostile at the indifference in Enin's voice. "Very well, I will call it an
empty threat."

"As I said, call it what you like."

Long silence gripped the space between the two magic-casters. Finally, Baannat spoke again, but this time with glee in his voice. "You have not left yet, so I take it you are willing to have a bit of fun."

"If you are intent on wasting your time, then I will not prevent you in seeing the outcome we already know."

"Excellent! What shall we work with today? Fire against ice?"

"We did that last time. If we are to do this, let us at least try to make it somewhat interesting."

The moment Enin finished his sentence, he could not see Baannat's glare, but he could most definitely feel it.

"Very well," Baannat responded with a cold chill. "Let us try something new and a bit different. We will both try to fill the space of my realm, as always, but this time I will cast light and you will cast shadow. Let us see if you can cast darkness with the same power as you cast the others."

"Shadow is not necessarily darkness or a dark power as you imply," Enin responded confidently. "Shadow is the by product of light, plain and simple. There is nothing inherently evil about it, only when it is corrupted by the magic-caster. Shadow is cooling shade on a hot day, shadow is relief to tired eyes from a bright sun, shadow is the contrast for even more vibrant colors. You see, Baannat, I can find the true power in all the facets of the magic we possess. That is why I always win this game."

Baannat giggled. "We shall see."

In an instant, the shadowed figure opposing Enin swayed his hands and two rings of white energy danced at his finger tips. They exploded in a blast of white hot light which flowed outward as if radiating from pulsating star. The white light quickly changed to a deep yellow as if the midday sun filled the room. The light began to swirl about as if it took the shape of a pinwheel twirling in a gale wind.

Enin raised his hands and two circles of pure white power flowed about his wrists. He threw his arms outward and the two circles flew from him in opposite directions. The moment they struck the yellow twirling light bathing the very air, the white circles turned gray and the darkness began to intertwine in the space between the ribbons of pale gold.

The pulsating light fought back against being invaded. It pushed to one side and then another, but as it did Enin's creation of shadow circled around and filled more areas between the swirls. Back and forth the two forces pressed against each other, twisting and twirling about this empty space like two intertwined tornados of completely opposite rotations.

Eventually the give and take between the two forces ebbed, and the areas of yellow
light and dark gray became fixed. The weight of the two were very close to equal, but
even to an unassuming eye it was clear that there was slightly more shadow than light.

"It was an interesting show," Enin offered almost apologetically, "but we always
come to the same conclusion, don't we?"

"So far," Baannat replied without bitterness in losing. If anything, the blurred figure
appeared to be smiling, but Enin could never be sure.

"If our game is over, I will be on my way."

"It is over—for now."

With that said, Enin simply walked out of this shapeless place and returned to his
study where he would await the entrance of another.

Chapter 6

Joel Portsmith found little comfort in escaping the Rock Beetle. After deciding to return to his home, the ever changing circumstances of the goblin attack continued to affect his movements. He stayed near building walls and behind as much cover as available, but never ventured fully inside a structure beyond a porch or an open stable area. As long as he remained moving on the streets, he kept his ultimate destination in mind. He feared the moment he entered a building that might seem to offer security, he would lose this focus. Confusion ruled Pinesway, and screams of torment continued to echo through the cluttered alleys. He knew there was no true safe place to hide, and he had no intention of lulling himself into a false sense of security by muffling the encroaching sounds of doom with four walls, a locked door, and a dark corner.

He encountered quite a few others in his path, many more people in fact than he ever expected. With each block he crossed, he witnessed one or two fleeing in senseless, panicked directions. Other remained hidden behind carts or under porches, and almost all wore a glassy-eyed, dumbfounded expression. These thieves and hooligans were no longer the predators of unsuspecting wanderers that ventured unwittingly into their hands. Instead, creatures of a nightmare now hunted them, and their minds were ill-equipped to deal with such irony. Many did not wish to speak to him, those that did often made little sense. A mix of fear, anger, horror, and confusion slurred their words as well as their meaning. When he was able to obtain viable information from a few of the less bewildered, he cursed at the news.

"They're herding us here like cattle," he grumbled to himself. "They've got us surrounded and now they're heading inward. No wonder everyone is running in every direction. Running east is as bad as heading west, same thing in every direction, bad news. I don't think there's anyway out of here. Ok, doesn't matter. I'm not looking to leave. I just have to get home, have to keep moving as long as possible in that direction. I wonder how far I can get."

He avoided contemplating this question again for as long as he could. Eventually, however, he was forced to a stop. His careful movements brought him a fair distance away from the town's center square and about six blocks from his home. Unfortunately, at this point he encountered a segment of the goblins' forward line. To make matters

worse, this particular group of monsters showed no sign of advancing. They stood in a
loose formation with clear lines of sight in several directions. They cut off every path he
could see that offered a way to his planned destination.

Joel crouched low and avoided attention, but it was not something he could do
forever. "I could double back, but that's not going to get me where I want to go. Ok, not
the situation I had in mind, but this ain't a festival parade, either. Face facts, it was going
to come down to a fight eventually. Might as well start it here, just don't want to end it
here."

Joel took a long look down the street towards a group of goblins that staked out a
crossroad in front of him. They crouched low and their small stature made them difficult
targets, but they seemed to show no care toward finding cover. For the most part they
stood out in the open, as if they held no fear of attack, or perhaps it was just their way of
being seen so that any panicked human wouldn't dare try to pass them.

Joel remained hidden from their sight as he contemplated the situation. "I got a clear
shot at a few of them right now. If I fire from here, though, there going to see me." He
paused to look back over his shoulder. "And no real good escape from here, either. Once
I take my shots, I'm gonna have to move, but I gotta move smart. Not going to get
trapped here."

Joel remained careful to stay out of sight and always remained mindful of the sounds
of the hook hawk that remained in the distance. The thought of the rock beetle gave him a
cold shudder, but there wasn't much he could do about that nightmare. If it was under his
feet right now, he'd never know it.

Instead, he focused on his main objective and toward that end he needed two things—
a covered spot to take out a few goblins with his crossbow, and then a safe path of retreat.
That path had to allow him a route away from the goblins not to a dead end. He wanted
his withdrawal to take him a safe distance away, but also allow him to turn back in a
direction toward his home.

Scanning the row of buildings, he found a secure spot to shoot fairly quickly. An
emptied and ransacked merchant store had two broken windows facing the goblin line. It
also fronted an equally empty warehouse that included a broken delivery door that
opened to a back alley. Calculating the distance from the storefront to the goblin position,
he believed he could hit his targets. The cover of the store would allow him to take at
least two or three clean shots from the windows, maybe even four. With the windows
already broken he wouldn't make much noise. Still standing in one spot, the goblins
didn't look too concerned with facing an attack at this particular moment, so he believed
he could catch them off guard. Once he fired, he hoped that before they could get a clear
lock on his position he could move back through the storefront, into the warehouse, and
then out into the alley.

The alley ran parallel to a street he needed to cross to get back home, so he could
follow this path for as long as necessary. If the goblins called for reinforcements, they
would have to close in tight, and that would open some holes in their line. He just needed
to create enough havoc to distract the goblins enough for him to get through.

He took his position in the store and stared down through his line of fire. He wouldn't
get a better chance then this. "It's getting darker," he whispered to himself. "Shadows are
getting longer, must be near sunset. Don't want to do this in the dark, that's their

advantage, not mine. Ok, best do it now and get it over with."

He carefully slid the crossbow down from over his shoulder and took hold of the stock. His hand trembled slightly at first, but with a quick breath, he steadied himself. He loaded the first bolt, and decided not to take any more time to think. His decision was made and it was time to fire.

The first bolt found its mark in the neck of an unsuspecting goblin. The creature spun around twice upon being hit before crumpling to the ground. The other goblins jumped at first and Joel thought they might scatter. Something, however, seemed to grip them in place as they stood frozen in dumbfounded awe of the sight. They looked back and forth from the downed monster to the streets as if trying to determine from where the attack came. The spiraled movement of the victim's fall, however, left them looking in the wrong direction.

Joel allowed himself a short nod to his luck as he loaded another bolt. He took aim, but this time his fortune did not smile with the same benevolence. The bolt flew straight and true, but it smashed against the thick metal chest guard of another unmoving goblin. The creature was stunned as it was knocked off its feet, but the bolt did not penetrate the armor and the goblin was unhurt. It appeared to peer right at the window from where the bolt came.

Joel ducked low, mumbled a curse as he loaded a third bolt and moved over to the second window. When he raised his head slightly to get a look at the situation, the curses faded.

The goblins remained unmoving and in the open, almost as if standing in a dazed stupor. They looked in all directions and none made a move toward his position. He decided to gamble at this point. He fired the crossbow once more and quickly reloaded, fired again, reloaded and fired a third time. He ducked down and moved back to the first window, popped his head up, and took another long look while he loaded yet another bolt. He could see that luck swung back to his favor. All three bolts found a victim and now there were four goblins on the ground already dead, or mortally wounded. The remaining goblins lost their stoic nature and now moved in pure panic. They hissed and growled as they dove for cover or ran in every direction. They appeared to care very little for determining the source of fire, and thus Joel did not make an immediate attempt to leave the store.

#

Sazar immediately sensed the attack on his goblins. He felt the loss of the minion almost as if someone plucked a scale from his skin. As he stood in a dusty warehouse, he peered out a half broken window toward the north.

"What's this?" he asked himself. He flipped through a myriad of images in his mind. He saw Pinesway from varying perspectives through the flashes of sensations he obtained from his goblins. He quickly categorized the different sections of town and immediately sharpened his focus on the area of the attack. He could visualize the goblin dead on the ground with a crossbow bolt in its neck.

"Crossbow fire, but just one shot," the serp mused. "I wonder where from. There will be another I'm sure." Sazar linked his thoughts directly to the goblins in this precise area. The images of the other sections of town quickly blurred out of his mind. With his attention narrowly focused on goblins near the point of the assault, his contact with the other monsters in town broke off. For these minions, the orders Sazar previously pressed into their minds would remain in the forefront of their thoughts, but they were also now more or less on their own.

"Stay as you are," the serp whispered to a thread of energy that instantaneously brought the command to the goblins that stood near Joel's position. They did not hear it with their ears, but it rang in their thoughts as if the order had been shouted from a mountain top. "Keep your eyes to the buildings toward the center of town. Look for movement."

At that moment, the serp actually felt the bolt that Joel had fired into the chest armor of the second goblin. So powerful was the link to this creature that Sazar almost lost his breath. He followed the gaze of this fallen but unhurt goblin, and Sazar believed he knew where the attacker hid. He focused more strenuously on the sight that came crisper into his mind. Seizing the very vision of the goblin at the scene, the serp saw movement of shadows through a broken window.

"Yes, there he is. This one is getting brave. Can't let that happen." He refocused his thoughts on the band of goblins. "Split into two groups and sur…"

His complete order never reached the goblins. Another bolt found a goblins ear and the creature screamed. The sudden explosion of pain and sound surprised the serp for only a moment, but it was a moment long enough. Another bolt found its mark and a goblin collapsed, dead instantly with a bolt lodged past the arm hole of its chest guard and into the creature's black heart. A third and final bolt also hit its target, piercing a goblins cheek and through its mouth. This goblin could not scream, but it gurgled in agony.

The serp endeavored to refocus his link with the goblins that were under attack, but the creatures' own delirious panic overrode such an attempt. They broke formation under the stress, ignored any whisper of the serp's commands that tried to enter their thoughts, their minds clouded with their own fear. Sazar's words could reach their minds, but it could not break through the haze of terror that now gripped their every concern. They ran and hissed, scrambled and screeched. They showed little regard for anything else other than searching for cover from the unseen attack. They moved without direction other than the desire to avoid the next bolt.

"Incompetent imbeciles," Sazar growled. He quickly ended his link with these goblins, deciding further attempts to corral them would be futile. Images from his other minions slowly began to filter back into his mind once more. He sensed no other calamity throughout the town and he drank in the relief that this instance of resistance appeared to be completely isolated. Still, he needed to address the issue to ensure that it would not spread. He immediately redirected the hook hawk to cover the area from above.

He considered sending the rock beetle as well, but quickly dismissed the thought. The beetle remained in its position chomping away on the remains of the two goblins the serp had commanded to be its meal. More importantly, the beetle remained stationed in a strategic position that cut off the river rogue from the rest of the town. With his ring of goblins tightening on the center of Pinesway, the serp wished to keep the territorial river rogue from venturing beyond its claimed land. The rogue could no doubt smell the rock beetle and would remain defensive of its position as opposed to curious about the upheaval near the town's center.

"Can't rely on the goblins, though," Sazar lamented to himself. "My other shag is too far across town. Best to send the big one."

With that, Sazar directed a mental command to the large shag that served as the serp's personnel body guard and was doing nothing more at the moment then standing guard outside the building. The shag grunted, crouched low, and bounded off toward the center of chaos that was all that was now left of Pinesway.

#

Ryson circled Pinesway from the edges of the surrounding forest before he even considered entering the town. He dashed through the trees in a blur of movement, quickly taking glimpses of each road that became visible as he traveled. The river that cut across the northwest section of town proved to be his only true obstacle. He could have cut across the shallow water with ease, but he did not wish to deal with the hazards of soaking his feet and lower legs with the bitter cold water. Just because the flowing river kept ice from forming didn't mean it wasn't dangerously cold. He also decided to avoid the bridge crossing when he spotted a river rogue crouched low beneath the span.

The creature seemed satisfied to remain still and let the events unfold in the town without its participation. It seemed content to guard its own small territory, so Ryson decided to leave it alone.

Instead, the delver scurried up a large willow tree, scampered over leafless branches and through vines that hung down and across the flowing river, then leapt across to the thick branches of a wild cherry tree. Once he darted down the trunk of this tree, he was across the river and continued his initial scout.

The delver cared little for what he saw. The goblins he visually pinpointed numbered at least a hundred. Since he could see only the outskirts of the town and not far into the center, he believed the true number to stand at a much higher total, perhaps three or four times as many. The creatures surrounded the town's outer boundaries, strategically covering each significant entranceway. The movements and sounds he could detect from deeper into the collection of structures indicated the devious monsters were closing in on the town square from all directions. Anyone trapped inside appeared to have little chance for escape just as he found little hope for a way to enter undetected. He knew he could bolt at top speed past the stationed guards at just about any point without risking injury, but his movement would be detected. At this point, he still did not have a precise plan, and thus, he wished to avoid being spotted.

Very early in his scout, he noticed the presence of a mammoth shag guarding a large warehouse near the southern entrance. Ryson recognized this monster. Sazar used this creature as a personal body guard, thus the delver remained certain Sazar was in that building and more likely than not directing the goblins movements.

Ryson now felt certain that Sazar was up to more than a simple raid for supplies or a blood hunt for his goblins to release their dark desires. Everything he saw pointed to the goblins securing the town. The problem remained that he could not truly know why. Sazar was not allowing anyone to escape, thus he could be targeting an individual or a group. Pinesway was now a haven for thieves and bandits, perhaps they stole something he coveted. Ryson also considered that the serp may have simply wanted to pick the town clean and his tactics kept any humans from escaping with possible treasure. The truth of the matter was that Ryson simply could not be certain of the serp's intentions without further information.

The delver quickly took a path south through the trees further into the forest. Once

past the southern edge of town, he circled back up and came to face the main entrance
where he first spied the large shag standing guard outside the warehouse. Remaining
hidden, he closed his eyes and focused his attention on what he could hear. Guttural
shouts of goblins mixed in with an intermittent human scream and a shriek from a hook
hawk off to the northeast. He tried to put a picture to the sounds and could only imagine
the uncompromising forward movement of the goblins against a terrified group of
humans.

Suddenly, he picked up sounds that were quite out of place. Grumbling growls of
goblins were replaced by new screams of pain, screams from a goblin, not a human.
Moments later, more goblin squeals of tumultuous confusion. Ryson tried to pinpoint the
area but could only guess it was occurring slightly to the west of the center of town.
Wherever it was, goblins were now in a fit of disorder. Adding to his curiosity over this
turn of events, the shag guarding the outside of the warehouse stirred from its statue like
stance and hurried off toward the direction of the commotion.

"Interesting," Ryson stated the obvious to himself. "He's going somewhere in a hurry. If Sazar is in that building, he just lost his guard."

The delver considered that point only for an instant. There were two goblins circling the building, but they were frivolous in terms of protecting the serp. Ryson could enter the warehouse and be out of their sight before the goblins even knew he was in town. A clear path to the serp offered itself right before him, yet his eyes focused on another path, that of the shag.

"He's going in the direction of the commotion. I'd bet on it. That means the goblins are having some trouble, or someone is giving them more than they can handle. The shag is going to clean up the mess. That's the only answer that makes sense."

In the end, the delver's curiosity regarding the shag's destination proved more enticing than the open path to the now unprotected Sazar. In truth, thoughts of the serp faded from his focus, washed out by the questions regarding this new turn of events. His delver instincts called for him to answer these questions.

As if to punctuate this desire, the movement of the hook hawk also caught his attention. Where it had been circling the eastern section of town, it was now curving its path to the west. It let out a spine shivering shriek when it passed the center of town, and its swooping, semi-circular flight path led it in the same direction as the shag was charging toward.

Thoughts of Sazar now disappeared completely from Ryson's mind. He eyed the path of the shag and quickly noted how the goblins guarding the streets cast a wary glance upon the loping monster. Their natural fear of the shag overrode the serp's order to keep a watchful eye on the entrance ways to the town. For a brief moment, their attention focused firmly upon the shag, and that was all the distraction the delver needed.

In a blur of motion, Ryson dashed across the open land that stood between the tree line of Dark Spruce Forest and the first structures of Pinesway. He darted behind one building and then around another before the goblins that guarded this area lost sight of the lumbering shag. They never saw the delver, and thus Sazar never gained an image of Ryson's entrance into Pinesway.

#

With the goblins in disarray, Joel watched with less worry over being spotted in the merchant shop. He peered through the broken window and watched as the goblins scattered in different directions. He raised the crossbow several more times and fired

bolts into their midst. He never hit his mark now that they moved in
haphazard fashion.
He tried to lead a target, but the goblins turned and twisted with each
racing step they
took. He never guessed correctly which way his target would turn and thus
all his bolts
ended up lodging into the walls of surrounding structures or the sides of
emptied carts.
Still, the continued crossbow fire added to the commotion. He noted that
several more
goblins began to appear in his view both further off to the north and
south of his current
position.
    "Ok, they're starting to take notice and they're moving in from other
directions to see
what's going on. If I'm going to find an opening, it should be soon."
    He crouched low as he tossed the crossbow back over his shoulder and
made a path to
the back of the store. He kicked away a loose panel that blocked his way
to the rear
warehouse and pushed through the litter of this larger open space. Before
he leapt out into
the alley, he leaned out slightly to take a quick look up and down the
path. He saw

nothing other than the debris of broken barrels and crates. Just as he took his first step out
into the open, he heard the shriek of the hook hawk.

"Not good!" Joel shook his head. The alley was narrow, but most of the buildings in
this area were only one story high and offered little cover overhead. "Can't change it
now, and can't get caught here."

Joel took off in a slow trot to the south, clinging to walls as best he could while still
keeping a respectable pace. He needed to create some distance between himself and the
point where the goblins were now congregating. He believed if he could get at least three
blocks down, he might have a chance to turn out of the alley and make a break toward his
home.

Another shriek of the hook hawk turned his skin cold. He braved a look up and back
over his shoulder. He caught the spiraling shadow of a large winged creature. The sun
was low in the southwestern sky, and with the shadow behind him, he calculated the
beast to be flying very low and almost directly over his head. He stopped dead in his
tracks. He believed he could actually hear the wind ruffling through twisted feathers very
nearby, much too close to give him anything other then a sense of his own mortality. He
flattened himself against the wall, offering as little a target to the sky as possible. A
breeze struck his face and he tensed, expecting to feel the cold hard talons pierce his
shoulders, but the pain never came.

The hook hawk shrieked a third time. This time the sound came further off to his right.
He heard the terrified squeal of a goblin in the same area. Joel moved away from the side
of the building and toward the center of the alley to risk taking a better look. Into the
sights of the sun, he saw the darkened outline of the hawk swooping further up into the
sky. He then saw the shadow pass along the ground in front of him and made out the
outline of a small figure clasped in the talons of the bird.

"Bad luck for that goblin, good luck for me. That had to scatter the others over there.
If I have a chance, it's now. OK, just have to make it over there as fast as I can."

Joel decided to bet the commotion of the hook hawk and his previous crossbow fire
might have distracted and confused the goblins enough to offer him his best chance at a
break through their lines. With the hook hawk now more interested in a meal than
watching the ground, he believed there was no better time for a quick sprint out of the
alley and toward his home. As he bounded out into an open street, the sight of the

monstrous shag running right toward him dissolved any confidence he had gained.

#

Ryson found it almost painfully simple to follow the shag without being noticed. The shag ran with a single minded purpose, always looking forward, moving at a steady pace. It never stopped to sniff the wind or to check its flank. It only ran onward in a northern direction. The monster took to the main roads and traveled with a confidence as if it had journeyed on these streets before. In reality, it simply followed the instructions the serp had placed in its mind, and thus, it gave no care to its surroundings or worries at becoming lost.

As for the goblins that Ryson ventured near, their attention would always fall to the giant shag. Despite knowing that this horrible giant was an ally as opposed to a threat looking to make a meal of them, they could not dampen their own instincts. It was simply impossible for them to remain calm when it bounded past them. The sight of the creature

demanded their attention as well as their caution whenever it was near. Every ounce of
their being commanded they remain watchful of this natural predator.

The delver used this distraction to his own advantage and dashed by any sentry points
with relative ease. As long as he remained a certain distance behind the shag, he could
count on extended moments of goblin diversion. Block after block, he moved in a
repetitive sequence. He would case the goblin positions, wait for the shag to catch their
attention, dart across any open area, take cover behind a new set of structures, and then
begin the process over again. Within moments, he closed upon the inner sections of
Pinesway and quickly became disgusted with what he witnessed.

The goblins had not raided this town for supplies, at least not yet. It was clear that at
this point they had focused solely on eradicating all the human inhabitants that remained
of Pinesway. The delver crossed several victims dead in the streets, some obviously
pulled from houses, others shot down while trying to escape. He saw no signs of mercy,
just the opposite. The goblins' trail of devastation showed a clear indication of their
savage strategy. They entered buildings quickly, breaking through doors and windows.
Their progress through town made it clear they spent no time searching for valuables.
They simply forced all inhabitants out into the streets, either to be killed on sight or to be
driven further into the center of town. Knowing from his initial scout that the goblins
completely surrounded Pinesway, he imagined this scene of brutality existed in a full
circle around the town.

Still, his attention remained on following the shag that continued its unrelenting trek
through the streets. Beyond avoiding their attention, Ryson dismissed the growing
numbers of goblins he encountered. He also almost ignored the swirling flight of the
hook hawk, but the appearance of this creature changed the dynamic of the situation. It
shrieked several times and the goblins were now less concerned with the shag and more
troubled by this flying beast. And for good reason as one goblin fell victim to the
gripping talons that carried it back up into the dying light of the dusk sky.

The delver watched this riveting scene for only a moment as his own instincts rang a
loud warning. Ahead of him, the shag suddenly veered from its forward path and turned
to the right. By its movements, Ryson believed the shag was now near its destination.
When the monster crouched low and its step altered from a traveling pace to a hunting

stalk, the delver knew the situation had altered dramatically. As if to confirm his
instincts, an elderly man looking somewhat winded and carrying a crossbow over his
back stumbled out directly in the monster's path.

The shag would have snatched the old man from where he stood in three heartbeats if
Ryson had not acted. The delver now completely ignored the surrounding goblins. He
bounded out behind his cover and dashed toward the shag in a blur of motion. His hands
came over the top of his shoulder to grab the hilt of the Sword of Decree that was
sheathed on his back. With a sweeping motion, he pulled the blade free at the same time
that he cut across the path of the monster. In one continuous movement, he slashed the
blade upward toward the shags shoulder as he twisted himself in a midair leap. The tip of
the blade struck the matted fur of the giant, and as it cut through the monster's coat and
sliced into skin, the shag screeched in pain as if the small cut had past through its very
core.

Ryson landed on his feet directly between the shag and the old man. He held tight to
the sword with both hands as he peered into the eyes of his adversary. The blade of the

sword glowed with the brilliance of the mid-day sun, but this was not the only
enchantment the sword released in this instant. As Ryson's gaze locked onto the shag, he
felt the link to the serp, and as was its power, the magical sword decreed Sazar's desires
as clearly as if the delver could read it on parchment.

Ryson saw what Pinesway would become under the serp's control—a breeding ground
for goblins, a growing threat to every human outpost, town, and city for leagues in all
directions. As the picture of this town in the future became clearer in his mind, he could
not fathom the number of monsters it would hold. Like an overpopulated anthill, the
buildings of Pinesway would burst near the seams with thousands upon thousands of dark
creatures. In this vision, he understood the true power of the goblin horde, a number so
large they could simply inundate any target they chose. And this nest of monsters would
grow as it overtook each human town. Ryson wondered if anything could stop such a
force, and he knew even Burbon might eventually fall.

With such horror, however, there was also hope. Through the sword's power of
declaration, Ryson now also knew what needed to be done to stop this nightmare before it
became a reality. He also knew he held in his hands the power to accomplish this task.

#

"The cursed delver from Burbon!" Sazar hissed. "What is he doing here?"

The serp took a moment to concentrate on all the images which passed through his
mind. He could visualize the entire town at this moment. His hook hawk stationed itself
on a tall grain tower near the center of town, and although it was busy shredding a goblin
into an easier meal to swallow, it continued to cast a wary eye in nearly every direction.
This panoramic along with the viewpoints of hundred of goblins that still encircled
Pinesway gave Sazar a complete picture of the situation. He then focused in on the rock
beetle, which was just finishing its own goblin meal. The giant insect stood above
ground, but all six legs remained anchored into the dirt street. Sazar could feel the
vibrations that the beetle sensed and this allowed his awareness to flow for a great
distance outward.

Other than the appearance of the delver, every other facet of the raid seemed in perfect
order. No other grouping of goblins reported any resistance from the still frightened and
fleeing inhabitants of Pinesway. His minions continued to make steady progress in
forcing out hiding humans and channeling them to the town center. The borders of the

town right to the trees of Dark Spruce that surrounded it remained clear. Through the
sensory perception of the beetle, he sensed no coordinated movement other than that of
his own forces. In every aspect, he remained in complete control of the battle.

The appearance of Ryson Acumen, however, left him with more than an uneasy
feeling. He hated this delver, for he knew what he was capable of.

"Why is he here?" Sazar cursed under his breath. "Burbon is his home now. Pinesway
holds nothing for him. He is alone to face a goblin raid in an abandoned town. This
makes no sense."

A realization struck the serp like a clap of thunder. "But is he alone? He is close with
the wizard, and the wizard is far too powerful. He could easily disguise himself from me,
or even an entire force of the human guard. They could be surrounding us now. As for the
wizard, he could be anywhere. He flies as easily as the hook hawk. He could be above the
town at any point. He could be above me right now."

The serp's words died off with this assumption. At that instant, Sazar understood what
is was like to be Joel Portsmith wondering if a rock beetle was directly underfoot, except
the serp now worried if an angry wizard was floating over his head. Sazar looked about in
a near panic. He also realized that other than the two goblins that patrolled the exterior of
the building he stood within, he was completely alone—unguarded and vulnerable. He
sent an immediate command to the monstrous shag that stood before Ryson Acumen.

Return to me at once!

#

Ryson stood unyielding between the immense shag in front of him and the old man
behind him. His eyes sharpened with a new found confidence. He now knew exactly what
Sazar hoped to accomplish, but he also knew exactly what to do to stop the serp. The
sword had given him the gift of insight as it had done in the past. There was no longer
any question over what he could truly accomplish, how many innocents he could still
save, or how he might be able to upset the serp's plans. His mind held a simple truth of
how to stop Sazar from gaining control of Pinesway—now or in the future. He grasped
the power to do so in his hands and his body held the capacity in the abilities of being a
purebred delver.

Ryson called back to the old man behind him. "Back away quickly."

Joel Portsmith didn't need a second request. He gladly complied immediately and
began back pedaling to the alley from which he came.

Ryson readied himself for the charge of the shag, believing the monster would move
once the old man began to retreat. Movement from the shag, however, was slow in
coming. It appeared almost distracted, its eyes nearly vacant. Eventually, it did move, but
not in the direction Ryson expected. The beast turned quickly and retraced its previous
path in the opposite direction.

Ryson held firm until certain the shag was indeed in full retreat. He then turned
quickly to the old man. "Get back in the alley. Stay under cover."

The delver scanned the area quickly registering goblin positions and their apparent
readiness to move forward. To his delight, this particular area remained empty of any
immediate threats, but even in the fading daylight he could make out dozens of the dark
creatures assembling together to the north and south. He darted into the alley to join the
old man.

Ryson sized Joel up quickly and for the most part liked what he saw. While the strain
of this day's events obviously took their toll, the man appeared unhurt and in control of

his senses. Considering the magnitude of these events, that in itself was a huge credit to
the man's inner strength. He was armed with a crossbow, but Ryson now knew the
weapon was no longer necessary.

"My name is Ryson Acumen. I'm a delver from Burbon."

"Figured you to be a delver," the old man said with a very small hint of animosity.

Ryson ignored the tone. "You alone?"

"I'm traveling alone, if that's what you mean."

"But you've come across others."

"'Course I have."

"Mostly in the center of town?"

"Yep."

"And where were you headed?"

Joel pointed over Ryson's shoulder back to the goblin line. "That way, was heading home."

"That will have to wait." Ryson stated firmly.

Joel's eyes narrowed and Ryson knew the man didn't like taking orders, so the delver spelled the situation out for him.

"You'll get home, alive and in one piece, if you wait. If you go now, the goblins will cut you down. There's a serp that's directing all of this. He's going to reinforce the line where the shag retreated. That's the direction you need to go."

Joel grunted in annoyance.

Ryson didn't wait for him to complain. "You can still get there, you just have to have a bit of patience. I also want you to do something for me. I don't think you'll argue too much seeing I just saved your life." Here, Ryson played on a hunch, a hunch that honor meant something to this man.

Joel nodded unhappily, but nodded just the same. "What do you need?"

"I want you to return to the people you passed," Ryson stated simply. "Don't take any risks, don't endanger yourself. Just go back to the center of town, it's safer there anyway. Tell everyone you meet to find cover and stay put. I'm going to take care of the goblin problem."

Joel appeared only mildly surprised, but questioned the delver anyway.

"Just you?"

"Just me."

"How?"

"Fear."

Joel eyed the delver and the shining sword that he grasped. He could not find it in himself to argue.

"Ok, I'll go back and tell everyone help is on the way and to stay out of sight. Getting dark now anyway, probably too dangerous to do anything else. You'll let us know when you're done doing whatever it is you're going to do?"

"I'll meet you at the town square."

Joel looked to the ground, spit off to the side, took a heavy breath, and simply turned around. He moved down the alley at a cautious steady pace, acknowledging this turn of events with sullen acceptance.

Ryson believed the man would not go back on his word, and thus quickly turned his attention to the goblins. The Sword of Decree shone brighter now as the light of dusk faded away into twilight. He held a beacon to the goblins that stood off in the distance, a target, but it would not matter. He would move at a speed that was beyond their comprehension.

He quickly eyed the growing number of dark creatures in the distance. Ryson

reviewed in his mind what he now knew to be the serp's forces. "Only goblins in this area
to deal with, but there's a hook hawk, a rock beetle, and at least two shags to worry about
as well. Shags shouldn't be too much of a problem, the big one is probably back with
Sazar. The hawk just ate and is more a reconnaissance tool than anything else. The beetle
could be a danger, just have to keep an eye on the ground so I don't trip. Sazar did me a
favor keeping the goblins in this formation. All I have to do is circle the city in expanding
rings working outward. Eventually, I'll clear them all out."

Ryson targeted the closest group of goblins which stood one block to the northeast. He
would hit them first. Ryson now better understood Sazar's power over these creatures. He
knew the serp kept them confused and fearful. The serp did not cast spells to influence
his minions, but the magical energies that flowed through the air allowed him to press his
will upon them. Once Sazar took hold of their minds, he used the magic and their own
emotions to keep their individual will in check.

The delver had enough contact with goblins to understand their minds as well.
Individually, they were weak and vulnerable, but as a horde they represented a threat to
even the largest beasts. The serp used this natural tendency to belong to a horde along
with the goblins weak will to maintain control over a large number. That control,
however, would last only as long as the goblins individual instinct for survival did not
interfere with the serp's commands. It was this weakness that Ryson intended to exploit.
The serp used fear to keep the goblins in check, but a creature of this character could
learn to fear many things. If a new fear became larger than the goblin's fear of the serp,
then all bets were off.

Ryson switched his grip of the Sword of Decree to one hand and held the point out in
front of him. The natural starlight around him magnified a hundred fold and he knew he
was now visible for great distances. It would draw crossbow fire almost immediately, so
he moved with greater swiftness.

Like a meteor streaking through the night sky, a ball of light advanced on the goblins.
They stood dumbfounded at the scene, totally unable to comprehend who or even what
was headed straight for them. A few found the courage to lift a crossbow to fire, but none
accomplished firing off a single shot.

The Sword of Decree spun like flaming pinwheel in Ryson's hand. He darted from
one goblin to the next in a blur of motion. He stabbed with his sword, but not at vital
organs and not with deep thrusts. He forced the blade forward just enough to cut through
the swollen rubbery goblin skin at a shoulder, an arm, or an upper leg. When the point of
the sword made contact, it burned. Such was the power of the Sword of Decree. It was
forged with magic to fight off the shadow trees, and within its blade it had the power to
burn souls, even the damned souls of twisted creatures such as goblins.

When these goblins felt the burning pain that went deep beyond the wound, they
gained a new fear, a great fear. Their thoughts of Sazar dissipated like droplets of water

thrown on a blazing inferno. They howled and cowered, most dropping to the ground in twisted, painful terror. So great was their fear, they could not find the strength to run.

Ryson decided to give them the incentive to do so.

When Ryson wounded all he saw, he yelled out like a raving mad man. "This town holds your ruin just as I now hold your souls in this sword. I can make them burn! Leave this place and never return. Leave now and tell all others of your kind what you have felt here in Pinesway! This town is cursed and all that enter will die painfully!"

The goblins of this pack needed no further encouragement.

#

"He is removing them from my control! The sword is enchanted. It's burning fear into anything it touches, so much fear that I can't overcome it. He is also moving so fast that before long he will have sent every goblin I command scrambling into the woods."

Suddenly, the serp gained yet another perspective that served to increase his disdain for the situation. The rock beetle sensed a new commotion, but this disturbance did not

come from the town, it came from the trees, from the areas where his minions now
retreated.

Sazar seized upon the last fragments of trace images he could obtain from these
goblins that surfaced through their panic. He viewed their last visions with increasing
alarm. Several fell into an ambush, slaughtered quickly and efficiently.

"Human soldiers waiting in the woods to attack! They are efficient in weapons.
Burbon guards!"

Sazar pounded the walls in growing frustration as he now knew that a contingent of
Sy's men had reached a position at Pinesway's edge. They simply waited patiently for the
fleeing goblins to fall into their range. It took little effort for them to dispatch all that
came into their path.

"That means the delver did not come alone," Sazar bellowed. The rage of frustration,
however, soon turned to distress. "These are soldiers of Burbon. If they have come, then
perhaps the wizard…"

Concern over the possible appearance of Enin to his midst caused the serp to break off
in mid-sentence. He blurted out his own realization, and the importance that it must not
come to pass.

"I will not be trapped here."

He sent out an order to his most prized minions. He ordered the rock beetle to burrow
underground and tunnel into the forest, and he commanded the hook hawk to
immediately take flight high into the night sky. The one shag still engaged in the battle he
ordered to escort as many goblins as possible to exit the town through the eastern gate.
The large shag was already on its way back to Sazar's side, thus the serp simply
encouraged the monster to move faster. To most of the goblins that still remained under
his control, he stopped pressing them forward and instead hastened them to make for the
trees in the quickest way possible. He hoped the scattering of the goblins throughout the
forest in different directions would make it more difficult for Sy's guard to eliminate
large numbers of them. Sazar sent a final command to twenty goblins that had not yet
been fallen upon by the delver. They remained to the southeastern outskirts of town.

"Move quickly to the square at the town center. You will find groups of humans
banded together. Open fire upon them. If you see one moving at great speed holding a
shining object, avoid it at all costs. Keep your distance, but continue to fire with your
crossbows at any humans you see. Continue this until I call for you."

Sazar, in fact, had no intention of calling for these goblins. He was sacrificing them
so he could make his own escape.

\#

Ryson's pace quickened, hastened by the fact that the goblins were now in full retreat.
He chased them down and continued to stab at them with his sword. He warned each
goblin he wounded to flee Pinesway and never return.

At this point, the goblins needed little incentive to run off. No longer did they feel the
pressing demands of the serp to take the town and kill its inhabitants. Instead, they sensed
the new turmoil in the air brought about by the delver's counterattack. They noted the
retreat of the shags and the hook hawk. Some were even aware of the rock beetle's quick
disappearance into the ground. Most of the goblins were fleeing in retreat even before
Ryson could reach their position.

In a spiraling pattern that continuously circled outward, Ryson became a blur of light
that flashed down streets and alleys. From the distance, he appeared like a flaming arrow
streaking through the air. He scorched well over two hundred goblins with his sword
before he reached Pinesway's outer limits. When his path led him around the southern
portion of the town, he bounded into the warehouse which he believed the serp used as a
hideout. As he expected, the building was now empty, Sazar gone.

Ryson quickly traced markings on the ground and walls and followed them about the
open space and back to the door.

"He was here alright," Ryson confirmed to himself as he stepped back out into the
night air and inspected more tracks on the ground. "He took off when the big shag
returned to him."

Realizing tracking the serp further into the forest at this point would gain nothing,
Ryson dashed off in a direct path toward the town square. With the sword still in his
hands, he lit up the areas he moved through like the welcome sight of the sun after a
terrible storm. When he reached the town center, he counted many people still hiding
under stairs, beneath broken carts, and within darkened, empty buildings. He found Joel
sitting on a bench, slightly hunched over, looking very tired and angry.

"You alright?" Ryson asked.

Joel looked up at the delver with an expression of sheer disgust. "Not hurt, but real
annoyed. Why does a serp attack an abandoned town?"

"He wanted to take what the thieves here already stole and he wanted a base." Ryson
responded confidently. "He wanted the whole town. He was going to use whatever he
could take here to buy more supplies, more weapons, and more food. Then, he was going
to make it a haven for goblins he could control."

Joel spat at the ground "Ok, and he was going to kill us all because I guess he didn't
want any humans as neighbors."

"Would you want to live next door to a goblin?" Ryson offered, almost a little too
lighthearted for Joel's liking.

"No, I like living next to abandoned houses. No neighbor is the best neighbor."

"Be that as it may…"

A familiar voice called out from the shadows that interrupted the delver in mid-
sentence. "Ryson Acumen! There are goblins to your left about to fire upon you!"

Ryson immediately recognized the voice, but took no time to acknowledge it. He
directed his attention to the few people that were slowly moving out into the open.

"Everyone get down!" he shouted.

Most everyone dropped to the ground or dove back to their original hiding places,
though some remained too stunned over the events of the day to have much comprehension of what was going on around them. A few stood unsteadily on their feet.

Whirling to his left, Ryson began to spin the Sword of Decree again in hand like a
pinwheel. The shimmering, spinning blade had a dazzling affect on everyone that
witnessed it. With the sword still twirling, he turned toward his left and the group of
goblins that had been ordered to advance on the town square. He leapt in the air and
quickly knocked several goblin arrows out of midair. When the first barrage of goblin fire
ended, six long arrows sliced through the air in succession, but these arrows came from
the opposite direction and all found their mark in a targeted goblin. Ryson leapt across
the remaining distance between himself and the surviving dozen or so goblins. He

quickly disarmed several of them, knocking the crossbows out of their hands before they
could react. Four more long arrows sizzled past Ryson and four more goblins crumpled to
the ground.

Now only half of the goblins remained standing and most of these were now
weaponless. The delver stabbed at those that still held their crossbows. They shrieked in
pain and he offered another warning to them.

"Leave this place and never return!"

Before they could move, yet another barrage of arrows cut into their numbers. Another
four goblins dropped from their feet, dead before they could hit the ground. The
remaining half dozen goblins turned and ran, spitting and hissing in abject fear for their
lives.

Ryson remained still, allowing them to leave and to hopefully spread his warning.
These goblins, however, never escaped Pinesway alive. A final salvo of arrows fell all
remaining creatures.

Ryson shook his head, but turned to greet the friend he now heard walking toward his
position. He returned the Sword of Decree to its sheath over his shoulder, as he put on a
tired smile.

Lief Woodson stalked carefully up to the delver, scanning the area for any more
goblins. His bow remained in his left hand and his right stood ready to draw several more
arrows.

Ryson extended his hand and placed it warmly on the elf's shoulder. He was surprised
at the tenseness he felt. The silence became surprisingly unsettling as the elf appeared to
almost ignore the delver. If anything, Lief appeared to almost thirst for more targets.

"Lief I'm glad to see you and thanks for the warning, but that wasn't…"

"Wasn't what? Necessary?" The elf's words were cold and seemed in diametric
opposition to the blazing hate in his eyes.

"Well, I'm just not sure if you had to kill them all," Ryson offered.

"They are dead and we no longer need worry about what they might do. You should
consider that the next time you use your sword upon them. When you strike, make it
count."

Ryson found the need to defend his actions. "I didn't want to kill them. I wanted them
to fear this place. I don't want them coming back, or any others for that matter. If they
reached the forest, they could tell others and rumors would spread through their ranks."

"Enough of them escaped off into the forest for that." Lief barked. "Too many, in
fact."

"Well anyway," Ryson offered hoping to change the tone of the conversation, "I'm glad to see you. Why are you here? How did you know I was here? Did Sy send you?"

"I have not spoken to your captain of the guard. I was traveling in the woods hunting a river rogue I knew to be in this area. From the distance I could see your sword and I heard the sounds of battle. I joined only a few moments ago. What has happened here?"

"It was the serp, Sazar," Ryson answered. "He wanted to control what's left of this town, use it to entice more goblins to join him."

Lief's eyes seemed to burn even brighter. "If I find this serp, I will end his days. Just as I will end the lives of any other despicable creature I come to pass."

Ryson found the hatred spilling from Lief's words more than a bit unsettling. "You don't need to kill him. He's powerless now. The goblins won't listen to him. They're now

so afraid of this place that even under his control they won't enter it. That's why I didn't
want you to kill those other goblins. The more that get out of here alive, the more will
pass on the story of what happened here."

"And the more that die," Lief retorted, "will mean fewer monsters we have to worry
about all together. It is time we all started realizing this and all started doing something
about it."

"What more exactly do you think should be done?"

"You have to ask?" Lief asked with near disbelief. "It is time to actively meet their
threat. It is no longer acceptable to wait and hope for the best, to simply to do nothing. It
is time we realized that these creatures are a threat and they must be dealt with." Lief then
eyed the delver with an expression that almost revealed suspicion. "You can't possibly
think we should just let these creatures take over?"

Ryson never thought of simply giving up to the likes of Sazar, that was why he was
here. Still, Lief's answer seemed to swing much too far. "We can defend ourselves
certainly, but hunting them down to simply eradicate them isn't the answer."

"Do not tell me what the answer is!" Lief growled. "Trust me, Ryson. This is not the
day to debate with me."

"It's not a debate, it's about unnecessary killing…"

Lief cut the delver off, allowed him to speak no further as his eyes blazed with fury
that Ryson had not seen before. "You're right, it's not a debate! This is no argument and
this was not unnecessary killing. It was very necessary. Fire upon you if you do not see!
How many did these creatures kill this day? How many did they kill yesterday? How
many will they kill tomorrow? You can't answer any of those questions, but I can answer
the last. They will kill no more after today. That is why this is not a debate and I warn
you I will not listen to any further of your doubts on the matter."

The angry outburst caught Ryson off guard. He stood even more stunned by the tone
and the expression then by the elf's actual words. Finally, he mumbled a question that
carried as much concern as confusion. "Are you alright?"

The elf's harsh expression faded a little but the emotion in his voice still boiled. His
eyes bore into the delver for a moment, but in looking at Ryson, he saw and remembered
a friend. The elf bit back his anger enough to offer a limited explanation. "No, I am not
alright. I have been banished from my camp, banished by the very same blasted fools that
did nothing when Petiole was in charge. Now they feel as if they must redeem their
inaction by blaming me. If you are curious as to why I am the way I am now, then I want

it to be clear. I hold nothing against you, nothing in any way, but I will no longer listen to
anything that defends inaction. Doing nothing when evil is committed is as wrong as
committing the evil. These creatures are loathsome monsters that exist to cause others
pain. I will not allow them to do so when it is in my power to stop them. Do you
understand?"

Ryson hesitated, he did not want to infuriate the elf further, but he also could not lie.
"No, I don't understand."

The elf nearly exploded. He actually turned his back on the delver as he gripped his
bow ever tighter. He exhaled heavily and spoke without looking back. "Then, you do not
need to understand. As I said before, I hold nothing against you. You have acted far
beyond what has ever been asked of you. You do not carry the failings of my camp. You
and I will simply have to disagree on the matter, but I will not argue the point with you

further. I will not ask for your assistance in what I must do, and you must not try to
interfere. I take my leave of you now, and when I find more evil creatures, I will send
them back to the darkness that spawned them as well. Good luck to you Ryson Acumen."

At that point, the elf simply stalked away into the growing shadows of nightfall.

Ryson took a quick glimpse around as Lief moved out of sight. He tried to piece
together everything the elf just told him, but he could not fully understand the emotions
he saw.

Suddenly, his thoughts of the elf were washed away by the same reoccurring sense of
emptiness he felt out in the forest with Enin. He felt something beyond empty, something
beyond hollow. Again, the word 'dry' seemed to fit the sensation, even though he could
not explain why. Somewhere—and in no particular direction for the feeling seemed to
exist outside of everything physical— somewhere he traced an inexplicable vibration to a
source of energy he could not define.

The sensation and his altercation with Lief left him frustrated. He turned about and
looked into the face of Joel Portsmith who had left his seat on the bench to join the
delver. For now, Ryson put his mind to the safety of those that remained in the square.
There were no goblins left in this area, thus for the moment, they were safe.

Joel Portsmith nodded to the departing shadow of Lief Woodson and decided to add
his own sentiments. "Not that it matters to you delver boy, but I kinda agree with him."

Ryson gritted his teeth. He didn't know this man well, but he didn't want to hear any
more of this. "Well, he was right about one thing. This isn't the time for a debate."

"Nope, arguing won't do any good," Joel allowed. And I don't want to stand out here
much longer. Thanks for clearing a path for me. I can get home from here."

Ryson's confusion now turned on this baffling man before him. "You're going
home?"

"Somewhere else I'm supposed to go?"

"I would think you'd want to go someplace else."

"You think wrong." Joel stated almost too simplistically.

"Listen, this town still isn't safe. The place has been abandoned. Just because the
goblins won't come back, doesn't mean something else won't come here looking for a
meal, like a shag, or a river rogue, or something else. There are worse things out there in
the forest, you know."

"There are worse things just about everywhere."

"Even so, there's nothing left here."

"My home's here," Joel stated firmly.

Ryson decided to point out a truth he just recently learned himself. "A home is where you decide it is, so don't tell me that. These are buildings, empty buildings that no one is going to return to, no one with any good intentions."

Joel shook his head. "I see where you're going with this and I really don't want to hear it. Let's be honest about this, delver boy, what the blazes else I got left to do, huh? I'm an old man."

"Not so old that you weren't able to survive this attack. You can go to Connel, you can come with me to Burbon. There are cities to the east and coastal towns to the west. You can make a new home."

"I've already lived on the coast, not going back. And what makes you think I have it in me to start over in Connel or anywhere else for that matter?"

"You can start over because you made it through this. If you were going to give up,
you'd be dead already. What makes you think you can't make it in a new town?"

"Don't want to."

"Don't want to? What is it you want? To stay here and keep fighting off one monster
after another? What happens if a shag comes back or that hook hawk? What then?"

"What then? I'll tell you what then. I fight them off or I die. What's the problem?'

"The problem is dying for nothing makes no sense."

"And who says it dying for nothing?" Joel demanded to know. "My wife and I came
here to live out the rest of our lives. You know what that means, delver boy? It means we
came here to die. Same thing, different words. She held up her part of the bargain. Blast it
if I'm not going to hold up my end."

Ryson looked into Joel's dark eyes and he remembered Enin's words before he left
Burbon, sometimes you really can't save people from themselves. And sometimes people
don't want, or even more importantly, don't need saving. Sometimes people do what they
have to do and you just have to let it go.

                                #

Sazar skulked away through the trees of Dark Spruce with the path of Pinesway to his
back. He remained attuned to the rock beetle that tunneled underground ahead of him.
Remaining cautious of ambushes, he commanded the insect to remain on guard for any
trembles of motion. The large shag walked in step directly behind the serp while the
second and smaller shag brought up the rear with only a few dozen goblins in between.

Looking over his shoulder in disgust at the remnants of his forces, he cursed to
himself over his losses.

"Where there were once hundreds, I now have but a meager few. Where I had the
opportunity to grow beyond measure, I now have to struggle to prevent further losses. I
have already lost far too much on this day. The goblins have scattered and now run in
fear of this place. I don't have the power to overcome this and the cursed delver knows it.
He did this on purpose, striking directly at what I could not control."

The serp hissed in anger as his tail shredded weeds in uncontrolled waves of anger.

"I don't think the wizard was even here. Probably felt I was not worth his time. Look
at me now, no longer even worth the delver's time, or the human guard from Burbon.
They let me creep away in retreat."

Sazar shook his head and hissed again, this time in disgust. "And so much is true. I am
no longer worth their efforts. It will take all my attention to keep these few that still

follow me from wandering off as well. My hope of Pinesway is gone, my hope of power
is gone."

Sazar stopped. He turned and looked over the meager group of goblins that moved in
his wake. He grew angry.

"No, I will not allow this day to be a loss. I must accept what happened, and use it as
well. This day has taught me that I can raid, but I can not conquer. Thus, I must choose. If
I am to be a raider, then these forces I have now are more than sufficient. I do not need to
grow in numbers to obtain what I need. If I am to be a conqueror, then I must change."

Sazar looked back down the path toward Pinesway, unable to even make out the
outline of a single building through the shadows and trees. He had ran from that town, ran
so far he could no longer see it. This realization did not make him happy.

"To be a raider is to retreat, to be a conqueror is to make your enemy retreat. I will
raid no more, thus I will change."

A decision made in his mind, albeit a dangerous one, Sazar walked with confidence in
his step once more. He hissed a happy consideration as he turned to the southwest.

"Perhaps one day I will be able to thank the delver in person."

Chapter 7

Holli appeared quite at ease standing in Enin's home. When a large, shaggy-haired
mutt romped up to her side, she confidently dropped a hand down to scratch its head.

"The dogs, they all seem to like you," Enin smiled.

"I've always liked dogs," Holli replied. "In some ways, I've tried to match what they
do. They use their senses in a very positive way and they don't just rely on one. Even
though many use scent heavily, they also watch and listen."

"They also have a natural sense of what they like and what they don't like." Enin
added. "They are happy when they are around things they like, and they are very tense
when they are concerned."

As if on cue, another two dogs bounded into to the room. They ran up to the elf, gave
her a sniff with wagging tails, and then leapt over to Enin to say hello. After he
acknowledged them both, they ran over to the large mutt and coaxed him to run out of the
room with them.

"Well, these three seem very happy here." Holli noted as she watched them gain speed
as they turned a corner and ran out of sight.

"Yes, they are, and it's funny actually. At first, I hated this house. Too big, too much
room for what I needed. It originally belonged to some well-to-do merchant. Of course
that was before the magic was released. The merchant took off for one of the coastal
towns, Alamatos I think, but I'm not really sure. Anyway, he left when the dark creatures
began appearing. There was a lot of that, people abandoning their homes. Well, not much
here in Burbon really. Most people stayed put here. Probably because of Sy and the
delver. It's been a blessing that Ryson decided to stay here. We should all probably thank
Linda for that. Uhmmm, where was I?"

"You were telling me how you hated this house," the elf reminded him.

"Ah, yes. It's not really my house, well I guess it is now. Anyway, I used to live on
the far side of town and Sy didn't think that was such a good idea. He wanted me to be
closer to the center. I told him it really didn't matter, that if my assistance was needed the
distance was quite immaterial. He said it didn't have anything to do with my powers, but
with the perception of the townspeople. Most of them saw what I did when the dwarves
of Dunop attacked us. Sy said that if people were going to feel safe here, they needed to
have me just about in the middle of everything. If I stayed in the corner of town,
eventually everyone would move to that corner as well. If I came to the center, for the

most part, people would stay put. I asked him how the people that lived at the edges of
town would feel, and he told me that those folks didn't mind as much. That's why they
chose to live there in the first place. Made sense to me."

"The strategy has its logic," Holli agreed.

"Well, it might have been logical, but that doesn't mean I liked it. As I said, I hated
this house at first. Much too much space for my needs. I felt lost here. I complained about
that constantly to Sy. I think he got tired of hearing it and it gave him an idea. He told me
the town needed a place to keep stray dogs. There weren't many strays, of course. Dogs
have become quite popular these days. Did you know that?"

"I know that dogs have a strong ability to sense danger and they naturally sense dark
creatures."

"You are quite right. And people around here realized that darn quickly. If the family dog was happy then the other family members knew they didn't have to worry about a goblin raid. Thus, not too many strays left running through town. Still, there were a few and they needed to a place to live, so Sy said they would stay here. Every now and then things get a bit crazy with the running around and all, but the house doesn't seem as big anymore."

The three dogs that had left re-entered the room with a fourth four-legged friend. All four ran about the room, excitedly re-inspecting the elf and saying hello once more to the wizard.

With the dogs leaping at his hands and face, Enin tried valiantly to pet all four at once, but he was short two hands. He looked back at the elf with a large smile. "In fact, sometimes now this house actually feels a bit small."

Holli dropped to one knee, putting her head at the dogs' level. Two of the four noticed this immediately and charged her with haste. They began licking both sides of her face.

"They welcome you here." Enin stated. "That's very important you know. It's not good when someone is suspicious of you when they first meet, sort of like how you were suspicious of me when we first met."

Holli stood up but kept both hands available for the two dogs. "At the time, I did not know you, nor did I know how talented you are with…"

"No, no, no, not talented," Enin stopped her in mid sentence, "gifted. There's a huge difference. Talent comes from within, and there are many that are quite talented at casting spells. I am not so arrogant that I believe for an instant that my abilities come from within, or that I should receive credit for what I can do. No, my magical abilities a gift from a greater power. I didn't earn them, didn't work long hours to perfect them. They were simply given to me at the outset. I don't know why, I simply accept it and take no praise for it."

"Very well, when I first met you I did not know how gifted you were." Holli tilted her head expectantly toward the wizard as if to determine if this choice of words was more suitable to his liking. When he nodded happily, she continued. "Magic was new to this world, especially new to humans that had little reference to it in their known history, and you must admit your manner did not, nor does it now, match that of a wizened spell-caster."

"I see, so because I did not walk around like a brooding, introspective, aloof human with very little to say, I appeared somewhat dangerous to you."

"That is not what I said." Holli responded in a rather short tone.

"Now, now, if you can't take a bit of fun, then how are you and I going to get along,
and that will be very important if I agree to what you want."

Holli frowned at this, and her tone turned slightly colder. "How do you know what it
is I want?"

Enin immediately held his hands up in front of his chest as if pressing away any
hurled accusations. The two dogs at his sides did not sit patiently for this and romped out
of the room, followed by the other two.

Enin's voice held a very conciliatory note. "Please do not get suspicious of me. I did
not read your mind if that's what you are worried about. I've learned that someone's
thoughts are very private, but it goes beyond even that. Over time, I've discovered that
reading minds is simply not worth the effort. There's too much chance for error. The

mind is the great cabinet of all thoughts, memories, dreams, and whatever else might
have you. There are things floating around in there that barely make sense to the person
they belong to. Can you imagine how confusing it would be to lift something from
someone else's mind and try to make sense of it? I'm not talking about perception, either.
You can perceive if someone is angry or happy or upset. I'm talking about actually trying
to read individual thoughts. Perhaps if I could guarantee that I could lift the very thought
you are focused on, it might make sense. The problem is that because there are so many
stray ideas floating around at any one time, I could pick up just about anything and it
wouldn't necessarily make any sense at all.

"Let's just say for argument's sake that I did try to read your mind just then. What if at
that moment you were actually thinking of one of the dogs that was in here, and perhaps
it reminded you of one that belonged to your great aunt. If I ended up picking up that
stray thought and gave it importance, where would that lead me? Would I think you were
here to visit me because I reminded you of your great aunt? Then I really won't appear
like that wizened old spell-caster."

"But you do appear to know why I'm here," Holli persisted not ready to relinquish her
suspicion.

"I believe I do, yes. I think I know what you want to request of me, but I needed to
make it clear that I did not steal your request from your mind before you made it. I had
the feeling that's what you thought, and I don't think you and I can afford to have that
kind of mistrust between us."

Holli's glare sharpened even further.

"I did it again, didn't I?" Enin sighed exasperatedly. "I'm speaking as if I know what
you want before you ask. I know I'm not explaining myself well, but the difficulty is that
I do know what you want. I've known you would be coming here for some time. In order
for me to explain how I know this, I think we need to speak about fate first."

Enin looked at Holli and then about the darkened wood walls that made up this room.
"Are you comfortable enough inside to have this discussion. I know elves don't care for
the indoors."

"It's not a problem. An elf guard learns to adapt quickly."

"Very good, then I will only ask you to please bear with me. Most people say that I
ramble on, and at times it will certainly seem that I might be babbling and not addressing
your true concern, but what we talk about now is very important."

Holli nodded and waited expectantly for the wizard to begin.

Furrowing his brow, Enin searched for exactly the right way to get his point across.

Unable to find a clear opening, he opted for two quick questions.

"Did you know that we all have a destiny? Did you also know we all have free will?"

He paused a longer period of time and watched her more carefully. She did not speak.

When she appeared to be waiting for further explanation, Enin nodded as if agreeing with her. "Very good, you're right in your hesitancy. The two questions alone could be debated on and on, but if I say them both together, I seem to contradict myself. To say that one has a destiny and then to say one has free will makes very little sense. They are, at first consideration, mutually exclusive. If there is a destiny for each individual, then there is no way we could exercise free will. Free will means making decisions, choosing between different paths. Destiny means our path is decided for us. How could we decide a path if that path is already set before us? Our decisions would reflect not our own free will, but the will of destiny that is guiding us toward our ultimate fate. Reverse it and the same problem arises. If we exercise complete free will, how in the world could we possibly have a destiny, a grand purpose that we are designed to fulfill? Any decision we make could easily send us in the opposite direction from where we were meant to travel."

Folding her hands in front of her, Holli wanted to quickly put the discussion in perspective. "Are you asking me if I believe in choice, or are you asking me if I believe in fate?"

"I'm asking you if you understand it's possible to have both. I want to know if you can accept that it's entirely reasonable to have a destiny and to exercise free will."

Answering quickly, Holli simply put her own conditions on the dilemma. "It would all depend on the degree of totality for each. If you are telling me that every single action in this world is completely based on fate, then free will would be near impossible. The reverse would also seem certain, that if every circumstance was completely based on the choices of the inhabitants of this land, then destiny would not be possible. As I understand fate, there would have to be some kind of guiding force necessary to set the stage. An external guiding force would be beyond individual choice."

Enin beamed with delight. "Excellent. You understand perfectly."

"I'm not sure I understand at all," Holli exclaimed.

"Yes, you do. You explained it better than I could. It all comes down to the degree of each. We have choices, absolutely. We can choose how we are going to live our lives, how we will deal with others, and so on, but we all have challenges we must face, obstacles to overcome, and events to handle. Some of these we create for ourselves by our choices, but others we will face regardless of how we live our lives. Just because we are destined to face some occurrence doesn't mean we can't choose how we get there. And, just because we can choose several different paths in front of us, doesn't mean we can avoid the same destiny that waits at the end of each path. That is in essence what you said."

"I suppose it is," replied the elf.

"I actually have a story I like to tell whenever I try to explain this to people. Do you mind if I tell it now?"

"Not at all."

Rubbing his hands together, Enin began his tale.

"Imagine there were two men. Each man was destined from the start of his life to be present at an important event where one of the men would die in a struggle. From the

moment they were born, each man had choices to make and these choices shaped their
lives, but they could not change the ultimate destiny they would eventually face.

"One man chose a dark and evil path. He became a thief and stole from many. The
other chose a respectable path and became a banker. He was trusted by his friends and
associates and became very successful. One day the thief attempted to rob the bankers
safe. The banker discovered him and one of them was killed in the struggle.

"If you are wondering which one died, the answer is that it was the one that was
destined to die. If you are asking was it the banker or the thief, the answer is it doesn't
matter. They chose their professions and that was based on free will. Their individual
choices made one a banker and the other a thief, but it was destiny that determined which
one would die that day.

"To take it even further, the two men could have both chosen a respectable path. To that end, they might have both become bankers. Eventually, they would become partners and one day one would mistake the other for a thief and the event would still come to pass. Or perhaps, they both would choose the lesser path and become thieves that fell in together. They would rob the bank together, argue over the money, and one would die. You see, they both had absolute free will to choose their own path, but neither could escape the fate of the event. Choice and destiny, both shaping two lives, existing together—do you understand?"

"Yes, I believe so."

Enin nodded and then came to the true point of his story. "Then, understand that is often within my power to see the destiny of others. I do not know why I have this gift, and I certainly did not ask for it. It is mine, however, whether I like it or not. That is how I know why you are here. I saw your fate the very last time we spoke. You were returning to your camp, but I knew you would not be able to stay, I knew you would be returning here."

Holli took long moments to consider this and Enin allowed her the time to do so. When she finally spoke, her tone remained guarded. "Are you telling me that it was my destiny to come here?"

At this moment, Enin did not shy from revealing even more of what he knew of Holli's circumstances. "Yes, I'm also saying you were destined to leave your camp. It was your choice how it would happen. Of that I am fairly certain. It is possible you elected to leave on your own, it is possible someone from your camp asked you to go, or it could be some combination of the two, or even something I haven't even thought of. It really doesn't matter beyond the fact that I knew you would leave your camp and your position as an elf guard."

Upon speaking this statement, Enin began to contemplate new considerations. "Actually, that brings to mind something else that is quite interesting. I'm really not sure if you were destined to be an elf guard, and I really can't say why. It might be that I can't see every destiny, or perhaps my abilities are limited to those events that occurred after the release of the magic. I don't think it has anything to do with past or present or future. I know destinies that are about to happen and some that are well off in the future. I also am quite sure of incidents of fate that occurred in past. All of these that I can think of,

however, are in the recent past, not far in the past. And yet, it seems to me that you were
destined to be an elf guard. It makes perfect sense. Even so, I can not say for sure."

"But you are sure I was destined to leave my camp?" Holli interrupted in an attempt to
bring Enin back to the subject at hand.

"Yes, of course. You were destined to leave your camp and come to me. I can say that
without doubt."

"And what is my destiny now that I am here?"

"That, I can't say."

Holli sensed something in the words of the wizard that made her doubt this statement
and she pressed the issue. "Can't or won't?"

"Perhaps both," Enin answered evasively.

"Now you are talking in riddles and that I do not like."

"If I am doing so, you will have to believe that I'm doing it with your best interest in
mind." Enin knew this would not satisfy the elf and he endeavored to explain further.

"Think of the story I told you before about the two men. What if I knew these men and their destiny and decided to inform them of it? If the banker knew ahead of time that he would die by the hands of a thief, perhaps that would cause him to alter his actions. Or if the thief realized the action of robbing the bank was dangerous, he might have chosen another target. Giving them this information might actually alter a destiny and change the balance of things. Balance is very important and should not be carelessly disturbed even for the best of intentions. Does that satisfy you?"

"Only to a degree," the elf answered. "Why tell me this at all, why tell me of your ability to see people's destiny unless you would be willing to reveal what you see?"

"That is simple. As I said before, I know why you are here. I wanted you to know how I knew this so that there would be no tension between us over this issue."

"Very well, I can allow that, but it seems to me that if you know why I'm here, then you already know the outcome of this meeting."

Here, Enin became stern. "Please never make that assumption. You must never for one moment believe that I know how all things will unfold. You see, that's where choice plays its part. We have a choice in how to deal with events, even events we are destined to face. We can not avoid our choices, just like we can not avoid our destiny. Since free will is just that, I can't state with authority how this meeting will end. All you need to understand is that I can see certain events in people's lives that they are destined to face. That doesn't mean I know how these events will unfold or conclude."

"Then how do we move forward?"

"Let us forget destiny and now treat this as we should treat all matters, with an honest discussion. I will begin by telling you why I think you are here. You have left your camp and you wish to become my guard. Yes?"

With a nod, Holli affirmed the wizard's prediction. "I must admit it is rather unnerving to actually hear this, because I have not spoken it to a single soul, but yes, that is why I'm here."

"Fine, we have that out of the way and we can talk of the issue plainly. The truth is I have questions for you and there are things I would ask of you if you were to take on this responsibility. If I don't like the answers, or if you don't like my conditions, then it is an arrangement we cannot have."

"What questions do you have?"

Enin furrowed his brow and did his best to place his questions in the best order. "The first one I have is why did you leave your camp?"

"The camp elders asked me to leave," Holli responded without emotion, as if the request had nothing to do with her personally at all. "They felt they could not lead effectively with my presence in camp. My role at Sanctum Mountain lifted my standing among the other elves. They feel that this puts me as part of elflore and would create confusion. It was not my place to question them. A guard simply does her duty. They said I must leave, and so I left. They also asked Lief to leave. Did you already know that as well?"

"That's hard to answer," Enin admitted. "I wish to be honest with you, but it's very difficult to describe what it is I see. It's not like I see this big image in my mind of you and Lief walking out of your camp. It's more of an understanding. For Lief, I know that he faces a challenging time ahead."

Holli nodded knowingly. "He did not leave under the best of circumstances."

"I imagine not," the wizard agreed. "Let us, however, return to you." A light hearted
smile quickly grasped Enin's lips as if he thought of a funny story. He laughed as he
explained. "You know, that's actually funny—that I'm the one refocusing the
conversation on the topic at hand. It's normally the other way around. People always tell
me that I can go off topic and get distracted. It's not like I mean to, it just kind of
happens. You see, I'm actually amazed at how I see things work. Every thing is
interrelated yet at the same time everything seems to be disconnected. One thing that
happens doesn't seem to have anything to do with another, but a few seasons later, the
two events come together in one way or the other. It's like you and I. When we first met,
you mistrusted me. Now, you want me to trust you enough to let you be some kind of
personal guard for me. It's not that I don't trust you, we will get to that later. It's just that
I'm trying to explain how I now see things. That's why it can seem as if I lose my focus
on things. You'll have to get used to it if you're going to spend time around me."

"Kind of like now," the elf added with a sly smile of her own.

"Aha, you got me. Seems like I went off topic right after I tried to get us back on to it.
Very good. Yes, let's get back to you. You left camp because the elders felt you would be
too much of a legendary figure and that would interfere with their ability to lead, yes?"

"Yes."

"Understandable, but what is not so clear is why you would come here?"

"Because I am a guard, it is more than what I do, it is what I am. I do not wish to
change that. My duty is to keep others safe, thus I considered where I might be most
useful."

"And you thought you would be most useful protecting me?"

"You are a very powerful wizard and while I do not believe you need protection,
having an elf guard with you would be beneficial to both you and those you serve. There
are many that might come to you seeking assistance or guidance. There are also the
curious that might come to you. Then of course, there are also other wizards that may
come here with less than desirable intentions."

"Hmmmm, you think I might be called out often by young eager spell casters wishing
to prove themselves? They might wish to challenge me to some kind of wizard's duel. If
they can defeat me, they might make a name for themselves? Actually, it's not like that at
all. Many have indeed shown up, but not to challenge me. Most of them just want to

learn. Others want to try and examine me from a distance. I can always sense them and
any confrontation is always rather minimal. I give them some things to think about and
they go on their way. So far, all of them have been satisfied with what I've told them."

"I doubt there is much I could do better in that regard." Holli agreed. "If I tried, I
would only get in your way, thus I would not even entertain the thought of actually trying
to protect you from a conflict with another spell-caster. That, however, is really not my
intended purpose. When a stranger comes to town to ask for you there are often
bystanders that become curious. I would endeavor to keep such innocents from putting
themselves in danger. A guard protects not just a single individual but the camp as a
whole."

"Well, we do have the militia guard for that. You've met Sy. He is in charge of
keeping the town safe."

"Again, I would not interfere with him as well," Holli conceded. "He is able and I
would only be a distraction to him and his soldiers. But I ask you, are there not times that

you are involved in your own matters of magic that you would like to ensure that no one
around you mistakenly puts themselves in harms way?"

"Hmmmm…"

"It is not a matter of me keeping an eye on you. It is a matter of keeping an eye on
those that might stumble upon your presence at the wrong time. This is what an elf guard
has done for ages. While the magic was encased in Ingar's sphere, we often directed
humans away from our camps without them ever knowing we were there. We kept
ourselves safe by keeping others away, and in turn, kept them safe as well."

"I understand that," Enin allowed, "and actually it raises another question. Rather than
come here, why not simply join another elf camp and continue as an elf guard there?"

Holli shook her head. "I discounted this idea the moment I left my camp. Being an elf
guard involves a tremendous amount of trust. There are times an elf guard's orders will
supersede the orders of the elf council. When the safety of the camp or an elder is in
question, quick decisions must be made and orders must be followed without debate. If I
were to join another camp, my loyalties would always be suspect, and thus, my decisions
would always invite questions, invite doubt. That is not acceptable."

"Couldn't they find a position within the elf guard that would give you less
authority?"

"It is possible they could treat me as a trainee, but I doubt I would be able to adjust to
that. While I believe I can adjust to most situations, I must understand certain limitations.
I have spent countless cycles of the seasons as an elf guard relying on what I have
learned, trusting my judgment, developing confidence in my decisions, learning to take
control when necessary. Returning to the level of a trainee would require me to ignore
what I have engrained in my being. It would be as if I asked you to cast nothing but the
most basic of spells and never trust yourself to truly tap into your magical powers."

"So you decided that if you could not guard another elf camp, you would try to find
someone else that could benefit from your training."

"Exactly."

With an accepting wave of the hand, Enin acknowledged the benefits of having Holli
as a guard. "I agree there are times I would like to make sure that no one unexpectedly is
put in any kind of danger. A set of elf guard eyes watching would indeed be an added
benefit. You are indeed well trained and so I doubt I would have to worry about your
safety too often. I am concerned about your level of potential interference."

"I'm not sure I understand that concern," Holli responded quickly.

"You just said your orders can sometimes come ahead of even those on your camp
council."

"Only when safety is a paramount issue."

Here, Enin shook his head. "That wouldn't do. You would have to understand that my
safety is of my concern only and your interpretation of a possible hazard to my well-
being must never override my own. As my guard, your priority would be on protecting
those around me, keeping me advised of surrounding circumstances, being watchful of
hazards I might not see—I can accept all of this—but you must never actively intervene
over my objections simply because you feel my own safety is at risk. In essence, I am
saying that I would always have the final word, even when you think my safety is in
jeopardy. Would you be able to accept that stipulation?"

"I will adapt to that."

"That is good, but I am also going to have to ask something else of you if you are to
be my guard. It may not make sense to you, but I have my reasons."

Holli became intrigued but remained quiet.

Enin spoke here with more of a gleam in his eye. "I want to be able to teach you how
to use the magic. Now I know you use the magic passively. You use it to increase your
awareness of what's around you, you use it to remain alert to possible dangers. I think
you even use it to steady your own inner strength. I must tell you this is all marvelous,
but I would ask more of you. I want to be able to teach you how to use the magic more
actively. There are certain spells I wish you to learn and after I show them to you, I
believe you will agree they will help you in what you view as your duty. If you allow me
to tutor you on casting certain spells, then I will allow you to follow me, guard me, until
your heart is content."

"I am not against casting spells, and I have done this in the past," Holli admitted. "I
simply have not had time to truly shape these skills."

"If you are to be my companion, it is something we will both have time to do. To tell
you the truth, I'm doing it as much for me as I am for you. If you're going to be around
me, and keeping an eye on me, I think it's a good idea if we have some common
interests. Otherwise, I'm going to start getting a bit nervous knowing that you're always
around keeping tabs on me."

"An elf guard remains inconspicuous," Holli asserted.

"I'm sure you will be, but it's better if we actually have some true interaction and I
really can't think of a better way. You're an elf and you're more open to the ideas of
what magic can accomplish than the people I normally talk to. This will give me a chance
to discuss things that I don't often get a chance to talk about. Such as, did you know
dwarves are very resistant to magic?"

Enin did not wait for an answer. He continued on never giving Holli a chance to
speak. "Of course you knew that, you're an elf. Sorry. Never mind. The thing is if you
tell that to someone like Sy, he would say 'Well then use something else on them.' But
there's more to it then that. You have to understand magic and how it works. Just because
a dwarf is resistant to magic doesn't mean he is immune to it. These are two different
things. Being immune is extremely rare. Being resistant means it's difficult for a magic
caster to hurt you, but it's not impossible.

"For example, if a sorceress stupidly sends out magic fire from her fingertips to blast
away at a dwarf, the dwarf would just stand there smiling. Of course, there are many

ways around that. You don't send magic fire at the dwarf, you send it at the air
surrounding the dwarf. Ignite the air and the dwarf won't be smiling. That's not just
magic fire any more, that's real burn-a-dwarf-all-over fire.

"The problem is that this takes more work to do, more power, more magic and
definitely more concentration, but it works where the old magic fire from the finger tips
is just a waste of everyone's time.

"It's the same with force blasts, too, you know. You can't just send out a regular burst
of magic force and expect it to work the same on everyone for all occasions. That's just
magical power—very strong against most things, but not against those that can naturally
resist it. Instead, if the force is focused on the air which is not resistant to magic, you
create a blast of true power that affects even the magically resistant. When you disburse
the air, keep blasting it forward and forward, that's a very powerful force. It's a tornado

that doesn't spin and if done with enough velocity, it can tear people apart. That's what I
did to the dwarves when they attacked Burbon you know. Hit them with light and a wind
driven force blast. They were lucky I took it easy on them, but if I didn't I guess I would
have knocked over every building in town. I don't think that would have made Sy
happy."

Enin looked expectantly at Holli.

"So the idea is to use magic indirectly," she stated simply.

"Exactly," Enin beamed. "This is what I'm talking about. If you are to be my guard, it
would help us both immensely if we had a common interest. So, what do you say? Are
you willing to learn what I am willing to teach you?"

"Yes. Are you willing to let me be your guard?"

"Absolutely."

Chapter 8

"Why didn't you tell me you were going off to Pinesway?"

Linda's question was loaded with danger and Ryson saw now way to avoid any of it.

"It didn't seem like a good idea at the time," Ryson offered.

"Letting me know where you're going is not a good idea?"

"That's not what I meant. You knew I was out on a scout, and I was continuing that scout, I was just doing it near Pinesway."

"No," Linda said flatly. "You WERE on a scout with Enin. That's where I thought you were, with Enin. You came back because you found out something was going on over there in Pinesway. You left without Enin, on your own, to deal with that. There's a big difference, and you know it, so let's try this again. Why didn't you tell me you were going off to Pinesway?"

Ryson tried not to give up so easily on his first excuse. "It's like I said. You knew I was out on a scout, you didn't expect me home until today. Even though I was near Pinesway, it really did start out as a scout of the town."

"Look, if you keep this up you're just going to make it worse." Linda's face became flushed as her anger rose. "You're playing with words here to try and avoid the issue. If you want to play this game, I can play this game as well. Yes, I know you were on a scout with Enin, but did you return to town yesterday or not?"

"I did, I never said I didn't, but…"

"Did you leave again?"

"Yes, to scout…"

"I didn't ask you what you were doing. I just asked if you came here and left. When you left did you leave with Enin."

"No, he said he shouldn't get involved."

Linda was about to continue, but then realized what Ryson just said and seized upon it.

"Involved? Involved in what?"

"I told you. Sazar tried to take over Pinesway. He wanted to use it as a base for goblins."

"So now you admit it wasn't just a scout. You went out, without Enin, to stop Sazar."

Ryson held his breath for a moment as he realized his misstep too late. He did his best to cover it. "Well, I didn't know what he was up to until I held the sword. I told you that, too. It started out as a scout. It really did."

"Godson, Ryson! You're doing it again. You're playing with words and trying to avoid admitting what you did. Fine, it started out as a scout, but it wasn't an ordinary scout with Enin out in Dark Spruce. And that's where I thought you were. But you came back from Dark Spruce because you found out something was going on with Sazar. You

were scouting Pinesway with every intention of interfering with Sazar and his goblins.
That was the plan from the beginning, even before you held the sword. Right?"

At first Ryson did not wish to answer.

Linda pressed him.

"Right?!"

"Yes, but…"

"But nothing! You can't even tell me you didn't have a chance to let me know because you came back here in between your trip to Dark Spruce and before you set off again. You were right here yesterday afternoon. And don't tell me you didn't have time, because we both know that's ridiculous. And even if it wasn't absurd, you could have told Sy to send me word. Speaking of Sy, did you know I went to speak with him last night?"

The delver wanted to groan but he held his breath. "Yes, he told me when I saw him this morning."

"Did he tell you I asked him if he knew where you were?"

"Yeah, he said he didn't say much, tried to be as hazy about it as possible. He said you didn't look happy."

"I'm not happy. Not happy when I talked to Sy, and I'm certainly not happy now," Linda stated firmly. "I asked Sy if he knew where you were. All he said was that you were on a scout. I could tell he was trying to avoid the subject. I guessed you told him not to tell me, otherwise he would have told me straight out. Am I right?"

Ryson saw the hole just keep getting deeper. There really was no way out so he just came clean. "You're right. I told him not to tell you where I went."

Linda wanted to scream. "Do you know how utterly stupid that is?! For Godson's sake, Ry, I work in a tavern. That means on some days I know more about what's going on in this town then you and Sy put together. I heard that Enin flew over to Sy's office yesterday afternoon. If Enin came back, that meant you probably came back as well. With a few nudging questions to a few guards, I found out you ran into town in a hurry yesterday afternoon and left again fairly soon after that in another great hurry. I also found out no one saw Enin leave with you. Now I find out you actually told Sy to hide the truth from me."

"I wasn't hiding the truth from you. I was trying to keep you from worrying."

"So that's what this is all about, huh? You think if you don't tell me exactly where you are that somehow I won't worry?"

"Well, if you know I'm heading into some place dangerous, you're definitely going to worry."

"Of course I'm going to worry!" Linda shouted with exasperation. "And if I find out where you went and realize you didn't tell me, then not only am I going to worry, I'm going to be angry about it as well! You know, this is really ridiculous."

The delver bit his lip realizing anything he could say at this precise moment would probably only make things worse. It was a wise decision not to speak at all.

Linda, however, had plenty to say.

"Ryson, don't you think I know what this is all about? I know you weren't trying to keep secrets from me, that you thought you were actually helping me by not telling me, but we've gone through this before. I don't want you saving me from my own concern about you."

Ryson attempted to swing that point to his favor. "Don't you think there's a difference between concern and outright worry? I mean don't you think you would have viewed this differently?"

"Absolutely," Linda responded quickly, "and if something happened to you and I found out your last thought of me was not to trust me enough to tell me where you were going, how would that have made me feel?"

"It's not about trust," Ryson replied with an edge of anger in his own voice.

Linda did not back down. "Yes, it is! You just don't understand that yet. I see perfectly clear what your intentions were, you wanted to protect me, not lie to me. I understand that. What you don't understand is that when you act like that, you're showing me that you don't trust me to understand what you are. You're a delver. I have accepted what that means. You're going to go out exploring; it's what you have to do. You'll do your best to tell me where you're going, but we both know we can never be sure where you're going to end up. That's what happens to you. You tell me you're going to scout the hills. Fine, but you and I both know that could last all of two heartbeats. Suddenly, you catch some strange scent or the trail of something you've never seen before. The next thing you know, you're out in the Lacobian Desert climbing a sandstone cliff looking at a razor crow's nest. You don't mean to put yourself in danger, but you also can't stop being what you are. When I agreed to marry you that was the biggest thing I had to face up to. I had to ask myself whether or not I could handle the fact that you would always be running off somewhere, most like somewhere dangerous. If I believed I could handle that, which I did and still do, well then, I have to live up to it. Do you understand what I'm saying?"

"I guess," Ryson said somewhat half-heartedly.

"No guesses, do you understand or not?"

"I understand, but somehow if I agree with you I feel like I'm admitting to doing something underhanded. That's why I'm not happy about this. It's not like I tried to hide something from you for my own benefit and it's not like I lied to you. Somehow or other you have me feeling like I did."

"I'll say it again then. I understand you did what you did for me and not you, but that doesn't make it right. Don't ever keep information from me because you think I'm going to worry. Of course I'm going to worry. I worry every time you walk out that door. You and I both know we can't stop that from happening. You're going to leave and I'm going to be concerned about you."

"So where does that leave us."

"Hopefully, it now leaves us with a new understanding. No matter how dangerous you think it is, I don't want you to keep things from me. When you don't have the opportunity to tell me what you're up to, I don't expect you to catch some pigeon and tie a note to its leg so you can send me word. When you do have the chance, though, like yesterday

before you went into Pinesway, I want you to let me know where you're going. You go
on being a delver and do what you do. I'll go on being a delver's wife and I'll do what I
have to do. But in the end we deal with all these things together."

Chapter 9

Sazar had no illusions of his status among those that utilized magic for their own
benefit. He wielded great power—this point was beyond debate. He was a master
manipulator, the magic allowed him to bend the will of countless dark creatures in one
moment. His devious yet quick mind categorized and segmented his minions into
different roles. He was never overwhelmed by the near infinite feedback he received from
their collective thoughts. Instead, he ordered them with perfect genius, prioritized them,
and laid them out intertwined with his own twisted desires. In this, he had no equal, and
that kind of power deserved considerable respect.

The serp also fielded unequal capabilities of strategy, deception and cunning. He
understood tactics with the same perception as a leathered old war general that had
suffered through countless campaigns. While he used logic, he was well aware that most
of his victims acted on emotion, thus he never separated the two from his assessments.
He balanced his decisions on a cruel but perfect utilization of the weaknesses of his
enemies against the strengths of his own forces.

Combine his intellect with his ability to control a vast league of monsters, and Sazar
represented a dangerous threat. To ignore him or treat him as inferior would be a mistake
of incalculable stupidity. An army of minions with powers of their own was at his
command. To anger a serp of this aptitude was to invite a plague of monsters to your own
doorstep—a plague directed with mind boggling genius and without compassion.

Dealing with other magic casters on a one-on-one basis, however, was a different
matter entirely. In a simple contest of spell casting might, the serp would almost always
end up on the losing end. Sazar knew his limits. His spells of pure offensive energy could
not match an even below average practitioner. His defensive skills ranked even lower. He
lacked the pure power to overwhelm, and he was deficient of the skill to outmaneuver.
Remove his near infinite power to manipulate other monsters and reduce him to a caster
of spells, and the truth of the matter was that he was no threat at all.

Yet, what he needed now was exactly what he lacked. While he could manipulate and
control monsters, his power to do so had certain limitations in duration and range. While
in his presence, dark creatures would remain under his will indefinitely. As they ventured
beyond his direct company to carry out his desires, however, they became open to other

stimulus. The further they traveled from him and the longer they were away, the more
likely they would be to fall from his control. In fact, the true size of an army he could
control knew no other limits, but these aspects would always minimize his true potential.

If he had the intrinsic ability to cast spells of power, he could offset these limitations.
The magic could carry his dominion over greater distances and could imprint his will
more firmly in the minds of his minions. In order for him to succeed in this venture,
however, he would need to cast certain spells, and quite simply, he lacked the ability to
do so.

Still, it was his nature and his strength to realize his shortcomings and determine ways
to achieve his objectives. If he lacked the power and ability to cast the proper spells, he
would simply find someone that had such power and ability. His needs were
straightforward. The situation called for both skill in certain aspects of magical power
and reserves of magical energy. He knew the human sorceress in the desert possessed

both. What he did not know was if the woman named Tabris would make the turn down
the path that would satisfy his own needs.

What further presented a challenge was the simple fact that Sazar needed an alliance
with the sorceress free of any manipulation. He had to have her assistance based on her
own will, not his. He did not doubt he could control her if she turned down the proper
path, but the control would only be temporary—the bane of his current weakness. The
moment she gained any semblance of her own cognition, she would attempt to obliterate
him. He could not afford that risk. No, she must be willing to give her assistance to him
freely. Otherwise, he would gain only an interlude of the power he sought. Thus, he
would have to restrain his own true power to manipulate and allow the sorceress to
decide on her own.

He set off to the Lacobian Desert clearly understanding his needs and his mission. He
took with him only the large shag, ordering his other minions to remain within the limits
of the Dark Spruce forest. He focused most of his will on the hook hawk and the rock
beetle. He did not wish to lose control of these two, and he hoped his resolve was strong
enough to keep them in line. As for the smaller shag and the goblins, he believed their
losses could be mitigated upon his return.

Sazar allowed his larger shag to follow as a guard for most of the journey, but as the
serp closed on the oasis deep in the harsh heat, he bade the monster back. If he were to
succeed, to gain the true crux of his plans, he would have to meet the sorceress alone.

The serp wondered if he should approach the oasis without hesitation or simply wait
outside its boundaries for an invitation. On quick consideration, he opted for an
immediate entrance. If he waited, he doubted an invitation would be forthcoming, and if
he appeared to be a distraction, it was most likely the sorceress would use him as target
practice for a lightning spell.

The sorceress appeared before him the moment he stepped passed the dry sandy rock
of the desert and on to the soft grass that surrounded a large pool of water. The oasis
stretched far in every direction. Large boulders that were part of the landscape for untold
generations now stood as silent sentinels seemingly out of place in a lush and cool haven
of thick grass, lazy circling streams, small trees, and a variety of plants and bushes. A
small structure appeared almost hidden among the vines that hung about some of the
larger rocks.

Sazar ignored the wonder of such a green place in the midst of such a harsh
environment. He bowed slightly to the sorceress and directed his gaze toward the ground
before her. He would not speak until spoken to. She would know who and what he was
and he would not risk even for one moment the appearance of trying to sway her.

The magic caster appeared annoyed by the appearance of the serp. Her tone was short
and uninviting. "What do you want?"

"To speak with you," he replied succinctly.

"About what?"

"About an offer that I have."

Tabris sighed heavily, obviously further annoyed by now having to waste more time
with the serp. "What might this offer be?"

"I hope you would consider an alliance. I need the assistance of someone with your
capabilities."

"And what capabilities do you think I have?"

"A very large reserve of magical energies, the ability to cast magical spells that are
focused on wind and storm—as well as spells that are fairly precise but more importantly
deep in range, a willingness to prosper without regard to the consequences it might have
on those that do not matter to you, and a desire to increase both skill and knowledge.
These are the qualities I seek and these are the qualities I believe you possess."

Tabris frowned but did not otherwise move. "State your offer."

Sazar had to be very careful indeed at this instant. He was about to request what he
truly needed, what he wanted very badly. At this critical point, he knew that he would
almost instinctively use his power to manipulate and to control. After all, that was how he
always got what he wanted. Unfortunately, he was forced to do more than control this
instinct, he needed to bury it. Success depended solely on him stating his offer as
succinctly as possible and allowing the sorceress herself to decide whether or not to give
him what he wanted.

The task was daunting, but his strength remained centered on his own concentration
and will. Just as he willed others to do his own bidding, he now willed himself to keep his
powers in check.

"I wish to control an army of dark creatures. I have the ability to do so within my
mind, but not the power within my body. I am limited by time and distance. Do you
understand?"

"Of course," Tabris sighed again, obviously becoming more irritated by the moment.

"Very well, then you understand I have the power to control an army. I do not lack the
concentration. An infinitely growing horde of simple minded creatures at my command is
not beyond my abilities. I believe you know that. The problem is distance, not numbers.
Once my minions move beyond a certain range, they are free to make their own
decisions. And they usually make poor ones. The other difficulty is time. As it passes, my
control also diminishes. It's almost laughable that I can not overcome these limitations on
my own, but I must admit that I can not, and so I am here."

Sazar noticed Tabris' growing impatient and hastened to the crux of his offer. "A
simple spell of wind drift would probably suffice to offset my difficulty in distance. A
sorceress in tune with the power of storm would have no problem with such a spell. If the
spell were cast in such a way that it would carry my very will in all directions, then
distance would no longer be an issue. The spell would need to be open ended and

constantly linked to my own mind, that is why I need a spell caster with great reserves of
magical energy. As for time, another storm spell would be necessary—this one along the
lines of pressure and imprint to allow my will to be more engrained in the minds of my
minions. Again, this spell would also require a constant tap into your powers, but again
only for the sake of that one simple spell.

"With the assistance of these two spells, my weaknesses would be removed, my army
would be limitless—in essence my power would be limitless. We would be able to
conquer as much as we desired. Further, opposed to conquerors that became weakened by
stretching their forces to thin over large areas, my army would achieve just the opposite.
The more we conquered, the stronger we would become. Control over one region would
not lead to conflict within. Instead, it would lead to a larger army and thus more power.
As long as I have the ability to shape the desires of those I wish to control and as long as
you kept that ability from waning over time or distance, there would be no end to our

conquest. As partners in this, we would share in the spoils of what this legion of dark
creatures conquered."

"This is your offer?" Tabris stared coldly at Sazar. If not for her surprise, she might
have simply obliterated him with the wave of her hand. Still, she could not refrain from
questioning the audacity of the serp. "You offer me nothing and you stand to gain much.
In fact, your offer is less than nothing. To give you want you want would require a
constant drain of my power, a link to you that would add to your strength and diminish
my own energy. This is insulting."

"No, you have not heard me in full. I will not deny the power I seek will cost you in
magical energies, but even you must agree the total cost would be negligible compared to
your vast reserves. My guess is you would not even notice the drain. I simply require a
boost in range and endurance of my own powers, nothing more. I require no library of
spells, no focus of your attention beyond the initial casting. It is just a simple extension of
my own influence. How much energy would it take from you to cast a continuous spell of
wind drift and a spell of imprint that would be linked to my powers of persuasion?"

"A shred would be too much because I say again I gain nothing from such an effort, so
why should I bother."

"You should bother because I do offer a gain, a substantial gain that would allow you
everything you currently desire."

"And how would you know what I desire?" Tabris eyed the serp almost dangerously.

"Simple. I understand logic. I need to in order to do what I can do. Do you disagree
with that?"

Tabris said nothing.

Sazar turned his back to the sorceress and peered out across the vast wasteland that
stood before him just beyond the oasis conjured by the sorceress.

"Why are you out here?" He did not let Tabris answer. "You are here for the same
reason many magic casters have come here, to practice your craft without distraction.
You are growing in power but you lack experience. With each day your understanding
increases, but you are also shackled, limited by the resources you have before you. You
test your skill on empty sand because it offers no resistance and little danger. Spells gone
wrong can do little damage out here. The truth is, however, you crave more. You wish to
build on your spells, build on your knowledge and build on your experience. If I am
wrong, then I shall leave now. Better yet, if I'm wrong simply cast your spell of
destruction on me and I will be no more."

Sazar waited a scant few moments. He did not worry for he knew his assessment to be
accurate. He continued on with his back still to the sorceress. "The real truth of the matter
is that I would be able to conquer only as long as you allowed it. The moment you felt as
if our bargain did not aid you in any way, you could simply cancel the spell and my army
would be gone, my conquests would be ended. It is, therefore, very much in my interest
to make sure you not only gain at the initial bargain, but continue to gain as time goes on.

"Since I know what you desire, and I know that it is in my interest to make sure those
desire are met, do you not believe that I would have an idea of how to ensure this?"

"I do not like playing in riddles, serp," Tabris stated, but her tone was not as harsh, not
as threatening. "I asked for your offer. If there is more to it, then I will hear of it now."

"The offer is as I said it would be. We will share in the spoils of my army's conquest.
What you fail to see is what those spoils include. With every outpost, town, and city I

take, there will be prisoners, prisoners I have no need for—prisoners I will send to you.
You may do with them as you wish, practice whatever spell you desire, utilize them in
whatever fashion necessary to assist you in gaining knowledge and power. Because these
will be humans from defeated and occupied towns, you will be able to carry out your will
without fear of consequence. There will be no war parties seeking justice, no vengeful
militia threatening to put an end to you. Just as you will give me an everlasting flow of a
very small part of your magical energy, I will give you and everlasting flow of a very
large number of experimental subjects for your magical endeavors."

Sazar understood choices. He understood them very well. When his true power was
broken down to its most basic principle, it all relied on his ability to manipulate, to steer
his target or victim toward a path that would benefit him the most. There were, however,
some choices that were beyond his power. The all important choices, the choice of faith,
the choice of love, the choice of loyalty, and ultimately the choice between good and evil,
these choices belonged to the individual alone. When an individual faced a choice such as
these, nothing the serp could do could sway that decision.

Sazar kept his eyes away for he knew that Tabris faced such a choice at this moment.
While it was not within his power to force her down the twisted path of dark desires, he
was not above the craving to try. He did not want to allow a lapse in instinct to cause
disaster. This was a powerful sorceress that could incinerate him with a wave of her hand.
He would not risk trying to persuade her in anyway, and he made as much known to the
sorceress without hesitation.

"I must say no more," he admitted with a candor that was not his natural character. "I
will admit I greatly desire to have this power, so great is my desire I might be willing to
attempt to sway your opinion. We both know we can't have that. There must never be a
doubt that you accepted this proposal on your own under no influence of my own. I will
give you as much time as you need."

"I need no further time," Tabris answered quickly, "and I know you did not try to
bend my will to yours. Had you tried, it would have been the last thing you did in this
life. No, I have decided on my own and I will accept your proposal."

Chapter 10

As Enin opened the front door, Ryson took two leaps back and urged the four dogs
that waited in the doorway to charge him. He slapped his chest and the one that reached
him first jumped into his arms as the other three clamored around his legs. After playfully
rolling the dog back in forth, he let the overjoyed animal slip easily to the ground in order
to let another one jump up into his hands. With that one still in his arms, he bent over low
to let yet another leap onto his back. Once these two were finished, he let them leap away
only to drop to his knees and say hello to the fourth and final dog that nearly knocked the
delver over onto his back.

Enin watched the display only slightly amused. "I am overjoyed you love them so
much, but I really wish you wouldn't do that. They now think it's ok to jump on everyone
that comes to the door. It's very hard on some of the visitors."

"Bah," Ryson replied with a grunt while still wrestling with the dogs. "If someone
doesn't want a dog jumping up to say hello, you probably don't want them as visitors."

"Hmmmm," Enin said while thoughtfully considering Ryson's reply. "Never thought
of that and you know what? You're probably right."

"Of course I'm right."

"Are you here to take them for their run?"

"That's one of the reasons." Ryson stood up and began walking back towards the door
which Enin swung open wider to allow Ryson and the dogs to come through. "I heard
Holli came to visit you and from all accounts she's still here. If that's true, I'd like to talk
to her first. Then, I'll take them for a few laps around the town's wall."

"Yes, she is still here. She is waiting for us in the library. And the dogs would love a
run around the wall."

Enin took the lead and marched halfway through a long hall and made an abrupt right
into a large room with an open door. Ryson followed, but slowed as he saw the elf staring
into a green mist that seemed to reflect his and Enin's presence like a mirror. Holli's
hands arched around the mist as if she was holding it in place.

"That's not bad, not bad at all," Enin stated with a satisfied smile.

"I wasn't able to hear anything," Holli noted as she collapsed her hands to her sides.
The green mist dissipated and soon all traces of it were gone. "I could see you open the
door. I saw Ryson step back and the four dogs went to greet him."

"Excellent. You saw everything. As to not hearing anything, well you're not supposed
to hear anything with that spell. It's a light spell. You are only supposed to see what I
see."

"For the most part, I could see clearly when I first cast the spell. As you moved further away and toward the door, the image became slightly less clear. In truth, it was only a small blur, but enough so that I could notice. As you walked back toward me, the image became stronger again."

"That we will rectify with practice and also when you realize to tap into more of you inner strengths. You have a natural ability to make the spell stronger, you just don't realize it yet. You need to focus more on the light that is part of your inner power."

Holli frowned. "But I cast green magic, not yellow. I thought my power focused on nature."

"Indeed it does, but doesn't nature thrive on the light? What is green but a combination of blue and yellow? Nature is water and light working together to give life. So, yes your true strength is in the druidic spells of nature, but you also have natural abilities for spells dealing with water and light. Casting green magic is a great gift and you should be thankful for it."

Holli smiled as she looked to the delver. "Hello, Ryson. It is good to see you again."

"It's great to see you. Is Enin teaching you how to cast spells?"

"Yes, he wants to help me with spells that would enhance my abilities as a guard. We both agreed that a sight spell would be a good start."

"I guess that will come in handy when you return to your camp. An elf guard that can increase her sight can only be a benefit."

Holli said nothing at first. She looked to Enin for possible direction. When he nodded his head without saying a word, she returned her gaze to the delver.

"I am not returning to my camp. My service there has come to an end. With his approval, I have now turned my service over to him. As I once supported my camp, I now avail my abilities as an elf guard to serve Enin, as well as this town."

Ryson did not appear shocked, but he did take long moments before responding. He looked back and forth from the elf to the wizard and then stared at the ground as if considering other details and trying to put them all in perspective.

"Holli, does this have anything to do with Lief?" Ryson finally asked.

"Yes and no," Holli responded. "Yes in that both Lief and I were asked by the elders to leave our camp. No in that Lief went his way and I went mine. I never got a chance to speak to him after he left. He did not leave under the best of circumstances."

Holli went on to explain all the details she could on what led to Lief's banishment and her own departure from the elf camp.

"I met Lief at Pinesway," Ryson stated after the elf was done. "I know he's not happy. He's actually quite angry. That's why when I heard you were here, I came over to find out what was going on. I wanted to…"

Ryson went silent. He said nothing as he stared into empty space. He brought a hand to his forehead as he tried to get a better feel of what he was sensing. He could not.

Enin had seen this look before.

"The dryness—that was how you put it last time—are you feeling it again?" the wizard asked curiously.

"Yes," Ryson admitted. "This is such a strange sensation. The real problem with it is I can't even get a hold of where it's coming from. It just basically appears out of no where.

It's fairly subtle actually, but when it happens, I can't miss it. That might not make sense
either, but it's how it is."

Enin spoke out loud as he considered his own thoughts. "I wonder if I could trace it.
What spell would it be? It's not light, but perhaps it's instinct. An animal spell might
follow it, but then I would have the difficulty of trying to determine which animal. Is it
prey that can sense a predator, or the other way around? It may not even be instinct. I
don't think it's elemental so I can discount wind, water, earth and fire. Illusionary also
seems doubtful, but it could be using dryness to hide its true qualities. That might
actually make some sense. What about shadow? But would a shadow feel dry? Maybe.
Then the question becomes how to detect shadow and trace it to an origin. My guess is
the feeling is from within you, so it might build on emotion, but dry emotions would be

no emotions. There are things I could try, but at the moment they would be guesses and I
don't wish to experiment until I know more. I think perhaps we…"

Just like in Dark Spruce Forest, Enin's focus on Ryson's feeling was torn away by a
feeling of his own. The wizard quickly gained an awareness that made him regretfully
cast aside any consideration of the delver's own sensations.

The wizard's expression became as serious as his tone. He looked to both Holli and
Ryson with a somber understanding of how the land had just changed. "I am afraid
something has just happened of enormous consequence. I can not explain fully how I
know this, but you must accept that I do. It has much to do with the balance of things and
I am very aware of elements of this nature. The sorceress Tabris, the one both of you
went into Sanctum Mountain with to obtain Ingar's sphere, has made an alliance with
Sazar. In one form or another, she is now linked with him and thus she has chosen her
path. I can not say where this will lead, I only know that I feel the weight of her power on
the side of evil and malevolence. Her power is great enough and her decision momentous
enough for me to sense this."

"Do you know where they are now?" Ryson asked.

"Near her new home in the Lacobian desert."

Ryson looked about as if trying to decide what to do next. "I don't understand how
you know this, but I'm not going to question it. Is Burbon in any immediate danger?"

"No," Enin answered with certainty.

"Well, that's something at least." Ryson then considered the power Tabris displayed
when she assisted those that entered Sanctum Mountain to retrieve the Sphere of Ingar.
The thought of someone that powerful teaming up with Sazar did not leave pleasant
thoughts in his mind. "The two of them coming together is not a good thing. You have
any idea of what they might be planning?"

"No, only that it will not be in the best interest of the land, but in their own selfish
interests."

Holli turned to her own training and immediately put the situation in perspective. "If
there is no immediate threat, then there is no need for immediate decisions. We should,
however, inform your captain of this turn of events. He needs to know without delay."

"I agree," Ryson added.

"Very well." Enin turned to Ryson. "I regret we must for the moment forget your
feeling of dryness and address it at another time."

"It's ok, it's gone now anyway. It only lasts for a few moments. We should all go to
talk to Sy. If this is as big as you make it out to be, we all need to figure out the best way

to handle this."

Ryson looked down at the four dogs that remained nearby. "I'll have to run with them
later. Sorry guys."

Enin looked to the animals briefly and then began to walk to the door. "They are
disappointed, but they understand."

Ryson allowed Holli to follow first but called out to the wizard as they moved down
the hall together. "Are you talking to them now?"

"If I answer that, you might think I was crazy."

#

Tabris took long moments of consideration before casting her two spells. A violet
colored diamond appeared around her wrists as she mouthed words in a whisper. The

diamond spun about her hands as it lifted from her hands. With a thrust of her arms the
purple diamond flew into the air. It maintained its shape, but it grew ever larger, its
boundaries expanding in all directions. As its edges rolled out of sight toward each point
of the compass, it left behind a faint shadow of itself. Eventually, this too disappeared.

Tabris looked upon Sazar and again mouthed words the serp could not understand,
words he could barely hear. Another diamond appeared near her hands, a smaller one.
This one held its tight size as she flung it at Sazar.

The serp's first instinct was to recoil at the motion, but he held his ground and the
diamond caused him no pain when it entered his chest.

"It is done," Tabris said. "Your will is now connected to the drifting breeze that can
no longer be seen or felt, but still exists. It will carry your power to bend the will of
others for greater distances then you would have hoped. Your will is also now enhanced
with the constant pressure of breath. Those that fall under your control will be reminded
of your orders with every breath they take. Both spells are continuous in their own nature.
The drifting breeze has no end and only death would stop the continuity of breath. They
are fed with my own energy, thus I can cancel them at will. Give me no reason to and you
will find that the creatures you place under your control will remain under your control
no matter how far you send them from you or how long they are away from your
presence."

"There will be no need to cancel them," the serp insisted as he stood unmoving while
trying to sense a difference within himself. At first he felt nothing. "You are certain the
magical energy is linked to my thoughts?"

"As certain as I am standing here. Test your new powers now. No doubt you left
creatures with some last orders other than the large shag that stands far out in the desert."

"Yes, a few."

"Establish a link with them now. Follow the shadows of your last contact with them in
your mind."

Sazar focused on the rock beetle. He sifted through the lingering thoughts of his last
contact. As it became clearer in his mind, he seized it and attempted to recreate it.
Instantly, he connected to the rock beetle that was burrowing right where he left it in
Dark Spruce Forest. The beetle became still as it waited for a command. Sazar felt the
presence of the rock beetle as if it stood at his side.

With this connection still strong and vital, he reached out his thoughts to the hook

hawk. Immediately, he linked his mind to that of the bird beast. The hawk perched
quietly in the trees and Sazar could see what the bird saw. Only a dozen or so goblins
remained in the area, and even a few of these were beginning to shy away from the area.

"You are now linked with a few of your minions?" Tabris asked.

"Yes. It is extraordinary that the link is so strong at this distance."

"You realize that you can use these links to acquire contact with other creatures?"

"No, I did not," Sazar admitted.

"The drifting breeze is now your vessel. Where it goes, your thoughts can go. You
simply need to focus on the target and your will can reach it. If the minions in your
control allow you to establish the location of a new target, you can flow your will through
them to that exact point. You no longer need to be in the exact presence of a creature to
bend its will to yours."

That consideration went beyond Sazar's furthest hopes. Without delay, he tested this new found power. Rather than attempting to re-establish a link with the goblins using a past thought from his memory, he concentrated on their location using the images given to him by the hook hawk. His mind sent out a command to the goblins trying to sneak away.

Return to your positions and await my instructions.

He watched with glee as the goblins stiffened with fear and quickly returned to the fold of the other creatures. He then bade the hook hawk to take flight, which it did without hesitation. The beast circled about at higher and higher elevations. All the time Sazar focused upon the images of the forest that came back to him through the mind of the bird. When he saw the second shag meandering west through sparse trees, he commanded it to return as well. The shag obeyed.

Gleefully, Sazar announced his success. "It is working!"

The sorceress appeared less impressed. "Of course."

With swift calculation of his newfound powers, Sazar considered one last effort to test. He had been able to reestablish his will on minions he previously controlled, but what of creatures with which he had no previous contact. He returned his focus to the hook hawk. Images of the forest returned to the forefront of his mind and he noticed two gremplings stalking together through the trees. Gremplings, small but agile creatures covered in fur with long tails were mischievous in nature and lacked any true power to be an asset to him, but for now they would serve as an excellent test. Beyond their nimbleness, they were also fairly intelligent, much more so than the common goblin. They also had stronger wills and lower levels of fear. With such characteristics, gremplings were often difficult for serps to control, and because they lacked the horde traits of the goblin or the sheer natural power of a shag, they were usually not worth the effort.

It was not, however, Sazar's desire to add these two to his army for their prowess. It was his wish to determine just how strong he had become. It would normally take a fair amount of concentration to bend the will of just one grempling when it was right in front of him. How would he succeed with two and at this far distance?

He focused his will upon the image of the gremplings in his mind. He reached out to them and ordered them to hold their position. In his mind, he could see them freeze. He then sent them an order to circle twenty paces about their current position and scout for

any other creatures in the area. Again, he watched them in his mind as they followed out
his orders.

The sensation was intoxicating to the serp. Not only could he now regain control of
his previous minions with very little effort, he could add to his army without ever having
to venturing out in the wild. The links he could create were far more powerful, the images
in his mind forcibly more vibrant. He could fix his concentration on a group of minions
in one area while still reaping the benefits of incoming sensations of creatures under his
control far off in the distance.

As he expanded his mind to incorporate the links with all his creatures, his own
perspective of the land around him grew with leaps and bounds. In essence, his awareness
of sights, sounds, and scents expanded beyond his own normal capabilities a hundredfold.

For one brief moment, the enormous flow of stimulus from outside forces into his
mind nearly overwhelmed him to the brink of unconsciousness or perhaps even insanity.

If he drank in too much of the inflowing information, he might lose his own place in
reality. He quickly seized on his own surroundings, anchored his physical being to the
actual point of his own existence. Then, he allowed the sensations from his minions to
take their place in his consciousness where he could utilize them but where they would
not overwhelm his own awareness.

"You have done me a great service, sorceress," Sazar admitted. "And in the process
you have opened great opportunities for us both. I will utilize what you have given me to
its greatest extent, and in return, I will send you whatever it is you need."

"I expect you shall," Tabris replied.

#

"You know, I woke up this morning with a bad feeling that I just couldn't shake," Sy
Fenden said as he gazed out into the rolling hills just outside the walls that surrounded
Burbon. Standing in the tower, he could see the edges of Dark Spruce Forest and he
wondered what new problems his town would now face. "You say this Tabris is a
powerful sorceress. Is she as powerful as you?"

Enin stood between Ryson and Holli and he answered Sy directly. "No, but do not
misunderstand. I am somewhat of an anomaly. I don't wish to sound as if I'm boasting
about myself, but my abilities with magic are on a different scale. You should never use
them in gauging the strength of a potential threat."

"I'm not." Sy stated flatly. "I've always listened to everything you said and I
understand you're in a different league, but the first thing I need to know is if this Tabris
is also an anomaly. Now, that I know she isn't, I still have to get a better idea of what
we're facing. Does she have the power to destroy this town on her own? I mean, if you
weren't here protecting us."

Enin took a moment to consider the question against what he knew of the town's
defenses. "She could cause considerable damage. She has a natural ability with wind and
storm, and thus she would be difficult for you to fight. She has a great reserve of magical
energy and she has been practicing for many days now. Still, she would have to
overcome much to destroy the whole town. She could destroy the walls and towers with
wind spins and tornados. Many of the buildings she could obliterate or set afire with
lightning. She would be difficult to strike from a distance with bows or slings since she
could deflect many with a wind shield. Your forces, however, would now be prepared for
such and onslaught. If you accepted the losses to the structures and simply remained

patient, you could wait her out. She would eventually tire and then your men would
indeed be able to take her. She could not hold out against you indefinitely."

"Alright so she can't just waltz in here and flatten us with a wave of her hand. That's
somewhat good news." Sy took another moment to gaze out over the wall and across the
lands that surrounded Burbon. "Considering what you know of her powers, is there
anything that immediately comes to mind that we can do to better our defenses against
her?"

"I honestly do not think she would attempt a frontal assault. She would waste much of
her energy and she would stand to gain very little."

The news was welcome, but Sy wanted to make sure there was nothing overlooked. "I
appreciate that, but I'd still like to cover my bets. What do you think, anything else we
can do or not?"

Enin joined Sy in looking out across the land. "The best thing to do is remember that
for the most part you would see her coming. Her power is not in shadow or illusion. It is
doubtful she would try to cloak herself. The strength of her magic is force, not deception.
Understanding that a woman walking alone toward the town would not necessarily be a
woman in distress would be the first step in guarding against her. Also, she would have
difficulty with barriers. Well, difficulty in passing them without using magic. With the
magic she can pretty much break through any section of the wall, but it's not like she can
fly over them like I can. That takes a skill she will not have yet obtained. Nor can she slip
past them in secret, as her power is not in shadow."

"You're telling me she can get through our wall, but she'd have to blast through it."

"Exactly," Enin said.

"So if she does show up with malice in mind, she'll have to expel magical energy to
get around any type of barriers we put up. She has—how did you put it?— 'great reserves
of magical energy' I think is what you said, but you also said we can wear her out. The
more barriers she has to bust through, the sooner she's going to run out of energy."

"Correct."

Sy nodded and again looked to the surround hills. "I was thinking of putting up a new
set of bulwarks. Now might be a good time. The traders aren't going to like another
obstacle to deal with, but that's the way it goes."

Sy took a moment to calculate in his mind where the best position for a new barricade
would be and how long it might take to construct it. He grunted a few unintelligible
words to himself about work details and wood from Dark Spruce.

"There are a few other things that I need to know," Sy continued as he turned back to
face Enin, Holli and Ryson. "You say that just this morning you sensed this Tabris had
joined Sazar and, as you put it, turned down a path toward evil."

"Yes, that is what I said," Enin admitted.

"Well, I have to admit this has me somewhat confused, so I need a bit of clarification
here. If I'm not mistaken you said that Tabris was the one that made Yave into that storm.
That didn't sound like a right benevolent action. In fact, if you weren't here when that
happened, Yave would have killed Ryson here and maybe destroyed the whole town. I
would have thought that action would have basically been considered an evil act on its
own. Why is it you think that this morning there's something different about her?"

"When she turned Yave into a storm, she did so with indifference," Enin explained. "It

was not her intention to cause harm to anyone. It certainly wasn't a decision that showed
compassion or kindness, but it was truly Yave that was dictating the path of wickedness
in that situation. For all intents and purpose, Tabris has been, to this point, neutral. She
was not good, nor was she evil. She simply studied her craft in the desert. When she
converted Yave to a storm she did so solely for the purposes of experimentation with her
own power. Today, however, she made a decision that altered her neutrality. Of that, I am
certain."

"Well, I can't say I follow you on that one. You've talked to me about this balance
stuff on several occasions and I think you're seeing things way beyond my comprehension. Still, I will never dismiss your judgment on these types of situations."

"I appreciate that."

"I do, however, have another question that regards are friend Sazar. This serp I know
is trouble. He's been bad news since the first time we encountered him. He led a fairly

significant goblin force into Pinesway just a few days ago. Now, he's joined forces with a powerful sorceress. This I know isn't good news for anyone. Still, he doesn't come across as one that would want a partner. From what I know of him, he seems to like being in charge. I'm guessing the sorceress is far more powerful than he is. Why would he risk joining up with someone who could order him around and there would be nothing he could do about it?"

Enin shrugged. "That, I can not say. I have never been very good at understanding what motivates those that choose a path of evil."

"Not even a guess?"

"I'm afraid not."

"How about either of you?" Sy asked as he looked to Holli and Ryson.

Ryson spoke out first. "I just know what I learned from the sword when I was in Pinesway. He wanted to take over the town to turn it into some kind of breeding ground for his minions. The sword made it pretty clear to me though that if I put the scare into the goblins, Sazar would lose out. I honestly believe I did exactly what I had to in order to kill that plan. I don't think the goblins are going back to Pinesway anytime soon."

"Alright, he wanted to expand his army by taking over an abandoned town. That failed so he joined up with a sorceress. I'm still not seeing the connection."

Holli offered her own view point. "It may be that he lost much of his forces to Ryson's attack and he had no other alternative but to find an ally. It may not be something he wanted to do, but perhaps he felt it was necessary. Or perhaps it was the sorceress that pressed the alliance and the serp truly had no choice. How could he fight her if she is as powerful as Enin says and he had just lost the majority of his own forces?"

Sy raised an eyebrow at the point. Quickly, he came up with a question to test the theory. "Enin, do you know where they are now?"

"Yes, they are in the desert."

"This is where Tabris created her home, so to speak, so she could practice, right?"

"Yes."

"Then I don't think Tabris forced the issue."

Enin displayed puzzlement and questioned the conclusion even as Holli appeared accepting of it.

"Why do you think that?" the wizard asked.

Sy answered rather matter-of-factly. "Well, if they are at Tabris' home, then we have to assume that Sazar sought out the sorceress and not the other way around. Otherwise, how would Sazar have gotten all the way to the Lacobian Desert so fast?"

"I see," Enin agreed. "Yes, it makes sense. If Tabris sought out Sazar they would be in Dark Spruce right now."

"Anyway," Sy continued, "what we have so far is that Sazar probably ventured out to
the Lacobian and met up with Tabris. He might have been looking for any magic-caster
or he might have been searching for her in particular. We can't be sure of which. Sazar
met Tabris who is a very powerful sorceress in her own right. Something happened which
led to Tabris making a decision to turn from being a neutral practicing magic-caster to
being an ally of a serp we know we can't trust and we know wants to cause some serious
trouble. At this point, we really don't know why he joined with the sorceress or what they
might be up to at this very moment. That's how I understand the situation. Am I missing
anything?"

"That sums it up very well," Enin responded.

Ryson perked up as he considered everything Sy just said. "Enin, when we were in Dark Spruce, you cast a spell that would allow you to see into Pinesway. When I came to your house this morning, Holli had just cast a spell to see me at the door while she was in another room. If you can do that, why don't you cast a spell that would let you see into the Lacobian Desert right now and maybe we can get an idea of what those two are up to."

Sy looked to Enin expectantly. "Can you do that?"

Enin frowned. "Not as of yet. I am still trying to figure out the proper way to bend light without an anchor point as well as avoiding detection."

Sy shook his head. "I have no idea what you just said. You seem to be able to cast some spells to let you look into other places, why not now?"

"Previously," Enin began to explain, "when I saw into Pinesway, and even when Holli watched Ryson from a distance, we both used a sight spell that requires an anchor. My sight spell into Pinesway used my web spell as the point of contact, thus I had already established a magical connection with certain aspects of the ground at Pinesway. When Holli cast her spell, she used me as the contact and I allowed her to use my sight. For me to look into Tabris at this moment, I would have to utilize a similar anchor, but I have no connection point. I could try to make one with a long ranged energy spell such as striking a point near her with wind or lightning. Unfortunately, she would immediately sense my spell. What good is spying on someone if they know you are watching? It would be better if I could actually see into that part of the desert without casting another spell first. What I am hoping to do one day is to bend light toward me so that I can actually see with my own eyes by simply capturing light from a great distance. The spell needs more work at the moment, but I am getting closer."

Sy looked intently at the wizard as he seemed to be playing with another thought in his mind. Enin wondered what the captain of the guard was contemplating.

"What is it?" Enin asked.

"You just said you could shoot a long ranged spell into the Lacobian to make some kind of magical connection. You said you could cast a wind spell or maybe lightning."

"That is correct, but Tabris would notice it immediately."

"What I have in mind wouldn't matter. If you know where they are and can hit them with some kind of lightning blast, then why don't you and we can stop worrying about this matter?"

Enin's expression turned to a gray mask of bitter disappointment. "You want me to just wave my hand and snuff them out like putting out a candle?"

"If you can, yes. That's exactly what I have in mind," Sy admitted.

Enin looked at Sy and then shook his head. "You know I get a bit tired of this," he
said with a huff. "Just because I know where Sazar is right now, I suppose you think I
should send a massive bolt of energy at that spot. It doesn't matter that I can't pinpoint it
exactly. All I need to do is make the bolt large enough to make sure it kills him and
hopefully Tabris, too."

Enin paused to look into Sy's eyes. When he saw agreement in the Captain's
expression, the wizard continued explaining his own disappointment.

"Do you really think I can do that? Well, I probably could, but I won't. I won't
because I would destroy everything around them as well, the innocent and the guilty.

There is life in the desert, just like there is life in Dark Spruce and just like there is life
right here. An act like that has great consequences, and I'm not ready to take that step,
that's a step toward disregard, power without responsibility. Do you really want me to be
like that? And if so, why stop there? I can protect every person in Burbon right now by
simply sending out a destructive force that will kill every shag, river rouge, vampire and
goblin within sight of the town limits. It would also kill every bird, every fox, every deer
and every traveling merchant that happens to be in the wrong spot at the wrong time.
Beyond that, there's the whole concept of balance that you seem to be forgetting. What
happens when I start indiscriminately removing creatures because of their choices? Do I
become the ultimate slayer of all things that don't choose the path we want them to
choose? And where do you think this evil will go, just disappear? I can tell you it doesn't
work like that. For every evil creature I destroy, that evil will find a new home, most
likely a more diabolical one. No, it's not a matter of can or can't. I won't do this."

The mood became somewhat uncomfortable as Enin folded his arms across his chest
and continued to look at Sy with something less than defiance but something more than
disappointment. The captain acknowledged the moment with a will to move on.

"Very well, I'm sorry I asked. I'll try not to do it again."

"I would appreciate that."

"I guess then there's not much we do about this," Sy stated. "Sazar and Tabris are out
in the desert and we can hope they stay there. I'll start planning the new bulwark and
inform all the guards of what we know. Other than that, we just have to hope we don't
see any trouble from them."

Holli agreed with the assessment. "It is a sound decision. If we do not go looking for
trouble, we have a better chance of avoiding it. It is also best to remain prepared in case it
comes looking for us."

Ryson jumped in quickly to shift the focus to a point of his own. "There's something
that's been bothering me about all this and I realize now what it is. I remember that when
I was in Pinesway, Lief showed up as I told everyone. Problem is he said he was going to
be hunting the dark creatures. I guess he thinks that's going to keep him occupied now
that he's been banished from his camp. But basically, he's taking just the opposite
approach we've decided on, he's out looking for trouble. Anyway, he said if he ran into
Sazar he would take care of him. He had the kind of look in his eye that indicated he

might not just wait to run into him accidentally, that he might go out of his way looking
for him. If he does that now, he's going to run into not only Sazar but Tabris as well. He
has to be warned about that. I don't think I would sleep well if I knew something
happened to Lief because of Sazar and Tabris, especially if I knew I could prevent it."

"So you're going to take off after the elf and try and find him and warn him?" Sy
asked with a raised eyebrow.

"That's the plan," Ryson said, but then realized Sy looked more than slightly
apprehensive. "You don't seem happy with this, what's up?"

Sy continued to press with a suspicious tone. "You're not using this as an excuse to
scout out the Lacobian and to find out what Tabris and Sazar are up to now, are you?"

Ryson answered firmly without a hint of anything but sincerity. "That's not my
intention at all. In fact, the truth is I have no desire to go anywhere near the Lacobian.
The only way I'm going to end up there is if Lief is somehow tracking Sazar and has
gotten that far, but I really don't want that to be the case. I'm hoping he's still in Dark

Spruce somewhere. Even if Lief is in the Lacobian, I'll try to get to him before he gets
anywhere near Tabris and Sazar. That way, I won't have to go near them, either. I have
no intention of getting involved with this sorceress."

"Let's hope none of us have to get involved with her." Sy added. "Are you going to
leave now?"

"In a moment," the delver replied. "I have to go tell Linda what I'm up to first, I
promised I would. And Enin, the dogs will have to wait for that run."

Chapter 11

"I know it's a lot to ask, and I don't know if I should even be asking it at all, but I thought I would at least talk it over with you. You don't mind, do you?"

Linda's question held a great deal of hope, and Enin's answer inspired even more.

"Linda, you have an open invitation to talk things over with me whenever you want. Well, as long as I'm not in the middle of trying to cast a new spell. You might want to give me a bit of space then. I'm always careful, but you can never be too careful. Anyway, you are a person I would never turn away. I have said it before and to more people than I can remember. This town owes you a great debt even though they don't realize it. Your Ryson is indispensable to us. Many think I am the reason this town still exists, but they don't truly understand. Burbon owes its existence to Ryson Acumen and we owe Ryson's desire to stay in Burbon to you."

"I don't think I want to think of it like that," Linda stated somewhat hesitantly, not sure on how to respond to such a statement. "I'm with Ryson because I want to be, not because I wanted him to save the town."

"And he is with you because he wants to be, and that's why he is in Burbon."

"Well, thank you." Linda paused as if trying to find the right words to move on to her request. She noted the elf's presence in the sitting room. "I'm glad she's here, too. Ry told me all the things Holli did at Sanctum Mountain and we all know how she helped out against the dwarves from Dunop. I think when good people are around, it makes you feel safer."

Holli nodded in appreciation of the comment but said nothing.

"What is it that's bothering you, Linda?" Enin asked. "You can come right out and say it, and if you can't explain it as well as you like, we can work with that, too. Remember who you're dealing with here. Most people don't know what I'm talking about half the time I say something. I just tend to keep blurting things out until it finally makes sense. It works for me, it can work for you."

Linda smiled slightly, but then remembered why she came and then any hint of a smile disappeared completely. "It's just that Ry told me about this Tabris sorceress today. He told me that she's helping that serp, Sazar. He's gone now, left to find Lief. It's not that he went out looking for Lief that's bothering me. I actually would have expected him to. He always worries about his friends and it's not a surprise at all. This Tabris, though, has me worried."

Enin pressed forward with a consideration of his own as Linda took a breath and a
moment to try and be more exact in her words. "You worry that Ryson will try to solve
the problem with Tabris on his own? I don't believe that is the case."

"No, I don't think Ry will initiate it, but I have a feeling Tabris will. I'm not even sure
Ry remembers, maybe he does and didn't say anything because he didn't want me to
worry, but I remember it. This sorceress didn't always call herself Tabris. At one point,
her name was Lauren and she went into Sanctum to help destroy the Sphere of Ingar.
Ryson told me that when everything was done on Sanctum, Tabris said she was either
going to kill him or thank him for what she had become. He told me this right after he
came back from Sanctum, almost as if it was an afterthought. I guess at the time, this
Tabris wasn't that much of a worry to him, just starting out as a sorceress. I think

everyone pretty much dismissed it, but for some reason I never did. Now, you think she's
doing bad things, joining with Sazar, and who knows what else. It was enough to get all
of you wondering what she might do to Burbon and enough to send Ryson out looking to
warn Lief. If that's the case, I don't think Tabris is going to want to thank anyone."

"So you think she will wish to make an attempt on Ryson's life?" Enin asked with a
raised eyebrow.

"Maybe, I don't know, I really can't say. I just know that the moment Ry told me what
was going on, I dreaded hearing it and I've been dreading it ever since."

Enin spoke with great sincerity as he attempted to do more than simply comfort Linda.
With all honesty, he wanted to convey his own certainty that Tabris would not be able to
harm the delver. "If you are looking for assurances that Ryson is safe from Tabris, I can
tell you that I am not concerned at all with the possibility of Tabris being successful in
killing Ryson. You really have nothing to worry about. You're only causing yourself a
great deal of unnecessary strain."

"I appreciate that, but you're not me," Linda replied quickly, almost as if she wanted
to explain her terrors more than she wanted to hear Enin's conciliations. "It's hard to
explain. There are things I can accept, things I need to deal with whether I like it or not. I
know I am always going to worry about Ryson. There are times I want to be able to help
him, but I know I can't. He has to go out on his own. He has to go exploring. That's the
way it is and that's the way it will be. I know what's in store for me being married to a
delver. I can live with that, but this thing with Tabris, I never bargained for this. This is
very different, not at all like what I'm used to, and I honestly don't know if I can handle
it."

Enin persisted in attempting to relieve Linda's fears. "Linda, I understand what you're
thinking, but again I can assure you that at this time Ryson has nothing to worry about
from Tabris."

"That's just it." Linda stopped as a wave emotion carried its affects across her face.
She swallowed hard and forced herself to continue. "I have no idea when it could happen,
when Tabris could strike. You tell me he's safe now, and maybe that's true. Maybe I can
even accept it, but what good does it do me for tomorrow or the next day or the next. This
is like a weight on my back that will never be removed."

Enin started to speak, but stopped before a word came out. He furrowed his brow and
tried again, but once more he couldn't think of the right way to explain to Linda what he

truly knew.

Linda interpreted this as an affirmation of her own fears. "You see, it really isn't easy to deal with." She paused only for a moment when she wiped away a quick tear. "I want you to understand that I'm not just being over emotional about this. The land is different now, and I've seen things—we've all seen things we've never expected. It's not like we can just make a wish and all the bad things will disappear and things will go back to the way they were. We all have to deal with it and I understand that, but this thing with Tabris—it's like it's haunting me. I keep thinking of all the things she might be able to do."

Linda turned to Holli. "Don't misunderstand me. I know there's good out there, too. I never knew elves existed. Now that I do, I'm happy to know there are elves out there like you and Lief. It's not like I want you to go away."

"I never thought that," Holli answered simply.

Linda turned back to Enin. "And I know you are truly a good person. I don't think we could have asked for a better person to be the wizard that we all depend on, but this magic changes everything and I don't even understand it."

After taking one deep long breath, she continued in her attempt to explain what was going through her mind. "It's going to tear me up inside knowing that some sorceress might want to kill him. When he goes on a scout, I know he's careful, I know he can look out for himself. That makes it easier. But this Tabris isn't something he can look out for. And it doesn't even have to happen when he's out on his own. It could happen right here in town when I'm with him and there won't be anything I can do."

Linda became more than tearful. She began to cry openly. "I remember when Yave showed up as a storm. After everything we went through, the town was almost destroyed by dwarves, Ryson was captured in Dunop, and I never lost hope, until that storm showed up. I thought to myself how do we fight that, how can Ryson escape that. He can't."

"But I took care of Yave, she will never be back," Enin stated still hoping to calm Linda's fears.

"Yes, but Tabris made Yave into the storm and Tabris is still here. Tabris could come at any time and create another storm or another magical power that I can't even describe. What can I do to stop that? What can Ryson do?"

Here, Linda steadied herself and looked right into Enin's eyes. "You saved Ryson from Yave. I want you to make sure you'll do it again, but I don't want to wait. I can't live like that, waiting and wondering when she might strike. I have too much to worry about as it is with him out there alone all the time. I can't have this on top of it, I can't!"

"What is it you would ask of me exactly?" Enin asked without hesitation.

"I want you to tell her. Tell this Tabris she is not to harm Ryson. Tell her you protect him. Everyone talks about how powerful you are. Even today, Ryson told me not to worry because this sorceress is nothing like you. I believe that. I also believe that if you tell her to keep away from him, she'll have to listen. I don't know why, but it makes sense to me. Someone as powerful as you has to be listened to, do you understand?"

Enin nodded. "Yes, I understand and I will do as you ask. In fact, I will do so right after you leave. I want you to go home and rest. Worry about Ryson in whatever way you wish, but don't worry about Tabris any further."

The room suddenly seemed brighter to Linda, the air lighter, and the world not so

dangerous. She leapt over to the wizard and hugged him gratefully. "Thank you, thank
you, thank you."

#

Ryson was both pleased and annoyed when he first returned to Pinesway. Pleased
because most of the corpses had been removed and were not left rotting in the streets.
The cold, dry dormant season air would have kept them from decomposing too quickly,
but the scent of death certainly would have attracted wild animals and who knows what
else from surrounding Dark Spruce. In truth, it almost appeared as if the goblin raid had
never happened. Along with the dead being removed, the crossbow bolts the goblins fired
had been taken from the ground and the walls.

The pleasure from the unexpected clean up was short-lived, and Ryson became
annoyed when he realized that the brigands had returned to claim the city, and thus
probably looted the bodies before they dumped them in the woods. Any weapons left
behind by goblins were now prizes for these bandits.

"So I get rid of goblins and what takes their place? Thieves," Ryson grumbled as he moved at a light jogging pace toward the last place he saw Lief Woodson. As he moved through one narrow street, he could not help but sense a trio of would-be bandits laying in wait for a wayward traveler. With his disgust surrounding the circumstances of this abandoned town still fresh in his mind, he decided to see if he could set them straight in the error of their ways.

He bolted toward their position before they even knew he was there. Two held rough clubs and the last held on to a crossbow. The bow was now of little danger to the delver as it wasn't yet loaded and Ryson stood too close for the thief to get off a practical shot. With swiftness that left the two club-holding bandits pale, Ryson struck at their wrists with the edge of his own palm. The stinging pain forced them to drop their weapons. He then reached over with near blatant disregard for all three of the thieves and plucked the crossbow from the hands of the leader. He flung it with force against the far wall of an abandoned building. It shattered, rendering it useless.

Ryson now stood stone still in the midst of the three dumbfounded brigands. He gave them a moment to collect their senses.

"There's still three of you and only one of me. Of course, you don't have your weapons any more. Oh, wait, let's make sure of that."

With speed the villains could not comprehend, Ryson shuffled his feet in two quick kicks and sent the clubs far out of reach.

The move actually angered one of the men as he felt the kick to his weapon was an insult to his manhood.

"Why you stinkin'…"

He reached for Ryson, but his hands found nothing but empty air. The delver dashed around the grapplers opposing shoulder and ended up behind him. With yet another lightning swift kick from the delver, the angry thief felt a blasting heel to his buttocks and ended up in a heap on the ground.

The other two decided to stay put. Ryson almost wanted to commend them for their intelligence, but he doubted they would understand.

"I want all of you out of here. I come back here from time to time and I don't easily forget faces. I was easy on you this time, next time I won't be. Move on."

Ryson moved right up to the brigand on the ground that had rolled over onto the seat of his pants. Before the thief could stand up, the delver put his face right to his. The cold chill in the air was apparent as Ryson's breath turned into a cloud of condensation around the bandit's head. "You understand what I just said?"

The challenge was clear. This wasn't even the leader of the three, just some muscle.

Ryson had his back to the leader. He did that intentionally. He faced the one he felt was the most emotionally unstable, the one he wanted to send a clear message. The leader would be just smart enough to find another town, but the one that initially attacked him might want to stay to exact some sort of revenge. Ryson wanted to leave no doubt in this man's mind that such an idea was not in his best interest.

"You don't like being on the ground, do you? Well, right now you can get up and walk away. Next time, maybe not. The two behind me, they don't matter. Forget them— forget what they might think or what they might say. Just move on."

Ryson never took his eyes from the man on the ground as he backed away and returned to his path toward the center of town. The thought of the now broken crossbow

made Ryson think of the old man he had come across during the goblin raid. He looked
about the empty houses and wondered if any of these were the man's home. He thought
for a moment about maybe trying to track him down to see if he was still alive, to see if
he needed anything. Then, he remembered how the old man left him and how Ryson
knew there wasn't really anything he could do for him other than to let him be.

Increasing his speed, the delver quickly reached the town square. Remembering
exactly the last spot Lief Woodson stood, Ryson reviewed the ground, examining it for
the clear signs of the elf's path. Delvers were not the best trackers as their focus often
wandered, but they had the natural eye to pick up specific traces of markings. Separating
the different paths of goblins, humans, and the elf, Ryson centered his concentration on
the tracks he needed to follow. The trail moved in the exact direction Ryson remembered
Lief used to make his departure, and thus the delver followed it with confidence. He
knew he could at least track the elf through this part of town.

The elf's tracks were old, but the lack of any true population in the town kept them
clear enough for Ryson to follow. The trail led him through many streets and in an almost
directionless path. Ryson realized why when he noted the elf had stopped on several
occasions to fire his bow, probably at the fleeing goblins. Remembering the anger Lief
displayed, Ryson doubted that any of the arrow shots were meant to do anything but kill.
Following Lief's path eventually led Ryson to the northwest section of town near the
river. The trail of the elf changed here, becoming more deliberate. Once Ryson crossed
the bridge leading out of town, he picked up a second set of tracks. They were the distinct
markings of a river rogue, complete with clawed-tipped, webbed feet imprints in the
sandy soil by the river's edge.

"So Lief went after the river rogue and it looks like the rogue took off into the forest."
Ryson looked into the trees and then at the sky to fix his own position. "Heading north.
At least that's no where near the Lacobian, and no where near Tabris."

Ryson headed off into the northern branch of Dark Spruce Forest following the tracks
of the rogue and the elf and hoping that he would find Lief before the trail turned in a
different direction.

                                    #

Once Linda left for home, Enin prepared Holli for two trips he now planned to take
this day.

"We might as well take advantage of this opportunity to test your new spells. First, we are going to see Tabris in the Lacobian desert."

"Before we go," Holli interrupted, "there is something I have to ask. It is something I actually suspect. You were very quick to tell Linda that she had little to worry about Ryson being killed by Tabris. I must admit I was surprised by that. I have always been of the belief that very little is certain in this land, there are no guarantees. It is something I had to live by while being an elf guard. We took nothing for granted so we could be prepared for anything. Yet, you seemed to have no difficulty offering certainty to Linda. Right now, we know Ryson is looking for Lief and it is not without reason that Lief could be looking for Sazar. That possibly could bring Ryson right to Tabris. Ryson is very skilled as a delver but this sorceress is also very powerful by your own admission. Is there something you know that allows you to be so certain that Ryson is safe from Tabris?"

"Safe? No, not safe. He may indeed have to face her. Of that, I am not certain."

"But you are sure Tabris can not kill Ryson; that he will not be taken away from Linda by the sorceress."

"Yes, Ryson has a destiny he must still face. I can see that in him. It is something he can not avoid. Thus, it would be impossible for Tabris to do anything that would keep him from that destiny."

"Do you wish to tell me what that destiny is?"

"No."

"Very well, but why not tell Linda what you just told me?"

Enin smiled at Holli. "You learn about people quickly, don't you? In the short time we have been together, I'm becoming more grateful that you are here. The truth is that I thought of doing just that, thought of telling Linda the real reason she need not worry at this time. Then I thought how do I word it? Do I tell her I see a destiny for Ryson that he must meet, and in order to meet it he must obviously be alive? Whatever way I thought of saying it, it just didn't sound right. It might have even scared her more than the thought of Ryson facing Tabris. What would I have accomplished then?"

"Very little," admitted Holli.

"I also have to remember that the magic is very different with Linda. I'm sure you've noticed that."

"I noticed the first time I met her," Holli replied. "She has no reception to the energy whatsoever. In fact, I believe her essence actually repels magical energies."

"Your perceptions are right once more. If I cast a spell at her, used every ounce of my energy, it would not affect her in the least. Magic simply can not enter her being. She may not acknowledge that she's aware of this, but I think deep down she senses it. It's kind of like everyone is in a rain storm and everyone is dripping wet, except her. She's completely dry and she doesn't know why. Because of that, she has a deeper fear of magic.

"It doesn't make sense really. She shouldn't fear it at all. She's basically immune to it. But since she can't touch it in anyway, she can't gain even a shred of understanding about the energy. So what do I do by telling her that the magic allows me to see certain things that must come to pass? I only make her fear the magic even more. No, it's much easier to simply go off and throw a warning at Tabris than to explain to Linda why the sorceress is not a true threat. If that makes Linda feel better, than it is time well spent. It may also serve a few other purposes."

"May I ask what they might be?"

"You may ask, and I will answer because you're going with me to two different places

today and I want you to know why. When we talk with Tabris, I want to get a better
feeling for her. I want to see if I can figure out why she chose to join up with Sazar. I also
want to let her know that we here in Burbon are aware of this. It's a pretty good idea not
only to warn her off from trying to hurt Ryson, but while we're there we might as well
tell her to stay away from Burbon. As powerful as she is, she still won't want to cross me.
This Sazar is a brazen creature, he moved on Burbon after the dwarves attacked. He
might have new ideas of how to take the town. I want to let them both know it's not
really something they want to pursue. Finally, I also need to get a sense for something
else. I need to know if someone else might be involved in this alliance of Tabris and
Sazar, and if I can get near Tabris, I might be able to sense something."
    "Who is this someone else? Can you tell me?"

"You will be meeting him in our second trip. His name is Baannat. I am not
completely certain of what he truly is, though I have my ideas. He is a very powerful
sorcerer, that much I do know. He is nearly my exact duplicate in what I can do with the
magical energies. He is also very evil."

"That's not very settling."

"Well, yes and no. It's never settling to have something that evil being that powerful,"
Enin admitted. "By the same token, evil has to exist for the balance of things in this land
to work. I hope I am on the side of 'good'. That being the case, there would need to be an
equivalent power on the side of evil. I believe this counter balance exists in Baannat. If he
did not carry this power, it would be carried by others. With Baannat, I know where he is
and I believe I can counter act whatever evil he might attempt. As long as I don't try to
intervene in this land and try to force my own concept of 'good' on everyone, that will
keep Baannat from intervening is his way. If he did, he would tip the balance and I would
have the opportunity to act. If he does nothing, and I do nothing, the balance is
maintained. I've tried to explain this to others without actually mentioning Baannat, and
for the most part I get rather perplexed looks. What do you think of what I just said?"

"I think I will be extraordinarily careful when you bring me to meet this Baannat."

"Yes, of course you would, that's what you would say. But what of balance, what do
you think of that?"

"I think I know far too little to have any valid opinion on that matter."

"That's a very careful response as well."

"Yes, it is." Holli hummed in agreement.

"Now, before we go to meet Tabris, I want you to understand how this will work. We
will go to the Lacobian first and deal with the sorceress. I will go first and you will
follow quickly after with a spell I will advise you of in a moment. When we are finished
with Tabris, I will cast a spell that will bring us back here together. I do not wish to leave
you alone in her presence even for a moment. When we have made our return, I will
advise you on our trip to Baannat's realm. Does this all sound reasonable to your elf
guard senses?"

Holli asked a quick pointed question before answering.

"Will we simply drop out of the blue on Tabris?"

"For the most part, yes."

"If she is startled or agitated by what she might view as an invader, she might respond
in kind. Will you be prepared to defend yourself against her if she does?"

"Absolutely."

"This spell I am to cast that will bring me there as well, I have no idea what state it
will leave me in. Will you be able to protect me as well?"

"Again, absolutely."

"Then I have no reservations at the moment to your plan."

"This is great; see how well we can get along." Enin beamed with a glowing smile.
"Now, let us first address the spell I want you to cast. We have talked about it before. By
now you should be much attuned to my energy."

"I am."

"Good," Enin smiled, "because that's how you will follow me to Tabris. I will cast a
spell I have showed you before—a spell that allows me to move across time and space.
This will bring me to Tabris in a very short period of time. While I believe you could cast

the same spell, it would take almost all of your energy and there is another way to
accomplish the same thing with much less power. I want you to cast an animal tracking
spell, say of a wolf, one that will allow you to track my path. I will leave a wake of
energy that will allow you to ride the waves of my movement as long as you are focused
on my energy. The tracking spell is the vehicle that will allow you to do just that, but it
will be my force that actually moves you. Imagine that you will cast the spell of the cart
and I will cast the spell of the horse. Do you understand?"

"Yes, actually I do."

"Excellent, then let's get started. Remember to ride the waves of movement I leave
behind for you, that way you save energy. All you have to do is follow in the wake."

Enin's smile grew broader as he turned his palms upward to face the sky. Two circles
of pure white graced his hands and quickly rushed upward in an arc toward the heavens.
His form quickly shimmered into a blurry fog and then disappeared.

"I guess he has faith I can cast the tracking spell," Holli murmured to herself.

Holli closed her eyes and focused on the head of a wolf and then its muzzle. She
thought of air flowing into the nostrils as she waved her own hands. An octagon outline
of green formed at her fingertips. She kept her hands still as the green energy took the
shape of a wolf's head that almost immediately darted upon the remnants of Enin's arc.

Holli felt her body being carried, not by her energy, but by Enin's. She simply had to
focus on the trail. She kept her eyes closed as she concentrated deeply on her own spell,
fixing an image of a wolf in her mind. The trail itself moved with great speed and force
and it mixed with her own magical energy as it carried her through space and time. She
felt the wind in her face and the temperature turn both cold and hot all around her.

Holli remember the Lacobian desert in her past treks through it with Ryson Acumen.
It was a harsh land, loose sand splashed over hard, sun-baked rock. The blazing sun
seemed to dry every inch of her body and wash out her keen elf vision as the distance
seemed blurred in a twisting, super heated haze. She remembered how the air blasted her
lungs like the opening of a furnace door and she hated thinking about those memories.
Thankfully, however, it was the dormant season and she hoped the place she landed
would be somewhat less hostile.

When Holli felt the movement stop and the land came into a new focus around her,
she looked around in startled amazement. Her surroundings were, in fact, nothing like the

desert she remembered and more like the green lush forest of her elf camp. More
perplexing, however, was that the surrounding plants and trees appeared to be in a stage
of enjoying the late spring as opposed to being in a phase of dormancy. She knew that
Tabris' magic created this environment, but it was no illusion. The sorceress controlled
the power of the storm and obviously used it to make her Lacobian desert home more
comfortable.

As the elf acquired her bearings, she realized she was near a still but crystal clear pool
of water surrounded by several trees as well as indigenous desert boulders. The air she
breathed felt cool and damp in her lungs as opposed to the searing hot dryness she
expected. Enin stood one step ahead of her and faced a sorceress that appeared very tense
and wore a suspicious expression that seemed to darken her features.

Enin had already begun speaking when the sounds of this place became clearer to
Holli's ears.

"I'm not here to interfere with your decision," Enin was saying. "It's yours to make as are the consequences that you will ultimately face. It is simply not my place to try to guide people down one path or another."

"But you find it your place to invade my home," Tabris sneered.

"Invade your home? Hardly."

"What then?" Tabris demanded. "I did not invite you here. You came here on your own and I don't want you here."

"Tabris, what you want is irrelevant to me."

"So you think you can ignore my wishes?"

"I can. I am here for the sake of others. It is their wishes and their well-being that I am most concerned—Ryson Acumen for one. The delver is under my protection and my watchful eye. Burbon is also under my protection, as you must already know. I will not take kindly to any action on your part that might put my home or my friends in danger."

"So you come here to offer threats!" Tabris cursed.

Enin grew tired of the sorceress' angry banter. "I am not going to waste time with you displaying my powers or challenging you to a duel. You are extraordinary powerful. One of the most powerful I have seen to date. Still, you are no match for me. A dozen of you are no match for me. A hundred of you are no match for me. It is no insult to you and not meant to be one. I am not boasting, and I am not threatening. You and I both know that if I wanted you removed as a threat from this land I could do so with a mere bat of my eye and there is not a thing you could do about it."

"Then why are you here?" Tabris asked with a more accusing tone.

"You faced a choice in which direction you are going to travel, a choice between good and evil. You chose evil. It was your choice to make and you will live with whatever comes of that decision. The delver, however, will not suffer from that decision."

The sorceress while understanding that she was no match for Enin still remained confrontational.

"Because you say so?"

"No, because fate says so. My time here serves no real purpose in this regard save one. There are those that think the delver needs protection from you. They want me to warn you to do him no harm. What they do not understand is that I do not have to protect him. He is protected by his own destiny. Those that are concerned, however, would not understand that. They want me to deliver a message to you and I am doing so. I do this only for their benefit. You and I both understand that my warning truly means nothing to you. But you do understand the power of fate, don't you?"

Tabris grimaced.

"Yes, you do. You will not harm him because you now know you can not harm him,
and I see in you that you will not waste your time in useless endeavors. You should thank
me for saving you time and energy.'
"I will not thank you for something I would have discovered on my own."
"Then perhaps you will thank me for this. I also know of your partnership with Sazar.
The people that guard my home are also aware of it. I do not like this Sazar creature and I
don't want him threatening Burbon. I may not like to act forcibly on matters, but I am
always entitled to defend my home. In that regard, I do not alter the balance, instead I
maintain it. If Sazar, or you for that matter, decides to attack Burbon, I will ensure that
you fail in the most devastating means available to me."

Tabris simply glared.

Enin turned his back on her and addressed Holli. "Your tracking spell was perfect.
Well done. My purpose here is complete. Now please allow me to take us both back
home together."

Chapter 12

"The place we are going to does in fact exist, but it isn't truly in this land, not truly
part of what we might consider our normal every day existence." Enin wanted to make
sure Holli knew what to expect when they reached their next destination and thus he
continued with his description. "It is a defined space with absolute borders, but it's
almost as if there's nothing there. If it made sense to say it was like walking through a
fog you couldn't see, I would say that, but of course that makes no sense at all. Still,
that's the sensation you will encounter. As much as you try to perceive anything truly
physical, your senses will be blocked. You will see the figure of Baannat, but he chooses
to cloak himself in the same type of fog. When you look at him, you will see something
of a shadow, but it will remain out of focus. This is really going to sound ridiculous, but
again, I have no other way to describe it. The area has no true light and has no true dark.
You have to remember that there is no sun or stars or bright moon or even a torch for that
matter. Therefore, there is no light. Still, there is magic and so there is no darkness,
either."

"So I will be able to see, unlike being in a darkened cave, but there will be nothing to
see other than the shadowed figure of Baannat?" Holli asked?

"You put it better than I do. It is not an entirely new dimension. It is more of a pocket
of space. Baannat carved out this pocket for himself so he could exist between our
physical land of Uton and the place where the dark creatures come from. Thus, I am
nearly certain he has some kind of connection to the dark creatures. The area seems to be
affected by most the physical rules of nature that my egghead scientist friend likes to talk
about, but then again, it is not truly a place of physical existence. You will feel as if you
are walking on the ground, but you are really standing and walking on magic. The space
is something like a magical duplication of an empty room right here, but it is not of the
same makeup. That's the best way I can describe it."

"This might be difficult for me," Holli admitted. "While I am trained to adjust to new
surroundings, adapting to such an environment will cause me some instinctive problems."

"Such as?"

"I am trained to search for dangers and threats, places of safety and paths of retreat
and exit. I will not be able to find any of these in what you describe."

"That is true."

"That is what I will find difficult," Holli admitted. "I appreciate you being honest with me and preparing me for this before we faced it."

"I like to help where I can."

"Thank you. As long as you are willing to be helpful and prepare me for this
endeavor, I have a question which I would like to ask."

"Fire away," Enin said.

"How did you find this Baannat, and if he created this space, why does he let you
enter?"

"That's two questions, but I'll be happy to answer them both," Enin replied almost too
lightheartedly for Holli's liking for a question she felt was extremely significant. "When I
began to understand balance, I actually went looking for him. I figured something like
him probably existed, and if so, it would be a good idea to find him. Searching for such

an entity was actually somewhat easy because of the vast magical energy he possesses.
Similar to the ability to see people's fate, I also have a deep connection to magic. The
pocket of space he created was fairly easy to find when I put my mind to looking for it.
As to why he lets me come in, I'm really not sure if he could stop me. He never put up a
barrier or anything. I just showed up one day and we started talking."

"So you don't really know why he lets you in."

"No, I guess I don't"

"Well, then that's not really an answer is it."

Enin furrowed his brow. "Hmmmmm, I guess it isn't."

"Then you really only answered one question after all."

Enin laughed.

"Yes, you're right again, but enough of that for now." Enin said as he turned slightly
more serious. "Let's discuss your spell casting. I want you to actually cast the spell that
will bring you to Baannat's realm. I will go first and you will follow, but you won't use
the wake of my energy to move you this time. Instead, you will focus on my energy to
guide you, but you will have to cast the spell to actually take you from this place to
Baannat's. You will be able to use me as a target once I am there. Focus on me and cast a
spell that will bring you to my side. The important thing to remember is that this time
you're not really moving through physical space as you know it. Baannat is not living in
an area that truly exists in this land. He is somewhat between physical space. You really
don't even have to concentrate on movement through space at all. What you need to do is
cast a spell that will transport your presence from here to a spot next to mine."

Holli stood still and quiet as she tried to get a handle on the aspects of the spell Enin
described. After a few moments, she voiced her concerns. "I think I understand what you
said, but I'm not sure how I can cast a spell to accomplish the task. In the other transport
spell you taught me, the one where I can move myself and others across the land in a very
short time, I learned to focus on channeling the magic to a specific area. From there, I
would form a straight line in my mind between the two points of where I currently stood
and where I wanted to go. When I had the line in my mind, I simply shortened it as much
as I could. Basically, in my mind I compacted the space between the two points while
still maintaining a concept of travel from one place to another. It worked for me, though
it wore me out, took most of my energy."

"That won't happen with this spell, at least it shouldn't take much of your energy at
all," Enin interrupted. "As I said, you're not going to require the energy to move you

across time and space. This is not a spell that will move you as we understand movement.
This should be a spell that simply transports you from one spot to another. You are here
and then you are there. No movement in between."

"That's the problem," Holli stated firmly. "With this spell you want me to cast, I can
see you as the target but I don't know how to draw the line between where I am and
where you will be. I won't have a true reference point in my mind."

Enin shook his head and attempted to be clearer in what the elf had to do. "That's
because you're still trying to force this into a time and space move as opposed to a sheer
transportation spell. You do not create a line because there will be no line. You simply go
from one point to another disregarding the space between."

"But if there are two points, then there should be space between them," Holli argued
holding to her own concepts.

"Not when one point is not in the same frame of existence as the other. Think of it this way, pretend you can only draw your line with ink on a piece of paper. That works fine when you want to travel from one spot on the paper to another. You can draw the line with ease. In this case, however, one point is on one piece of paper, but the other point is on an entirely different piece of paper. You can't draw your line under these circumstances, but the two points still exist. You just have to transport yourself from one piece of paper to the other. Does that help?"

"Slightly," Holli allowed, but continued to voice her difficulties with the spell. "My problem is that if I don't draw the line in my head, I honestly don't know how I get from one point to the other. That's my sticking point."

"I see," Enin allowed as he rubbed his chin. "Well, the truth is this is a difficult spell for you to cast. It is a combination of different magical aspects, and they have little to do with your primary powers. Shadow is prevalent in the spell because you are in essence transporting yourself to a place that is a whisper reflection of this land. Light is involved slightly as an offset to its natural opposite shadow but more importantly in how the yellow aspect is included in the orange aura of energy and movement. The orange power of energy will guide and bring you to me while the gray essence of shadow will let you pass into this other plane of existence. I know that doesn't sound very clear but that is the essence of the spell. Because you cast with a green aura, it is difficult for you to see the underlying aspects of the gray and orange energy types that are involved in the basics of the spell. Let me see if I can help you with that."

Enin took a candle off the desk in front of him and lit it. He held up the flame for Holli to see. "We know the flame exists because we can see it and feel the heat from it. Still, I can pass my finger through it as if it were not there. If I take another candle and hold the wick to this one, another flame is born. If I then hold the two candles apart, there are two separate flames. When I bring the candles back together and hold the wicks next to each other, the flames merge into one again."

Enin walked around the desk toward Holli. "Now, look at your shadow on the ground. It has no substance, no depth whatsoever, but you can see it is there. When I stand here, my shadow is separate from yours. If I walk toward you, my shadow combines with yours and neither of our shadows is the same as it was. When I step away, our shadows return to the outline of our individual shapes."

Enin stepped back and let Holli examine the change in their shadows on the floor. He then pointed to her shadow. "The source of light that creates your shadow is in front of you, so where is the shadow?"

"Behind me," Holli answered.

"That is correct, and if I circle you with a candle, the shadow rotates around you. It moves on the floor. Now let us change the conditions of the light. If a candle that was in front of you is immediately extinguished and another light is instantly lit behind you, where would the shadow be?"

"In front of me."

"Think very clearly on that," Enin pressed. "The shadow was in front of you and then behind you. It did not move in a path around you to get from one place to the other. Your shadow shifted from one place to another without actually moving through space. Though it did not actually follow a path, or a line, it did change positions. It was here, and then it was there. Do you understand?"

Holli nodded and her expression appeared as if a cloud was slowly lifting from her mind.

Enin continued. "The concepts I tell you should let your mind gain a spark of understanding of energy and shadow. They are certainly complex topics when it comes to magic. What should help you in casting this spell is understanding that just because something has no substance doesn't mean it can't exist. Also, the lack of substance allows for shifting motion that is not bound by the same restrictions that objects of solid material face in this existence. So, when I ask you to consider the spell of transporting to my side, you have to think in terms beyond the movement spell you have already learned. You must focus on allowing the magic to do what it is capable of doing and that's bringing you to me without actually traveling though space and time. Just like a shadow can jump from place to place, you can jump. In this case, the magic will be like the light source. Let the magic worry about the details of how it happens."

"Are you saying to simply focus on the desired results and not the method?" Holli asked with a new glint in her eyes.

Enin's eyebrows shot up. "Yes, that's an excellent way to put it as long as you understand that you have to shape the magic in your mind to do what you want. You can't simply say 'Take me to Enin' and poof you will be by my side. Anyone can do that. The question is can you grasp the concepts of energy and shadow magic in such a way that you can cast a spell that will bring you to me, wherever I am."

"Yes, I believe I can. As long as I don't worry about the mechanics of how it's being done, I believe I can call on the magic to bring me to your side. All I have to do is focus on your magical essence, as long as you keep it open to me."

"I will indeed," Enin allowed. "Are you ready to give this a try?"

"Yes."

"Excellent. I will transport myself to Baannat. Once I am gone, you can cast your spell and you should immediately appear in Baannat's realm. If for some reason you fail, do not worry. I will give you a few moments and if you don't appear, I will summon you to my side. I don't think that will be necessary because looking at you now, I believe you know what you have to do."

"I believe so as well," Holli stated confidently.

"Before we go, let me warn you not to speak to Baannat. Listen to everything he says, but say nothing. Ok?"

"Will I be able to speak to you if necessary?"

"Absolutely. If you have something you need, or a question, don't hesitate to ask. I just would prefer if you didn't speak to Baannat."

"Very well."

"Then let us get this over with."

Enin raised his hands above his head and two circles of white quickly encased his
entire body and he disappeared.

Holli immediately focused on Enin's magical essence. She could feel his power but
could not place it in any particular location. It was almost as if he was in the air over her
very head. She ceased trying to put a known location on Enin's presence and simply
focused on appearing at his side, as if she wanted to send her own shadow next to his
with a bright flash of magic. She mouthed a few whispers and she disappeared in a mist
of green.

Holli appeared in a space of bland white with no other color. She could see, but other then herself, Enin and a shadowy figure off in the distance in front of them, there was nothing else to focus on. It felt as if her feet stood on solid ground, but she could perceive no floor. There appeared to be walls, but she could not gauge how far the walls were from her current position. She considered pulling an arrow from her quiver and firing it off into any direction simply to see where it might stop, or if it stopped at all before it flew out of her range of vision. She decided quickly against the action, for she could not be certain of how the magic of this space would affect the path of her arrow. She wondered if it might end up coming right back at her.

Holli's contemplations over this strange place were brought to an end by the first words she heard from Baannat. These words did more than echo through this magical space, they vibrated, and she could feel them to her very bones.

"Hello, Brother. I didn't expect you to visit again so soon. And how are you this day?"

Enin wanted to ignore Baannat as he concentrated on what he could sense around Baannat. He filled his being with the magic that made up the place. He felt for any whispers of deeds that might link Baannat to Tabris. Still, he responded for he knew Baannat would only continue to harass him.

"I'm fine, Baannat."

"You bring a new visitor with you. An elf, how wonderful. And you are teaching her. Splendid. Of course you know that doing so will only make you weaker by your own theory. If balance must exist and you strengthen this elf, then you would have to become weaker, or there would be no balance. Or perhaps instead of you getting weaker, I would get stronger. That is what you believe and that is a pleasing thought, is it not?"

Enin answered with near disregard, as if he was talking to nothing more than empty space. "She has always had the power to cast spells and she has always been on the side of virtue in the balance of things. Yes, she will grow in power but not so much to make a true difference in the scales."

"Has he spoken to you yet of balance, my dear?" Baannat's words were clearly directed at Holli now, and they were both hot with desire and cold with hate at the moment he spoke them. "He loves to speak of balance. One might say it even consumes him."

"She is not here for your amusement," Enin intervened.

"Then why is she here?!" This time Baannat's words carried nothing but anger.

"Because I want her to see this place, to know it."

"And why is that?!"

"Does it really matter?" Enin asked.

There was complete silence for just a moment that was quickly shattered by Baannat's nearly uncontrollable laughter. The bubbling howls of mirth rumbled through the air like rolling thunder from incessant lightning strikes.

"No, it doesn't matter at all," Baannat finally said through his slowly dying giggles. "And why are you here again so soon?"

"Events continue to occur that make me suspect you are up to something, Baannat."

"Checking up on me again, making sure I'm being good. Isn't that wonderful? Or perhaps maybe you're trying to provoke me into interfering in your activities so you can do some interfering of your own? What are the events you speak of this time?"

"If you are involved, you would already know. If you are not involved, then it is none of your concern."

"You think you can keep secrets from me?!" Baannat shouted.

"I simply have no desire to tell you anything."

"But you tell me everything by just being here."

Enin brushed aside the comment with his own understanding of reality. "You can see into the land as easy as I can come here. If it is truly important for you to know, look into it yourself. I won't bother to stop you."

"Perhaps I don't need to look, perhaps I already know," Baannat offered deviously. "And now that you are here, do you sense anything that gives me away."

"No, I do not," Enin admitted.

Baannat waited. "It seems you are done with your task which means it is time for you to leave, and yet you make no attempt to exit. Normally, you are quick to try and go before I make my request for our game. Not this time, eh?"

"If you wish to play, I'm ready. I always humor you."

"Humor me?" Baannat growled. "It is not humor that makes you stay this time. No, you are worried because you think that by teaching this pathetic elf you have given away too much of your power. You want to play this time to see if you can still win, but now you worry you can't. You think you have changed the balance."

"The balance has most definitely changed, but not in the way you think," Enin stated confidently.

"Has it?" Baannat suddenly giggled. "Then let's truly test this. You will cast black magic, the aspect of death. And I will cast white magic, the constant of all magic combined. I admit I am giving myself an advantage. I will cast what is my natural gift, and you will cast that which you oppose the most."

"I do not oppose the black aspect of magic," Enin countered. "It is not just death. Death is only a part of it. It is change."

"And I am well aware that you dislike change," Baannat shot back. "Change upsets you. Change brings turmoil and takes away that which you like most, consistency."

"Not all change is bad. Learning is change. Teaching is causing change. Helping is creating change. I've never opposed these things."

"Then let us put this to the test," Baannat demanded.

Baannat brought his hands together to two tight fists in front of his chest. Two rings of white hot power encircled his shadowed figure. They revolved about him in opposite directions until they met at his fists. When they did, they formed a glowing white axe, massive in size. The blade shone sickly pale as if covered in angels' blood. It began to swing back and forth, then up and down. With each pass, it left a trail of white energy that gleamed brighter then the rest of the pale space.

Enin nodded and quickly cast his own spell. The wizard's own circles of white energy
quickly turned black and melded together to form a large block. The rectangular shape
swam out into the empty paleness of space that surrounded them and headed for the axe.

The axe head swung through the black shape, cleaving it in half. The two now
separate shapes quickly ballooned in size, each now matching the width and height of the
original block. Both blocks again moved through space following the white hatchet.
When the blade swung again it sliced through two blocks instead of just one, and thus,
there were now four black pieces. Again, all four grew back to the size of the original

block. The process went on for long moments and countless swings of the blade. The
number of blocks grew exponentially and began to erase the bright whiteness left behind
by each swing of the Baannat's magical weapon. Before the cleaver completed its final
swing it was clear that Enin's dark blocks overpowered the white remnants of Baannat's
blade swings by an obvious margin.

"This can't be!" Baannat wailed. "You should be weaker, not stronger!"

Enin shrugged. "It is rather appropriate you asked me to cast the magic of change, for
that is what has truly happened. The balance between you and I has been altered to offset
the new evil that now resides in Uton. It is nothing less than I expected."

"But what of your elf witch beside you?" Baannat protested. "She should have swayed
the balance to me!"

"As I said before, she was always on the side of righteousness. Her increased strength
did little to alter the scales."

Enin turned to Holli. "I have learned what I wish to know here. I will take us back."

The wizard placed an arm around Holli's shoulder and with a simple step of will he
guided her back to their home in Burbon. He looked her in the face as he tested her
awareness.

"Are you alright?"

"I'm fine," Holli answered.

"Very good. I am happy to see you were able to cast the spell. Your power is
growing."

Holli ignored the compliment and instead focused on the wizard's expression as she
asked a question of her own.

"Why did you bring me to see Baannat?"

"Because I believe it was important for you to see him for yourself, to know that there
is evil out there. You can never be blind to that fact. Awareness of it will allow you to
defend yourself against it."

Enin said nothing further.

Holli realized it would be futile to press him for greater details. Instead, she asked a
new set of questions

"Why does he call you brother?"

"Because he knows it irritates me. I am not his brother. I am not related to him in
anyway. He just likes to point out that we have similar powers."

"Do you think he's involved in Tabris joining Sazaar?"

"No, I do not think so. I scanned the magical energy that was in the room when we
entered. I could find no echo, no whisper of a link between Tabris and Baannat. I also
sensed nothing when we visited the sorceress. If he had intervened in some way, I believe

I would have sensed something, a trail of his magic. I did not and so it appears as if she
made the decision on her own. It is also as I suspected in that Tabris' decision has altered
the balance of things here in our existence. Her previous neutrality had no affect on the
struggles between right and wrong, mercy and torture, forgiveness and vengeance—
basically good and evil. That is now changed and as a counterbalance to that change,
Baannat has weakened."

"Or perhaps you have gained strength," Holli offered.

"Maybe. Either way, I now hold the advantage over him."

The two said little more about the encounter, but back in the Baannat's pale realm, in
the fading residue of black and white magic, Baannat snickered.

Chapter 13

The majestic Colad Mountains stood in the far distance and Ryson enjoyed gazing at
their imposing outline whenever such a view became possible through the thick woods.
The crisp, clear air of the dormant season and the bare trees allowed him more than a few
passing glances at the northern ranges whenever he ventured up to a treetop to get a better
view of the surrounding terrain. With each glimpse to the northwest, the delver knew the
mountains saw far more than their normal share of extreme weather during this dormant
season. Heavy snows filled not only the peaks but also far down the mountain sides. Even
at the tree line, the thick white snow cover blotted out nearly all signs of green, brown or
gray.

These were the days Ryson loved to travel in this region. The daylight was short, and
the air was brisk, but the land around him sparkled with life even as much of it slept in
dens, burrows, or under blankets of crusted snow. The normally thick underbrush of vines
had withered and fallen away during the end of the harvest season as did the leaves of the
low hanging branches. Paths for roaming existed in nearly limitless directions, and the
delver felt the call to explore many new trails several times during his excursion. With a
mind toward finding his friend, however, the delver ignored these calls and kept an eye to
the fresh tracks on the ground.

His journey kept him in Dark Spruce Forest, and though Lief's trail continued in a
round about pattern, it remained to the northwest of Pinesway. At no point did Ryson
ever fear that the elf had made a turn to the south and a possible encounter with Sazar and
Tabris. Heavier snows in this region made the trails easier to follow as it seemed neither
the river rogue nor the elf took the time to cover their tracks.

Still, the tracks of the elf appeared somewhat confusing. Lief's trail followed that of
the river rogue, apparently stalking it for a kill. It seemed quite clear to Ryson that many
such opportunities arose for the elf to strike, but as far as the delver could tell, Lief never
made the attempt. All the markings indicated that Lief simply continued to follow the
beast, making no sincere effort to end the chase. Adding to the confusion, there were
signs the elf had indeed fired his bow, but when the delver strived to learn the target, he
always found the corpses of goblins, tree rakers, bloat spiders, hobsprites, and once even
a snow ogre that must have ventured far from its natural mountain habitat. Every monster

appeared to be felled by one of Lief's arrows, yet the river rogue continued unabated on
its own path, at times even feasting on some of Lief's kills.

The afternoon sun hung low in the western sky when Ryson slowed his movements.
He heard rustling sounds in the distance and the cackling squawks of tree rakers. Such
shrieks had become common in this area of Dark Spruce since the return of dark
creatures, and Ryson knew enough to remain careful when he heard them.

Tree rakers depended on the heavy growth of forests to do most of their work for them
and on the panic of their prey to make their hunt successful. Thick and bulky as well as
slow and ponderous, rakers hunted knowing they could never catch even the slowest of
their intended victims. Instead, they created traps on well worn paths, and their cackles
frightened potential prey into making mistakes that would cost them their lives.

As powerful as full grown shags, tree rakers were enabled with the strength to knock
over small trees no matter how well rooted into the ground. Rakers normally worked

together in small packs, usually numbering four or five. Pushing together small trees that
sprouted up along the sides of wild deer paths, they quickly turned a once free and long
standing trail into a corral that led to a dead end trap of intertwined branches and
impassable tree trunks. As rakers where not choosey in their diet, they would wait for any
potential prey—human, wild animal, or even dark creature—to venture into the area.
They would then begin their shrieks sending the intended victim into a panic. Taking
strategic positions to block off other exits, they hoped to compel their prey down their
prearranged path. The frightened victim would become so distracted with the clamoring
cries, it would never notice the trap that awaited at the end it until it was too late. The
group of rakers would fall in behind their victim, blocking off any escape.

Short in stature, wide in girth, and with the thick wrinkled hide that looked much like
tree bark, rakers could blend in with the forest during any season. Still, they made more
than enough noise to make their presence known. At the moment, they were not close
enough to the delver to present any immediate danger, and as long as Ryson moved with
reasonable care, he would be able to avoid them with ease.

On previous trips to this region of Dark Spruce, the delver spent time becoming more
acquainted with the calls of rakers. Ryson had now listened long enough to this pack to
know they were not hunting. They had caught the scent of a danger and were trying to
frighten it away.

"Probably the rogue," Ryson whispered to himself, "or maybe even Lief, but whatever
it is, they want it out of here."

Quickly gauging the tracks on the ground and considering what was most probably
ahead of him, Ryson took to the trees. He grabbed a low hanging branch and hoisted
himself up into a box-elder. He jumped another two branches upward before moving
along a thick limb to a neighboring cottonwood. He gauged the distance to the rakers
cries and moved with a greater speed knowing he would not fall into one of their traps.

After but a few moments, the delver closed upon the clamor. He quickly spotted the
river rogue that appeared particularly agitated over the noises of the tree rakers. Though
visibly tense over the chaotic sounds, the rogue remained in a fixed position, slightly
hunched over and using a fallen, rotten log that was lodged between two full grown white
pines as cover. It showed no desire to retreat or to bolt for better cover. Instead, the rogue
continued to peer to its left toward a thick grove of spruce trees.

Ryson followed the rogue's gaze to the same spot. As he eyes fell upon the thick
branches, he noticed the barely visible signs of slow, steady movement from within.
Almost immediately, Ryson witnessed an arrow fly from out of the spruce trees and with
deadly malice toward one of the rakers. The arrow stuck clean on the side of the
creature's head, and the dwarf-constructed metal arrowhead penetrated the raker's skull
with ease. Only half of the shaft remained visible after impact, the rest burrowed deep
into the monster's brain. The creature dropped to the ground with a dull thud. Death was
instantaneous.

Ryson shook his head and then bounded through the trees towards Lief's position in
the spruce grove.

"Lief!" he called out.

The elf's head popped out behind cover just as the screeching of the other rakers in the
area ceased. The pack members that remained alive scurried off as fast at they could
deeper into the cover of the woods.

As for the rogue, it appeared somewhat uncertain of its next move. It didn't like the
smell of the delver that now approached, nor did it have any desire to follow the
remaining rakers into the woods. In the end, it appeared satisfied to remain behind the
rotten log, and it simply crouched lower to the ground as it waited for any further signs of
action.

In mere moments, the delver was in front of the elf as he extricated himself from the
thick branches of the spruce.

"Ryson?" Lief asked, revealing more surprise than any other emotion. "What are you
doing here?"

"I've been tracking you. I heard the noise of the rakers and then saw the arrow and
realized I found you."

The elf looked over toward the dead raker. "One less monster to worry about. These
dwarf constructed arrowheads can break through rock, so they have no problem with the
tough hides of tree rakers."

"Or the hides of goblins, bloat spiders, and even a snow ogre," Ryson added with a
hint of displeasure.

Lief didn't notice the tone, or he chose to ignore it. "That was a pleasant surprise—the
ogre that is. Didn't think I'd chance upon one of those so deep in the forest."

Ryson found Lief's rather upbeat response somewhat perplexing. "What are you doing
out here?"

The elf raised an eyebrow as if the question was unnecessary and the answer obvious.
"I told you exactly what I would be doing when I left you at Pinesway, and if you've
been tracking me, you should be able to tell by the trails. After dispatching as many
retreating goblins as I could find, I set my sights on the river rogue that setup a territory
near Pinesway's northwestern bridge. It was already highly alerted to much of the
disturbance when I came upon the bridge. Once it smelled my arrival, it took off for the
woods. He was obviously spooked by the goblin attack, perhaps also by your activity,
and thus made haste to leave the area almost immediately. I have been tracking it since
that time. He has proven to be a difficult quarry. He left his territory in quite a hurry and
has showed no great desire to return quickly. At least on two different occasions, though,
he did try to double back to Pinesway. I had cut him off and almost had him, but both
times the blasted wind changed and he caught either sight or scent of me and fled further
into the forest."

Lief pointed the top of his bow at the creature as he continued. "He's over there now,

much more used to my scent at this time. He's probably wondering about you, though.
Still I don't think he wants to leave my vicinity too soon as I've been providing him with
several easy meals lately. I'm actually quite happy it got away. It seems to have given up
on returning to its river bridge by Pinesway. Instead it has staked out a rather large
territory here in the woods. There is a small stream off to the west where it started
digging out a new den. There's not a lot of water for it, but the forest has enough snow on
the ground here for it to make due. I've been using him to track goblins and other such
creatures. The rogue stalks when it senses prey nearby but does not strike. It leaves that to
me now, almost as if it knows I will take care of the killing for it."

Ryson looked over to the rogue. He felt sadness for the creature, but said nothing.

"You were tracking me I assume for a purpose," Lief stated. "May I ask what it is you
want of me?"

"Mostly, I wanted to warn you," Ryson acknowledged.

"Warn me?"

"Yes, when we met in Pinesway, I told you about Sazar the serp. It seemed to me you might go out of your way to hunt him down. After I returned to Burbon, we learned that he has teamed with a sorceress and I wanted you to know that. If you started hunting the serp, you might have stumbled on a dangerous situation."

Lief frowned then glared at Ryson. "You see what happens when you don't act? You let evil get away and it only gets stronger. Perhaps I shouldn't have wasted so much time on the rogue or perhaps I should have taken care of the serp first while I was still in Pinesway. The rogue would have waited. Blast all of this!"

Ryson did not know what to say, and thus, said nothing. Lief, on the other hand, just seemed to get angrier.

"Why is it that evil is allowed to prosper? Why must it be that creatures like Sazar can not only get away with directing the death of innocents, but can then benefit by the help of a sorceress. Where is the justice in this?" Lief bit down hard in frustration but then turned his questions directly to Ryson. "Does anyone know the power of this sorceress, who she is?" Lief demanded.

Ryson, knowing the answer, was now even more hesitant in responding, but he eventually spoke honestly.

"Actually we both know her," the delver finally admitted. "It is Lauren, the one that was with us at Sanctum. Remember? She changed her name to Tabris when she left us."

"Yes, I remember well and I'm not happy about this, either." Lief then shook his head in absolute disgust. "It seems every time I turn around I am reminded how things tend to only get worse. If I remember correctly, she began at the outset with a great capacity to utilize the magic. How much of a danger is this sorceress now?"

"Enin says she's not in his class, but that she is quite powerful, powerful enough to cause a great deal of damage if she put a mind to it. Beyond that, I can't say."

Lief's hands clenched into tight fists. "Well, at least I know what I must do now."

"What's that?" Ryson asked quickly, and then wondered if he really wanted to hear the answer.

Lief spoke as if his next actions would be as simple and as obvious as crossing a road in the deserted town of Pinesway. "I will track this serp and this sorceress and I will put an end to their evil before too much damage is done."

"Well, they really haven't caused any damage yet. I'm not sure if it's the best idea to go looking for trouble."

"Looking for trouble?" Lief appeared nearly baffled. "Is that what you think I'm doing
is looking for trouble? Who caused the trouble in Pinesway?"

Ryson decided to be forthright and pointed out what he saw to be the truth. "I won't
argue that Sazar and the goblins started it, but you didn't have a problem with finishing it.
It seems to me both you and the goblins caused your share amount of death there."

Lief's eyes narrowed. "What would you have had me done, Ryson Acumen? Perhaps I
should have just swatted them on the back side as they raced back into the woods after
killing a dozen or so humans. Would that have been a fair punishment?"

This time Ryson could not find the words to answer the elf, but Lief continued without
waiting for an answer. "And what do you think I should do now that I know this serp that
controlled these goblins is now in league with a powerful sorceress? Would you have me

just sit back and wait for them to destroy everything in Dark Spruce before someone does
something to stop them?"

"But we don't know if they're going to destroy Dark Spruce," Ryson finally protested.
"In fact, the last I heard, they were still out in the Lacobian."

"Then I will go to the Lacobian."

"Do you think that's really necessary?"

Lief's frown grew deeper as he could not fathom why he had to explain this to the
delver. "The magic has only returned for a few short seasons and already this serp has
caused nothing but evil. This Sazar creature threatened your own home town of Burbon
to gain access to the tunnels dug by the dwarves. It plundered Dunop when it had the
chance, then it moved on to try and take over the town of Pinesway. Its minions left many
dead in the streets, or did you already forget?"

The image of the dead became even clearer in Ryson's mind. "I didn't forget."

"Should the serp not pay for his crimes? Should he be allowed to simply do whatever
he likes without consequences?"

These words struck Ryson rather hard. He clearly remembered what the serp did at
Pinesway. It was Sazar's orders that led to many killings, killings that were barbaric in
nature. Ryson certainly believed Sazar should face repercussions for his actions, he just
wasn't sure if Lief running off to the Lacobian was the right way to go about it.

"That's not what I said," Ryson finally spoke out. "I didn't mean the serp shouldn't be
dealt with. Sazar is a threat and he does have to answer for what he's done."

"Then why are you trying to stop me?"

"Because it just sounds wrong how you're going to go about doing it."

"Then tell me your answer as to how it should be done. Will this wizard of yours, this
Enin, will he handle the situation?"

Ryson looked down to the ground becoming more frustrated by the moment. "No, he
doesn't think he should get involved."

Lief almost laughed. "Not get involved? That's what Tun said when the sphere first
freed itself. He didn't want the dwarves to get involved. He would have had all the
denizens of Uton destroyed by the dark magic if he had his way. Not get involved? That's
what the elders of my camp insisted when I wanted them to intervene in Petiole's absurd
behavior. And so they did nothing. So do not tell me that that's your answer, that you
think I shouldn't get involved."

"Look, Lief, I don't know what the answer is. I just came out here to warn you of
what's happening. I didn't want you to get caught by surprise. I guess I've done that. As
to what you do next, I guess that's up to you."

"Indeed it is up to me." Lief exhaled heavily and then seemed to lighten in mood ever
so slightly. "I appreciate what you have done for me here. You have done so out of
friendship. I realize that, and I thank you. What I do now, I do because I feel I must. It
has nothing more to do with you. Do you understand that?"

"I guess so, though, I don't understand much of anything anymore."

The elf looked about the forest, momentarily stared at the corpse of the tree raker, and
then cast a wary eye toward the river rogue. "These are complex times for us all. Still, I
can not simply do nothing now. I had a chance to deal with this Sazar and I missed that
opportunity. I now feel it is my obligation to keep him from doing as little damage as

possible. I assure you I will act with care and hopefully I will succeed in doing what must be done."

Ryson looked across the forest at nothing in particular. He felt almost ashamed of what he was about to say, but he knew he had to say it. "I can't go with you, you know. I don't know how to argue with what you're doing, but something about it just doesn't seem right."

"I am not asking you to join me," Lief said with almost a shrug. "I will track these villains in the Lacobian on my own. I am not sure how I will deal with them as of yet, but I must at least try. First, I must dispatch this rogue."

Ryson's gaze quickly shot toward Lief in utter dismay. "You're going to kill it?"

"I'm responsible for leading it out here into the forest," Lief responded flatly. "I won't leave it here to wreak havoc."

"Wreaking havoc? What are you talking about?"

"A river rogue is a dangerous creature with the ability to kill many innocents. It must be dealt with."

"Why? Because it has the potential to kill? You can't kill it just because it might do something in the future."

"What else will it do? You think it has the ability to offer any thing constructive to this land?"

Ryson would not give up this time. He believed killing the creature would be a dastardly act and made his feeling evident. "You worked together with that creature. Dark creature or not, it does not deserve to be killed so callously. You call these things monsters, fine, but they have their place here just as the rest of us. It was hard for me to argue about Sazar because he has committed crimes, but tell me what this creature has done that you haven't. It has hunted to survive. In its last few days, it hasn't even killed. It has left that task up to you. If you want to send it to its death simply because it's dangerous, then maybe you should save an arrow for yourself."

Lief stood with eyes blazing, but said nothing.

"Here's what I think, Lief. I'm not exactly sure why you're so angry at the land. You want to be angry at the elves in your camp, that's one thing. From everything I've heard, it sounds you have the right to be more than just a little annoyed. Godson, I was furious with your camp when they allowed Petiole to drop the seeds. Still, I don't see how that gives you a free hand to become a cold blooded killer. If you kill this river rogue, that's what you will become."

Lief's voice was cold and any glimmer of friendship in his eye vanished as if blown

away by a bitter wind. "And when this rogue ventures back to Pinesway and maybe all
the way to Burbon and kills some child, who will be the cold blooded killer then? The
monster for one, but what about you for defending this thing when I could have dealt
with it appropriately?"

"Did you hear what you just said?" Ryson asked nearly overwhelmed by Lief's
reasoning. "You think this creature is somehow going to travel all the way back to
Burbon just to kill a child. That's more than a stretch, that's an outright fairy tale."

"Fine, it stays here and kills a traveling merchant. Does that please your sense of
reality?"

"It might be more realistic, but it might never happen either. You seem to want to
damn this creature to an act just so you can justify your wanting to kill it. You know as

well as I do this creature may do nothing more than hunt goblins and tree rakers like the
one you just shot. You can't punish something just for what it's capable of. We're all
capable of doing terrible things, that doesn't mean we're going to actually do them."

"Rogues are killers and thus deserve to be treated as such," Lief stated with near
disdain.

"Are you becoming a killer?"

"You think I take some kind of joy out of doing this?" Lief shot back quickly. "That I
am doing it for a thrill? I hate each time I have to fire my bow, but I would hate it more if
I did not. I didn't ask for these creatures to return to the land, but they have, and so they
must be dealt with. In truth, I am as much responsible for anyone for their return, or have
you forgotten that I was with you in Sanctum?"

"I didn't forget, but I also didn't forget that the magic returned to the land before we
even set foot on Sanctum's base. The sphere somehow blew a hole through the side of the
mountain and dark creatures had returned before I even met you. We had nothing to do
with this, so if you're trying to take blame…"

"I take no blame," Lief interrupted fiercely. "I take responsibility! And because I
realize my responsibility I have to act. I will not be like the others, others that I've
watched and done nothing while everything around them screamed for them to act."

"So you're going to save Uton all on your own and that starts by killing that rogue?"

"It starts by me doing what is necessary even though I might hate having to do it!"
Lief screamed. "Have you heard nothing I said? Fire upon you, delver. I don't wish to kill
the blasted rogue, but I will not have its acts of murder on my conscience."

Lief said nothing further. He pulled an arrow from his quiver and prepared to nock it
in his bow. He spit upon the ground in angry frustration as his hands shook slightly from
his emotions.

The delver watched wide-eyed for only a heartbeat. In a flash of movement, he dashed
to his left and grabbed a solid broken branch from the forest floor. The branch was long
and sturdy, freshly broken off a nearby maple tree, probably by one of the tree rakers.
With this crude staff in his hands, Ryson ran toward the river rogue, remaining well out
of its reach, but between the dark creature and the elf.

It seemed almost as if the elf did not understand the delver's intentions. Lief raised
his bow, took aim at the rogues head, and fired his arrow. It never reached its target. As it
sizzled through the air with deadly accuracy, Ryson turned his weight to one side while

he swung the heavy branch upward in a long arc. The lower end of the crude staff
shattered the arrow in mid-air.

Ryson quickly turned about to gauge the reaction of the river rogue. It remained
crouched and unmoving, but watching the delver with a hungry stare, as if it expected
Ryson to become its next meal once he was stricken by one of the elf's arrows.

Realizing the rogue would stay put, Ryson turned his attention back to the elf. "I
won't let you kill it. I can protect it as long as I have to. How much time and how many
arrows will you waste trying to do what you know you can't?"

Lief's response was as quick as it was cold and hateful. "Fire upon you, delver! If it
was not for your past, I would seriously consider firing the next arrow at you. Fine, you
wish this monster to live, then you take responsibility for it. I leave any future evil it does
on your conscience, not mine. The blood is spills will soak your hands as well as its own.

At the very least I can say I tried to remove this monster before it committed any further
acts of violence. It was you that saved it. Think hard on that."

Lief disappeared into the trees, heading south with the Lacobian desert as his ultimate
destination.

The delver looked first upon the elf's back as Lief climbed into the trees above. He
then cast a glance to the river rogue that appeared more confused that the delver had not
yet fallen. Ryson looked at the claws and the razor sharp teeth and knew the thing had to
eat. He sighed heavily and wondered if he made the right decision.

Chapter 14

Sazar left Tabris in her desert oasis as he returned to Dark Spruce to begin his new grand designs of conquest. He promised the sorceress that he would not take long in culminating his plans into action and fulfilling his part of the bargain. He did not, however, wish to utilize the desert as his base of initial operations. His conquests would begin with the humans, and for that he would drive eastward.

Even as he trekked back through the outskirts of the Lacobian and into the western span of Dark Spruce, Sazar utilized his new found powers to expand his small group of minions into a massive horde. The hook hawk under his control soared over vast regions of the forest. When it spotted small camps of goblin raiding parties, Sazar focused his persuasive will through the gaze of the flying beast. The members of the goblin cluster immediately fell under his spell. Once he gained access to their consciousness, he obtained information on the location of competing goblin packs. He directed his winged monster toward these new locations and his minion army grew as fast as his hook hawk could fly.

He sent his smaller shag into the rocky hills in search of more of its kind. Shags in the area would immediately sense the invader and come out to meet the challenger to protect their territories. The smaller shag would never have to fight the larger and more massive monsters that railed against it. Once the small shag locked its gaze upon the targeted creature, Sazar's conniving mind would take the will of the monster and another powerful beast would be added to his army. Within days, Sazar controlled over three dozen shags. Their combined destructive strength could destroy a dwarf constructed barricade in a matter of moments. He now had a mobile battering ram capable of dismantling any barrier.

The two gremplings he first tested his powers on also became very useful. These furry almost imp-like creatures bounded through the forest, swinging from tree tops searching for bloat spiders, the perfect nightmares to add an edge of fear to his multitude. After all, in order to be ultimately successful in his plans of conquest, he needed not only to defeat the initial resistance, but to break the will of those he intended on ruling. Bloat spiders were almost too easy to control. They spun thick webs and waited for days for prey. Their minds never focused on anything beyond that. Persuading them to move with his army required little more than the promise of endless prey.

As the serp walked through Dark Spruce, he kept his own eye upon the skies always
watching for razor crows and hook hawks. Whenever he spotted one, he immediately
placed it under his control and sent it to reconnoiter more and more of the forest. With a
murder of razor crows and numerous hook hawks delivering images to his own mind, his
awareness of the forest and his perception of the surrounding lands grew to god-like
proportions. Secret entrances to dwarf mines, hidden trails to elf camps, and guarded
meeting places for the two races became as obvious to him as the full moon in a cloudless
night sky.

He moved his horde with precision, keeping the mass spread thin. He no longer needed
them near his physical presence to maintain his control of their thoughts, and he used this
to his advantage. Ensuring that he would alert no one that he now controlled massive
army of countless creatures with varied strengths and abilities, he kept small detachments

separated across the vast forest. He would bring them together eventually, but only when
he was ready to attack. For that, he needed to move them further eastward and equip his
forces for an overwhelming onslaught.

With a desire to make his first assault one of such overwhelming fury, Sazar's greatest
obstacle was arming this vast horde of goblins. Most had some sort of crude weapon
when he persuaded them to join his league of minions. For what he had in mind,
however, this was not enough. He wanted each goblin to carry a crossbow and a short
sword of iron at the bare minimum. He wanted the bolts made of metal as well. The
number of goblins he controlled soared into the thousands and equipping them beyond
simple daggers or crude clubs proved to be a near impossible task. Though they raided
several human outposts and two dwarf underground mining stations, he still had many
more goblins than weapons. In the end, he ordered many to construct short bows from
tree limbs and to carve wooden arrows from broken branches. Not quite what he first
envisioned, but it would be enough, enough to obliterate the defenses of his first target
and enough to make it clear that his army was never to be trifled with again.

#

When Linda recommended they take a walk outside Burbon's walls, she thought the
open air would lift Ryson's spirits. Instead, it only seemed to take his focus further away.
As they walked about, Ryson often turned from her and stared out into the distance. She
grew tired of looking at his back and so she walked around in front of him and looked
him in the eye.

"Alright, enough of this. You've been like this for days now. What's bothering you?"
she demanded in a caring yet serious tone.

"It's hard to explain really."

"Try."

"I guess I'm worried about Lief. I'm sure he's reached the Lacobian by now. I can't
help thinking something might have happened to him."

"That's not all of it and I know it," Linda pressed. "I know you've been worried about
Lief since you got back. I understand that and we've already talked about it a lot. You
know you can't stop him from doing what he wants to do. You even talked to Holli and
she thinks he won't do anything too risky. You agreed that now that he knows this Tabris
is with Sazar he's going to be extra careful. That seemed to make you feel better for
about half a day, but then you went right back to moping around again. That has me

completely confused because as far as I can tell you've accepted the situation as it stands,
but something is still eating at you and I want to know what it is."

"The whole thing is eating at me," Ryson offered as if hoping that a general statement
of concern would suffice.

Linda would not let it stand that way.

"That's not a big help to either of us. Look, I'm going to keep badgering you until you
finally admit it, so you might as well save us both a good deal of aggravation and start
talking about it to me instead of keeping it bottled up inside."

Ryson kicked at the dirt. Part of him wanted to take off in a flash and not deal with
what was on his mind, but he knew Linda would simply wait for him to return and she'd
be back at it again. She was persistent and so he began to explain.

"For the most part, you're right. I'm worried about Lief, but it's not like I really have
a choice about stopping him. He made that perfectly clear."

"So what is it then?"

"It's about why he said he was going to the Lacobian," Ryson finally offered. "I've been thinking about what Lief said to me. What he's doing is dangerous, there's no doubt about that, so there has to be a reason for it. I really think part of why he's doing it has a great deal to do with his anger over his own camp. But he didn't explain it that way to me. He gave me some solid reasons for going after Sazar. The thing is that when I think about those reasons, I start wondering."

He paused and looked over to the southwest. He grew quiet again as his expression turned more sullen.

"Don't stop now," Linda insisted. "What is it you're wondering about?"

"What bothers me most is that he might be right," Ryson admitted. "Sazar had a lot of people killed in what's left of Pinesway. He shouldn't be allowed to get away with that. He needs to be punished. That's not all he's done, either. He threatened our town, looted the dwarf city, and who knows what else. Still, it's almost as if he's not on our doorstep right now, we don't have to worry about him. Like it's not our problem. Something seems very wrong with that."

Ryson went even further with his analysis of the situation. "Maybe what Lief is doing is something we all should be doing. If a member of this town did what Sazar did, he wouldn't be allowed to walk around free. Even if he left town, Sy would send out a party of his men looking for him. If he got away, they would make notices of the man's name and a description of him and send them with other mail to town's all across the region. We don't let people that commit crimes just walk away, why are we letting Sazar get away with what he's done?"

"So you think you should go out and join Lief and hunt this Sazar down?"

"No, that doesn't sound right to me, either," Ryson said with a shake of his head. "Lief is going too far, taking too much responsibility for what's going on and doing far more than is necessary. He's out on some kind of mission thinking he should kill every dark creature in the land. What Lief is doing didn't start with Sazar and it's not going to end with Sazar. He's on some kind of crusade. I'm not ready to go that far, but then again something should be done about that serp."

"Well, what do you think should be done exactly?" Linda asked.

"Like I said, he should be punished for what he did in Pinesway. He can't be allowed to get away with that."

"You're setting yourself in a circle you know," Linda pointed out. "You think Sazar

has to be punished, but in order to punish him you would have to capture him. Lief is
going out to capture him, but you're not sure if that's a good idea."

"He's not going out to capture him. He's going out to kill him."

"Well if you think Sazar is captured, do you think he should be executed?"

Ryson didn't answer.

"Don't go silent on me again. You need to get this out. What do you think should be
done with Sazar?"

"I guess if I had my way he'd be taken to the dwarf town of Dunop and thrown in the
dungeon that I was in under the palace. He looted their city and that's where he should
pay for his crimes. Let him rot there until he dies."

"In my mind, that's the same as executing him. It's just a longer duration. The serp
would probably prefer being killed."

"Well, I wouldn't want to be the one that had to swing an axe down on his neck and so I wouldn't ask anyone else to do it, the dungeon sounds like a good alternative."

It was now Linda's turn to look out in the distance to the southwest, in the direction she thought the Lacobian desert to be.

"So I guess the problem is that Sazar is out there and not here in chains."

"That's certainly part of the problem," Ryson agreed, "and now he's tied in with Tabris who is powerful enough not only to protect him but to make him more of a threat. I'm still not sure if Lief is right in trying to hunt Sazar down on his own, but if he does somehow put an arrow in the serp, I don't think I'll lose any sleep over it."

Linda thought for a moment on what Ryson said and then questioned him on one part of it. "You said that you aren't sure if Lief is right in trying to hunt Sazar down on his own. You also said that if someone here in town committed the same crimes that Sy would send a party of men out to capture him. What's the difference?"

"I guess because Sy is captain of the guard and it's his responsibility to protect the town."

"Lief is an elf," Linda countered. "Maybe his job is to protect all of the land or at least protect Dark Spruce. Much of what Sazar has done has been in or near the forest. Why doesn't that give him the right to exact justice?"

"I'm not sure that it doesn't," Ryson admitted. "Like I said, I don't know what to think of this thing. In a lot of ways, I think Lief is right. At the same time, I don't like what I think is motivating him, but I'm not sure if I should try to look at it that way. If you look at just the basics of this mess, Lief is actually justified. I'm not even sure it would be wrong for any one of us in this town to go hunt the serp down. We have the right to defend ourselves. Sazar brought this on himself."

Ryson then turned and nodded back to the town. "The truth of it is I wish Enin would do something about it. That's another reason I went to talk to Holli. I wanted to make sure Enin knew about what Lief was up to. I thought maybe it might get him thinking like I'm thinking. If it did, he could stop this whole thing in an instant, but he just keeps on talking about balance and not interfering in people's choices. It's frustrating."

Linda considered that point for a moment and wondered how she would have felt if Enin turned down her request to warn Tabris not to hurt Ryson.

"I see what you're saying," Linda offered. "We have this wizard here that's like a god. When he helps us, we know we're blessed. When he doesn't, we wonder why he won't."

"Especially when we're dealing with magic," Ryson continued. "If it was just Sazar out there, I think I would have wished Lief luck and figured that would be all we'd have to worry about the serp. The fact that Tabris is now involved changes everything. We don't know what she's done, if she's done anything at all that warrants basically calling an assassin out on her. I'm not sure if Lief can actually kill her, but that's his basic intention."

"If she joined with Sazar, then she's an accomplice to whatever he does."

"At this point, we don't know what they're up to, and we don't know why she joined Sazar in the first place."

"You told me that it was Enin's belief that she had now turned evil."

"Exactly, and I have no reason to doubt him. He knows things that will happen before they actually do, I can tell that much. He won't say it, but I can see it. I don't know if he

reads the future, has some kind of visions, or what, but I definitely know that he has some
idea of how things are going to play out."

Linda remembered how certain Enin was that Tabris would not be able to harm
Ryson. She did not feel that his guarantees were enough at that time. Listening to Ryson
talk about the wizard's power made her think that maybe his assurances should have
relieved her more than they did. Suddenly, she started feeling much more secure about
the future.

"Maybe that's how you should look at it," Linda said with renewed optimism. "You
admit that Enin is powerful and has abilities we really can't understand. Don't you think
that if his assistance was truly necessary, he would give it freely?"

"But it is needed."

"Is it? How do we know?"

"We don't know, but there's certainly enough going on to make us realize we might
need some help."

"Need help or want help?" Linda asked. "There's a big difference. Just because we
want something or ask for something, doesn't necessarily mean it's the best thing for us.
Maybe we can't always have some higher power help us out. Maybe sometimes we have
to figure things out on our own. I don't know if that's balance, but that might be what
he's talking about when he goes on about our choices we have to make."

"So we just go out and do what we can and hope for the best?" Ryson asked.

Linda smiled reassuringly. "Maybe that's all we can do."

#

Lief noticed the strange goblin activity before he even set foot in the Lacobian Desert.
His travels brought him through the heart of Dark Spruce Forest and while he moved
with a mind toward the southwest desert, the activities within the trees could not go
ignored. The existence of goblin packs wandering the forest had become commonplace
now that magic had returned to the land, and detecting the diminutive monsters became
natural practice for all elves that ventured through the trees.

At first, the elf simply tried to avoid the goblins, but their persistent movement was
the first hint that something was not quite right. Goblins were not transient, nomadic
creatures that constantly ventured across the land. If anything, they moved only when
necessary and normally not far from an established source of food and water. During the
dormant season when food remained scarce, many goblins even dropped into a near state
of hibernation.

Lief, however, found the exact opposite behavior in every group of goblins he

encountered. As he ventured further into the heavy trees, he continued to come across
roving bands of the dark creatures that showed anything but normal activity. These small
groups showed no desire to remain still, but moved with purpose and without squabble
over direction. That in itself was almost too much to believe as it was a goblin's nature to
argue and complain within their ranks, especially if they were doing something against
their instincts.

He realized that while they were moving in small packs and did not congregate into
one horde, they still moved as if they had the same goal in mind. They were all arming
themselves, apparently raiding human outposts and possibly even a dwarf mine. Still,
even as they collected weapons, they did nothing to establish a territory or even a zone of
safety. The latter was the most confusing as the normally suspicious and leery creatures

ignored obvious signs of potential predators. They moved about the forest as if they did
not have to care about potential threats. Even when hook hawks soared above their heads,
the goblins simply continued moving eastward as opposed to shrieking in fear and diving
for cover.

"Odd," the elf noted to himself. "They move as if they have come together, yet they
remain apart. This is not like goblins at all."

The elf knew full well that goblins were capable of combining into a massive horde
and moving of like mind and desire. It is at this time these creatures are their most
dangerous and prove that they can not be ignored as some weak insignificant pest that
can be swatted away. Elflore describes past legends and battles that include a sea of
goblins attacking in waves of a purple-gray, pulsating mass that could fill the hillsides
like ants on a drop of sugar. Their sheer numbers of incalculable size could overwhelm
the best defended castles of men or the tallest tree fortresses of elves.

Still, for goblins to reach this level of a threat, they would need to combine. An
underlying need or desire must bring them together into one conjunctive mass. For all the
Lief could see, they remained in their small packs, but acted as if their aims were the
same.

Remaining high in the trees and deep within the cover of pine branches, Lief avoided
being seen by goblins below or flying beasts above.

"Why would they all be moving in the same direction? They could fear something to
the west, but they do not act as if fleeing. They are moving with purpose, not with fear."

In considering a danger to the west, Lief's mind returned to his own objective of Sazar
and Tabris. He wished to waste no further time on the likes of goblins when such a true
threat existed out in the Lacobian Desert. He almost dismissed what he witnessed until he
realized the actions of the goblins might indeed be related to his own objective.

"Could the serp be directing them?" the elf wondered aloud. "No serp has the power
to control this many goblins separated by such a distance. But what other explanation is
there? They do not flee from the hook hawks. If anything they ignore them. Even if they
numbered thousands, the arrival of the bird beast would at the very least provoke a
response. If the serp was indeed guiding their actions, as well as the hawk, they would
indeed ignore the bird."

Lief considered all he knew and all he saw. "No serp alone has the power to do this,
but what of a serp combined with the power of a sorceress? And if Sazar were to gain

such power, what would he do? Would he stay in the Lacobian wasteland where prizes
are few and far between? No, he would not. He would move either west to the coastal
towns or east through the forest and into the plains that hold so many human cities."

Putting the pieces together in his head like a puzzle that becomes easier to solve at the
end, the elf visualized Sazar creating an army of minions just as he had done before
attacking Pinesway. This time, however, the army would be massive in size and scope.
With the aid of a sorceress' power, the serp could control thousands upon thousands of
goblins as well as hook hawks and other monsters. From the desert, Sazar would have to
cut through the rocky hills and then Dark Spruce, but eventually he would come to the
open plains and one human town after another where he could finish what he started in
Pinesway. Realizing that the goblins were indeed linked to his own objective, Lief
understood he did not have to go to the Lacobian to find his target.

"These creatures will lead me to Sazar, eventually."

Chapter 15

"Raid the farmhouses and the barns, leave the animals alone, allow the humans to escape. When they have fled, search all the buildings quickly for weapons and food," Sazar commanded the goblin in charge of the raiding parties. He would also send these orders by thought to each minion surrounding the outlying farms, but as he discovered the goblins actually responded better to a chain of command, he elevated a certain number of them to higher ranks and communicated with them directly.

It truly wasn't necessary for him to speak with his minions to get his orders across. His powers of control enhanced by Tabris' magic allowed him to communicate his directives completely through mental links. Allowing a few goblins access to his presence and speaking to them directly, however, elevated these creatures to a higher status. It was a status all the goblins desired, and they would compete with each other to gain the serp's favor in order to move up the ranks. While the serp found repeating his orders verbally somewhat tiresome, he realized the effort actually enhanced the goblins' willingness to follow his directives exactly. With so many dark creatures under his control, Sazar quickly learned how to manipulate and influence them with the greatest degree of efficiency.

For the most part, the goblins showed a great desire to belong to his horde, and as his army grew, it actually took less exertion to place them under his command. Many of the diminutive creatures actually began seeking him out, as if they could sense the growing power of the goblin horde now under his direction. They bickered and argued constantly. They fought and backstabbed for any advantage they could obtain to move up the ranks, and this proved to be an annoyance as he began to lose goblin soldiers to their own infighting. Still, Sazar found that establishing a dominant order within the goblin ranks increased the zeal and willingness of each individual goblin to work toward promotion. This more than made up for the moments of turmoil.

"Remember," Sazar continued, "force them out of their dwellings or lure them out, but do not kill them in their homes. Let them see you, let them panic, and let them run. Make sure the fleeing humans head toward the city, not out toward the wilderness. If they head for the trees or toward the grassy hills, redirect them to the roads heading back to the city. If they continue to seek refuge elsewhere, then you may kill them. Some of them must reach the city guard posts alive."

Sazar's long thin tongue quickly darted out of the side of his mouth as he looked toward the east from a small window. He sat in a large chair in front of a desk that had one leg smaller than the others. It wobbled slightly when he leaned upon it. The building he now used as shelter from the night and the coming snow storm was one of three structures that comprised a small outpost to the northwest of Connel's outlying farms. The bodies of the humans that used to maintain this outpost lay stacked in a haphazard pile in back of a small shed like structure. The dead humans previously served as clerks monitoring goods shipped from Connel to the northern passage routes that led through the Colad Mountains and into the northwest valley regions. Their journals and papers now fed the fire which kept Sazar warm.

"I will let each raiding party commander know when to begin their individual
assaults," the serp informed his raiding commander. "I want you to remind them of the
importance of waiting for that order."

The serp then gazed deeper into the eyes of the goblin commander. Sazar's eyes
seemed to swirl as if the dark oblong pupils floated in unsteady waters. His voice
hummed with a near musical tone as he detailed the first part of his plan to the raid
commander.

"The raids will begin in three farms due south of Connel's main entrance. The farmers
will not want to fight goblins alone in the dark. They will also not want to risk losing
their supplies this early in the dormant season. Most will run for the nearest guard post.
The human sentries will alert their superiors and they will almost definitely respond with
a forward patrol on horseback to drive off what they will view as an ordinary raid of
simple goblins looking for food. The mounted patrol will investigate and they must be
allowed to see the goblins about the farm houses, thus your raiders will not hide at the
sound of the incoming horses. They must be seen, and then they must flee, but they are
not to respond in any other way."

Glaring at the goblin commander and pressing even deeper into the mind of the
diminutive monster, Sazar made sure the goblin understood his strategy. "More raids will
begin just west of those first three farms as well as further south once the first human
patrol has been sighted. The escaping farmers of these additional raids will come across
the horseback patrol and announce the new activity. Unsure if these are the same raiders
that scattered or another raiding party, the patrol will call for reinforcements. That is why
the raids must be staggered."

Once certain that the goblin commander understood Sazar's intentions without
question, the serp announced the rest of his plan. "At the point, the humans will
undoubtedly send reinforcements to the south. When this detachment reaches the outlying
farm lands, the primary raid will occur at all the farms to Connel's east. Again, let the
farmers escape to the city, let them reach the guard posts. When their militia learns of this
new larger attack, they will believe we bypassed the city in order to gain access to the
dormant season food stocks. Upset that goblins have moved well past the city limits and
to the more important farmlands of the eastern plains, the humans will most assuredly
dispatch the majority of their forces. It is at this time their forces will be out in the open

and most vulnerable to attack. The main body of my army that has already surrounded
Connel will fall upon them with force. When they are decimated, I will then call on the
shags and bloat spiders. You will also begin to hear the calls of the razor crows and hook
hawks. That will conclude all raiding activity on the outlying farms and you are to
withdraw and redeploy your forces to cover the main road that extends east out of
Connel."

The goblin did not speak. It simply nodded and waited to be dismissed. Sazar waved
his scaly hand and the raiding commander scurried out the door.

A handful of goblins remained in the shabby office with Sazar as he began to
telepathically communicate his orders to his army as a whole. These goblins within the
outpost office earned the right to extricate themselves from the mass that made up the
horde and stand by Sazar's side. They normally fulfilled meager tasks to keep the serp
happy. For the most part, they served as nothing more than messengers and gophers, and
they would do anything to retain that position and avoid returning to the horde as simple

foot soldiers. One of these goblins was Chal, a goblin that had no real duty other than to serve as Sazar's listening board.

Not the smartest, the most cunning, the strongest, or even the most kowtowing goblin, Chal gained Sazar's favor by being the most able to listen. His attention span far exceeded the normal goblin and it allowed him to remain focused on a conversation with the serp even as Sazar was forced to take long pauses to communicate with his army of minions. With other goblins, Sazar could never start a conversation, take a pause of more than a few moments, and return without having to start all over again. Chal for some reason could actually keep a thought in his balloon like head for more than a wink of the eye, a trait that was most unusual for goblins and immediately elevated him to a high status.

"Chal," Sazar called out. "I'm interested in your opinions on this action. This is my first true conquest and as it begins, I wish to analyze it further. To this point, I have been quite successful in keeping this huge number of goblins undetected. That in itself has been a monumental task. The approaching storm has undoubtedly assisted in this matter. Traveling in Dark Spruce gave us natural cover. Getting across the hills and farmlands was another matter. In order to get this close to the city without being seen, we have had to use much of the night already. We do not have long now before the sun rises. When it does, we will obviously be discovered. Still, I have the city surrounded and they don't even know it yet. I have numerous raiding parties ready to attack, thus we are now committed. Still, it almost seems too easy, but as there is no turning back, I am wondering if I might be overlooking something. What would you do at this moment?"

Chal responded as he often did, simply and without much thought. "There are enough goblins at your command to simply take the city and kill everyone. That is what I would do."

Sazar expected this over simplistic response, but in truth, he did not really want Chal's advice. He simply used Chal as a way to talk to himself. By explaining to Chal the basic principles of his approach, Sazar often found potential flaws that might be so obvious that they were earlier overlooked.

"So you feel I have wasted too much time and placed too much effort in keeping my forces concealed. I have enough raw power to simply march into Connel and destroy the city. That is probably true, but I would lose more goblins that way."

"They can be replaced."

"It is good to see that you have such love for you fellow goblins. Still, you mustn't be short sighted. Yes, I can find replacements, but I want this army to grow not to shrink or to remain stagnate. I plan to control far more than this city. The land occupied by the humans extends far to the east, very far indeed, most likely beyond your wildest imagination. There are countless towns and cities that extend through the farmlands and grasslands. Uton is only a small region of an even larger expanse. There is another ocean to the east and cities of massive size on its coast. One day, I may wish to take these cities as well. To do that, I must grow in power, not lose power out of impatience."

Sazar clicked his long sharp nails on the desktop. The desk wobbled momentarily and Sazar sighed as he sat back in his chair away from the unsteady table.

"Also, by concealing my forces the humans were never alerted and given a chance to escape. It is not enough to simply take an empty city. That was my objective when I attacked that pathetic town of Pinesway. I will no longer think so small.

"The second mistake you make is in wanting to kill all the human inhabitants. That is just plain foolishness. I have told you of my bargain with Tabris. I am bound to honor that bargain and fully intend on doing so. If I kill everyone in the city, what will that leave me to send to Tabris? Goblins? I doubt that would make her happy, to say nothing of my goblin army. No, it would not do to simply march in and kill them all. I must control them. To do that, I must show them that I am more than a marauding army. The battle must not only be won, it must be won in such a way that they understand I am not to be underestimated.

"I also have to think about supplying my forces," Sazar continued. "I am no longer interested in simply raiding and stealing what I can get my hands on. I will conquer this city and I will hold it. Once I am in control, I will need food for my forces as well as metals to make new weapons. I certainly can not depend on the goblins or any other of my minions to farm or to mine. I will need the humans to do that. I will offer them life in exchange for their servitude. In order for that bargain to work, they must remain alive after I take the city."

Sazar nodded his head with a degree of satisfaction. "No, I believe the initial designs of my plan are sound. I don't want the inhabitants of Connel to escape and I don't want them all killed. I simply need to make sure their ability to fight is extinguished. I will do that by coaxing a large portion of their forces out into the open and destroying them. The ordinary inhabitants of the city will then be more willing to accept their fate."

Chal shrugged. "Goblins don't like the open land. When the sun comes up, we will look for cover from the light."

"The storm clouds will keep it fairly dark for a while," Sazar hummed. "I believe it will also snow for some time. The sun will not be too much of a problem."

"We do not like snow, either."

"Goblins don't like much of anything," Sazar responded with a weary sigh. "But I must say I should consider that. I can not allow the battle to drag on for long. A heavy snow might slow my army's forward movement into the city. If the humans can regroup with archers, it might allow them to cause heavy casualties, not enough to change the ultimate outcome, but as I said, I wish to minimize my losses. It is best if I begin the first raids as soon as possible."

#

"Humans always cut down the trees," Lief grumbled to himself with disgust.

Watching from a small grove of trees that long ago used to be part of sprawling Dark Spruce Forest but was now nothing more than an isolated patch, Lief's sharp elf eyes could peer though the distance as well as the darkness to make out the movements of several goblin packs. He stayed within the safety of the trees as razor crows continued to fly overhead. The cold air became still as the night grew darker. The elf could smell the snow in the air, waiting to fall and cover the tracks of the moving horde.

The goblin packs had moved past the trees just as night fell and their numbers had swelled to alarming proportions. They continued their eastward movements and it became all too clear to the elf that Connel must be their ultimate destination. Scurrying over hills, darting down dark dirt roads, and skulking through dormant farm fields, the goblins moved in an orderly fashion with that one apparent destination in mind. The number of goblins in each pack increased ten fold, and the number of these packs grew at the same staggering rate. They did not yet combine into one massive throng, but as they

closed upon Connel, they did less to spread their numbers across the vast land. With their
raids on outposts and mines now obviously complete, they now moved with a bigger goal
in mind.

During his previous travels through Dark Spruce, Lief had kept a casual eye on the
trail of the marching monsters. He stayed alert, high in the trees, and was spotted on
numerous occasions, both by goblins below and flying beasts above. When spotted, he
remained calm as he followed a pack for a short distance and then eventually turned and
moved off to find another band. He acted like nothing more than an elf guard keeping
tabs on a goblin threat invading the lands too near an elf camp. Such encounters had to be
common to these creatures as they traveled by so many other elf camps. As long as his
sightings remained consistent and revealed nothing beyond causal forest reconnaissance,
he believed he would be disregarded by the dark creatures, and so far, he was.

With the goblins now out of the forest, however, Lief's options dwindled. An elf spied
out in the open farmlands would now be looked upon with much greater suspicion. He
could not yet afford to bring that kind of attention upon himself. As of yet, he was unable
to get a fix on the serp that he knew was behind all of this activity. He believed Sazar was
close, but the outlying farms of Connel spread over great distances. There was little else
he could do but wait.

"This is as close as I can get… for now."

#

The new mayor of Connel was very tired, but seldom was able to sleep. When a strong
knock came on her bedroom door, she was already awake considering more rebuilding
plans for the next few days.

"Give me a moment," Helen Flisher responded. She rose from her bed and pulled on
her clothes. She knew she would not sleep any further this night, so there was no need to
pretend she would return to bed. When she opened her door, she found her assistant
waiting for her with a look that revealed more fear than concern.

"What's wrong?" Helen asked firmly.

"Guard Captain Tevor is here to see you. He says it's urgent."

"Where is he?"

"At the door, he wouldn't come in."

Mayor Flisher moved past her assistant and toward the front of the house. The door
was open and a cold wind greeted her. She grabbed a coat that hung crumpled over a
chair, threw it over her shoulders, and stepped outside.

A heavyset man with a sour face only glanced at her and then returned his gaze toward

the south of the city. "Sorry to disturb you, mayor, but I'm following your orders." The
career soldier's voice was thick as if the words from his mouth weighed more than those
from other men. "We have reports that goblins are raiding farms to the south. More than
one farm family has made the report so I believe the claims are legitimate. I have no
scouts at that position at this time so I can not verify beyond these reports. Based on what
I have heard, I believe three farms have been attacked. I have no reports of casualties at
this time. These farms are beyond the city limits, so I have executed your standing orders
for all goblin raids outside the city. I have placed all interior guard posts on alert, recalled
all outer patrols and placed them at watch within the city's main quadrants, dispatched
additional watch to the roofs of our tallest structures, and placed the cavalry at the ready."

His initial report complete, Captain Tevor turned and awaited the mayor's response.

Helen Tevor stepped carefully down the front steps of her house and looked to the
south and then up at the sky. She pulled her coat more tightly around her as she inhaled
heavily the cold air.

"It's going to snow," she remarked.

"Probably," the soldier agreed.

The mayor played out the possibilities in her mind. "Goblins are small, they probably
don't like the snow. They would move like children, struggling through it if it got too
deep. They're probably hungry and worried the snow might prevent them from
scavenging food in the forest. If I were them, I might try a quick strike on a farm to get
what food I could."

"I could send out a patrol on horseback, find out what they're up to and clear them
out," the captain offered.

The mayor looked up at the sky again and shook her head. "No, it's still dark and a
storm can be unpredictable. Dawn will be here soon, let's wait for more light. If the
farmers protest, let them know they will be compensated for their losses. The dwarves
never hit the farms so we have more food then we have people now. We can afford to
lose a few barrels of grain to a handful of goblins, but I don't want to lose any more
soldiers to goblin crossbows. It's just not worth the risk."

The captain found the concern for his soldiers quite refreshing and nodded in
acceptance. "Will you be remaining here in case I have to send you updated reports?"

"No, I'm going to head over to town hall—well the temporary town hall—to my
office. I'm not going to get anymore sleep tonight, so I might as well make good use of
the time."

"Very well. I will keep you updated."

"Thanks."

#

Sazar sat quietly with his mind focused on the sensations he received from the half
dozen rock beetles that were now under the town. Through them, he could feel the
movement of the human troops, sense their alarm, but none of it matched what he
expected.

"The farmers reached several guard posts within the city limits quite a while ago," the
serp said more to himself than to Chal, but he wanted the goblin to listen as well.
"They've had plenty of time to rouse their forward scouts. Indeed they have already
recalled their outer patrols and have mounted several soldiers on horseback. These
soldiers are not moving out. Why not?"

"They are afraid," Chal said.

"No, they are moving with great certainty and purpose, not panic, but they are staying
much too cautious. Could they know I already have them surrounded? No, that doesn't
make sense, either. Everything I feel indicates they are simply waiting, not truly
preparing for a battle. It's almost as if we don't exist to them, as if the small raids never
took place."

"Maybe they don't care about these farmers," Chal offered, and at that, Sazar turned a
head toward the goblin.

"They do not care? Hmmmmmm. Humans tend to be an excitable lot. When they feel
they are threatened they either run or attack. A few of the more intelligent ones show a bit
more caution, but in the end they also would meet a raid with some type of action. But

what if they didn't care? They might indeed ignore the claims of a few farmers and
simply do enough to appear as if they are prepared to meet any additional threats. Very
good, Chal. Let us give them additional threats."

Sazar began sending new orders by mental command, first to his raiding commander
and then to the individual pack leaders. He began narrating his new plans as he continued
linking with the minds of the goblins in the fields. He spoke out loud to Chal as he
completed most of his commands.

"Since there is no patrol to respond to the first raid, it is a waste of time to try and
confuse them with another smaller raid in the same area. I'm calling for an immediate
attack by all goblin raiding parties in the fields to the east of Connel. I am also directing
them to force the humans to flee to the city by whatever means necessary. Let us see if
the humans remain so cautious when many of the farmers to the east reach their guard
posts with warnings of a larger raid. I think then they will care, they will care a great
deal.

#

Even in the dark and over great distances, Lief could see the turmoil in the farmlands.
The first raid to the south of Connel was smaller in scope. When he watched the goblins
allow the farmers to flee toward the city, he realized he had a chance to enter Connel. He
would be seen, but probably not noticed if he appeared as a fleeing farmer as opposed to
an elf.

Pulling his cloak out about him to cover the bow and quiver of arrows on his back,
Lief looked over his own appearance to see what he might do to be more convincing.
Making small tears in the lower portions of his shirt and pants, his clothes fit more
loosely making him appear wider, especially in the dark. Satisfied, he dropped out of the
sparse area of trees, and upon the ground. He began to trot toward Connel, not with the
speed and grace of an elf, but with the hurried and frantic gait of a fearful human. He kept
crouched over and a hood pulled down well over his head. He remained on the main road
as this was an area the goblins remained watchful over but had dared not encroach.

As he passed over several hills and past many of the southern farms, he peered to the
east. Well past the city limits, the outlying farms in this region suddenly came alive with
panic. The elf could see small fires being lit across the lands, and he spied the shadows of
both goblins and humans running frantically about. Many of the humans took to the roads

heading toward Connel and it appeared again as if the goblins were allowing them to
make it safely to the city, though Lief could not imagine why.

The raids to the east grew in scope and intensity. The shouts became clearer. The fear
grew more apparent in the human screams just as the hate intensified in the goblin
shrieks. It appeared as if hundreds of farm families had been rousted from their beds and
were now fleeing for the protection of Connel.

Lief quickly came to the area that he knew presented the greatest challenge. From his
previous position, he knew that Sazar had surrounded Connel with his multitude of
goblins. This ring, however, was not complete. In order to hide his horde, Sazar utilized
the surrounding farmlands as cover and kept the monsters off the main roads and low in
the fields. This presented several breaks in the goblin lines including one on the road that
the elf now traveled.

The goblin position was also fluid and it moved with cunning to avoid previous
human patrols. Lief did not know how it that was possible, but the goblins appeared to

gain advanced warning to patrols, almost as if somehow they could sense the soldiers'
movement the moment they left the confines of the city. Retreating and parting to allow
humans to pass, the goblins showed much more diligence in avoiding the guards than on
seizing or attacking them.

As Lief approached the area he knew to contain the greatest concentration of goblins,
he realized if he were to be stopped, it would be now. Still, he hoped he could avoid an
encounter simply by appearing to be nothing more than a fearful human running toward
the safety of Connel.

"If they let the farmers make it to the city, perhaps they will do so with me," Lief said
quietly trying to convince himself he was not running toward his own death.

He moved with a labored unsteadiness as he remained crouched over. He exhaled
heavily almost to the point of wheezing, and he even threw in a few groans of despair as
he looked over his shoulder appearing to fear what might be behind him. Every fiber of
his being told him to move faster, to utilize his swift elf abilities to avoid the danger that
he knew was all about him. To do so, however, would surely mean his death, and thus he
fought down his own instincts. He rambled onward, even falling to his knees on the hard
road. He scrambled up with all the contrived imbalance he could muster as he continued
onward toward the lights of Connel.

Throughout his ungraceful run, he expected to hear the sizzling whistle of a crossbow
bolt whizzing through the air. He waited for the burning sting of penetration into his
back. The pain never arrived and he quickly neared the first outer buildings of Connel.

As much as he did not wish to be seen by the goblins, neither did he wish to confront
the humans on guard. Several remained on watch peering out into the darkness.
Attempting one last charade, Lief stumbled to the ground rolled over into the ditch and
quickly slid on his belly away from the main road and into matted grass.

No longer needing to fool the goblins, he moved with his elf grace. Rolling silently
through light underbrush he made his way to toward a dark building just off to his left.
He climbed up a post as if climbing an oak tree. Avoiding the notice of the guard, he
rolled up on to the roof and surveyed the area around him.

                                        #

Running out of the old town library that now served as the town hall and the office of
the Mayor, Helen Flisher reached the outside air just as Captain Tevor began leaping up
the stone steps.

"I was just coming for you," he said with an out-of-breath huff. "More trouble."

"I hear. What's going on that we can be sure of?"

"More goblin raids, this time to the east."

"The east?! They've bypassed the city?" Mayor Flisher questioned in surprise.

"Unless they came from somewhere else other than Dark Spruce, it looks like it."

"I didn't think goblins liked the open lands."

"I didn't either, but we really don't know too much about them."

The mayor frowned. "Never mind, we'll deal with that later. It sounds bad out there,
what kind of goblin numbers are we looking at."

"Too dark to get a good look," Tevor admitted, "but it's clear they're hitting just about
every farm that's within walking distance on our eastern side. In order to do that, they
would need at least two hundred maybe more."

"Casualties?"

"No reports of any as of yet. Every farm family that has made it to the city has said
that the goblins didn't harm them or their family members and they didn't see any dead
on the road into the city."

"They're letting them escape?"

"Seems that way. I have the full cavalry waiting at the eastern border of the city for a
full charge to repel. Even if there's four hundred out there, we can send them into retreat
and clear the area."

The mayor considered what she was told and listened to the clamor in the distance.
She wanted to give the order, but a great doubt weighed upon her mind. She hesitated and
revealed her concerns. "Something about this isn't right. They hit us to the south and now
they hit us to the east with greater numbers. We didn't respond to their first attack. If they
just want food, why not use their numbers to sack everything they could from the
southern farms? Why move up to the east? If they are from Dark Spruce, they put the city
between them and their escape. If not, why did they break up their forces to hit the south
first?"

"Two possibilities that I can think of, the first is that the two attacks are not related.
Maybe these are two different goblin packs that have nothing to do with each other, but
because of the storm, they both got the same idea. They just attacked from different
points."

"Do you believe that?"

"Not for an instant," Tevor admitted, "but it is possible."

"The second possibility?"

"The second is that they know the eastern farms are larger. When we didn't respond to
their first attack, they got brave and went for the bigger prize."

Mayor Flisher shook her head. "If they know that the eastern farms are larger they
should also know that it's the dormant season and we moved most of the food from those
farms into the city."

"We also kept a good deal out in the farms in case the dwarves attacked again so we
wouldn't lose all our supplies."

"True, so you think they just want our reserves?" the mayor asked.

"They're goblins, they don't farm themselves. Why not?"

"I don't know. Something still doesn't feel right about this."

At that very moment, the first few snow flakes began to drift out of the night sky.

"It's starting to snow," the mayor said.

"Aye, what's your order on the cavalry?"

"Hold them," Mayor Flisher said quickly, but then she altered her position slightly.
"Actually, no. Have them ride out and assist the escaping farmers, but they are not to
engage the goblins—just a rescue mission, nothing else. It's going to be light soon

enough and it's already starting to snow. We have enough food in the city that we can afford to lose those reserves, but I don't think we will. They don't have enough time to take everything. Pretty soon it's going to be light out here and the snow is going to pile up and slow them down. If the goblins are still out there when it gets lighter, we'll see them and know what we're really up against. If they're loading up with supplies and trying to run back to the forest, we can send out your forces then. What do you think?"

"I admit I don't like running from a fight…"

"Well, we're not really running. We're just waiting for the right time."

Tevor smiled lightly. "Aye, I can wait and I'd like to see just what we're up against as well."

#

Frowning and shaking his head, Sazar's normal flowing and hypnotic voice dropped to a grumble. "Why are they not counterattacking? They are allowing us to move unimpeded. Their cavalry is doing nothing more than gathering up some of the farmers."

Throwing a fist down on the uneven table, Sazar threw himself out of his chair and stormed to the door. "I need to have better view of what is going on."

He threw open the door and stepped out into the cold night air. Ignoring the snow flakes falling on his head, he sent a mental command to a hook hawk perched in a tree far off in the distance.

Lowering its head slightly, the beast turned about on a thick branch, spread its uneven wings and leapt into the air. With but a few beats of its thick wings, the monster gained altitude higher then the trees. It began to shift and swerve in the air as it headed in a jagged path toward the city of Connel. As the flying beast came close enough to view the full breadth of the city, the images it gained in its mind traveled through magical waves back to the serp.

"Much of the city is in ruins!" Sazar noted. "I knew the dwarves of Dunop attacked, but I had no idea that inflicted so much damage. The outer ring is in fair shape, but the inner city has been crushed. Over half of the buildings are near demolished. The dwarves must have struck from the city center. The human forces on patrol are few and far between. No wonder my rock beetles felt so little movement above them. I wonder how many humans are even left in the city. This changes things drastically."

Chapter 16

Fires from torches lit up the darkness all around Connel. Even as the snow continued
to fall, fear of what now surrounded the city replaced any worries about a simple dormant
season storm. The goblins also set several of the farmhouses ablaze, and the flames licked
the darkness of the waning night. To the east, only a dull, faint glow could be noticed on
the far horizon, but the sight of what stood between that horizon and the city limits
destroyed any ray of hope from the coming dawn.

Sazar himself was on the march toward the northern entrance of the city. With his
small contingent of goblins at his side, he appeared as nothing more than another dark
creature joining the ranks of the monsters that now encircled the city. His horde made no
further attempt to hide their presence, to remain quiet in the darkness, or to avoid the
approach of enemy scouts. Just the opposite, Sazar had ordered his minions to make their
numbers quite clear to the human inhabitants of Connel. He ordered all torches lit, several
farmhouses set ablaze, and every goblin to shriek with murderous delight.

The main body of Sazar's goblin army closed ranks, blocked all roads surrounding
Connel, and formed one continuous circle around the doomed city. No longer did they
skulk in the shadows or crouch low against the dirt. Not a single clear path existed
through their dark ranks. As the torches and surrounding fires danced with hell-like glee,
the snow that reached the flames sizzled into steam. Newly wet wood gave off a white
smoke as it burned, and the host of goblins appeared as if blessed by some unholy
dragon's breath.

"Chal," Sazar called out to the goblin behind him. "Does this meet with your
approval?"

"I like that we are not hiding, but why don't we attack?" the goblin asked almost
innocently, if that were possible.

"Because I do not believe we will have to," the serp answered firmly.

Sazar then channeled his commands to the razor crows and hook hawks that remained
near the trees to the west. In mere moments, the dark, thin, almost knife-like crows
circled the goblins overhead. Their V-shaped bodies floated in the glow of the fires
beneath them and their black wings accented the white snow falling out of the shadows
from above. The hook hawks took to flight at a much higher altitude and soared in
swooping patterns over the center of the besieged city. Shrieking upon the serp's orders,
their calls penetrated every dark alley and every basement shelter. No one in Connel

could ignore the horror they now faced.

"I am ordering the shags and bloat spiders to move as close to the city as possible without coming in range of any foolish archers. I am also calling for several goblin raiding packs to advance forward ahead of our main line. We will do the same and appear as just another pack of goblins. I want to be ready to enter the city when the time is right."

#

"It's very early, still dark outside," Enin professed as he looked up at the night sky. As he looked into the blackness above him, hundreds of snowflakes seemed to materialize out of nothingness.

"I know," Ryson said as he waited on the grass in front of Enin's home which was
now dusted with a thin layer of cotton soft snow, "but it's snowing and I wanted to take
the dogs out to play and for a run before it gets to deep—or muddy if it warms up and
melts. I didn't think you'd want a house full of muddy dogs."

"I don't mind that much. Actually, I'm very glad you're here. I would like a moment
to talk to you. It won't take long and then you can be on your way with the dogs." The
wizard looked back behind him at the four tail-wagging canines that waited at the front
door. "They won't mind as long as I don't keep you too long. Please come into my study.
Holli's already there and I would like her to hear this as well."

This piqued the delver's curiosity and that was all it took to get him inside. He
followed the wizard down the hall and into a large room where Holli waited near a
window. Ryson nodded and the elf returned the greeting.

Enin began immediately, not even waiting to sit down.

"Ryson," he began, "I want to make sure you understand something. I see in you
someone that cares very much of what happens to others. You involve yourself because I
believe you think it's your responsibility. I admire that and I wish more people would
have even a slight degree of your willingness to help and contribute."

The wizard let that statement stand for a moment and then continued what he believed
was an obvious truth. "I'm sure you're thinking right now that you wish I was more
willing to contribute, and that is what I want you to understand. We have talked often and
at great lengths about things like choices and balance and interference. I never try to read
your thoughts, but I do believe I can sense your reactions now and then. In the past few
days you have helped in Pinesway, and gone out of your way to make sure a friend did
not stray into danger. At the same time, I did nothing to stop Sazar in Pinesway and I
make no attempt to stop Tabris from assisting this monster now. You must wonder why I
do not do more. Am I right?"

Ryson simply nodded.

"You have always gone well beyond what is expected of you," Enin continued. "You
do so much for so many. When I see what you can accomplish, I am envious and I really
wish I can do more. Unfortunately, I must be very careful." Enin stopped and sighed.
"There I go again. I am not saying what needs to be said, going in circles, saying the
same thing over and over again. Let me try this again with as much clarity as possible."

Enin rubbed his hands together and focused his thoughts clearly on what he wanted to

say. "When I talk about balance, I am often referring to the equal weights of all things,
especially good and evil. I have done my best to remain on the proper side of events. I
have strived not to use my power for selfish desires, or out of anger, and especially not
out of arrogance or pride. That being said, I think it's time you understand there is
another being that exists that does not have that same outlook. I believe he is malevolent
in spirit and would certainly act without the care I have tried to exercise. In many ways,
he is to evil what I hope I am to good. It is a way that the balance can be maintained
throughout the land. I believe this creature exists to keep me in check, to remind me that
if I start to interfere in the choices of humans, elves, dwarves, and so on, it would then
give this creature the opportunity to intervene in his way. Holli has now seen this creature
and I believe she can verify some of what I'm saying."

Enin turned to the elf and raised an eyebrow. "Well, not clearly seen him, but has been
in his presence. He is not a figment of my imagination, yes?"

"He is real," the elf responded simply.

"And what do you think of him?"

"I believe he can and would do great harm."

Enin turned back to the delver.

"You see? I never was making excuses. For whatever reason, there must be balance and if I break the balance by interfering there will be consequences. In fact, it is actually very simple. Whatever good I do, it will assuredly be offset immediately somewhere else by something very bad. There are times I can act, and there are times I don't believe I should, otherwise I might invite disastrous results elsewhere. This part is hard to explain, in truth because I don't really understand it myself, but if I do something like say interfere with Sazar and Tabris, it opens the door for this other being to interfere elsewhere. As long as I am responsible with my actions, it keeps the balance."

"But there are times you acted before," Ryson pointed out. "You stopped the dwarves from destroying Burbon, you destroyed Yave, you warned us about Sazar attacking Pinesway, and there are countless smaller things you do daily to keep us all safe. Isn't that interfering?"

"I don't think so, then again perhaps it is," Enin answered in his usual and somewhat confusing fashion. "It all depends on how you look at it, and it all depends on the results. With the dwarves, they attacked us, they made a choice. I responded to that choice and to their actions. I never took away their ability to attack before they chose to do so. It was also not a struggle between right and wrong or good and evil. The dwarves that attacked did so because they felt threatened. The people of this town and the elves that fought with them did so to defend themselves. I ended that battled but I did not intervene in the struggle between good and evil."

"That's where you're going to lose me," Ryson proclaimed. "I didn't see anything good about the dwarves attack."

"That's because you're not a dwarf," Enin replied. "Anyway, let us not get sidetracked from what it is I want to say. I want you to understand that there is evil out there and if I act out of haste simply to do what I think is right, I believe that evil will be given an opportunity to gain strength. I can not let that happen. You may not understand that fully, but perhaps it is enough. What do you think?"

"Well, the fact that you're telling me there's something out there as powerful as you that is evil isn't going to make me sleep any better," Ryson admitted, "but at least it gives me an idea of why you're as careful as you are."

"I am very happy to hear that," Enin reflected with a smile and then thought of a way
to reward the delver. "I also want to share something with you I know that is important to
you. I will give you the answer to a question that has plagued you for some time now.
You have wondered why Dzeb and the other cliff behemoths came to your aid in the
tunnels of Dunop. You even asked him why he came to help and he ignored your
question. You tried to push it aside, but you are a delver and such a task is not truly
possible.

"The truth of the matter is that Dzeb and the other cliff behemoths were vehemently
opposed to intruding in the affairs of other races. It was not their place and they knew it.
They have faith, and in their faith they believe that it is Godson's will that will determine
the fates of other beings. Even with their grand power, they would not dare to impose

what they thought is right or wrong on other beings. In the end, however, they did
intercede, and the question is why?

"They did so because of you my friend. Not because of your pleas or your arguments,
but simply because they see something in you, something that I see as well. You, whether
your like it or not, are a person of destiny. Do not feel embarrassed by this or even be
surprised by it. It is rare, though it is not completely unheard of to say the least. There
have always been and always will be a handful of individuals in this land that always
seem to be in the thick of important events. Of course there are individuals that only have
one moment of historical significance and then fade in to the background. Then again,
there are others that make important contributions over and over again, and they never
tend to fade away. They keep reappearing. Some say that they do so because they insist
on thrusting themselves into important events even when they do not belong. They live
for fame and power. Sadly, this is true for many such people.

"There are others, however, that do not seek such a position, but neither can they
escape it. They are continuously pressed into service whether they like it or not. They are
people of destiny, and you are such a person.

"Remember, the cliff behemoths always remained true to their faith. They entered
Dunop to stop the sand giants, but ultimately it was you that saved the city from the
shadow trees and stopped the war. Thus, the cliff behemoths did not truly intervene in the
actions or choices of other creatures. They simply gave you the opportunity to do what
you were destined to do and nothing else.

"I won't ask you if you understand and I don't wish to try and debate the details. The
only thing I want you to know is that the cliff behemoths entered Dunop to give you a
chance to do what you had to do. Whether you failed or succeeded in the challenges you
faced then, or for that matter in the challenges you still must face, that always remains up
to you."

Enin looked deeply into the delver and though he still sensed a great deal of confusion
in Ryson, he did not wish to explain any further. "Now, do me a favor and take the dogs
out to play, they are getting impatient."

                    #

As if she simply faded in from the darkness and took form where there was none
before, a woman in a long black cloak appeared off to the side of the road where Sazar
and several goblins stood watching and waiting. Her cloak billowed at the bottom and

appeared to have no true end as if she was an extension of the darkness around her. Her
appearance so stunned one goblin that he fired off a crossbow bolt before he knew what
he was shooting at. The woman stepped forward and leaned into the incoming bolt,
allowing it to plunge deep into her shoulder. Without even a gasp of pain, she pulled the
protruding bolt from her flesh and threw it to the ground.

"Hold," Sazar commanded to the other goblins. He would not step forward, but he
turned slightly to face the woman.

"You are the serp in control of these creatures," she stated as a simple fact.

"Indeed I am," Sazar answered as he stared into the eyes of the woman before him. He
did not like what he saw and for the first time since he gained his new powers from
Tabris, he felt a chill whisk through his very bones.

"Do not try to work your will on me, serp. I understand the strength of will as well as you do, and though my power to control an army would never match yours, your influence over me dies in my veins."

"Vampire?" he questioned.

She said nothing, but the dancing shadow in her eyes made the answer clear.

The serp gritted his teeth. "What is it I should call you?"

"You may call me Janindise"

"Very well, Janindise, how did you find me?"

"For me, I can taste the vibrations of your controlling thoughts. The outflow of your will is like a guide. I had no trouble following it back to its source."

"Do you guard this city?" Sazar asked somewhat concerned about what the answer might be.

"I hate this city," the woman answered. "Do to it what you will."

"I plan to," the serp responded simply. "What is it you want?"

"I have extremely little time before the sun rises, thus I shall waste none. There are two things you must be made aware of. One is that I am bound to attack goblins, shags and the like in order to satisfy my thirst. Normally, I would travel into the hills or the forest to hunt what I need. Now that you bring so many here to me, I find it absurd to waste time hunting them down in the wild. If it is any solace to you, I will not kill what I feed upon, thus you will not lose any of your followers. I tell you this out of a courtesy."

"I appreciate your advanced warning," Sazar noted. "What confuses me, however, is why can't you attack the humans of this town?"

"I will not discuss that."

Her tone made it very clear that pressing her would be a waste of time and Sazar did not wish to make an enemy of this woman, certainly not at this point in time.

"Very well. You did say there were two things you wished to advise me of, what is the second?"

"I have a friend that dwells in this city," the vampire explained. "I plan to return to him now. I will not let you hurt him, thus I suggest you advise your goblins, your shags, your hook hawks, and whatever other monsters you plan to unleash on these other mortals, to leave us be if they happen to stumble upon us."

"Does your friend have a name?"

"Edward Consprite. I have already informed him of your arrival here and of the horde this city faces. He believes he might be of some assistance to you. He has very in-depth knowledge of this place and its inhabitants. It seems he used to lead them once. He has been replaced and now also has nothing but contempt for this city as well. I can not imagine how he might be of help to a serp that wishes to plunder a city, but he has

surprised me on many occasions and so he might surprise you as well. Eventually, he will
come to you on his own. Whether you listen to him or not, that is your business. If you
kill him, then it will become my business."

"It is not my intention to make anything your business. I will leave you and your
friend be, and I will listen to this human if he does seek me out. I do, however, have a
question. If both you and this Consprite hate this city, why do you stay here?"

"He has no where else to go and I have come to enjoy his company."

"I see," Sazar responded simply.

"The sun is rising and I have only moments left. Remember my warning, do not harm
Consprite."

She took one step back and simply faded into the swirling snow and waning darkness.

#

"We have to surrender," the mayor stated with a tone of desperation.

"Surrender? To Goblins?" Captain Tevor found this solution to be no solution at all.

"We have no choice," Mayer Flisher responded while casting a frantic look out to the
goblin horde that surrounded the city. "What can we do against this? We can't run; they
have us surrounded. We can't hold them off; we have no walls, they would be on us in
moments."

"We can fight," Tevor offered stubbornly.

The mayor pointed out to the throng of goblins. "Against that?"

"The cavalry is ready and my infantry is entrenched. We've been training the civilians
in case of another attack by the dwarves, we might as well call them in now. It may be
enough."

"It'll be enough to start a panic and make things a hundred times worse."

"With all due respect, you're wrong about the panic. Most of the people already know
we're surrounded. It's not like the goblins are making themselves hard to notice any
more. We sound out the alarm just as we planned to do under another dwarf attack. Some
people will go to where they're supposed to go and be ready to fight, some will hide. At
least we'll know what we've got. The sun is starting to rise, so even with the snow, it's
getting lighter. The snow is in our favor, too. It will slow them down."

"And with all due respect to you," the mayor responded, "how much do you think it's
going to matter if they have to march through ankle deep snow? They're already on us.
They've even moved shags, spiders and small goblin raiding parties almost up to our
doorstep. They've got those strange hawks flying over our heads right now and those
crows waiting right above the goblins. We didn't train our people to fight against that.
How many experienced soldiers do you really have left? The dwarves decimated our
forces. Look at the number of goblins out there. Do you honestly think we have even the
slightest chance of avoiding annihilation? Tell me with all honesty you think the forces
under your command can possibly find a victory and I'll pick up a sword and join you,
but it can't be a suicide charge."

"Surrendering may be the same as suicide," Tevor offered with a dark expression.
"They might not take prisoners, and even if they do, we have no idea how they might

treat them. Godson, they might eat us, we just don't know what they will do. Look, I
appreciate what you're thinking. You've already saved most of my men. I would have
sent out the cavalry when they started raiding the farms. They would have all been
slaughtered and I probably would have marched out there to die with them, but if it's a
choice between fighting and surrendering, I think all of them would rather fight."

"Do you think there is any kind of chance we can stop them if they attacked?" the
mayor asked flatly.

"There's always a chance," Tevor stated stubbornly.

"Yes, there's always a chance for a miracle," the mayor allowed, "but there also has to
be time for realism. This time I'm not going to ask you if there's a chance, I want you to
be honest with me, as honest as you can be to your soldiers when their life is on the line.
What do you believe will happen if the goblins move forward?"

Tevor bowed his head and looked at the snow covered ground. "I will order the
cavalry to charge their weakest point which I believe is to the southwest. I believe if they
concentrate their charge, they can break through the goblin line, though they will suffer a
fair amount of casualties. I will also order them that once they break through to harass the
enemy flank to the best of their ability, but if they come under heavy crossbow fire,
which they will, I will tell them to retreat south then turn due east and head to the plains.
Hopefully they can hook up with forces at Fort Nebran, and warn them of what went on
here."

"What about the rest of us here in the city?"

"I will order the infantry to remain entrenched and fight to the death, which I believe
they will. That will hopefully cut deep into their numbers. At least they would if it were
just goblins. So many shags out their have me worried. Those monsters can plow through
our trenches with ease. That's probably why they're up front. I will have my best archers
try to pick off the shags and that might help."

"And if the hawks or the crows interfere with the archers?" Flisher asked.

"Let's hope they don't. In the end, even if we do cut into their numbers, there are still
too many goblins to defeat. They will eventually overrun us and move into the city
streets. If we get some luck with the shags and if the infantry can kill as many goblins as I
hope they can, they might not want to venture further into the city where we can have the
civilians armed and ready."

"And what would happen if they didn't stop?"

"They'll wipe us all out," Tevor answered solemnly.

The mayor heaved a heavy breath. "Even with all the hope in the world, you just
admitted we can't fight them off. In fact, you admitted we would be dooming our entire
guard force."

"As I said, we may be doomed anyway. At least, maybe we can get some of the
cavalry out, and if we inflict enough loses, there may be some small hope that we can
save the interior part of the city."

"I'm sorry captain but that's not good enough." Mayor Helen Flisher made a final
decision quickly. "I want you to pull your infantry back, but you may leave the cavalry
where they are. We will raise a white flag and send out four unarmed riders in each
direction of the compass to stop just before they reach where the shags are positioned.
Ask for volunteers, they might not come back alive. If they are approached, they are to
tell the invaders we surrender, but that we have women and children and we need to

understand their terms. They are to ask for representatives to come to the city's border. I
will then meet with them so they can deliver their terms directly to me so I can have them
followed out. If they will not let us surrender, we will know then. At that point, you can
order your cavalry to make an attempt to escape to the southwest. The rest of us will all
fall back to the city center and fight together, to the death if that's what happens."

Captain Tevor knew there was no point in debating. "I'll see to it."

#

Immediately after Ryson left with the dogs for a romp in the snow, Holli turned to the
wizard with an expectant look.

"You know something, don't you?" she asked.

Enin looked to the floor with a grim expression.

"Ryson is destined for more challenges," he said with a hollow ring.

"That's not what I'm talking about," Holli quickly responded. "I already know Ryson has yet another moment that he must face that is probably important to us all. I gathered that from your discussion with Linda when she asked you to warn Tabris. This doesn't have to do with Ryson. Something else is happening that's weighing on you, something that is happening right now, something that is very bad. You have the power to stop whatever it is, but you believe such an act would be a mistake. Am I correct?"

"You are. I have always acknowledged your perception, and it appears to be serving you well yet again."

"We're all going to find out what this is, that's why you told Ryson. We're going to eventually hear about this and you knew he would wonder why you didn't do anything to prevent it. Whatever it is, it must be rather large in scope."

"It is," Enin acknowledged. "With Tabris' help, Sazar is about to take Connel.

Holli considered this news carefully. "This does not bode well for anyone in this region. A city that large in the hands of a serp and a sorceress has treacherous consequences. All of the elf camps in Dark Spruce will view this as a major shift. Normally, goblins would keep to the cover of the trees and thus were more of a threat to my kind then the humans, but not anymore. Connel is a gateway to the plains of the east and the human farms. There are forts to the east, but the goblins will simply avoid them. This will be clearly viewed as a start to a goblin-human war. Will you do nothing to prevent it?"

"I believe there is little I can do."

"No," Holli stated clearly and without hesitation. "There is little you are willing to do. There is a difference."

"Didn't you hear what I told Ryson?" Enin shot back. "Anything I do is an open invitation for Baannat to act in an opposing fashion. If I interfere here, where will he interfere?"

"Let us leave Baannat for a moment and talk about you. Whether you wish to admit it or not, Ryson was right. You have acted in the past. You have even possibly interfered, but perhaps you just don't realize it. Every time a spell caster comes here seeking guidance from you and you give it, you have inserted yourself in what may come to pass in the future."

"But I don't actually guide these people," Enin insisted. "I give them something to think about and send them on their way. The choices they make are up to them, and thus I

don't interfere. I also don't make good magic casters stronger or evil ones weaker. I treat
everyone equal."

"You made me stronger; considerably stronger in fact. My power as a magic caster
has grown significantly since I have joined you."

"That is true, and for that we can actually thank Tabris."

Holli cast a doubtful eye at the wizard. "And why is that?"

"Tabris was neutral, then she turned to evil. That opened the way for me to make you
stronger and yet maintain the balance. And that is exactly what I'm talking about. Tabris'
actions allowed me the opportunity to make you stronger as a force of good just as my
actions might allow Baannat an opportunity to act in a terrible way."

"You were determined to increase my power before you learned of Tabris' choice,"
Holli noted. "You made that a stipulation of my being your guard and that occurred
before Tabris joined with Sazar."

"Yes, I did, but there was a reason for that as well. At that time, I was still slightly
stronger then Baannat and could afford to work with you. If I tipped the balance slightly,
it would not have been enough to affect the total balance because it was already in my
favor. However when Tabris turned, it opened the door very wide. Even though I have
been able to enhance your powers far beyond what I originally planned, Baannat was still
unable to gain strength because evil was strengthened through Tabris' choice. In fact,
Baannat actually lost strength compared to me. That in itself should illustrate why I must
be careful in what I do."

"This is all very confusing to me," Holli admitted. "You're trying to tell me you can't
act in some ways because it will allow Baannat to counteract what you do. If you
overreach, you will make Baannat stronger."

"That is precisely what I mean."

Holli remained doubtful and made such sentiments clear. "I will have to think on
this."

#

Sazar had sent Chal to listen to one of the human messenger. When the serp heard the
offer of surrender, he commanded Chal to change certain provisions. He would not meet
the mayor at the border of the city, but rather several roadways deeper just north of the
city center. In order to guarantee his safety, he would have his shags and spiders move
from their current positions to the very edge of the city limits. That way, if anything
happened to him, his followers would be in position to exact retribution. His hook hawks
would remain overhead, but would stay at high altitudes, and his massive goblin horde
would not move one step closer to the city. The mayor could either accept these changes,
or expect the entire horde to enter the city within moments. Sazar knew the answer before
another human messenger returned with the acceptance of Sazar's demands.

The serp now stood in front of Mayor Flisher listening to her chatter on about women
and children within the center of the city. The useless sentiments bored Sazar, but he
appeared to be interested in order to carry out the final stages of his plan. He nodded here
and there, raised an eyebrow and did his best to appear considerate.

During the meeting, the sky became much brighter and the sun appeared to fight for
dominance through the cloud filled sky. The snow storm quietly diminished into a small
flurry and though the ground was fully covered, the depth of the snow lacked any true
significance. The light wind that made the earlier snowflakes dance had since died

completely away, and the air was silent and still. Everything appeared peaceful and calm,
covered by a thin blanket of white, everything of course but the dark horde that encircled
the city.

"I would also like to send our cavalry out of the city and past your goblins
unmolested," the mayor remarked. "I will order them out of the area completely. They
will not attack your followers. Instead they will leave through the south and then turn east
and head out into the plains."

This was the first thing the woman said that actually sparked an ounce of interest in
the serp. His head nodded back and forth for a moment as he made certain considerations
of his own.

"Granted," Sazar allowed. "Send word to them immediately. They must leave now
without delay."

Captain Tevor could not remain silent. "May I have a moment with you mayor before you agree on this?"

The mayor looked to Sazar for his approval and when the serp nodded to her, she moved back several steps to confer with the guard captain.

"Why would you send our elite forces out of the city?" he demanded with a tone he tried to keep respectful. "You are leaving us defenseless."

"We are already defenseless against these goblins. Look, I'm actually doing this based on your recommendations. You said if we were going to fight, you would have sent the cavalry out in an attempt to escape, so I'm just following your plan."

"That was if we were going to fight," Tevor corrected, "not surrender. Many of the men you expect to leave have families here. They will not wish to go."

"I appreciate that, and for the sake of their families you have to order them to go," Mayor Flisher stated in an almost pleading fashion. "We have one chance to get out of this and that's to give the serp what he wants and hope he leaves us alone. If he doesn't, we are going to need help. If your cavalry can get to Fort Nebran without casualties, they can warn the forces there of what we are facing. Perhaps they can come to our aide and the cavalry can return in full force. What other choice do we have?"

Realizing that with dozens of shags and nearly twice as many bloat spiders already at the city borders, there were no choices left for them and the captain agreed.

"Give the order right away," the mayor demanded. "I want to get them out before he changes his mind."

While the mayor and the Captain Tevor discussed their options, Chal could not restrain his own curiosity.

"Why would you allow the human forces to leave?" the goblin asked of Sazar.

"Very simple," Sazar said in a tone that almost hummed with satisfaction. "I wish to conquer and control this city, not destroy it. This cavalry she speaks of is the most dangerous contingent of humans I face. If I remove them from the area without violence, I reduce casualties on both sides. I also diminish their forces without diminishing my own. Finally, with less of their militia within the confines of the city, there will be less insurrection among these humans. They will be much more willing to follow my orders."

The mayor returned to the serp before he could say more.

"I have instructed Captain Tevor to give the order to the cavalry. They are already mounted so they will be leaving in moments. Please instruct your forces to let them pass peacefully."

"I shall do so now."

The serp did not move. He sent a command to all his forces not to interfere with the
human contingent on horseback. He also sent another command, one to his bloat spiders.
With this complete, he turned his attention back to the human leader of the city that was
assuredly now under his control.

"What else is it you would like to propose?" the serp asked.

"Will you not send a message to your forces regarding our cavalry?" the mayor
demanded with an alarmed expression.

"I have already done so," Sazar responded as he raised an eyebrow. "Perhaps all of
you here should understand that I do not need to move from this spot to command my
entire army. I do not need to speak to communicate my desires. If you doubt this, then all
you have to do is listen. You will hear no clamor to the south, no screams, no sounds of

battle. Your cavalry is moving right now as we speak out of the city. I see what my forces
see and so I know it is true."

Both the captain and the mayor eyed the serp with suspicion but then turned an ear to
the south. Indeed, they heard nothing that would indicate any disturbance. They allowed
long moments to pass and still all remained quiet.

"I will ask again," Sazar interrupted them, "what else would you like to propose?"

The mayor appeared momentarily flustered but quickly regained her composure.

"I would ask that you leave the citizens within the city center alone. They are
civilians."

"They are humans, I will do with them what I will."

This answer stunned Mayor Flisher even further. At first she didn't know what to say.
Eventually, she hoped to make another plea toward mercy.

"You asked what my proposals were. I will turn over whatever supplies you require
without resistance. I will restrain the citizens and the armed forces to the center of the
city so that you may take what you want without harassment. I will have supply carts
gathered for you and allow you as much time as needed to load them with whatever you
want. Take what you will, but leave the citizens unharmed."

The serp stared into the mayor's eyes and almost laughed.

"I will take the city itself," the serp stated gleefully. "You think I am here simply to
raid your supplies and be on my way. I have some very unhappy news for you. I am here
to stay. That was my intention from the beginning."

"But what would you want with our city?" the mayor asked frantically.

"Everything. The structures of this place shall house my minions, your supplies will
feed them and arm them. The people of this place shall serve them. This place will
become the first human city to fall under my rule."

"You can't be serious!" the mayor cried.

Captain Tevor said nothing. He considered all that had happened in the past few
moments and realized that if the serp wanted the city, there was very little he could do to
delay him, let alone stop him.

"In fact, it is truly already mine," Sazar stated with confidence. "I want you to see
something. Walk with me now."

Sazar turned about and headed north back to the outskirts of the city. After passing a
few alleys and side roads, he could see one of his bloat spiders apparently dangling in the
air suspended over the main road that led out of this section of town and into the northern
plains. As they walked closer, it became apparent that the swollen body of the spider was
actually clinging to an enormous web that stretched across the street from one end to the

other. The few remaining snow flakes that drifted out of the sky stuck to the web strands,
making them appear thicker and of uneven size.

The mayor and Captain Tevor stared at the hideous creature in the center of the web. Its dark brown body was heavy and very round with small patches of thick hair
protruding from different areas. Its six legs were narrow and seemed inadequate in
strength to hold the disproportionate sized body. At its mouth waited the tips of two small
fangs that protruded out of protective sacks.

"A bloat spider can make a web of this size in a very short amount of time. This one
started the moment you gave your order to the cavalry to leave. Others have since begun
making similar webs all around your city. At this point, they are close to successfully

blocking nearly every road exiting the city. You could not escape if you wanted to. I
know which areas remain unblocked and I have order my shags to guard them. My
goblins will now use these to enter the city."

Sazar then gave a mental command to the enormous shag that served as his body
guard. The monster dashed out of a dark alley and quickly took hold of the bewildered
mayor. As the monster ran toward the web, she froze in terror in the grip of the shag.

"Captain," Sazar commanded, "do not do anything rash. For the sake of your men that
are waiting at the city center, you need to be alive to ensure their survival."

Captain Tevor was forced to watch as the shag threw mayor Flisher into the web very
near the face of the bloat spider. The creature's two front legs pulled the mayor closer
toward it as the remaining four limbs clung to the web to keep it supported. The spider
wasted no poison on its victim for it was too hungry. The fangs pierced the mayor at her
left side just above her waist and the insect began to feed immediately.

Without poison to numb her, the mayor felt everything and her screams could be
heard far into the distance. She flailed with the one arm that had not been caught in the
unbreakable grip of the spider's web, but it only made dull thuds against the creature's
thick hide. After agonizing moments that seemed more like an eternity, her screams died
down to whispered cries and then silence.

Sazar looked to Tevor and spoke without glee, without satisfaction, but with a tone of
unheralded seriousness.

"Captain, I'm allowing you to live because of all the people in this city, I believe you
will understand the situation the best. You would have preferred to fight then to
surrender, even if it meant death. Death in the clutches of a bloat spider, however, is not
quite the same as death in battle. The truth of the matter is that I now control your city
and battle is no longer an option.

"Your elite fighters are now gone. Access to the city is under my complete power. The
spiders have restricted access and shags now control the streets. My hook hawks and
razor crows provide surveillance and can strike at any point in the city. The full
compliment of my goblin horde is now entering the city through the only clear passages
my spiders have allowed. They now take cover in your very structures.

"I am aware you have foot soldiers that were moved from outer entrenchments into
the center of the city to protect the civilian population. They are truly insufficient in
force. There is no way they could possibly break out of the city to escape, thus they are

stuck where they are. The interior of your city has suffered the most damage from the
dwarves and it is not truly a defensible position. Put simply, I would not even have to
attack the remnants of your militia. I could cut off the supplies, pick off your inhabitants
from a distance with goblin crossbow fire, send in my hawks, or simply burn the interior
of the city to the ground. I'm telling you this so you understand the situation."

"I understand it fine," the captain growled with hate.

"Actually, you don't," Sazar corrected him. "I am aware that humans cling to hope,
even when hope is small. The hope I give you is this; I will allow the people of this city
to return to their normal activities, at least for the most part. The farmers will return to
their farms to grow food, miners will return to the hills to mine metals, and your artisans
will be set to do the work they are trained to do. The only difference is that they are now
doing their work for me.

"Your city suffered a great loss in numbers from the dwarf attack. That much is obvious. With a reduced population, your farms around the city provide a great surplus of food. The people of this town will continue to be fed. The surplus, however, will belong to me and my army. What the miners take from the ground will be used to make armor and weapons, and again, they will belong to me. Those humans that do not farm or do not mine will be required to work toward making weapons, supply carts, armor, or anything else I need.

"Do not mistake my offer as a chance for escape. The goblins will patrol the farms, the shags the hills, and my flying minions will remain in the skies over and around the city. Anyone that is caught trying to escape will be thrown to the bloat spiders. Anyone unwilling to work will be thrown to the bloat spiders. Anyone trying to disrupt my supplies will be thrown to the bloat spiders. If anyone disobeys any of my rules, they will be… well, you get the idea now don't you.

"You can look at it that I am taking everything from you, or you can look at it as I'm giving you a chance to live. You will wake, work, eat, and sleep, and yes it will be toward my benefit, but you will live. As long as you live there is hope that one day you might be freed. I suggest you take the proper perspective."

Chapter 17

Sazar eyed the human before him with a great deal of puzzlement. Normally, the serp
gained a keen insight simply by looking at a person. He could judge their character, their
honesty or lack thereof, and their personality within the first few moments, and he would
usually be fairly accurate in his assessment. He already knew a bit about this man,
however, and what he knew didn't fit with what he saw.

He knew that Edward Consprite gained the favor of a powerful vampire. He also knew
that at one time this man was the mayor of the city the serp now occupied. This should
indicate the human had guile, savvy, as well as strong leadership qualities. Further,
Consprite's association with the vampire would have made Sazar bet most of his goblin
army that the man was gifted with a great deal of charisma; that Consprite would have
filled any room he entered with a great presence of personality. Sazar would have lost
that bet.

Consprite had made his appearance known by simply walking out into the open. He
had moved directly to a goblin in the streets as if walking up to a town guard to ask for
directions. This particular goblin was under orders to assess the human occupation of an
undamaged dwelling close to the city's western border. The ex-mayor stepped in front of
the diminutive monster and grumbled that he was Edward Consprite and wanted to see
Sazar. The goblin almost made the dreadful mistake of plunging a short sword into the
man's belly. This would have certainly caused unnecessary conflict with Janindise.
Luckily, however, Sazar caught the exchange in his mind and commanded the goblin to
send the human forward before any damage was done.

Consprite had walked through the streets with a determined pace, but his legs
appeared stiff and his feet shuffled across the ground. With clothes that appeared far too
large for his frame and a slouch in his shoulders, he appeared more of a transient hobo
than a man that once held the position of leadership in this city. And though his
appearance would seem to indicate a severe lack of self-confidence, in absolute
opposition to this, he walked by shags and packs of goblins with utter disregard.

Sazar had kept an active mental link to the minions that watched Consprite pass
through the streets. The images he captured contrasted greatly with what he anticipated.
When Consprite had reached his final destination, a large merchant's home that the serp

now called home, he saw the man enter without fanfare or grace, but with all the dignity
of a pauper entering a soup kitchen. Sazar could not fathom how this man gained the
favor of a vampire, and with Consprite now standing right before him, the concept was
even more bizarre.

Consprite appeared more of an empty shell than a vibrant living being. The skin
around his eyes and cheeks hung heavy with many wrinkles as it did around his neck and
hands. This loose skin along with a gray pallor made the human look like a man that had
been lost at sea for days on end. What was left of his hair hung long and loose about his
head as if long ago he decided not to bother cutting or combing it.

Truly, this was not what Sazar expected, and the serp gained another surprise when he
looked in the man's eyes. He did not see the bubbling spark of life there, or charisma of
any type. This was not a man that could hypnotize you with his eyes and thus didn't
worry about the rest of his appearance. What Sazar saw in the eyes of this man was a

single-minded focus, a disregard for everything else that went on around him. Consprite
was here to talk to Sazar and anything else was simply irrelevant. Sazar acknowledged
the man before him with caution as well as curiosity.

"Good day, Mr. Consprite. As you must already know, I am Sazar. As I am also sure
you already know I have met your friend. She told me you have the idea that you might
be of some assistance to me. I must be brutally honest, I'm not quite sure of what
someone like you can do for me."

"What I can do for you all depends on what you want," Consprite spewed his words
with gruffness.

"What I want I am well on my way to achieving. The city is mine."

"Yes, it seems to be," Consprite replied with almost a tone of sarcasm. "You have
them surrounded, you have taken the outer limits, but you have not yet moved into the
inner portions of the city. Why not?"

Sazar seemed a bit taken aback by Consprite's question. First, when the ex-mayor
spoke of 'them', he clearly differentiated himself from the rest of the citizens of Connel.
Second, he appeared to be questioning Sazar almost as if the serp was a subordinate.
That, the serp did not like.

"Are you in some rush?" Sazar asked.

"How long it takes is irrelevant to me, but when you say the city is yours you need to
be a bit more specific. You said you weren't sure what I could do for you. I am quite sure
I can offer you something. The problem is I don't know what you really want. I know the
people of this city. I know how they will react."

"Then you know if I simply rush my army into the center of the city, it will only create
panic. I'm not looking to do that, panic is messy, and it lacks control."

Consprite squinted at the serp, mumbled something incoherently and then began to
pace around the room.

"So you don't want to just kill them all," Consprite said as he continued to move
about. "If you did, you wouldn't care how messy it was. Actually, I'm guessing the
goblins you have at your beck and call would enjoy it more if it was very messy."

"That's very perceptive of you," the serp hummed.

"And don't bother trying to compliment me. I really don't care what you think of me."

"Is that so? It is you that came to me," the serp pointed out. "You are the one that said
you can help me. If I don't think highly of you, why would I trust you to help me?"

"Because I know I can help you," Consprite replied brusquely. "It's just a matter of
figuring out how. If you did want to kill everyone here, I'm sure you can handle that on

your own, but if you want to know where they keep their most valuable supplies,
wouldn't it be easier if I simply told you rather than have your goblins waste time
searching for it."

"Yes I suppose it would."

"Is that what you want? Do you want to claim this town's most valuable possessions?"

"That is certainly part of it," Sazar confirmed, "and perhaps you can help me with
that. There is, however, more to it than simply taking the material items of value."

"What else are you looking for?"

Sazar saw no true danger in making it very clear what he wanted, and so he spoke
without hesitation.

"I am going to take everything this city has to offer me, both substantial and insubstantial. I will not be leaving it in the foreseeable future. It will become the center of my operations as I focus on growing my army. When my forces become stronger, which now they certainly will, I will begin to move eastward. I do not limit my ambitions to the borders of Connel."

"I see, and what do you plan to do with the humans that live here now?"

"I plan to have them serve me. They will grow my food, mine my metals, and fashion my weapons."

"If they resist?" Consprite asked but showed no true concern.

"They will die most unpleasantly. I have already made an example of one of them, their mayor, a human named Flisher. Do you know of her?"

"I do," Consprite grunted. "She's dead?"

"Most painfully, I assure you."

In truth, Consprite hated Flisher, though there were others he hated more. Still, he wondered aloud if it was such a good idea to remove her so quickly. "If you plan to keep the inhabitants of the city under your control was it such a good idea to kill their leader? She wasn't a real threat to you and she could have been used to keep order."

"I did not like her," Sazar admitted. "While she appeared to understand the situation, I don't think she would have effectively conveyed the seriousness of the situation to her followers. By dying as she did, she served my purposes much more efficiently."

"So who's going to keep the people in line now that she's gone?"

"Are you volunteering?" Sazar asked with an almost challenging tone.

"Absolutely not," Consprite replied resolutely. "While I still believe I can help you, I'm sure it wouldn't be in that way. These people mean nothing to me any more and they know it. They wouldn't listen to me any more than they would listen to one of your goblins."

"Very good," the serp nodded. "At the very least, I can see you have a grasp of the situation and do not waste my time in making promises you obviously couldn't keep. As it stands, I have someone that I will use to keep the people in line, as you put it. I already have utilized your Captain Tevor to carry my message to the humans. He will be much more convincing when he explains to them what they face and what they must do. He will also keep his men in check, at least for a while until he realizes there really is no hope left for them. Then I will probably have to throw him to the bloat spiders as well. By then, I will have taken full control of the city and it will no longer matter."

It was Sazar's turn to pace across the floor, and as he did his tail swayed back and
forth with his own thoughts. He considered what he just learned of Consprite. Here was a
human that did not like the people of Connel, and they probably shared no love for him.
Consprite developed a close relationship with a vampire and showed no reservations in
dealing with shags, goblins, or even a serp. In every way, this human appeared to be
acting in a very non-human way. This consideration brought to mind one of Sazar's more
immediate problems.

While Sazar needed Captain Tevor to keep the humans in check, at least for the
immediate future, he also needed someone to help him in another area. For Captain Tevor
to remain useful to Sazar he needed to be respected and, even more so, trusted by the
humans that the serp wished to control. This other role that Sazar required necessitated
characteristics of just the opposite. Sazar believed that Consprite offered him exactly

what he needed, and he offered up his considerations freely in order to judge if his
estimation was correct.

"Actually, Edward Consprite, there is something that you might be able to do for me. I
have one problem that I am somewhat concerned about. You see, some of the people of
this town must be, oh how shall I put it, perhaps sacrificed is the proper word. I made an
agreement with a sorceress in the Lacobian Desert. My part of the agreement requires
that I supply her with subjects so that she may test her spells. I clearly plan to send some
of these humans to her, but I have not yet figured out the best way to do this. I wish to
maintain control here, and I want the humans to believe that they will ultimately be
allowed to live even if it is under my rule. As long as they believe the life I offer them is
better than being thrown to a bloat spider, I believe they will remain useful to me. If,
however, they realize that many of them will be sent to their deaths at the hands of an
experimenting sorceress, they might get other ideas. They might actually rebel, and that is
my problem."

"So you need to select humans that you can send out into the desert without alarming
the entire population?" Consprite asked with little regard to the implications of such a
dilemma.

"You understand very well," Sazar said.

"That is a problem I can solve for you without hesitation," Consprite answered with
almost a note of glee in his voice. "I know exactly where to get your first group of
subjects, and the rest of this town will not care one bit. They may even be pleased to see
them go."

"Really?"

"There is a Church of Godson in this city," Consprite now noted with more disgust
than cheer. "I suggest you start with them."

The serp showed a sign of amazement at such a suggestion.

"You think I should base the selection of people on some religious segmentation? Do
you really think that is wise? I like to believe I understand humans, at least to a degree.
Their beliefs in religious matters tend to stir some rather interesting passions. To me, that
seems very dangerous."

"Don't kid yourself. This is not some established, respected church. They are nothing
but a bunch of loons. They will not be missed. And it certainly will not stir any kind of
concern in the rest of the people here."

"I would imagine the Church of Godson might have gained new respect," Sazar
wondered aloud. "After all, their beliefs contain such creatures as goblins, and shags, and

even serps. Now that the people face such creatures in reality, I would have guessed that
more humans might have sought out this church."

"Oh yes, they have grown in number," Consprite admitted, "but not so drastically that
they outnumber those that mistrust them. Many in this city even blame them. Not many
here are happy with what has happened since the sphere was destroyed. I'm sure that now
you're here, they're even more unhappy. But the followers of that church, they were
ready to accept all of this before it even happened. A lot of people think they even
welcomed it. How do you think people that are surrounded by goblins are going to feel
about a church that welcomed the return of dark creatures?"

"You have a point. Still, I believe care is required. I don't want it made known exactly what is going on. I would like to see these people removed from the city without alarming the rest of the population."

"That's the beauty of it," Consprite said. "They keep to themselves as it is. All you have to do is go to their church and you can probably find several dozen there right now. Keep them isolated and send them out to the desert in small groups. No one else has to know or will even care what's going on."

Sazar placed a finger to his chin and tapped a long nail against his cheek and began to pace once more.

"It's certainly an easy way to start," Sazar hummed to himself. "The first few days will pose the most challenges in maintaining control. I doubt Tabris will be patient enough to give me more time. No, I have to prove to her that I will maintain my part of the bargain, so I must begin sending her something immediately."

Sazar turned about and faced Consprite directly. "Ahhh well, it seems the best alternative I have. I stand corrected; you have proved to be of assistance to me. I also wish to make further use of you. I will send you to this Church of Godson with a small party of goblins and two shags. You will see to it that a number of humans, let us say ten to begin with, are removed from this church and sent to the western outskirts of the city. I will instruct my goblins to transport the humans from there to the desert."

"I have no problem with that."

"That might be, but I'm not quite finished just yet. If I'm going to fully trust you with this endeavor, however, there are things I must know about you."

"Such as?"

"How is it that you have fallen under the protection of this vampire, Janindise?" Sazar asked.

"I have no problem telling you that, either. No problem at all. I was the mayor of this city when the sphere of Ingar freed itself from Sanctum. I learned a great deal about things at that time. I learned there is power far greater than political power, that being mayor of a city really meant nothing—as Ms. Flisher apparently found out today. The magic the sphere contained was power, but only if you have the skill to use it. Unfortunately, I do not have such a skill."

"Does this story have a point, and if so, will it answer my question?" the serp interrupted.

"Fine, you want the short version. There was a delver named Ryson Acumen that was hired to find out about the sphere. I had this delver followed. My first tracker died, but I

never give up easily. After an encounter with this delver right here in Connel, things
spiraled downhill quickly. I was removed as mayor. I decided to hire additional trackers
to pick up the trail of Acumen to find out every place he had traveled. With nothing else
to do, I followed along, learning as much as I could. During these travels, we happened
upon Janindise. She would not attack us, so I was able to speak with her. She asked what
brought me to her, and I told her the truth, that I had been retracing the steps of Ryson
Acumen. It seems she hates the delver as much as I do. In this, we found common
ground, and I make no effort to hide that fact. I was out of money and unable to convince
the trackers to work with a vampire that could only move at night. The trackers left me. I,
however, understood that Janindise could be a great asset. I stayed with her, even
convinced her to return with me to Connel."

"And why does Janindise hate this delver?" the serp inquired.

"That is her business, and I do not speak of it. One of the reasons she graces me with her companionship is that I respect her wishes. She has no problem with me revealing our mutual hate for Ryson Acumen, but she has made it clear she does not like to speak of her experience with the delver."

"I see. I do have one last question before you leave. Why do you wish to be assistance to me in the first place?"

"When you cut me off before, I tried to tell you I have a new understanding of power. I see such power in you. I do not fear you because Janindise protects me. When I prove my worth to you, I will gain yet another ally. Power is in the friends you keep, even if you might not be able to trust them."

#

The mood in the Church of Goodson did not quite match that of the rest of the human population in Connel. Certainly, there was fear and anxiety over the encroaching goblin horde, but not to the same extent as from those that hid in dark basements or empty alleys. On the faces of the followers that sat in the unassuming church, there hung a simple acceptance, as if these people almost expected what was happening on this terrible day.

If this were any other place within the city limits, when Edward Consprite walked through the large doors accompanied by two large shags and followed by a half dozen goblins, panic would have exploded throughout everyone present. In this church, however, the followers simply remained silent and began to pray silently.

The spiritual leader of the church, Reader Matthew made no attempt to calm the other followers of Godson. There was no need. Instead, he simply took a deep breath, and with the help of two canes, hopped up to the ex-mayor with grudging acceptance of who was before him. It didn't take long for Matthew to recognize Consprite. Though the ex-mayor was thinner and older in appearance, Matthew could always recognize the deep seeded hate that languished in the eyes of this man.

"Hello Matthew," Consprite said with obvious contempt to the Church of Godson's leader. "I can see by the look in your eyes you remember me, even though my appearance has changed somewhat. That's good."

Reader Matthew simply nodded as he eyed the ex-mayor and the two large shags that stood on either side of him. The stench of the two monsters began to fill the room and in order to keep from gagging, the reader was forced to take short shallow breaths through his mouth.

Consprite looked over Reader Matthew and regarded the stump that took the place of
his left leg. "I'm going to guess that occurred during the dwarf attack. Am I correct?"

Reader Matthew bit down any anger and answered with an even tone.

"Yes, I lost my leg to a dwarf ax. I still manage to get around."

"Yes, with two canes and a good deal of hopping. It must get rather tiring."

"I manage. Now, if you don't mind, the people here are very alarmed with what's
going on. The presence of these two shags is adding to that concern. May I ask what you
want here?"

Consprite looked over the rows of benches that were half full with silent followers of
Godson.

"They don't look alarmed."

"Would you prefer they ran screaming out any exit they could find?"

"All exits are blocked on the outside," Consprite remarked with a smirk.

"How comforting."

"Still I am curious," Consprite admitted. "I would have expected much more concern among your followers considering what's going on outside. You have heard of what's going on, haven't you?"

"We are well aware of the situation," Matthew replied, but his calm demeanor made it seem as if nothing of any great importance was going on outside the walls of his church.

Consprite continued to find the reader's reaction most perplexing, even slightly annoying.

"And here I am with two shags at my side and you walk right up to me as if I'm an invited guest. You don't think that's surprising?"

"As I said before, what would you have me do?"

"I would have you explain to me what's going on here before I decide to have these shags start tearing your church apart." Consprite warned.

Reader Matthew looked over his shoulders to those that remained seated but now appeared a bit more anxious over the shags in their midst. He nodded his head and turned his attention back to the ex-mayor.

"This is from the Book of Godson," the reader offered, and he began to quote text from the book that represented his faith. "'And the dark ring will come to the last plain city, diminished but not destroyed. In the whiteness of night, that which was silent shall be heard. Not an arrow shall fly, not a blade broken and still the city shall fall.'"

Reader Matthew paused as he raised his eyebrows toward the ex-mayor. Consprite did not reply, other than a shrug, and Mathew explained further.

"That may sound confusing to you, but we knew what those words meant before this serp of yours even came to this land. 'The last plain city' is Connel, the final city of the farmland plains before the Colad Mountains. 'Diminished but not destroyed'—certainly the dwarves put great damage to the city, but we were not quite destroyed. 'The whiteness of night', I'm sure that sounds very confusing until you think of the snow that fell last night. And for the last part, the goblins were silent, but then they shrieked when they wanted us to see them. Connel has fallen into the serp's hands and yet there was no true battle. This prophesy was explained clearly to us many seasons ago, by a special person who is no longer with us. He understood the prophesies clearly and he told us what they meant before the sphere ever broke free from Sanctum Mountain. You see, we knew this would all happen long before this day ever came."

"So you think that because your book of fairy tales told you the goblins would take the
city that this would somehow save you?" Consprite questioned with more than a hint of
sarcasm.

"Save us? No, only Godson can save us, but that's not what you asked. You wanted to
know why we could appear so calm in the face of such danger. We are not happy about
what is going on, but we realize it's all part of Godson's plan. Giving in to panic would
not help us, only faith can help us."

"I'm happy to hear that," Consprite laughed. "I didn't want to ruin any false hopes.
The truth of the matter is that you are anything but saved. You wanted to know why I was
here. I am here for a good long time, and no one is leaving this place until I send them
away. You see, the serp that now rules Connel is in need of some humans. It seems he

made a deal with a sorceress out in the desert. This sorceress wishes to practice her
newfound craft, but there really isn't anything out in the desert other than some
scorpions. She needs something a bit bigger. Knowing you as well as I do, I felt you and
your followers would be perfect for the task. The serp asked me to select ten of your
followers and send them to the Lacobian so they might assist the sorceress in her practice.
What do you think about that?"

Reader Matthew adjusted his stance so he could hold both canes in his left hand while
he kept his weight balanced on his remaining leg. He pulled a worn book from his pocket
and he began to read.

"'A snake will walk out of the sand but to the hot wind he pays his mind. Those of
faith must retrace the path to appease a witch's bargain.'" Upon completing that passage,
Matthew looked back to the former mayor. "Would you like to read that yourself? It's
right here."

Matthew opened the book wider and held it out for Consprite to see. The ex-mayor
slapped it out of his hand, but Matthew simply watched it fly to the floor and did nothing
more.

"That's not a problem," Matthew revealed. "I have the book memorized by now.
What's important is that you understand that none of this will weaken our faith."

"Is that so?" Consprite growled. "Well, since you're so prepared for this, I will give
you the honor of selecting the first ten. You will go back to your followers and pick out
six men and four women, make one a child, I don't care which, and these ten will be sent
to the Lacobian."

Matthew stiffened his back and looked defiantly into Consprite's eyes. "I will not.
You can order these beasts to rip my arms off, and then my remaining leg. You can throw
me to the bloat spiders I've heard encase this city. I will not do what you ask. You can
threaten me with anything, but I will not do your dirty work for you."

In a moment of pure defiance, Reader Matthew held out his right arm to the largest of
the two shags and waited for Consprite to give whatever order came to his depraved
mind.

Consprite, however, showed his depravity went much further then Matthew would
have considered. He turned to the large shag and gave his order.

"Take him," Consprite then yelled to one of the goblins behind him, "but he is not one
of the ten. He will go to the Lacobian with the ten and all that follow. He is to watch as
every member of his church is turned over to the will of the sorceress. You are to make

sure that message is given to her. He is not to die until the last of this church's followers
are exhausted. Then hopefully she will test a particularly painful spell on him."

Consprite then looked into the eyes of Matthew as he hung in the tight clutches of the
shag. "I will pick the ten and then ten after that. I will review the logs of this church and
make sure that every member of your church is located no matter where they are hiding. I
will send them all and you will watch them die."

Reader Matthew threw no curse at the ex-mayor. He simply asked a question.

"Don't you want to hear how this is all going to turn out? Aren't you interested in
what's going to happen to this city? Let me give you one last quote. 'An enemy past, a
friend in the future, a debt repaid in full. Cities linked, one below saved by the light of
speed, one above rescued by what moves in shrouded passage.' I know what that means,
but I have no desire to tell you. May Godson have mercy on your soul."

"No one is going to have mercy on yours," Consprite retorted. "And I could care less
what's in your book of fairy tales. Get him out of here."

#

Up in the dark rafters of Connel's Church of Godson, a silent Lief Woodson watched
with an anger growing within him. His fury boiled until he felt the rage running further
up in his throat, but he managed to remain quiet. At one point, he took an arrow from his
quiver and readied his bow to fire at Consprite's heart. Unfortunately, he also knew a
very real truth, and so he never took the shot.

Even if he killed Consprite at this very moment, he would only gain the people of this
church a momentary reprieve. He could not defeat the whole goblin army or get these
people past the shags and bloat spiders that surrounded the city. Sazar remained beyond
his reach, always protected by hook hawks and other dark creatures. Killing Consprite
would not free Connel, and thus the people of this church would still end up being sent to
Tabris.

He returned the arrow to his quiver and cursed silently. If he was going to truly save
these people, he needed help.

Chapter 18

Sy considered what he heard so far from the elf. The news was grim, but not
completely unexpected. The captain of Burbon's guard knew something of significance
had transpired to the east, and he made it clear that the report the elf gave him was not
truly a surprise.

"I've had reports come in from all different sources over the past day and a half," Sy
confirmed. "I've heard from scouts and merchants traveling the roads. It's been pretty
clear Connel was the target of something big. None of the news was good, and most of it
came from fairly reliable sources. It's getting rather common to hear about strange events
and strange creatures, especially from those that travel this far out. When reports start to
pile up, though, you know it's time to worry. I was just about call to for Ryson and ask
him to go scout the farmlands to the west of Connel when I was sent word you were at
the gate."

Lief Woodson waved aside any need for such an endeavor. "I can tell you anything
you need to know. I have been tracking the goblin movements for some time. I was
hoping they would lead me to Sazar. Unfortunately, I never was able to pinpoint the serp,
though I am absolutely sure he is in control and currently in the city."

"From what you've told me, I would have to agree." Sy shook his head in disgust. "I
knew this serp was going to be a problem the first time I saw him. I just didn't dream he
could cause this much trouble."

"Indeed, he is now a great danger. His army is large and well coordinated. They
moved through the forest with a single purpose, and yet they never formed into one large
unit until they hit the hills outside of Dark Spruce. When they came together, they moved
with care and avoided detection until they were ready to attack. They took over the city
without resistance. "

"The fact they took the city without having to fight isn't really a great surprise to me,
either," Sy said. "Connel was pretty much devastated by the dwarves. I know they were
focusing on rebuilding their army ever since the dwarf attack. They seemed to be moving
fairly well along to that end, but there's no way they could have trained enough soldiers
in this short of time to really form an effective brigade. From my reports, the only unit of
any true experience that was not decimated by the dwarves was their cavalry."

"Their cavalry left the city under the banner of surrender. They were allowed to leave

without casualties. They moved out of the city from the south and then turned due east.
They rode out well beyond the farmlands, beyond my sight."

Sy raised an eyebrow. "Really?"

The conversation was interrupted as three individuals quickly entered Sy's command
post. Lief Woodson had asked for Ryson and the wizard Enin, but he was more than
somewhat surprised to see Holli. The sight of her opened up a painful wound.

"So here is where you've decided to live out your exile?" Lief asked of the elf guard.

"It seemed reasonable," Holli replied simply.

"An elf guard living among humans? Even if it is a human town you have previously
helped protect, even if there are those here that you can call friend, it seems very wrong.
You were trained to protect the elves of the forest."

"Now I am training in a different way. While I do feel I help protect the people of this
town, my true duty is to the wizard."

Lief eyed Enin, but Sy cut off the conversation.

"Lief asked that I bring you here," the captain stated with authority. "He has some
rather bad news. We were all wondering what Sazar would do when he teamed up with
the sorceress, well now we know. An exceptionally large force of goblins reinforced with
shags, hook hawks, and razor crows has taken Connel."

"Connel was attacked?" Ryson blurted out in obvious concern.

"Attacked is not the appropriate word," Sy responded quickly. "From what I have
heard, the goblins encircled the city and forced a surrender. Every report I have,
including from Lief who was in the city at the time, indicates that the people in Connel
surrendered and there were very little casualties."

"This can't be right," Ryson argued. "How could he force Connel to surrender? He's a
lousy serp."

"A serp with the assistance of a powerful sorceress," Sy reminded him. "Lief has
reported to me the size of the goblin army was massive enough to completely surround
the city. You know how big Connel is. Think of how many goblins it would take to
encircle the whole city. Now add some shags for support and hook hawks for aerial
assaults and it's not unreasonable to believe that Connel surrendered, especially after the
beating they took from the dwarves."

"But why Connel?" Ryson persisted, "And what's he doing there now?"

"As your captain stated," Lief answered, "I have been in Connel. The serp appears to
want to hold the city for his own gain. He has used the goblins not to kill the inhabitants
but to control them. He has herded them into Connel's center. Bloat spiders encircle the
city at its very edges. They have spun vast webs to block access to the city. Those few
roads that are clear are guarded carefully. I have heard his orders as they were delivered
to the people that live there. They are to toil for the serp's behalf. For the most part, they
will be allowed to resume their daily lives, as long as what they do serves the better good
of Sazar. Just call them slaves."

Ryson grew more enraged by the moment. "He's just going to take over Connel and
work the people to a slow death?"

"I'm afraid for some death will come much quicker," Lief continued with what he
knew of Sazar's plans. "While most will be allowed to live in order to benefit Sazar, the
followers of Godson, they are another matter entirely. Sazar needs to send humans to
Tabris so that she may test her spells upon them. I assume it is payment for the power she

has granted him. The human that was mayor of Connel when we were dealing with
Ingar's sphere—the one named Consprite—he has somehow joined the ranks of Sazar.
He has convinced the serp that this group of Godson followers would be the best to send
to Tabris. Of this, I am sure. I heard it myself and saw them take the first prisoners from
the church to be brought to the Lacobian Desert. This included their leader, the Reader
Matthew. They left before I did and are therefore already on their way to Tabris. And
when those followers are no more, you can bet he will send another group and another
group, and on and on."

"We can't let this happen!" Ryson demanded.

"No, we can't," the elf answered bluntly. "That's why I'm here. I could do nothing
alone. In fact there is little that anyone could do except…"

Lief turned to Enin. He was about to continue until he looked deeply at the expression on the wizard's face. He then looked at Holli and his suspicion was confirmed.

"You knew this!" Lief accused. "You knew Connel had fallen to Sazar."

"Yes, I did," Enin admitted sadly.

"And you did nothing to stop it?!"

"No, it is not my place."

Lief's eyes opened in wide shock. "I came here to gain your assistance. I thought once you knew of what was going on you would be more than willing to put an end to this. You have the power to wipe the city clean of Sazar's filth."

"Power?" Enin questioned. "People say I have been blessed with power. That is only partially true. What I really have been blessed with is a true and complete understanding of that power. That is the true gift I have received. I understand what I can and can't do; what I should and shouldn't do. I understand the gift can be changed at any time or taken away completely. I always act within the boundaries of that understanding."

"What in the name of Godson does that mean?" Lief demanded.

"It means I can't interfere."

Rage filled the elf. "Interfere?! This is not interference. It is your responsibility, your duty! Fire upon your soul if you do nothing! You alone have the power to destroy this dark army and you would stand there and tell me you won't because you think it would be interfering?!"

Enin held to his position. "It would be."

At this point even Ryson regarded Enin's words with bewilderment, and he made as such known. "Enin, this isn't interference. Sazar attacked Connel. We can't just stand here and do nothing about it. At some point, you have to accept that this serp can't be allowed to get away with anything he wants. People, good people, are going to die. You can stop it."

"And when I do and free Connel, where does it end?" Enin asked. "Tomorrow I hear that goblins are raiding an outpost near the Colad Mountains, do I go there and destroy them or is an outpost too small to care about? The next day I find that river rogues are attacking a small elf camp, do I assist them or should I just worry about humans? The day after that I hear that razor crows are swarming over an algor desert community, do I wipe the air clear of them, or should I simply keep my attention on these surrounding lands?"

He paused only for a moment to look around the room at the faces that revealed more surprise than understanding. He continued with his own concerns of the consequences to his actions.

"And when I'm done providing my assistance to all those I deem worthy, what
happens next? I have opened the door for every spell-caster in the land to do the same.
The problem is that each spell caster may not be of like mind. Perhaps there are sorcerers
out there that wish to help the dark creatures. Would that be just as acceptable?"

"Help the dark creatures?" Lief asked in absolute disgust. "What are you talking
about?"

"I'm telling you there are consequences to my decisions, consequences you don't
understand."

"What I don't understand is how you will allow an army of dark creatures to run free
and cause great harm to others. You have the ability to save these people and yet you
deny them that aid!"

"I can't tell you how much I feel for the people of Connel," Enin replied with great
empathy. "I wish I could help them, but I can not act solely on sympathy."

Sy stepped in between the elf and the wizard just as Lief was about to explode with
anger. The captain, however, turned his attention to the wizard.

"Enin, this isn't just about Connel. What's going on has put everyone here in danger.
The elf is more right than probably he even understands. It's not simply just a matter of
saving the people of Connel. We also have to save ourselves. We face all kinds of threats,
some of them direct, some of them indirect. I swore to protect the people of this town.
Keeping them safe also means keeping them alive. No one is going to be left living here
for long with Connel in Sazar's hands"

"If Sazar is foolish enough to attack here, I will defend my home." Enin stated simply.
"If it comes to that, then it is not interfering. If I am brought into the conflict, then I am
free to act. There is a difference, however, between defending and attacking."

Sy stood silent as if trying to comprehend what the wizard just said to him. He
revealed that he could not.

"I have to admit, I don't understand your logic at all," Sy stated firmly. "You're not
making any sense whatsoever, but that doesn't even matter. If you're telling me you can
defend your home, then you best start thinking about doing it now. I was serious when I
said we were in danger. I meant all of us, everyone in Burbon."

Holli presented a question of her own at this point. "You think Sazar would attack
Burbon in greater numbers to offset the wizard's power?"

Sy looked at Holli only for a moment. He looked back at the wizard with a discerning
eye. He spoke of Enin with brutal honesty.

"I'm not even sure how to answer that right now. I've got the feeling Sazar could
increase his numbers a hundredfold and he still wouldn't be a true threat to Enin. Truth is,
I wonder if anything could offset his power, if he's willing to use it. But it seems like he's
unwilling unless he's attacked directly. The problem is Sazar doesn't have to attack us
directly. He doesn't have to come to Burbon's walls, he can starve us out. We depend on
Connel's farms for food and supplies. With those cut off from us, we don't have many
options. I mean really, what can we do? How long can we last? Maybe we can start
farming the surrounding fields and hope to protect them, but how long will that take?
Maybe we can even hunt in Dark Spruce, but that's going to be tough going during the
dormant season. What then, Enin? Will you help us destroy Sazar's army when we start

to starve?"

Enin said nothing.

Sy simply turned away from the wizard. "Well, I'm not going to wait for an answer
from you because I already know enough of what's going on out there." Sy then pointed
to the map on his wall. "Even before the dormant season began, I've had my scouts go on
long patrols. I've sent Ryson out dozens of times to cover areas throughout Dark Spruce
and up to the Colad Mountains. Each time I ask them to report on the number of goblin
raiding parties they come across. I've been keeping track of their movements and
numbers for some time and the information is anything but encouraging news. Their
numbers are swelling by leaps and bounds. I have no idea how they end up appearing in
this land, but I know more come each day. Before today I thought they were broken up,
splintered in hundreds, maybe thousands of small groups all over Dark Spruce, the Colad
Mountains, and Godson knows where else. But now it seems like Sazar is bringing them

together. He's apparently brought enough together to take Connel, but the thing is, I don't
think he's done yet. I think he's only got a fraction of what's out there.

"Now, think for a moment what happens when all these goblin packs that are spread
over the forest, the mountains, and maybe even the desert hear that a serp has taken a
human town the size of Connel. You don't think for a moment they're not going to seize
on this and head for Connel? How many will end up there? Would anyone have the time
to count that high? And once they're there, what do they do? They storm every
surrounding farm and take everything they can lay their hands on. And what do we do?

"The simple point is we are not in an enviable position anymore. I don't care how
powerful Enin is. We now sit with Connel controlled by Sazar. He's got Godson knows
how many goblins and who knows what other creatures. Our supply lines are now in very
grave danger. We have Pinesway abandoned, so no help there. Dark Spruce is right on
our doorstep, past that to the Northwest is the Colad Mountains and more dangerous
creatures. To the southwest is the Lacobian Desert and I don't even want to think what
might be waiting for us out there. Yes, we had it good for a while thinking that none of
these creatures would dare anger our good wizard, but those days ended when Sazar took
Connel."

Sy paused then turned to the delver. "Ryson you told me about what you saw at
Pinesway, when that sword of yours gave you a vision of what Sazar wanted then. He
wanted to make Pinesway a breeding ground for goblins to grow his army. Do you think
he wants any thing different now? Problem is it's not an abandoned little town at the edge
of Dark Spruce. It's Connel on the edge of some of the richest farmland around. He's
going to make humans work on those farms for him. Put this all together and it's not a
good story for anyone, especially us."

"So what do we do?" Ryson asked.

Sy looked one last time at Enin, but when the wizard offered nothing further, the
captain took control. "We need to hit the serp now. We hit him with whatever we can
muster. We either drive him and his forces out of Connel, or we have to actually start
thinking about evacuating Burbon, moving east out of his reach."

"And how do you intend on forcing his goblin army out of Connel," Holli asked. "I
have seen your guard in action against the dwarves and I know your current strength.
They are excellent defenders, but this action would call for offensive tactics. They would

be vastly outnumbered with the goblins fully entrenched in the city. These are not
welcoming odds for you."

"No, they are not," Sy admitted, "and I have no intention of leading my soldiers on a
suicide mission. There is, however, sufficient help to the east. Fort Nebran lies within a
days ride, additional outposts exist less than a day away from the fort. Lief has also told
me that the contingent of Connel's cavalry escaped to the east when the city surrendered.
I would bet my best horse that they went to Nebran as well. When they hear what's going
on at Connel, they're not going to need much incentive to return.

"I've had dealings with the officers at Nebran before, and believe me they know the
score. They're thankful that our town sits between the farmlands and Dark Spruce. Word
has spread of Enin and they know Burbon serves a nice buffer. When they hear an army
of dark creatures has bypassed us and taken Connel, they'll know that they're the next
target in line. If we consolidate all our numbers, we can assemble a sufficient force to at
least have a chance. With a little luck, we might be able to take back the city."

Holli offered one last bit of concern. "What of the bloat spiders? Lief said they have encased most of the city with their webs. How can we attack the city if we can't get through the webs?"

"Actually, I believe the spiders will at first work to our advantage. It's not just a matter of limiting what enters the city, it's also a point to consider how fast Sazar can get his forces out of the city. He may not be able to meet us in the open field. If we know that in advance, we can make it work to our advantage." Sy turned to Lief. "This does, however, raise a question. If the city exits have been covered by the webs of bloat spiders, how did you manage to get out?"

Lief responded without hesitation. His tone held the simple ring of truth as opposed to any arrogance in what he was able to accomplish. "I am an elf, not a human. I can climb up and down the sides of your structures. The spiders only covered the free paths of the streets knowing that humans would not be able to jump rooftop to rooftop to avoid their webs. They did not know an elf was present within the city."

It was then Ryson that raised a concern of his own. "What about the people trapped in Connel?"

Sy frowned and did not answer.

Ryson pressed with his own understanding of the matter. "If you attack Connel, those people in there are going to be trapped with the goblins. Sazar could use them as hostages or simply kill them to keep them from getting in the way."

"The city is surrounded by webs, Ryson," Sy reminded him. "I can't get them out. There's no secret passage way that's going to get them out. I don't have that kind of magic."

Everyone looked at Enin, but the wizard simply stared at the floor. Ryson, however, quickly ended the uneasy silence as his face lit up like a flare.

"But there is!" Ryson exclaimed.

"Is what?" Sy demanded.

"A secret passage, there is a secret passage. Remember the dwarves attacked Connel just like they attacked Burbon. They dug tunnels under the city and attacked by appearing in the city's center without giving Connel's army advanced warning. We can use those tunnels to get the people out."

Sy stood silent, but only for a moment. Then he quickly dampened the delver's proposal. "The dwarves blocked those tunnels after they left the city in ruins."

"They just block sections, so the humans couldn't use them to follow them back to Dunop."

"Exactly, that means we can't get through them to get to Connel. It's enough of a

block that we wouldn't be able to dig through in time. We can't wait forever to hit Sazar.
We have to do it now."

"We couldn't dig through, but the dwarves could."

"You think the dwarves are going to help us?" Sy questioned. "The dwarves didn't
just attack Connel, they attacked Burbon as well. And it wasn't just a small disagreement,
it was a nasty battle. We lost a lot of lives and they lost much more. Our wizard here
decided to help then and we forced them to retreat. Now I know you told me that they
attacked because their queen ordered them to and I know she's gone now, but it's hard
for me to believe the dwarves are going to be willing to assist us after all of that."

"They owe us, or at least they owe me," Ryson said simply. "I saved Dunop from the
shadow trees. I also asked for the Cliff Behemoths to come to Dunop. They did and
stopped the sand giants. All I'm asking is for them to do is to clear a few tunnels so we
can get to Connel. They owe me that much."

"They may not think they owe you anything at all," Sy responded flatly.

Lief turned to Sy and declared his own considerations. "No, they are stubborn, they
are greedy, they are arrogant, but they are also very proud. They understand that the
delver saved their city. That, they can not deny, and thus they can not deny the debt they
owe him. For them to turn down a simple request would be beyond my comprehension. I
believe they will have to do what he asks out of their own desire to clear that debt. To
deny him that simple request would be an act of dishonor. I believe that would be beyond
them."

As Sy looked silently at the map on his wall, he considered the many factors they now
faced. In his mind, he calculated the risks of involving the dwarves and the advantages of
freeing the humans of Connel. At the same time, he ran through different scenarios in his
head regarding the possible upcoming battles with the goblins entrenched in the city.

"Let me just think about this for a moment," Sy stated as he continued to review his
map. "Maybe, just maybe we can use Sazar's own tactics against him. He surrounded the
city to cut them off from any hope of escape. We can cut them off in the same way, cut
them off and keep them focused on what's happening just outside the city."

Sy made a quick calculation of the forces he would need and the soldiers he believed
would be available for the attack.

"Actually, this could all work in our favor if we time it right," the captain offered as
he turned his attention to Ryson and Lief. "If you really think we can get the dwarves to
open up those tunnels for us, we might have a chance to get those people out of there. We
all have to realize that you're not just going to be able to guide them all out under Sazar's
nose, but if I can get a sizeable force to attack the city, Sazar can't afford to watch over
the people they've got caught in there. We start the attack right at nightfall at the
perimeter and Sazar is going to have his attention on us. At the same time, you can start
moving as many people out as you can. Even if we fail to initially defeat Sazar, we can
still succeed by removing his work force. On the outside of the city, we would have him

surrounded. Maybe we can't get him out of Connel, but at least we would have him
contained, and with no prisoners, no hostages, and no way to get out to the farmlands.
Also, he won't be able to send humans to Tabris. If we're right about what's going on
with her, that's going to hurt his relationship with her. If she suddenly decides to break
off the deal and strip him of any extra powers, I'm guessing he goes back to being a
regular serp and he won't be able to control that many creatures scattered all over Connel.
Even if that doesn't work, we can even think about just burning the city to the ground."

Holli nodded. "It is a sound plan. You would also succeed in cutting off any new dark
creatures from joining Sazar."

"Exactly," Sy agreed. "We're still going to have to try and do everything we can to
engage the goblin horde to keep them occupied, but at least now we have other options
available to us if we can't get them out of the city."

Ryson now offered his own understanding of what needed to be done. "It has to be me
that goes to Dunop. I'm the one that has to make the request. You also can't send any of

your soldiers with me through the caves. It will slow me down and I need to rely on
speed."

"I don't intend to. I agree with you and I also can't afford to spare any. The few that I
can leave behind will have to guard Burbon. I was hoping, however, that Lief would go
with you. You can use another pair of eyes, and from what I've seen, an elf won't slow
you down that much."

"I can live with that," Ryson stated as he looked to Lief expectantly.

"I shall accompany you," Lief agreed with little fanfare.

Ryson considered the events that transpired the last time the two were together and
wondered if Lief would be able to control his anger in the midst of so many dark
creatures. "You realize we have to go unnoticed, especially when we are in Connel, so
you can't simply run off and start attacking the goblins. Our objective is to get everyone
out alive, not to start a war once we get in there."

Lief's eyes narrowed. "You might no longer believe this, but I can maintain control
when necessary. I was able to get in and out of Connel without being noticed. Do you
think I could have accomplished that if I just started attacking goblins?"

"No, I guess not," Ryson conceded. "I just wanted to make sure we agree on what our
main purpose was here."

The elf simply heaved a heavy sigh.

"I wish to accompany them as well," Holli interjected. "I can help them and while we
need to keep the party small, I think three is better than two. We can all move swiftly and
quietly. When we reach the inner streets of Burbon, I can assist in guiding the humans to
the tunnels."

Enin finally spoke up. "You wish to go with them?"

"I need to go with them," Holli answered. "I feel it is my responsibility."

"How so?" the wizard asked.

"You said that when Tabris decided to join with Sazar it represented her turn toward
an evil path. By your own admission, you used that decision as the reason you were
willing to make me stronger. If she did not turn toward evil, I truly wonder if you would
have trained me at all. That being the case, I believe that I must do all that I can to
counteract any evil this sorceress does. She is responsible for Sazar gaining control of so
many creatures. Without her power, he would be left to raid abandoned outposts in the
northern wilds. Do you understand?"

"Whether I understand or not is immaterial," the wizard said revealing little emotion.
"If you wish to go with them, that's your choice."

"It is not my choice alone. I came here to be your guard, thus my first duty is to you. If you do not want me to go, if you don't see the need, then I would stay here. I have to answer to my duty, and that is to you."

"No, your first duty is to yourself." Enin looked about at everyone in the room. "I know all of you don't think to highly of me right now, but perhaps this will help explain, even if it is only slightly." The wizard turned back to Holli. "I've spoken at length about choice and not interfering. You have a choice, as does everyone in this room. If you believe it is important for you to go with them, then I would never stand in your way. I will not take that choice from you. Everyone here wants me to solve this problem. I've tried to make it clear that there are consequences in that action. I know my arguments

seem weak in the face of what everyone is talking about, but you all need to decide for
yourselves what you must do."

Enin turned and walked to the door. "I still want you as my guard when you return,
but more importantly, I want you to do what you think is right. Good luck to all of you."

Without waiting for anyone to respond, he walked out the door.

Sy did not let the silence last. He had already begun working out his plans and he now
wanted to move quickly. "How long do you think it will take for you to get to Dunop,
convince the dwarves to help get the tunnels cleared, and get into Connel?"

"Getting to Dunop is easy," Ryson answered. "Not sure how long it will take for us to
see someone of authority to convince them to help us. That's the true unknown. When I
left last time, Jon Folarok was basically comatose. He had withdrawn in the wake of
Yave's rebellion against him and he showed no sign of coming out soon." Ryson turned
to the elves. "Do either of you have an idea of what's going on down there?"

Lief spoke up first. "When we delivered Petiole to the dwarf city, Jon Folarok was still
king. There appeared to be order in the city and we have heard no further rumors about
the dwarf separatists that wished to end the rule of the monarchy."

Holli concurred. "Every report I heard revealed stability has returned to Dunop."

"Well at least that's good news," Ryson replied with a show of relief. "Just about
every dwarf down there is going to remember me and my sword. I ran around the whole
city to kill the shadow trees, so I don't think there will be a problem getting in. Once
we're in we need to accompany the dwarves to the tunnels to Connel and allow them time
to clear them."

"Dwarf construction is a marvel to watch," Lief added. "It will take little time for
them to clear a path."

Ryson made a quick calculation based on that. "Dunop isn't that far from Connel, so if
everything goes smoothly, it should only be three or four days."

Sy nodded in satisfaction. "I'll give you a couple of extra days as a buffer. I'm going
to need time to assemble the forces I need to take care of my part. I'll organize the guard
here today, determine what I need and what I should leave behind to guard Burbon, and
then we'll ride for Fort Nebran. With their aide, I can have the force ready to move on
Connel in three days. It will take another day to reach Connel from the Fort."

Sy tapped his fingers on the desk in a counting fashion before continuing. "We will
begin our attack during the evening, right before nightfall, six days out from today. You

should already be under Connel at that time. When you hear us attacking and you believe
its dark enough, you can begin. Get topside and start sending as many people as you can
to the tunnels. Hopefully, in the cover of darkness, Sazar's attention should be focused on
us. If they do spot the humans fleeing, they will think they are seeking shelter from the
coming battle. I doubt Sazar will care about them."

Sy tried to play out the battle in his mind. He considered the sequence of events and
revealed his own hopes. "I honestly believe we can raise enough of a force to surround
Connel. That will be more than enough to keep Sazar focused on us. Whatever happens
during the battle, we won't make any attempt to move toward the inner sections of the
city until daylight, if at all. Some of this is going to depend on how Sazar reacts, but all of
our assaults will be focused on the outskirts of the city. As we attack, it should draw more
of their forces to the city's outer boundaries. With just the three of you, you're going to
have to move fast, but I've seen you all move and if you coordinate it well, I think you

have a good chance of getting a large portion of them out of there. Is there anything I'm
overlooking?"

Lief pointed out one potential problem. "We must all be wary of the hook hawks and
the razor crows. With their ability to fly over the city, Sazar will have eyes that can see
great distances."

"Good point. Not sure if there's anything we can do about them, but I'll work on it.
Anything else?"

Holli offered what she knew. "Bloat spider webs are difficult to cut, but they will
burn. They will not burst into flame, so the surrounding structures should not be in
danger of catching fire, especially with the current cold in the air. The problem is it takes
time for the smoldering strands to break apart, by that time, the spider is aware of your
presence and will attack."

"Good to know, anything else?"

No one responded. Sy offered his last sentiment. "We know what we have to do. As
Enin said, good luck to all of us."

Chapter 19

"I don't want to seem like an ungrateful person," Linda began as she spoke to Enin
alone in his library. "I asked you to go to speak to Tabris and you did. I was grateful then,
and I still am now. The problem is I need to know why you did this."

Enin began to speak, stopped, fumbled with his hands, and started over. "I did so
because, as you said, you asked me to. I believe everyone in this town owes you a debt of
gratitude."

"You told me that last time. I appreciate it, but there's something missing, something
you're not telling me."

"How do you mean?"

Linda circled about the room as if she was getting her words in order before she spoke
them aloud. "Before Ryson left for Dunop, he told me what was going on. He told me
Connel had surrendered to Sazar and that with Tabris' power Sazar was now a great
threat. He also told me how Sy and most of Burbon's guard are riding out to Fort Nebran
to get aide so they could try and get Sazar out of the city. From what I'm hearing, we're
all in a lot of danger, from Burbon to Fort Nebran and maybe beyond that. Many people
are going to risk their lives again."

"Are you worried about Ryson's safety again?" Enin interrupted.

"Actually, no, I'm not. He told me he was going into the center of the city through the
dwarf tunnels. That he was going to help people escape from Connel, not fight the
goblins. I guess if I'm worried about anyone, I'm more worried about the soldiers that are
going to have to fight. They're the ones that are going to be in the most danger."

"I'm not sure I'm following you," Enin admitted. "What is it exactly you want to
know? Is it why I warned Tabris or why are so many people in danger?"

"Actually, it has to do with both." Linda did her best to come right out and say what
she knew. "Ryson told me you wouldn't help the people of Connel; that you said it would
be interfering."

"That is very true," admitted Enin sadly.

"Then why did you help me?" Linda stepped closer to the wizard and looked straight
into his eyes so he could not avoid her. "Why did you warn Tabris not to hurt Ryson?
Isn't that interfering?"

Enin for all his magical power did not know how to answer that question. He stood
and looked back at Linda, would not avoid her stare, but he could say nothing.

Linda pressed him. "You tried to tell me that Tabris couldn't kill Ryson, that I had
nothing to worry about, but I persisted and you agreed to help me. It seems to me that

more people need your help now, but you are not as willing to help. You're telling people
they have to deal with their own problems. If that's true, why didn't you tell me I had to
deal with my fears?"

Enin struggled for a moment and then did his best to convey his own understanding of
what he did and why he did it. "I did not truly interfere when I warned Tabris. It is not
within her to kill Ryson, it's just not a possible course of action. When I went to warn her
on your request, I told her something she would have found out on her own. She even
told me as much. Nothing I did by going to the desert affected anyone's choice."

"That's not true," Linda said firmly. "It affected my choice. I could have simply listened to your advice and tried to deal with my fears, but I didn't. I insisted you go, and you did. Why would you do this for me and not help the people that are trapped in Connel? And please don't tell me it's because I'm the reason Ryson stays in Burbon. I know that's not the whole story. You did this for another reason, something that has to do with me. I know that, and I need to know what it is."

Enin folded his hands in front of him. He would not try to avoid the matter any further. As Linda had done her best to speak directly to the point as possible, it was now his turn.

"You know you can not touch the magic?" Enin asked.

This simple question forced Linda to look away. Enin, however, was now the persistent one in driving the conversation.

"You wish to know why I helped you."

"Yes," Linda answered in a trembling voice, "and yes I know I can't touch the magic."

"You are an amazing force in that manner. It is beyond being resistant. You are immune to it, you actually repel it. I do not think it can affect you in any way."

Linda attempted to end the discussion of this particular topic. "I don't want to talk about how I can or can't use magic. I want to talk about why you helped me."

"That is what I'm talking about. I'm trying to explain why I felt it was necessary to go to Tabris for you. Because you have this special gift, there are things…"

"You call it a gift?" Linda interrupted him.

"Absolutely, just as I am gifted to use the magic in extraordinary ways, you are gifted to be completely immune to it. That means it can not harm you. In this new world we now live in, that is a tremendous advantage. Think about that for a moment. Magic is a powerful energy. It is making sweeping changes across the land that no sane person could have expected. Go back to the last dormant season when we didn't know about Ingar's sphere or magic beyond a simple card trick. Try to tell me that anyone could have imagined the dark creatures that now walk the land would actually exist in anything other than a fairy tale. And look at me. I'm a wizard with power on an unimaginable scale. And now look at you, for all of my power, there's not a spell that I can cast that can harm you."

Linda did not wish to discuss the magic and refocused on the purpose that brought her here. "I don't know anything about that, but I know it doesn't explain why you would help me and you won't help others."

Enin appeared to grow more than slightly irritated at this comment. "First of all, I'm
more than willing to help others. I'm just not willing to interfere on such a large scale.
Second, if you allow me to finish you will understand that it does explain why I went to
Tabris for you."

Linda bit down on her lip and remained quiet as Enin continued.

"I realize that because you can not feel or touch the magic in any way, it is more of a
mystery to you than perhaps any other being in this land. Very few have the ability to cast
spells of any significance, but even those that are not spell casters can at least sense the
magic. Perhaps that's why there's not mass chaos. In the backs of their minds, people
know that the magic is present and that this explains to them the reason for the enormous
changes we face. There really is no other answer. You just can't take a bunch of goblins,

shags, river rogues and Godson knows what else is out there, throw them into the midst
of reasonable people and not expect them to wonder about their own sanity. But if they
already know something in the very air is different, then they can step back from the
chaos and not lose their minds.

"Now, let's consider someone that can't sense the magic—someone like you. You are
holding onto reason simply because everyone else is much more accepting of the
situation. Still, it has to be beyond unnerving to you. You can't sense the energy because
you can't touch it in anyway, and it can't touch you. You have no inner connection with
the magic. If you did, you would have some insight that the power itself is not inherently
evil and that it is not meant to harm us. The rest of us that can touch the magic, even in
small ways, understand that this energy can be used for great things. Magic does not
cause pain, does not cause hardship. It is corrupt beings that use the power with evil
intentions that cause the troubles we face. You, however, can not touch the magic, so it
remains an absolute unknown to you.

"When you came to me and explained your worries of Tabris, I understood them far
better than you realized. Tabris threatened Ryson and Tabris is a very powerful sorceress.
The magic she controls is an aberration to you. It was as if your worst fears were coming
to life. Now I knew that Ryson could not be truly hurt by Tabris, but because of your
fears, you could not accept that. As I have said before, by warning Tabris I did not
interfere in any way in what might come to pass. All I did was assist you in facing
something you did not have the ability to face on your own."

Linda stared at the ground. She did not look up when she asked the question she now
very much needed an answer to.

"How do you know that Tabris can't hurt Ryson? How do you really know that?"

Enin almost cursed. In the end, he decided to reveal what he knew. "The magic allows
me to see the destinies of others. I often see what people must face in the future. I am
aware that Ryson must face another great challenge. He can not avoid it. It must happen.
Because of that, I can predict that nothing will prevent him from facing that challenge.
Tabris understood this as well when I told her that. If she indeed had any plans to seek
out Ryson, they died at that moment because she knew it would be a waste of her time
and effort. Do you see? I didn't interfere. I didn't sway anyone's choice. I simply told her
what was obvious to me."

Linda appeared to accept this at face value, but then asked the obvious question.
"What is this challenge Ryson has to face?"

Enin turned stoic, his voice flat with simple determination. "That is something I can not reveal to you, at least not now. I was not against warning Tabris for you for all the reasons I explained, but I can not begin revealing things without considering all the consequences that might follow. Anything I say might change your outlook, or Ryson's, and that would indeed be interfering. It is not my place to simply divulge these things on a whim, so please do not ask again."

Linda was certainly not happy with this answer, but for the moment, she did not press that specific issue. There was, however, more she wanted to know. "Do you see destiny in all people?"

"Most people, but not all," Enin stated plainly enough. "I'm not sure why. That's just the way it is."

"Do you see a destiny in me?"

"No, but understand that means very little because of your gift. You are immune to the
magic and thus your destiny might simply be guarded from my sight because the energies
I interact with can not touch your essence. What I believe, however, is that most people
eventually figure out their destiny. They make choices based on who they are, what they
have become, how they have lived their lives, but in the end, we all tend to reach a point
where we have to face something whether we like it or not. At that point, we face our
destiny by dealing with it the best way we know how."

With this, Enin had finally said something that might not have made complete sense to
Linda, but she was able to take hold of it in her own mind. She seized upon it and made
her own understanding clear. "You're talking about knowing what we're supposed to
do," she stated with renewed confidence. "Sometimes we don't know what we're doing
or why we're doing things, but at some point, certain things become very clear to us. I
don't need magic to do that. My destiny is to help Ryson. I know that deep inside."

Enin smiled. "I won't argue with you on that."

#

"I am Ryson Acumen. I am a friend of Jon Folarok and I wish to see him." With that
one statement and the Sword of Decree in his hand, Ryson, Lief and Holli were allowed
to pass through the streets of Dunop with a full dwarf escort. He held the weapon low at
his hip with the tip pointed to the ground. The blade magnified the light that was reflected
into this deep underground city through an elaborate configuration of mirrors.

The dwarfs they passed eyed the elves suspiciously but most bowed their heads
slightly in acknowledgement to the delver. There was no clamor of hostility, there were
no shouts of rage. Tensions were noticeably reduced since the last time Ryson and Lief
walked upon the roads of Dunop.

The delver and two elves remained calm as they traveled the impressive underground
tunnels through the city of Dunop. Even though Ryson had seen these vast caves before,
he still marveled at the impressive dwarf architecture. The most amazing structure of all
was the grand palace that stood at the heart of Dunop. It's cascading, spiraling towers
stretched from the lowest visible bowels to the highest points of the rock ceiling
overhead. They stood like mammoth pillars that supported the entire weight of the land
that rested above this city of engineering audacity.

As the three visitors were escorted into the palace, Ryson recalled the layout of these halls and realized they were being brought directly to the throne room. He wondered if he would be greeted by Jon Folarok, he wondered if Jon had perhaps recovered from his state of utter withdrawal, but all such speculations ended when he spied a dwarf woman sitting at the head of the room.

The three walked directly up to this woman and briefly bowed their heads in acknowledgement of the woman's obvious standing of authority, but none of the three recognized her.

Surprisingly, the woman smiled upon them all.

"Welcome my friends," she said in a deep, thick voice. There was sincerity in her words, that much was clear. The easy stance of her short, stout body gave every indication that she held no animosity to any of those that entered. She sat relaxed and waved her arm toward the delver with open enthusiasm. "A grateful salutation to you, Delver Acumen. You are always free to enter Dunop for its people know you as honorable. I am Therese Folarok, Queen of Dunop."

Ryson appeared very much bewildered, but tried to speak through his confusion.

"Thank you, uhmm, please don't take this the wrong way, but I didn't think there was another Folarok to take the throne. When I left, it was just Jon, and he was not in the best of conditions."

A brief hint of sadness washed across the dwarf queen's otherwise animated face.

"Unfortunately, Jon's condition has not changed since your last visit. He remains very much within himself. He will not talk to anyone and shows little regard for anything that goes on around him. As for there not being another Folarok, that was true then, but no longer true now. My great grandfather married the niece of a Folarok prince. Although I did not carry the name, I have always carried the blood. In order to bring stability to Dunop, it was conceived that I should marry Jon Folarok to take the name as well. Though Jon is still king and the acknowledged ruler of Dunop, I am accepted as the leader."

Lief kept his own tone respectful, but he could not refrain from asking the question that burned his own mind. "And do the dwarves of Dunop accept your authority?"

"There is no challenge to my role," Therese stated as a matter of fact. "Dunop has much to recover from, and the mistakes of Yave and those that wished to destroy the monarchy have received the appropriate blame."

"That's good to hear," Ryson stated with a sense of relief. Then his mind turned over the series of events described by this new queen and a curious question popped into his mind. "I don't mean to pry into your affairs, but I am confused. Jon wasn't married when I left and he was in no condition to do much of anything. If he's still withdrawn from everything, how was it possible for you to marry him?"

Therese showed no sign of holding back, no desire to try and hide the circumstances of her partnering to Jon. "Jon was able to walk with only slight assistance to the sacred alter of Krajkar which is the required setting for royal weddings. While he did not speak, he was able to nod at appropriate times. I believe he understood exactly what was going on and welcomed the situation. Since the ceremony, he has shown very slight signs of recovery. He still has a long way to go, but somehow I think he knows a great burden has been lifted from him."

"And put on you," Ryson offered.

"Fah, I was aware of that burden when I was approached by those loyal to the Folarok name. Times were, and remain, very difficult. We lost many dwarves due to Yave's misguided intentions. The sand giants caused great damage to Dunop before the Cliff behemoths arrived, and we lost an entire section of Dunop due to the shadow trees."

Therese would not look upon Lief or Holli, but she did bow her head to Ryson. "We would have lost the whole city had it not been for you. For that, I and all of Dunop wish to thank you."

"There were many mistakes made during that time, by many different people," Ryson offered. "I just did what needed to be done."

"We are still grateful."

Ryson nodded and then decided it was an appropriate time to come to the point of his meeting. "Actually, I'm glad you're grateful because I'm here now for your help."

"And what does the Delver Acumen need?" Therese asked without hesitation.

"The human city of Connel has been overrun by a goblin horde. Actually, overrun isn't the best word. The city was surrounded and forced to surrender."

"Truly? The goblins surrounded the city? They were able to amass such a number? The vermin normally do nothing but bicker among themselves."

"They did not act on their own," Ryson acknowledged. "They were led by a serp named Sazar. He brought them together and he coordinated the attack. It is by his will they control Connel and he aims to grow stronger."

"Fah, I know of this one named Sazar." Therese nearly spat upon the ground, but she remembered where she was and swallowed hard instead. "He is the scoundrel that slunk into our city and stole what his miserable hands could carry. I have made it my business to know what lowly creature took advantage of our misfortune. I was not surprised to learn it was a despicable serp."

"He is despicable, and now he's dangerous as well," Ryson said. "With Connel in his hands, he now threatens the entire region. We can't have that. We also can't let him keep the prisoners he has in the city. This is where I need the assistance of the dwarfs of Dunop."

Ryson paused only for a moment and decided not to try and dance around the subject.

"When Yave ordered Dunop to attack Connel, tunnels were used to allow the dwarf warriors to enter the center of the city. While we know sections of these tunnels have been collapsed to prevent humans access to Dunop, we still hope to make use of them.

"Our main objective is to free the human captives. This will isolate Sazar and his dark creatures. The prisoners are held in the center of the city and Sazar's minions control the outskirts. There is no access to the city above ground that is not blocked. If, however, we can reopen the tunnels, the three of us here hope to guide the prisoners out of the city through the underground passages.

"Right at this moment, the human guard of Burbon is joining forces with others in the east. They will attack the outskirts of the city while we manage the escape. What we need from you is permission to use the tunnels for our plans, and we need your dwarves to clear the blocked areas so that we can utilize them. We are not asking for anything else."

This time Therese did hesitate in answering. She took long moments to consider the proposal and during her reflections, she asked small pointed questions.

"Will anyone else accompany the three of you to go from here to Connel?"

"No, it will just be the three of us," Ryson replied. "We need to move fast and not draw great attention."

"At what time of day will the evacuation start?"

"Right at nightfall."

"How long will it take?"

"Probably the entire night. I'm not sure exactly how many people are trapped in
Connel, but it has to number in the thousands."

"How many days until this counter-assault by the human forces on Connel is planned
to begin?"

"It's also going to begin at nightfall, five days from now."

Therese seemed in absolute acceptance of the request and willing to assist the delver,
but she did place a restriction on the evacuation. "I have no problem whatsoever in
granting your request other than making one condition. You may use the tunnels to
evacuate the humans of Connel, but you can not bring them into the city of Dunop.
Understand, Delver Acumen, that I request this out of respect for the dwarves of this city.
What occurred during Yave's unlawful rule was not the true will of Dunop or the

majority of the dwarves themselves. Still, dwarves of this city attacked Connel. We
attacked unsuspecting soldiers and citizens alike out of hate and prejudice. Many realize
this now and they know shame. I can not have that shame deepened by parading the
victims of that city through these streets."

"I understand," Ryson responded. "In truth, I don't need you to offer them sanctuary
here in Dunop, just passage through the tunnels so they can escape the city."

"I am grateful for your understanding," Therese said. "These humans from Connel,
they can go anywhere the tunnels allow, do you have a preference?"

Ryson thought for a moment. "Yes, if we can send them east of Connel further into
the plains that would probably be the best alternative, the safest."

"Our tunnels do not extend very far in that direction. That is the prairie land and
controlled by the humans. There is very little of interest to us there and we have only a
few passages beyond Connel's eastern borders. Those we have do not extend very far."

"Do they extend out of sight of Connel?"

"A dwarf's sight, a human's sight, an elf's sight, or a delver's sight?" asked the dwarf
queen.

"How about the sight of a hook hawk flying directly above Connel?"

"Yes, they extend that far."

"Then that would be enough." Ryson then addressed the timing of what was needed to
be done. "How long will it take a contingent of dwarves to reach the areas that were
collapsed to seal off the tunnels to Connel?"

"A day, perhaps two."

"And to clear them?"

"Another day."

"That's better than I could have hoped," Ryson said with a smile. "The sooner we can
start the better."

"Then we shall start immediately," Therese waved over a guard and issued some
immediate orders. When he left with haste, she turned her attention back to Ryson. "I
shall have you and your two friends escorted to the Connel tunnels right now. You will
be given maps of the corridors so that you know which tunnels to utilize under Connel
and then which to use to evacuate the citizens of Connel to the east. Since you will be in
the corridors for at least 5 days, we will provide you provisions to last several days as you
wait for the proper time to enter Connel.

"A team of excavators will accompany you to the points where the tunnels were
collapsed. As I said before, it should only take them a day to make clear passage. A small
contingent of dwarf guards will also accompany you to these points, but not beyond.

They will simply ensure that no creatures use the free passage to attack Dunop. We
allowed that to happen when Sazar looted us the first time. I can not let it happen again."

"I understand."

"The dwarf guards will not accompany you into Connel. For that, you must go alone,
but rest assured the path will be obvious to you. You will not get lost in the tunnels."

"That's all I can ask for."

"Then let us begin."

Queen Therese called for an assistant to escort the three to the tunnels and provide
them with everything they needed. She thanked Ryson again as he and the two elves left
the throne room.

With the visitors now gone, Therese walked over to a table with the stride of
determined purpose. She threw herself in a heavy wooden chair and grabbed writing
materials that were placed neatly about the table top. She stared at blank parchment long
enough to organize the words in her mind. When she started writing, her hand moved
with flowing continuity. She never paused, and once finished she raised herself up from
her chair and walked over to her military advisor with the same resolve.

"I want you to prepare what's left of our assault forces for immediate action. I also
want every member of the palace guard to make ready for battle."

"May I ask why?"

"I see… an opportunity," Therese explained. She handed the parchment she completed
to her advisor. "This will explain it better."

The advisor quickly scanned the paper in his hands. He looked up at the queen with a
question. "Do you think many will join us?"

"I do, actually," the queen replied. "But this time the dwarves of Dunop must
willingly choose to join in this attack. I do not wish to order them or threaten them like
Yave did. This time Dunop must act as one without excuses and without any blame to
place on any one individual."

"I hope you are right," the advisor remarked with a dubious tone.

Therese pointed to the parchment. "Please have the scribes make copies and post them
throughout the city once the elves and delver have moved into the tunnels to Connel. I
don't want them reading this."

"It will be as you wish."

Chapter 20

The trip through the Lacobian desert was as harsh as the surrounding lands. Reader Matthew and the other ten humans forced from Connel's Church of Godson faced a painful journey. They were given little rest, less to eat, and only enough water to keep them alive. The goblins that pressed them onward were tasked with moving them as fast as possible to Tabris' oasis without having any die. Beyond that one condition, the goblins could care less if the trek was painful beyond comprehension. A suppressive dry heat nearly roasted their skin during the day and a biting hollow cold left them shivering in the dark of night.

It was at night, however, that the reader and his followers found the strength to go on. In this dark place, they saw stars they had never seen before. The sky stretched out before them and even in the empty coldness, they beheld a beauty that the goblins that pushed them or the sorceress that waited for them could not dampen. It was almost as if they could see into the very heavens where they believed Godson awaited them. In truth, many of them understood a glorious message of hope in these stars. In the vast nothingness, the dark emptiness, the stars glowed white and painted the sky with an undying belief that something so vast would contain so much more for them than an empty ending in this barren place. The desert tested their bodies, but it also strengthened their faith. That faith would serve them well once they reached their destination.

The oasis was pleasant to the eye and afforded much more agreeable conditions than the surrounding desert, but in truth, it did more to offend the followers of Godson than offer any form of relief. They understood that such a haven was not a gift out of the goodness of Godson, but a phantom sanctuary created by the will of a sorceress. They found the place repugnant, a twisting of the natural order of Godson's will.

Tabris met the members of Godson's church with indifference to them as a group but keen interest toward their individual traits. She seemed totally apathetic toward the struggles of their journey, offered them no solace. The only time she truly displayed any emotion was when she was informed that the one named Matthew was to be kept alive to watch Tabris test her powers on the other humans. She could only use him when all the other members of his church were extinguished.

"Which one of you is Matthew?" Tabris demanded.

"I am," Matthew said simply.

"Why is it that I'm now inconvenienced in having to keep you alive?"

"It's not by my request," Matthew answered.

Tabris seethed. "Making me angrier is not going to help you or your friends."

Matthew knew what he was about to attempt was pointless, but he tried to reach the woman before him anyway. It was as much an attempt to save her as it was an attempt to save those members of his church, and thus he had to try. "Don't you remember me, Lauren? That was your name when you went into Sanctum Mountain, only after you left did you take the name Tabris."

The sorceress stood silent, staring at the man before her with a mix of swirling emotions.

"I'm the Reader Matthew. I was at the Church of Godson when Stephen Clarin brought you to us. You remember Stephen, he was killed by Ingar."

Tabris continued to display only indifference even as she now clearly remembered the reader. "The Reader Matthew, yes I remember you. You had both legs back then. What happened to you?"

"I had the misfortune of meeting a dwarf axe with my thigh."

"It seems your misfortunes continue."

"Will you let them continue, Lauren?"

"My name is no longer Lauren, it is now Tabris. If this is some attempt to try and sway me to offering you mercy, don't you think it would be best not to annoy me?"

"Very well, Tabris. If you remember me, you must also remember Stephen. He brought you to us when we needed you, when the whole of Uton needed you. He had great faith in you."

Tabris shrugged. "He also died foolishly. As for my assistance at Sanctum, I now realize that it was necessary for me to become who I am. Had I not joined those fools, the sphere would have killed us all. Still, it is a shame such an artifact had to be destroyed. Knowing what I know now, I wonder if the sphere could have been altered in a way that it would not poison the land. Imagine what power I could possess if I controlled all the magical energy inside the sphere."

"When you first went to Sanctum," the reader reminded the sorceress, "it wasn't about power. Stephen brought you there to save Uton, not control it."

Tabris shrugged again. "Yes, well that was then and this is now. And now I'm learning to control the magic that is free. That is why you and your friends are here. There are spells I need to test. I wish to experiment in different ways of shaping the magic. There is only so much you can do with empty sand or snakes and scorpions. The spells I have in mind require more complexity and thus require more complex subjects. Living beings can be mixed with the magic in different ways. The magic can be used to harm or kill them, but it can also be used to change them. Twisting and shaping the energy in different ways will mean different changes. Unfortunately, until I really understand how the spell will affect an individual, I won't be able to cast anything safely. That is why you are all here."

Matthew considered the horrifying truth just revealed to him. The people of his church would face an unknown and potentially agonizing death as this sorceress treated them as nothing more than meaningless test subjects. He could not bring himself to imagine what sort of painful transformations the magical spells would have on their bodies. Hoping to stave off such a fate, he did his best to reach her once more.

"When I first met you, it was obvious you were scared of what you were becoming.
Stephen found you and you trusted him. Do you remember that trust? He would not
believe that you would hurt these people here. In fact, he knew you had great power and
that you could use it to help people. You helped get everyone through the human tier of
Sanctum. Remember what you were! Remember how you helped Ryson and the others!"

At the name of the delver, the sorceress bristled and finally emotion found her voice.
She nearly trembled with anger.

"I remember the delver well. You wish to remind me of what I was? I remember it
clearly. I did not ask for this power. I tried to stop it, but your friend the delver would not
allow it. He forced me to become what I am."

She felt the desire to cast a spell of lightning and obliterate the reader where he stood,
but then she brought her emotions under control. "I see now why you must watch while I

practice my craft. You must learn what the magic can do, what I can do. Let me show
you now."

Tabris pointed indiscriminately at a man that stood with the other believers of Godson.
She ordered those goblins that had escorted the group to separate him and place him just
outside the border of the oasis but still in clear sight and within earshot of her own voice.
She bade the goblins to leave him and move out of the way. Then, she called to the man
in an almost lifeless voice.

"What is your name?"

"Avery," the man replied without moving. He stood still and watched the sorceress
intently. It was obvious that fear began to creep into his mind, but he held his ground and
remained standing. He made no attempt to flee. He waited with his feet on the gritty hard
surface of broken rock, feeling the desert heat all around him. Only brief waves of cool
air flowed into his face from the oasis before him.

"Avery, there is a spell I've been working on for days now. I can harness the energy of
a storm. That is now child's play. It is a simple feat to bring the necessary elements
together to create a tempest of any quality. I have also already been successful in
combining the essence of an individual with the power of a storm. In truth, that was also
fairly simple. It was just a matter of transference. Build up the energy of the storm and
then meld it to the inner energy of the individual. The problem is that in that scenario the
physical body is lost to the greater power of the storm. I wish to accomplish more of the
reverse. I want to capture the power of storm and maintain the body of the individual. Do
you understand?"

Avery did not answer.

"Well, it doesn't matter if you understand or not. What I'm going to do is try and give
your body the force of a storm as opposed to giving a storm the essence of your being.
The first thing I'm going to try is a wind spin. It's basically a small tornado. I will focus
on the bottom half of your body. Your head and arms will remain untouched, but
everything below your waist will begin to spin just like a miniature tornado."

"You should not do this," Matthew pleaded. "It is wrong!"

"Be quiet," Tabris commanded but never looked at the reader. She instructed the
goblins to take hold of Matthew and to watch the others to make sure they did not
interfere. She returned her attention to Avery.

"Try to stay conscious as long as possible. I'm afraid there's not going to be much left
of you when the spell is over. I will work on that once I get the right configuration of the

spell. You see, eventually I might even like to cast this spell on myself when I have it
under full control. I envision myself crossing the desert at much greater speeds when I
can actually combine myself with something like a hurricane wind. Of course, I can only
do this when I'm sure I won't destroy myself in the process. Thus, I have to practice."

Tabris now did turn to the reader. "Anything you wish to say to Avery before I cast
my spell?"

Matthew only glared back at Tabris for a moment, then he turned his full attention to
Avery. "What she does will not last for long and then you will be with Godson forever.
Hold to that thought, and keep your faith."

Avery heard these words and actually smiled.

Tabris shook her head at the display. She concentrated deeply on the man standing in
the desert and then pulled her hands together and closed them toward her chest. She

muttered a few words as she mingled thoughts of spell fragments in her mind. In image
of what she hoped to construct took shape in her thoughts as a violet diamond of energy
appeared at her breast. Her hand took hold of the magical shape and she threw her arms
forward toward Avery. The purple magic flew from her and exploded about the man's
legs.

Avery gritted his teeth and bit back a scream for as long as he could, but as his legs
began to fling wildly in the air, he could hold back no more. He yelled in great pain as the
bottom half of his body disappeared into a swirling mass of sand and debris. His legs
were no longer visible to those that witnessed this atrocity. The upper half of his body
appeared to be centered upon a spinning top, a tiny tornado that remained in place.

The screaming continued for long drawn out moments until Avery's head went limp
and drooped over his shoulders. His arms also fell lifeless down the sides of his torso. His
hands bobbed about as his fingers fell into the swirling mass that consumed his lower
body. Very soon after he lost consciousness, the spinning ceased and the remnants of his
legs collapsed into a mound of twisted flesh and muscle as well as splintered bone. The
upper half of Avery's body crashed into the sandy rock of the desert. He was dead.

"I have learned much from this," Tabris noted, completely disregarding the remains of
Avery's body. "I believe my deal with Sazar will indeed be a bargain for me." She then
turned to Matthew with apparently great interest. "What have you learned, reader?"

At first, Matthew did not wish to answer, but then found the strength to offer his own
opinion of what just happened. "I've learned that faith is stronger than magic."

The statement momentarily caught the sorceress off guard, but she found her anger
again quickly. "If that is so, why don't you use your faith to defeat me now?"

Matthew did not move.

Tabris continued to taunt him. "If your faith is so strong, stop me and save these
others that depend on you. Save those that will be coming in the future."

Matthew looked to the ground. "It seems their faith is stronger than mine."

Tabris laughed and called for another follower of Godson.

Chapter 21

Ryson kept track of the passing days by monitoring the change in light in the tunnels.
Dwarves used thin, tubular channels that rose to the surface throughout their matrix of
catacombs, corridors and tunnels to bring air to their underground passages as well as
sunlight. While even during the height of day, the corridors would be considered dark by
most humans, the delver, elves and dwarves could see easily in the diminished light.
When night fell, the passages turned eerily dark and Ryson often pulled out the Sword of
Decree to magnify the starlight. He didn't need it to see, but at least the light chased away
the strangling darkness that consumed these tunnels.

As the dwarves finished clearing the last blockades of the corridors that led to Connel,
Holli considered the darkness as a possible hindrance to their plans.

"When we direct the humans down here, they're not going to be able to see. It's going
to be well after sunset when the evacuation should begin. There are thousands of humans
that need to be evacuated, that's going to take the entire night. That means they are going
to be in the caves, even during the greatest darkness of midnight. There will be much
going on above them and asking them exit through such a dark passage is to invite
panic."

Ryson sheathed his sword and examined the dim light of the tunnels.

"You're right," Ryson agreed. "They're not going to like what's happening as it is and
if it's this dark, many will probably panic. I could stay in the tunnels and help direct
them. With my sword unsheathed that would give more than enough light. Anyway, we
need someone down here to guide these people to the right caves."

"That task should fall to me," Holli stated. "You know Connel far better than I do.
You also have speed I can't hope to match. Connel's center is large and we have to
assume the people are spread out. You must be on the surface to spread the word of the
escape plan. Lief also must go as he has the best knowledge of the city's situation directly
after the goblins took over."

Ryson considered the point and he could not argue. "Would you argue with taking my
sword? I'm not going to want to draw attention to myself when I'm out in the open, so
I'm not going to be using it. Seems to me it would serve a better purpose down here."

"The idea has merit, but I don't like the idea of you going unarmed up into the city."

At this point, a dwarf in charge of the excavating moved forward to the elves and
delver.

"Do not concern yourselves with the lack of light," the dwarf stated gruffly. "We have anticipated such a problem and already have the answer. We have brought several light gems that we will setup in but a few moments. These tunnels are constructed to direct the light forward and redirect it down many shafts. Based on how we station the gems, we can send the light all the way to Connel as well as to the far eastern end of the corridors which will be your final destination."

Ryson nodded, but then for the first time began considering other potential problems he did not think of before. He questioned the dwarf further on what to expect.

"The tunnels that we plan on using that go eastward beyond Connel, how will we exit? Is the tunnel open at the end? If so, where will the people end up when they come back out on the surface?"

"It is open," the dwarf replied. "It breaks into a dry stream bed. If it were the start of
the growing season, it would be half filled with water. At this time, the waterways that
feed it run low before the snow melt. The humans leave it alone since it floods during
their planting season. For your purposes, it should be fine. Once your people are in the
open, they will be in the prairie lands east of Connel, not very far from several farm
outposts."

Ryson nodded happily, then he thought of his own needs.

"What about getting from the tunnel up into Connel? The people of Connel had to fill
in the outlets by now. I'm sure they didn't just leave open holes all over the place."

"They probably have, but not all. We created many access points, some of which lead
to the sub-basements of older buildings. We kept these exit points hidden so that we
could move in and out of the tunnels without being seen. They are marked on your map."

"That's actually going to work in our favor," Ryson remarked as he considered what
he was told. "We can guide people to these points and they can escape under cover as
opposed to dropping into the ground in plain site. Even if the serp and the other dark
creatures are occupied with Sy's attack, one of them is bound to notice lines of people
dropping into the ground in the middle of some road."

Lief had opened the map and was already reviewing certain sections. "This will hasten
our work. We will not have to guide the humans directly to the openings. We can direct
them to these buildings here, here and here," he said as he pointed to the map. "They can
enter the tunnels themselves and Holli can direct them down the proper passage to the
east. With luck, we may be able to pull this off. The most difficult part is going to be
spreading the word and keeping the humans from making a panicked escape."

The dwarf turned about. "The clearing is nearly complete. In but a few moments, we
will set the light gems. Your paths will be clear to you. Simply follow the direction of the
light." The dwarf kept moving but he pointed his arm out to his right side. "Remember
that direction is north. These tunnels do not curve. They are built in straight lines. Turns
will be obvious, so keep your point of reference about you and you will always know
which way is east."

"Looks like we get moving," Ryson said as he gathered up their supplies.

#

Sy rode side-by-side with Colonel Haravin the commander of Fort Nebran. Haravin
had already heard what happened to Connel from the cavalry that reached the fort days

earlier. He needed little convincing to assist Sy in his plans. In less than two days, they
combined their forces with every outpost in the region.

The entire militia rode upon horseback as it set out for Connel. For the most part, the
eastern farmlands were flat, wide open plains which allowed for the battalion to stretch
across the horizon. They moved in unison, a long unbroken line, several horses deep.
They carried spears and bows and mulled over the coming battle. Those that belonged to
Connel's cavalry took the lead. They vowed to free the city or die.

Sy looked over the impressive array of men, horses, and weapons. "He's going to see
us coming, no reason to hide. Might as well let him see our numbers and give him
something to think about."

The colonel grunted. "He won't need scouts, either. From every report I have, he's got
those blasted hook hawks circling the city. With those foul creatures in the air, he's going
to see us before we see them."

"If you were Sazar, what would you do?" Sy asked.

The colonel didn't need time to answer. "I'd stay put. He knows we didn't come out
here to just free the farmlands or retake supplies outside the city. With this many men,
our mission is pretty clear. We're going to attack. Now from what I've heard from
Connel's cavalry, he has thousands of goblins in that city. They're armed with crossbows.
If I were in charge of that force—keep them in position, that's what I'd do. If he comes
out to meet us in the open field, he gives up the advantage. He may be a bastard of a serp,
but he's not dumb. We need to give him the credit he's due. I would bet the 4th regiment
he's going to force us to come to him."

"So we're going to have to face him in Connel's streets."

The colonel had already accepted that as fact. "Indeed, and that's not going to be
easy."

"Well, it might not be easy, but if you're right, and I'm sure you are, we can make
time work for our advantage. From what Lief told me, he's going to be having the
farmers work the fields. We can start by freeing them first. We hit any goblin packs
guarding the farms hard. We can do that while it's still light. Once we have the farms
secure, we do what he did. We surround the city. Hopefully, we can make him sweat a
bit. Let's focus on our strengths."

"Aye, that's never a bad idea," the colonel replied as he clicked on his mount.

#

"It's got to be around noon," Ryson said as he inspected the light coming through the
cave and calculated the time in his head. "Sy's forces should already be advancing on the
city. They're going to hit tonight."

Holli reviewed one of the maps given to them by the dwarves. She looked down one
tunnel that led to the east and then up another that followed directly under Connel toward
its center.

"Those that will be evacuating will be coming down this tunnel and they will have to
turn here. This will send them to the east. According to the map, this tunnel goes due east
right to the exit point. Once they're moving in this direction, they can't get lost and will
have no problem getting out. That makes things much easier. We just have to make sure
they make this turn."

Ryson looked about the rock walls that made up these elaborate caves. He pulled the
Sword of Decree and pressed its point into the stone. On the opening to the eastern
passageway, he wrote the words 'Exit this Way, Go to End!' and an arrow pointing in the

proper direction. On the wall that led back toward Dunop he carved 'Do Not Enter,
Danger!' The sword left deep etchings that were clear for everyone to read.

Holli grabbed several stones and with them created a large arrow on the stone floor off
to the side that pointed in the right direction. "Yours is better, but another sign won't
hurt. It will also probably get scattered as more travel this way, but once we get the
people moving in the right direction, they will simply follow each other."

Looking back toward Connel, Holli considered the task ahead of them. She then took
another glance at the map that revealed the locations of hidden entrance points into
Connel. "Assuming the humans never discovered these two passages, I would suggest
that Ryson take this one and Lief you take that one."

She pointed to the two corridors as Lief and Ryson stood by her side. "Ryson, yours
should come up several blocks northwest of the city center and Lief's will provide access

more to the southeast. You will be several blocks apart and can thus cover more of the city. If you both move clockwise for a half circle and then turn inward and move counterclockwise you will not end up covering the same ground."

"Works for me," Ryson agreed.

"I will be waiting for them very near these passageways," Holli continued. "I will move back and forth to each as fast as I can. Tell the first few that you send to wait for my instructions once they are inside the tunnels. After that, simply tell the rest to follow those that have gone down before them. We should be able to create a constant flow. That will, in fact, be the only way we can get most of the people out by sunrise anyway. May I suggest that you take care in the first people you contact. It is important that they are capable and of strong will. I will most likely choose several of the more competent to assist in offering instructions to those that start moving down the tunnels. If any show panic up on the streets, do not approach them until much later. We can't afford panic in the tunnels, especially in the beginning."

"What of those that do not wish to leave?" Lief asked

"Move on and let them stay where they are," Holli responded firmly.

Ryson was about to argue and Holli sensed it before he spoke a word. "Ryson, we don't have time to try and convince these people what is best for them. By doing that, you risk the lives of others that are willing to leave. It is not fair to them. If there is time, we can return later, but we deal with that situation after we get as many as we can to safety."

Ryson didn't like how that sounded, but deep in his heart, he knew she was right.

"Once the evacuation is progressing and I am confident in the people I have assisting in the tunnels, I will also come to the surface. I will use this passage." She pointed to a spot at the center of the map. "While you two work inward, I can work from the center out. When we meet, we can then move to points closer to the outer edges of the city. This will be the most dangerous areas and at that point we should move together."

Ryson heaved a heavy sigh. "I guess that covers everything. We should probably start moving to our positions under the city. We'll have to separate and be ready to surface when we hear Sy attack the outskirts of the city."

#

It was late afternoon six days after Sy Fenden left for Fort Nebran when the full force of Nebran's extended cavalry struck the outlying farms within sight of Connel. Small bands of goblins patrolled the outer fields. As they turned to the east to view what

sounded like thunder, they beheld a large dark mass low on the horizon. It stretched
across the hilly fields and extended beyond their sight. One thing was very clear, it was
moving fast and moving directly toward them.

The echoing thunder grew in intensity and soon it became clear that this storm was the
force of soldiers on horseback. The rhythmic galloping of the horses pounded fear into
the black hearts of those goblins unfortunate enough to be patrolling the far eastern limits
of Connel's farmlands. Knowing there was no possible way to outrun or outflank the
angry mass of soldiers that rushed toward them like a flood during the great thaw, most
goblins dropped to the ground in balled up heaps hoping to somehow miraculously avoid
the fate before them. Miracles, however, would not belong to these goblins on this day.'
They were saved for others more deserving, and these creatures had earned their death.

If it wasn't the tip of the spear that skewered them, it was a mighty hoof that trampled them. Death was sudden and instant, the goblins unable to even scream for mercy. Every goblin in the field that could not retreat to Connel's safer borders was annihilated in that massive, angry rush.

The soldiers made no shouts of joy, no cries of victory. They knew this was only the first and easiest part of their task ahead. Instead they wore grim expressions of determination, blinking back the wind, dust, and debris that battered their faces as they rushed onward with Connel clear in their sights.

In Connel's north side within a large elegant home, Chal stumbled into his master's quarters. He moved hesitantly to the serp that stood near a window that faced west. Chal stole a quick glimpse out that window and could only see the fading red and orange of a brilliant sunset as the sun dropped below the peaks of the vast western mountain ranges.

"I'm quite aware of the attack from the east," Sazar stated before his lackey could speak. "Do not look so concerned."

"But there is a great number," Chal blurted out.

"Of course there is, did you think they would return with five soldiers in a wagon drawn but a three-legged horse? I can see what the hook hawks see, never forget that, thus I know their numbers. None of this is unexpected, actually. When I allowed the cavalry to flee to the east, I knew this was a distinct possibility. Why do you think my first act was to have the supplies in the farms moved into the city? The humans don't want us here and they're going to try and make us leave, but I have no intention of leaving."

Even in the face of Sazar's calm, Chal could not contain his growing apprehension.

"What will happen when they reach the city?"

Sazar sighed. "I assume all goblins are probably reacting like you, that's why I am receiving so much fear. Your passions are sometimes very tiring. I supposed it is time to reassure you all."

Sazar concentrated deeply and grasped every link within his mind to literally thousands of goblins within the city and beyond. He sent one blanket message to them all.

Every goblin outside the city must return at once if possible. Those to the west, flee to the forest and wait my command. Those inside the city, take your posts behind the webs. Disregard the number of humans, they can not break through into the city. When they come within range, fire upon them.

"Does that make you feel better?" Sazar asked.

Chal nodded but Sazar already felt the wave of relief flushing into his mind from
goblins throughout the city, and thus, he knew the answer before Chal replied.

"We have some fortune in this," Sazar continued to Chal. "We did not send the
humans to the mines today and so every shag is here in the city as opposed to guarding
miners in the hills. I am impressed with the contingent of soldiers the humans raised, but
it will not avail them. The shags will guard the few unblocked entrances into the city and
the humans will not be able to enter. It is surprising, however, that their timing is so poor.
The sun sets and the darkness is ours, not theirs. Still…"

Sazar stopped in the middle of his thought. He said nothing further as he grasped
tightly to the links of several special minions. He opened his being to their senses and
took hold of new knowledge.

"Something is below the city," Sazar stated with an angry edge to his voice.

                              #

Sy could see the goblins closer to the city scrambling toward the structures that made
up the outer edges of Connel. They darted quickly out of sight, and at that distance, he
could not make out where they entered the city. Still, he watched intently waiting for any
sign of the enemy creatures, wondering if they would rush out of the city to repel them.
He saw nothing to indicate such a strategy.

Sy yelled to Colonel Haravin as they raced closer toward Connel. "They're doing
exactly what you said they would! They're staying put, they're not going to meet us out
here. They're going to stick to their positions. Shame, we would have decimated them."

"Aye, I think the bastard serp figured that out when he saw us. Regardless, our initial
attack has been successful. It is time to institute the next phase." With that, the colonel
raised his hand with two fingers held upward.

A rider to Haravin's left raised a green and white flag. As he did, the long line of
galloping horses broke at the center. More and more horses dropped back away from the
middle of the line, increasing the size of the gap. As these horses moved away both to the
right and the left in an angled direction, the once unbroken line began to form two
separate and distinct V-shaped formations that pointed at each other. These formations
began to spread apart even further as the soldiers closed on Connel. The break between
the two formations widened to the point that the whole of Connel could fit through the
gap. As the riders continued forward, one formation moved to the north of the city and
the other to the south, and neither would come close enough to be in crossbow range of
any goblins waiting at Connel's edge.

Both Sy and Colonel Harkin remained together at the formation that would cross past
the south of Connel.

"That probably surprised him," Sy grinned.

"Aye, at the very least, he has something to think about." With the formation now
passing beyond Connel, the colonel raised three fingers to the flag bearer. "Time to begin
phase three."

The soldier to the colonel's left now raised a green and red flag. Those riders that
pulled back and formed the back shaft of the V-formations now raced back to their
original positions to reform one unbroken line.

"Let us now clear the western fields and let the serp wonder if we are bypassing him
to take a flanking position at Pinesway."

The thundering line of riders romped through the western lands just as they did the
farmlands to the east. They cleared the area of all goblins and even those that had
attempted to reach the trees of the forest were caught by the speeding horses. Before the
last glowing strands of the red and orange sunset died away below the mountains, the
western lands were cleansed of any dark creatures.

The cavalry line slowed and pulled to a halt. After turning completely about, the long
stretch of soldiers on horseback paused for long moments to give their mounts a
momentary rest. They cleaned their weapons, readjusted their armor and checked their
equipment. Connel now stood before them to the east as darkness now came to rest upon
the land.

Sy nodded his head toward the city. "His hook hawks are still in the air. If what I've
been told about him is true, he can see whatever the creatures he controls see. That means
he knows we haven't left."

"Aye, let's make it clear we're not going away." The colonel then gave an order to his
flag bearer. "A steady trot to the city. Surround it out of crossbow range."

The soldier replied by first holding a solid green flag that he waved twice toward the
city. He then raised a yellow flag that he twirled about like a pinwheel. The long formed
line of cavalry now moved steadily back toward Connel.

Chapter 22

Ryson's sharp delver hearing picked up the thunderous beat of horse hooves even
from his position well below ground. From the roaring vibrations, he knew that Sy had
succeeded in convincing many to join the assault. He wondered about this awe-inspiring
sight, what that many soldiers on horseback racing to the city must look like. His delver
curiosity almost got the better of him, but he recalled his true mission and buried the
desire to look upon the charge of soldiers. He would ascend through the access tunnel,
but remain focused on leading those trapped in Connel to safety.

As he began to climb toward a new light overhead—a light from an opening that
would lead to the basement of some storehouse in Connel's northwest section—Ryson
picked up another tremble in the ground, one that did not originate from the distant horses
racing toward Connel. This disturbance rattled the ground very close to him. Half-way up
the access tunnel, he stopped his own movements to better sense what was going on
around him. Moments later and just a few steps ahead, dirt and rock erupted into the
passageway as the black, grime-filled pinchers of a rock beetle burst through the narrow
cave walls.

Ryson jumped back just as the beetle pressed itself out of its own burrowed passage.
As the narrow high-jointed legs twirled the giant insect about to get a new hold of the
access way, Ryson stared in uncertainty at the large rounded body of the monster that
now blocked his path to Connel. When the creature started to propel itself forward in a
rambling motion, the delver backtracked with ease. He kept a safe distance from the thick
pinchers that glistened in the sparkling beams of light that flowed through the lower part
of the cave. Knowing he could not leave this creature alive if he hoped to evacuate people
down this passage, he had little choice but to draw the Sword of Decree.

As the glow of the blade magnified the light in the tunnel, the immense insect
recoiled. Without spinning about, it retraced its own steps backward at an alarmed pace
of frantic motion. Before the delver realized the insect's intentions, the beetle reached its
own burrowed tunnel and darted out of sight.

Ryson cursed as he deftly raced back up the access way and toward the beetle's escape
route. The delver peered into the hole and allowed the blade of his sword to enter the new
cavern, filling the passage with brilliant light. Ryson saw three different paths breaking
from the opening and could not fathom which the insect might have taken. Still, he could

not simply allow the creature to escape. It could easily return when people filled this
tunnel. That would be beyond catastrophic. He was about to venture a guess as to the
beetle's path when he heard Holli shout out.

Ryson cursed again in a moment of indecision. The elf was calling out to him, not in
fear or in panic, but in a tone that demanded his immediate attention. He took one last
glance down into the beetle's den, shook his head in disgust, and then bounded back
toward Holli.

In but an instant, Ryson saw Holli with her bow drawn. She stood between two rock
beetles. She aimed at the one in front of her. With steady precision, she released the
bowstring and let the arrow fly at the creature's head. Unfortunately, the insect dropped
its body low against the ground and the shaft shattered against the thick round shell that
covered its massive body.

"There's another one behind you!" Ryson shouted a warning.

"I'm aware of that," Holli replied. In the blink of an eye she ran directly at the monster that she had fired upon. She dove upward and forward, extending her body as high above the beetle as the cave ceiling would allow.

The large insect lurched up quickly on its two hind legs with its thick pinchers poised to attack, but its movements were no match for the nimble elf. The pinchers closed on empty air. The miss left the creature off balance and it toppled forward. It landed on its legs, however, and it twirled about to face Holli once more.

"Use your blade on the one nearest you," Holli commanded. "The sword can break through the armored hide."

Ryson did not act immediately. Instead, he set his feet below him, taking a deep breath in preparation for the strike. Almost as if the beetle could sense what was happening behind it, it rose up on its legs and skittered off to the side. Without looking back, it dropped low and propelled itself through a hole just wide enough for its body to fit through.

"Blast!" Holli shouted. "Cut the other one off! Don't let it reach that tunnel!"

This time Ryson moved swiftly and without delay. He leapt to a clear spot between the remaining beetle and the passage the other insect used to escape. He held the Sword of Decree firmly in front of him waiting for the monster to turn. It never did.

Holli drew another arrow, but before she could even place it in the bow string, the beetle's six legs thrust it toward her with unexpected speed. She had to drop the arrow as she leapt to one side of the tunnel and then used her hand against the cave wall to thrust her further away from the lunging pinchers.

Ryson leapt forward at the creature, but the instant he moved, another pair of pinchers exploded through the cave wall and nearly closed around his neck. Only his delver speed saved him as he dropped to the ground and rolled away. Completing the tumble and leaping back up to his feet, he faced the new attacker with his sword ready to strike, but the insect's head withdrew back into the darkness of yet another break in the cave wall.

At that moment, Lief appeared and without hesitation fired his bow at the beetle that continued to move toward Holli. The arrow sliced through the air and slammed into the upper joint of the insect's rear left leg. The leg quivered and then fell limp.

The loss of its hind leg left the beetle unsteady in its movement, but also much more alarmed. It no longer focused on Holli and instead skittered and skipped about on its

functioning legs, leaving the damaged one to drag along the ground. It flattened itself
against the ground and its forward legs dug furiously against the dirt and rock. Within
moments, half of its body was submerged out of sight.

Ryson stood uncertain as he watched the monster make further progress in burrowing
out of sight. "What do we do?"

"There is little we can do," Holli offered dejectedly.

Ryson pointed back down from the way he had come. "There was another one that
came at me by the northern passage. It escaped down a path that opens very near the
entrance point we were going to use."

Holli moved up and quickly inspected several of the holes made by the beetles. "That
means there are at least three, probably more. We have no idea how many. We have to
call off the evacuation."

"But we can't…"

Before Ryson could argue further, Holli explained the simple truth. "What we can't do is send defenseless people into this cavern. The serp has a connection with these creatures. Since they know we are here, he knows we are here. Regardless of what is going on near the outer edges of the city, he is not going to ignore these tunnels any further. He can use the beetles to attack, or have them collapse the tunnels. Trying to bring people down here would be the same as sending them to their death."

"Then what do we do? Getting the people out of there is part of the plan. We have…" Ryson stopped suddenly and peered down the tunnel toward Dunop. "Wait, there's more movement down there, but it's not beetles."

Both elves turned their own attention back down the cavernous passage. Their keen elf vision revealed the truth.

"The dwarves are coming and they are dressed for battle," Holli stated and quickly took a position in the center of the tunnel.

Indeed, swarming up through the cavern from Dunop came a great host of dwarves moving with grim determination. They wore full battle armor and carried mace and axe. At the front marched the dwarf queen. As she approached the three, she unexpectedly offered a smile and bid those dwarves behind her to hold their progress. She immediately acknowledged Ryson.

"Leave the beetles to us, Delver Acumen, and there is no longer a need for your evacuation." The queen then raised her left hand, pointed forward, and made four distinct clicking noises with her tongue. Several groups of dwarves charged further up the tunnel, disappearing into the various passages used by the rock beetles. The queen then turned back to the delver. "Be assured the insects will not escape us."

Ryson looked from Queen Therese to the two elves. Lief was eyeing the dwarf queen suspiciously while Holli stood stoic. Ryson could read little from her expression. Without knowing what else to do, he asked the obvious question.

"What are you doing here?"

Therese Folarok actually laughed—a throaty, hearty laugh. After a few breaths, she finally answered, but in the form of a question. "What do you think we are doing here?"

"I don't have the slightest idea," Ryson admitted honestly.

"Your elf friend here believes we are here for no good reasons," the queen said as she nodded to Lief. "And that one will not reveal her assumptions. She is well trained. I would play this game with you longer, but time is short. We have a city to cleanse of dark creatures and we wish to do it before the sun rises."

"You're going to attack the goblins?" Ryson blurted out in obvious surprise.

"Indeed, as well as any other dark creatures that must be removed."

"But why?"

Here, Therese's face lost its mirth and her tone turned deadly serious. "It is quite simple. We have wronged these humans. It is time to make amends for that wrong."

Therese looked upon the delver and saw only more confusion. She did her best to make her point clear. "You yourself pointed out these tunnels were created for us to attack the humans of Connel, and attack them we did. We offered no quarter and allowed no mercy. We took the lives of many in that battle, many that did not deserve to die. We did all of this because we wanted to believe they were a threat to us, when in truth we were the ones creating the threat. These humans had never done anything to us. In truth,

they did not even know Dunop existed until we rose upon their streets for the sole
purpose of trying to prove our own superiority."

Ryson tried to interject his own understanding. "But Yave…"

The delver was not allowed to continue as Queen Therese cut him off in mid sentence.

"…was not the only one to blame," Therese said with finality. "Yave was not alone,
and we can't simply hang this totally on the separatists that aided her for their own cause.
We all have blood on our hands. Dunop has blood on its hands, and it must be cleansed
just as we will cleanse the streets above of the horde that now infests them. You see,
Delver Acumen, sometimes it's not enough to simply acknowledge you've done great
harm. Sometimes you have to do more to rectify those mistakes."

She paused as she waved her arm behind her to the throng of dwarves that waited in
the tunnel for her orders. "Behind me is nearly every dwarf in Dunop and they are here of
their own volition, not because I ordered them here. So you can understand the weight of
what I say, understand that these dwarves volunteered for this action. They accepted it as
their duty, their responsibility. Once you departed, I posted declarations throughout
Dunop that Connel had been captured by a horde of goblins. I asked for any that wished
to assist the city to appear before the palace gates prepared for battle. This is what
showed up."

Ryson stared down the tunnel and realized the line of dwarves continued beyond his
sight. It really must have been nearly every citizen of Dunop.

"But we didn't ask for your help beyond clearing the passage," Ryson said still
amazed by what he saw.

"Fah, that barely makes up for the extensive damage we caused to the city above us.
In essence, the goblin's ability to take the city is also our fault. We weakened the
human's defenses, and thus, it is even more imperative we redeem ourselves. How can
clearing a few tunnels even begin to erase the stains on Dunop's honor?"

"I don't think anyone blames Dunop for what happened in the past," Ryson offered.

"You think not?" The queen shook her head strenuously. "I'm afraid it is not so. We
could try to place the blame on Yave and those misguided dwarves that arrogantly
desired to show dwarf strength at the expense of others. Unfortunately, the attempt would
be in vain. You can not separate the dwarves from the deed, or the deed from the
dwarves. They become one and they encompass all of us, not just a select few. Dunop
will always be known as the city of dwarves that attacked the helpless without true cause.
That is not a legacy we wish to have endure."

"But things have changed," Ryson said. "You have new leaders. Yave is gone, those
that followed her appear to be out of power. You can move on."

"I am grateful for your willingness to forgive, but you are not like many others. Know
this Delver Acumen, you showed us true honor when you saved Dunop from the shadow
trees. You did not have to do this. You were aware the dwarves of Dunop had attacked
humans in Connel. You were aware we were about to attack the town of Burbon. You
were thrown in the dungeon as a reward for trying to stop that madness, and still, you
found it within yourself to put those transgressions aside and save our city. In that
moment, you proved yourself far more worthy of admiration than any dwarf in Dunop.
That is not only a credit to you, it is a credit to those who serve with you, those you call
friend, whether they be elf or human. When we consider what we have done in the face
of such honor, we are humbled."

Therese's face suddenly brightened and she spoke with renewed vitality. "But now you give us an opportunity, a chance to remove the stain on our honor and possibly allow us to gain your friendship and respect. If so, we can then respect ourselves once more. It is our intention, all of the dwarves of Dunop, to rid the city above of those despicable creatures. Now please, I understand your curious nature, but any further questions must wait. As I said, we wish to complete this task before the sun rises, and I need your assistance."

"What do you require?" Holli asked.

The dwarf queen nodded in appreciation to the elf guard. "The evacuation is no longer necessary since we shall free this city, however, the humans above must be informed of our intentions. The last time dwarves rose up to the streets of Connel, we did so to attack, we did so to our shame. The three of you must inform them that we mean them no further harm. We will dispatch these dark creatures that plague them, and then, we will return home. While I would understand their apprehension, I do not wish the sight of dwarves returning to their streets to incite further panic. Understand this, these dwarves that follow me are under strict orders not to harm a single human, even if we are attacked by them. You cooperation is most needed in this regard."

Ryson considered what was said to him, and quickly welcomed the plan. It was obvious that Connel could no longer simply be evacuated and here before him was the perfect solution to their problem. Sy and all the soldiers surrounding Connel would face unparalleled difficulties in pressing the goblins out of the city, but these dwarves were much better suited for the task.

With the thought of Sy in his mind, the delver paused and listened intently to everything about him. While he heard the movements of the small dwarf groups pursuing the rock beetles, he could no longer hear the charging hooves of horses overhead.

"Alright, and thank you. This is more than I can ask, and I'll do everything I can to help. From what I can hear, Sy must have his forces in place around the city. The charge is over. If we're going to do this, then we need to go now."

Holli spoke up to the delver. "You and Lief can return to your initial passages you planned to use before. I will not have to wait here to guide the humans, thus I can take the center path now."

Ryson shook his head strenuously. "No, you take my passage. I need to go more to the southwest. I have to get to the Church of Godson."

#

The slow trot of the horses drew to a close. The soldiers of Fort Nebran along with the cavalry of Connel and the guard of Burbon now surrounded Connel. The edge of the circle remained well out of crossbow fire from any structure within the city. The soldiers sat patiently on their mounts in the encroaching dark of early evening. The air grew ever colder as any faint glow of light completely disappeared behind the gray wall of mountains to the west.

Colonel Haravin eyed the city and his soldiers that surrounded it as he considered the next phase of the attack. He spoke to Sy openly of what they had to do.

"I have six squads mopping up both to the west and east and securing those farmlands. We will not need them in our initial attack, but we now deal with our biggest challenge. I do not want to risk casualties, but we must make Sazar believe that we are focused on entering the city and not acting as a diversion."

"Agreed," Sy said. "At this point, things have gone better than I would have dared
hope. I'm guessing that Ryson knows we have the city surrounded."

"How sure are you of this?"

"It's amazing what that delver can hear. Even below ground, he had to hear the charge
of the horses. Even the elves probably heard that."

"That is assuming the dwarves did as the delver asked and cleared the tunnels. If they
did not, then the delver and elves may be no where near the city."

"He would have gotten word to me if he wasn't there. In fact, he'd probably be right
here now ready to scout the city for the openings."

"Unless the dwarves threw him in their prison."

Sy frowned, but then stopped himself. "Can't think like that."

The colonel nodded, "You are right. We can't. We must believe that the evacuation is
about to start, so we should begin with our initial assault plans." Colonel Haravin turned
to the flag bearer to prepare the next set of signals. "Fore and back, every other solider!"

The aide next to Haravin raised two red flags. He kept the first one still as he thrust the
other forward. He quickly pulled it back and then kept that one still as he waved the first
one forward. He did this several times in quick succession.

Once the signal was called, the soldiers carried out the orders. In the large circle that
surrounded Connel, every other rider urged his mount forward at full speed. Those that
remained stationary prepared their bows and waited for the first rush to conclude. From a
hook hawk's perspective high in the sky, the original circle now looked more like a
dotted line that lost small segments of its mass as half of the formation members broke
from its ranks. The soldiers that rushed forward now created a second circle which
appeared to be collapsing inward with Connel as its central focal point.

Those that charged forward strung arrows in their bows. In the thickening dark, it was
difficult for them to locate their targets. They had been instructed earlier to first look for
the bloat spiders nestled in the webs that sealed off the city. In some cases the riders
spotted dark masses in the center of a spun web. These made easy targets, but in other
areas, the spiders had moved to dark corners or clung closely to the shadowed walls of
buildings. For these creatures, the soldiers would have to take their best guess and hope at
least some of their arrows might find their mark.

The riders also knew the goblins would be waiting with their crossbows. Again, the
night assisted the defenders for their positions were cloaked in dark and shadow. Still, the
riders knew a barrage of crossbow fire would welcome them the moment they came in
range. At the moment they believed the exchange would occur, they urged their mounts

on faster in hopes of racing beneath the arc of fire. The tactic worked with amazing
success and as the hail of crossbow fire sailed over their heads, the soldiers released their
own arrows.

All around the city, the barrage of shafts split the night air. The bloat spiders centered
in their webs died instantly from numerous impacts. Even those monsters clinging to the
shadows did not escape the accuracy of the first volley. So many arrows littered their
webs that well over three quarters of the bloat spiders were either killed or mortally
wounded. Those that survived were now trapped where they hid. Their webs remained
intact, but the cascade of arrows plunged into the threads made them impassable for the
spiders' movements.

Those riders making up the first assault turned about and headed back to the outer
circle before the goblins could reload. As they returned to the perimeter, those soldiers
that had held steady now moved forward with hopes of matching the success of the first
attack. Again, a second inner circle formed and tightened about the outskirts of the city.
As this group reached the ground marked by the goblins' bolts, they prepared for the next
volley of crossbow fire.

The goblins anticipated a similar tactic from this second assault. They believed the
riders would increase their speed to avoid casualties. The diminutive monsters had
lowered their aim in hopes of turning the tactics against the human riders. They fired with
glee, but this soon turned to curses of hate spawned anger.

The second wave of riders did not urge their mounts forward. Instead, they pulled up
their horses to a near halt and allowed the bolts to fall upon the ground before them. They
fired their own arrows into the darkness, letting them rain down on the heads of where
they believed the goblins would be hiding. They quickly turned about and returned to the
circular formation that surrounded the city.

"Call for a hold!" Colonel Haravin ordered and the signal caller raised a solid yellow
flag that he held firm above his head. The colonel turned to Sy. "Let them think on that
for a while."

Sy pulled a spyscope from his pocket and peered into the edges of the city before him.
He reported his findings of obviously dead bloat spiders to the colonel and informed him
as well as to the condition of their webs. He could not venture a guess as to the casualties
of the goblins and wishing to remain conservative he stated that most probably escaped
injury.

With the break in movement before him, he urged his horse slightly to the left and
then back to the right. He tried to get a clean view down one of the wider roads that led
further into Connel. He didn't expect he would see anything, but he hoped he might get a
glimpse of humans moving toward cover. That would at least give him an indication that
Ryson had begun the evacuation.

As his horse sidestepped further to the left at Sy's urging, Burbon's captain let out a
grunt of surprise. He pulled the horse to a halt, and peered deeper into the dark streets,
then pulled the spyscope away from his face. He looked at the city in absolute
bewilderment and then returned the scope to his eye.

"What is it?" the colonel commanded.

Sy shook his head and at first said nothing. He quickly handed the spyscope to the

Colonel. "Take a look down the wide street straight ahead of me" Sy then pointed in front
of him.

Colonel Haravin took the eyepiece and moved his own horse into a better position.
"What in blazes is that?!"

"Those are dwarves," Sy said.

"Are you sure?"

"Beyond sure, I've seen them before, I've fought them before. I know what a dwarf
formation moving down a street looks like."

"What in blazes are they doing here now?" the colonel barked. "They attacked Connel
before."

"Yes, right before they attacked Burbon," Sy confirmed.

The colonel urged his horse further off to the left and looked down another street. "There's more of them. Good Godson, a great many more!" He handed the eyepiece back to Sy for him to take another look. "Could they have used this as an opportunity to take the city for themselves, or perhaps even joined with the creatures?"

Sy took a quick look and then shook his head. "Doesn't appear that way. They're attacking the goblins, and they're attacking in great force."

The dwarves began swarming into Connel from dozens of points all across the city. In some cases they used existing access tunnels. Some of these were clear, never sealed by the humans because they were not found or because they were located beneath the rubble of a collapsed building. Dwarves, however, could move rubble like the wind moves dried leaves. Others that had been sealed proved even less a deterrent as the dwarves plowed through the dirt that filled the holes as if it wasn't there. They also quickly dug new passages to the surface, passages that would bring them closer to the outskirts of the city and directly upon the goblins they sought.

Once in the open streets, the dwarves dropped into battle formations. They drew close, their armor locked together, forming wedges that pressed forward with undeterred power. Though they lacked natural speed, they marched in union at double time. Soon nearly every road leading to the outer edges of Connel was filled with dwarf battle groups looking to smash their intended foes.

The goblins at first had no idea what was coming for them. Their backs were to these streets, their attention on the humans that were engaged outside the city. The hook hawks, however, patrolled the skies, and as they screeched warnings, eventually the goblins took heed. As they turned to witness this spectacle of doom that now charged toward them, their eyes widened in terror. In their haste, they fired their crossbows wildly. Most bolts missed their targets completely. Those that managed to hit a dwarf simply bounced harmlessly off thick battle armor.

In this moment, the outcome of the ensuing battle was already clear. No matter what the size of a goblin horde, it was no match for a fully armored battalion of angry and determined dwarves. Dwarves worked and fought together in unison. They understood war and battle tactics and they did not know fear. This was a combination of assets that stripped the goblins clean of any potential advantage.

The goblin horde had no such harmony. Though their strength lie in numbers, they could never boast of being a truly cohesive unit. They moved in waves of bedlam and

used chaos and turmoil to confuse and demoralize their victims. On this day, they faced
dwarves and dwarves laugh at such attempts. The goblins could not intimidate this foe
through fear and though their ranged weapons might have given them an edge against the
slow moving dwarves, they lacked the proper discipline to use that advantage effectively.
Eventually, the dwarves would fight through any barrage of crossbow fire and turn this
into a battle of close quarters, a battle the goblins could not possibly win.

Those shags that guarded the few clear passages in and out of Connel and others that
protected the goblin flanks would fall first. Shags possessed the strength and size and
could match a dwarf in a test of sheer power, but one shag against thirty dwarves with
mace and axe was not a fair contest. Those shags that charged the dwarf formations head-
on were dispatched with frightening speed. While their thick fur was ample protection
against most hazards, it could not save them against bone crushing mace blows or the
powerful swings of a dwarf axe.

The dwarf battle groups marched unimpeded toward the final positions of the goblins
when they met their first true challenge. Attacks from the air began to impede the
dwarves' progress. Hook hawks began to swoop low from the sky and grab and scratch
with sharp clawed talons. Though razor crows joined the fray by flying in maddened
circles, they did little more that distract the dwarves. Still, they proved an annoyance and
allowed the hook hawks greater time to make more passes that slowly began to cause
casualties.

From their position outside the city, Sy and Colonel Haravin witnessed the battle with
growing enthusiasm. It was clear the dwarves were attacking the dark creatures, and it
was now their attention to assist in any way they could.

The colonel called for his closest lieutenants. He had new orders and they could not be
delivered with flag signals.

"Disperse this order throughout the ranks. We will move to the very edge of the city
and keep circling it at attack speed. Keep the goblins sandwiched between us and the
dwarves. If a hook hawk swoops down into range, open fire with bows. The same goes
for any goblins trying to escape out of the city. Make note of any clear entrances you see.
Do not enter the city at this time, but we will need to make use of them later."

The soldiers urged their mounts forward and came to the very outskirts of Connel,
almost within arms reach of the webs that encased the outer edges of the city. They no
longer feared crossbow fire for the dwarves were now engaging the goblins in close
combat. The horses began to move at a furious pace always circling the city. Whenever a
hook hawk attempted to swoop in for an attack, it received a barrage of arrows that
swiftly dropped it to the ground. Even the razor crows were quickly dispersed by the
flood of arrows that now swam through the dark night air over the heads of dwarf and
goblin.

Trapped between the human cavalry circling the city and the dwarves storming
through their entrenchments, the goblins panicked. They broke ranks and ran with
disregard to their ultimate fate. In the end, this simply hastened their demise.

With the goblins routed, the dwarves turned their attention to the bloat spiders. Their
axes made quick work of any web threads that blocked a city street, and their maces
ended the threat of those few creatures that remained alive. Once all the webs were
cleared, the dwarves turned about with a mind toward destroying every last goblin

retreating back through the streets.

As most streets were now cleared and entrance into Connel could occur unimpeded, Colonel Haravin could not pass up the opportunity. "Signal an entry into the city, secure the main roads and follow inward to engage any fleeing goblins."

The soldiers followed these orders gladly, especially those belonging to the cavalry of Connel. They moved through the streets quickly passing the dwarves and closed upon the heels of the few remaining goblins. As they secured the roads, Sy and Haravin pulled to a halt to size up the situation.

"Do you think your team even bothered to evacuate anyone?" Haravin asked.

"I doubt it," Sy replied. "They would have had to use the same tunnels as the dwarves. I'm sure Ryson would have seen what was going on and put a halt to it even if they started. My guess is most of the people are probably taking shelter inside their homes."

"Once we secure these main roads, we can begin searching the inner sections of the city. The dwarves didn't leave much of the goblins to be any threat."

Sy nodded and then looked about curiously. He realized the number of dwarf battle
groups in the streets was dwindling fast. Those he could see began to drop into holes in
the ground and fell completely out of sight.

"They're leaving," Sy pointed out. "I guess they did what they came to do and are
going home. Maybe Connel has turned an enemy into a friend."

Chapter 23

Once Ryson was above ground, he moved swiftly to the surrounding houses. He didn't
expect too many people would open their doors if he simply knocked, especially with the
city infested by goblins. Instead, he peered into windows and when he spotted anyone, he
quickly and quietly called for their attention. He explained that dwarves were
approaching, but this time they were here to attack the dark creatures and no one else.
Many he spoke to reacted to this news with downright disbelief, and the delver truly
could not blame these people. He told them to sit tight indoors, stay out of the way, and
watch for themselves as to who the dwarves would attack.

He moved as fast as possible but the streets were deserted and most people were
reluctant to be seen. He had spoken only to a few when the dwarves began appearing in
the streets. Ryson hoped that the citizens of Connel would stay indoors and allow the
dwarves to meet the goblins unimpeded. As he watched the progress of the dwarf battle
groups, he realized that hope would be met.

With the dwarves topside and ignoring the humans and their structures, Ryson felt that
this was far more proof then anything he could say to those trapped in Connel. He
believed Lief and Holli could do enough to warn anyone that might come out on the
streets to cross paths with the dwarves, and so he turned his attention to reaching the
Church of Godson as quickly as possible.

He moved near top speed through the backstreets and alleys in order to avoid any
dwarf formations. In a blur, he dashed through the darkness and covered the distance in
mere moments. He came to a sudden halt at the steep stone steps of the Church of
Godson. As he did, he realized there were several small groups of goblins crouched about
the doors and corners of the church.

Leaping forward without hesitation, he never gave these creatures a chance to know
he was there. He never drew his own sword, left it sheathed across his back. Instead, he
pulled a short sword from the grip of a surprised goblin. Using the flat of the blade, he
swung it down hard on the tops of their heads. When he completed his path around the
entire building, over a dozen goblins lay in unconscious heaps scattered about the church
grounds.

Ryson crept up to the large oak doors at the front of the church and pushed one open
slowly and quietly. Carefully peering inside, he saw several people that appeared to be

members of the church sprawled uncomfortably about the benches of the church. They all
looked tired, disheveled, and most appeared withdrawn as if they waited for the swing of
an executioner's axe they knew they could not stop. The condition of these people left the
delver angry, and he threw open the door with disgust.

As the door banged open loudly against a wall, the people inside jumped with a start.
They looked at the delver with darkened and confused expressions. None of them made a
move to approach him. They appeared as if they could not trust what they saw.

"Don't worry, I'm not here to hurt you. Is anyone or anything inside here guarding
you?" Ryson asked firmly.

No one answered aloud but many pointed to an open archway that led to a darkened
passage. Ryson began to move toward that doorway when a figure stepped out of the

shadows and into the light of the church's main hall. Ryson recognized him immediately
even though he was much gaunter than the delver remembered.

"Hello Edward, or would you prefer me to call you Mayor Consprite?" Ryson asked
with an edge of anger to his voice.

"Thanks to you I'm no longer the mayor, but also thanks to you I now have a position
of power among these pathetic people."

"Thanks to me?" Ryson asked.

"Yes, you see you introduced me to the fairy tales of the Book of Godson," Consprite
offered with a sarcastic grin. "I, however, was able to separate the fantasy from the fact in
that book. When the Sphere of Ingar was destroyed, I understood better than most what
that would mean now that magic changed everything. The book, though humorous
throughout, gave me some idea of what to expect. I learned where to find power that
didn't require me to obtain a position such as mayor."

"Is that it?" Ryson asked with a near growl. "You suddenly pick up a book, then you
turn on the people that believe in that book and you blame me for what you've done? I
know what you've done to the people of this church. I know how you sent them to the
desert. You can't put one ounce of that blame on me. You are totally responsible and you
will pay for it."

"I'm not blaming you at all," Consprite retorted haughtily. "Blame implies that I've
done something wrong, and I've done nothing wrong. I've simply changed my perspective to be in better alignment with how things now work in the land."

Ryson was becoming more disgusted with this man with every word he spoke, but he
could not refrain from asking more questions. "And how do you think things work now?
How is it that you can possibly justify what you've done here?"

"It doesn't need justifying beyond me standing here as I am. I have not been affected
by the goblins taking over this town. If anything, I've benefited from it."

"That benefit is about to end," Ryson stated confidently. "Right now an entire army of
dwarves is rushing through the streets to remove the goblin horde. Where is that going to
leave you?"

Consprite actually laughed. "It happened sooner than I expected, but it's not a
surprise. Well, that's not completely true; the dwarf thing is a surprise. Who would have
thought those little bastards would come to Connel's aid. But it's no surprise these
goblins are going to get their turn at the stake so to speak. They couldn't tie their shoes
without help. Actually, I don't even know if they wear shoes, never looked down that far.

Their faces are bad enough to look at. That Sazar has more power than I would have expected, helped out by the witch in the desert, but I always knew his grasp exceeded his reach, or is it the other way around? I never understood that statement. Anyway, basically he seemed to want way more than he could really handle. Eventually, he was going to be taken down. That's why this doesn't change things for me. Whether he and his goblin horde get annihilated or not is immaterial. It leaves me in no different place than I stood before. I don't need the goblins, just as I no longer need the pathetic people of Connel. You see, I don't have to worry about being a politician anymore—about saying the right things, making it seem like you're giving them something for nothing, or bailing them out of a disaster of their own making. The new inhabitants of this land understand one thing and one thing alone, power."

Ryson shook his head. "The problem with that is you don't have any power."

"Power is what you make it," Consprite said smugly, "and I know how to make
alliances of power. You see I have a friend now."

Suddenly, Ryson sensed something behind him, something that wasn't there a moment
ago. It was almost as if a very angry and evil presence simply appeared in the shadows.
As if to confirm that sensation, Ryson felt a sharp tug at his back. Something sliced the
belt at his shoulder that kept the Sword of Decree on his back, and the delver felt the
sword and sheath pull free. He twirled around in an instant and witnessed a familiar face,
a face he did not wish to see again.

"I see you remember me," Janindise growled. "When we last met, you used this horrid
sword along with the coming dawn to force me into a bargain. Do you remember that as
well?"

Ryson stared angrily into the eyes of the vampire. At first he did not wish to even
acknowledge this woman, but his anger was growing hotter still. He realized that
somehow the ex-mayor had joined with this vampire and it disgusted him beyond reason.
Now, she was here in Connel and causing pain beyond her dark powers.

"I remember it very well," Ryson finally responded. "You promised you would only
hunt dark creatures. You promised on what was left of your soul you would keep to that
bargain and now you are here terrorizing these people. I can only assume you do not
honor your word."

The vampire's eyes blazed with hate. "You vermin! I have kept to that bargain and
regretted every moment of it! Do you know how long I have drunk the foul swill of
rancid blood from goblins, shags, and river rogues?! But that ends tonight. There is much
time before the sun rises again, and you no longer have your precious sword to help you."

Janindise held up the sword in victorious glee, and then quickly tied it about her own
waist. "It will remain sheathed at my side until I find the proper means to destroy it. You
will no longer have use of it again." She peered deep into the delver's eyes, her own eyes
becoming a mesmerizing mirror of the delver's deepest fears and desires. She pressed all
of her will upon him as she now spoke in a more soothing tone. "You no longer need the
sword because you have no desire to use it against me, just as you no longer have the
desire to hold me to the promise I made so long ago. You wish to release me from that
promise now, don't you?"

Ryson stared back in cold defiance. Even as the face of this monster twisted into
illusions of fear and fantasy, the delver remained firmly attached to reality. "No, I do not!

I hold you to that promise. Drink from an innocent at your own peril. You made that
bargain to save your life and there's nothing you can do to make me free you from it."
Ryson stared back even deeper into the cold abyss of Janindise's eyes. He took no
comfort in what he saw there, but he took strength in his own beliefs, his own faith, his
own understanding of right and wrong and good and evil. He focused on the faces of his
friends, his feelings for Linda and her feelings for him. He took hold of his inner strength
and pressed it back against the nightmare in the vampire's eyes. "You took my will once
before. I remember what that was like and I will never, ever let that happen again. If you
wish to try harder, you have my blessings. Just like you, I have all night, but unlike you I
can last through the dawn."

In a scream of rage, Janindise lashed out at the delver. "Very well, but I will not be
denied. You will release me from my vow! I made my bargain with you. When I drink

from your veins, I will control you despite your strong will. I will make you relieve me
from that bargain even if I have to break it first."

She reached out with the razor sharp claws of her fingernails, but she found nothing
but empty air as the delver leapt clear of her swing. Revealing her own swiftness, she
jumped toward him with her hands at his throat, but again she failed to take hold of her
target as Ryson easily dodged around her.

Ryson turned his back to the vampire and hopped up on an empty bench. He then
bounded toward a wall and used it to propel himself higher into the air where he grabbed
hold of a rafter in the ceiling. He swung himself around as he perched himself far out of
reach.

"You think just because I don't have that sword that I'm defenseless?" he taunted her.

Janindise hissed. "And do you think you are safe up there?" She said no more as her
body faded into a dark, inky mist. The vaporous cloud floated upward with surprising
speed. As it reached the rafters, the vampire's body solidified once more and now she had
a firm hold of the wooden beams. With one quick rocking motion, she launched herself
toward the delver.

The move surprised the delver, but only for a moment. A being that moved with his
speed was used to reacting to an ever-changing environment nearly instantaneously. He
dropped low, swinging forward on a single beam, and then released his hold to fall
gracefully to the floor. He landed on his feet and bounded over three benches as if they
were nothing more than blades of grass. He whirled about and leapt across the entire
expanse of the open room and landed at the front door. He stopped and twirled about.

He shook his head in defiance as he faced the vampire once more. "I was going to take
this outside, but I don't have to. We can stay right here."

"Arrogant fool, you have so much confidence in your own speed that you
underestimate mine!" Janindise flew from the rafters to the back of the church and the
doors where Ryson stood.

"Speed? You have no idea what speed is," Ryson yelled and in a flash barely visible
he ran up toward the front of the church and stood right by the alter.

The vampire turned with another hiss and ran wildly after the delver like the demon
she was. "You will release me of my vow and you will then die at my hand!"

Ryson jumped up into the rafters once more as Janindise barreled into the front wall.
As he hung over her head, he called a question down to her. "Just to make sure I

understand this, I have to ask. If you ever do get a hold of me, which you won't, but for
argument's sake, let's say that you do. Once you feed on me, you will have broken your
word. What's left of your soul is lost. Why bother having me release you of your promise
once you've already broken it?"

The vampire looked up and bared her teeth at the delver. The white fangs sparkled in
the candlelight of the alter. "It won't matter if the bargain is broken if you release me of
it. It doesn't matter which happens first."

"I think it does," Ryson countered.

"I don't care what you think! I will feed on whatever I like once I am finished with
you!"

"The only thing you're going to feed on after this night is over is the sun."

"You will never survive that long!"

"I don't tire, certainly not from being chased by you," the delver scoffed.

Janindise leapt with her arms stretched toward the delver. She never reached him. An arrow with a wooden shaft pierced her heart at its very center. The strike sent her sprawling back against the wall. Her eyes widened in disbelief. As she took her last glance of this world, she saw Lief Woodson stepping further into the church with his bow in his hand.

Edward Consprite stumbled to Janindise's side. He tried to hold up her body to keep her from hitting the floor, but he lacked the strength. Her body was already cold to the touch as it folded through his arms and sunk to the ground. As Consprite looked down upon his fallen ally, he watched in dismay as her skin began to shrivel and fall loose around her bones. The flesh and muscle behind it decomposed at an unbelievable rate, almost as if her body was deflating. In mere moments, there was nothing but a grey leathery hide that sagged around her skeletal frame. Soon after, even these remains began to disintegrate until there was nothing left but hair and clumps of loose debris that could be easily scatted by the slightest wind.

Consprite turned to the elf with both sadness and fury in his eyes. His own frame was haggard and his gate uneven, but he stalked toward the elf with evil intentions. The sight was almost humorous until another arrow from Lief's bow pierced his heart as well. Consprite crumpled to the floor with a low groan and died right there in this Church of Godson.

Ryson dropped down out of the rafters and on to the floor. He inspected the granular remains of the vampire as he picked up his sword and returned it to its place on his back. He then moved to the corpse of the ex-mayor. He looked upon the body with a shake of his head. Finally, he looked up at Lief.

"Thank you," the delver said surprisingly.

"Are you not going to argue with me over necessity of the death of these two?" Lief asked almost too perplexed to offer the question.

Ryson looked about the room, looked into the hollow faces of those that spent the last few days trapped in this church. Though there were traces of joy in being freed, it did little to chase away their extreme exhaustion.

"No, I'm not going to argue about it. I would have let the sun take care of her. Your way was quicker. As for him, you only get so many chances. He more than abused his."

"I am pleased to hear that."

Ryson nodded to Holli who was now standing next to him. "Is everything going alright outside?"

Holli answered without hesitation. "The dwarves have the situation well in hand. They have dispatched the shags and are now closely engaged with the goblins at the outer limits of the city. Lief and I met not far from here. We agreed it would be futile to try to explain the situation to the humans here any further. If they do not believe their own eyes, they would not believe the word of an elf. I do not expect there to be any conflict between human and dwarf, at least not on this night."

"What about the cavalry outside the city?"

"They have Connel surrounded. They have already dispatched nearly every bloat spider. I doubt they will allow any of the goblins to escape. Eventually they will make it through the webs and enter the city to assist the dwarves."

"I guess that takes care of that. That means there's just Sazar to deal with now."

Holli did not answer but looked to Lief. Her expression was not lost on the delver.

"What is it?" Ryson asked.

Lief became almost rigid as he began to explain. "I believe Sazar can be left to the
dwarves or the human soldiers that enter the city. He is not the true threat here anyway.
Instead, I now have another proposal that Holli has forced me to discuss with you. She
and I have conferred about it briefly, but she demands that you be included in this
decision."

"What decision?" Ryson pressed with greater curiosity.

"It is the sorceress Tabris that is truly responsible for what has happened here. She
must be dealt with and I believe she must be dealt with before she learns of what has
happened here. Holli has told me that she knows where Tabris is in the Lacobian Desert.
Not only that, she has the ability to bring us there utilizing her own magic powers. That
may give us the opportunity we need."

"You want to go right now?" Ryson asked with slight amazement.

"We may never have such an opportunity," Lief stated grimly. "Very soon she will
learn that the goblins have been defeated here in Connel. Once that occurs, she will
realize that many will connect her to the crimes that have been committed here. If she
does, at the very least she will make stronger preparations for those that may seek her out
for justice. She may even decide to leave the area she is at now. If she does that, we will
not have the same ability to reach her with such ease."

"So exactly what is it you want to do?" Ryson questioned.

"I would have Holli transport us to a point immediately outside her oasis. I would then
move upon her with as much speed as possible in hopes of catching her unaware. I would
strike with the same speed and end her as a threat."

"So you want to kill her," Ryson stated as his voice died off.

Lief controlled any rising anger. He would not argue with the delver openly, but he
decided to ask simple questions instead. "Do you think we have the power to capture
her?"

"No."

"Do you think she's a danger to this land?"

"Yes," Ryson admitted after a long pause.

In his own mind, Lief believed that was enough to justify his intended actions. The
delver, however, would need more. "More importantly, because I know you don't wish to
act based solely on what someone is capable of doing—which is what you once told
me—do you believe she should be held accountable for what she has done?"

Ryson looked around once more and wondered how many of the people in this church
had lost a friend or a family member to satisfy the trials of Tabris. He thought about how
many had suffered in Connel beyond these walls over the past few days. He knew Sazar

brought the plague of goblins on this city, but ultimately he was enabled by Tabris'
power. If she had not chosen to assist him for her own benefit, he would not be here
today. He knew she was as responsible as the serp for all the misfortune that was caused
in this place, and yet he was not certain what to say. The delver, however, did not get the
opportunity to answer at that moment.

Enin stepped into the center room as if he walked through a doorway that materialized
for his own personal benefit and then faded at his whim. He walked up to the two elves
and the delver. "You have done well here. Connel is now free. Sy is well and already
within the city limits. The soldiers that ride with him are hunting down the stragglers of

goblins, razor crows, and hook hawks. The dwarves are even now returning to their
home."

Holli could not contain her surprise. "You've been watching us all?"

"Watching and listening," Enin admitted.

"Then you heard what Lief just said?" the elf guard asked with a questioning glance.

"I did."

"And what is your opinion of this idea?"

"It is not for me to say."

Lief spoke in a disgusted tone. "Then say nothing and stay out of our way."

Enin looked upon the elf with a puzzled expression. "I am not standing in you way.
Do what you think you must."

Holli could not leave it at that. "And what if I say I must do more than simply bring
them to Tabris? What if I say I feel I have to help them in this cause, that I have to do
whatever is in my power to stop this sorceress?"

This caught Enin somewhat off guard. "You wish to battle Tabris? Do you understand
the consequences of such a decision? No matter what happens, there will be a shift in the
balance. There is great weight in what you intend to do, it will affect many things. You
can't simply do this on a whim."

Holli shook her head. "It is not a whim. And as to the balance and the effect, that is
how you see it. I have never been able to accept that. What I do is based on what I think
is the best course of action. Though I am no longer allowed to protect my camp, I am still
an elf guard. That is what I am. I look at this situation and realize that it's not about the
balance of magic power. It's about what should be done, what needs to be done. You
wish to try to break everything down to some kind of philosophical question regarding
interference and people's choice. It is indeed about choice, but it is not as complicated as
you wish to make it. It's about my choice and what I think I should do. Tabris has done
great harm here and she will do it again. Even if she doesn't do it again, she has to be
held accountable for what she has done here. She has to be stopped."

"You are not powerful enough to defeat her on your own," Enin said in a warning
tone.

Here Holli became resolute. "Sometimes you don't need to be more powerful to do
what needs to be done. There is more to any battle than that. I will also not be on my
own. I will be with Lief and Ryson, if indeed the delver agrees to accompany us."

Ryson, instead of answering the questioning glance of Holli, turned a plea to the
wizard. "You can stop this right now, Enin. I know you have the power."

Enin looked into the delver's eyes, and though he found it extremely difficult to deny

Ryson's request, he made it clear he could not bring himself to intervene. "Yes, I have
the power, but do I have the right? You wanted me to remove the goblins from Connel.
And yet, you all seemed to handle that quite well on your own. In fact, the way I see it,
much good has come from me not interfering. The dwarves choose to use this
opportunity to come to the aide of Connel. The people of this city once believed the
dwarves to be their enemies, now they think differently. The dwarves now feel they have
restored their honor and have let go of their collective guilt. It seems to me that my
decision to stay out of the way was the correct one, but you quickly forget this. Now, you
want me to go to the Lacobian and deal with Tabris."

Ryson did not give up so easily in the face of Enin's argument. "But this is different.
This isn't freeing a city, this is just one person, a powerful sorceress. You're the best
equipped to deal with her. You don't even have to kill Tabris. You can contain her, place
her in a magical prison or something. Why can't you do this?"

Lief turned on the Enin as well. "What say you wizard? You really can not hope to
argue with his logic. You of all people know how much a threat this sorceress can be. Are
you going to just stand by and let her empower another serp just so she can gain more test
subjects for her spells? Or will you finally act?"

Holli added her own thoughts. "You yourself said Tabris turned to evil. Those were
your own words. She has done a terrible thing here and she must not be allowed to simply
walk away."

Enin felt as if he was being unfairly outnumbered, that those he called friend were
now completely disregarding his own understanding of the situation. He appeared
shocked and sounded more than angry. A fury was growing in him and it became
apparent in his words. "How many times do I have to tell you people? Am I speaking
some strange language? Is it so very difficult to understand? Really, I want to know? For
the love of Godson, it is not that complicated! Why is it you wish me to insert myself into
the paths of others. I am not some god that you can come to in order to solve every
problem that comes into existence. There are certain things we all must face—events,
circumstances, people, life paths that we can not escape. We will face them whether we
want to or not. That is destiny. How we deal with these events is our choice. No one
dictates these decisions. We make them on our own. We can meet our challenges with
honesty, faith, determination, honor, integrity and courage, yes courage. Or we can
choose to deal in deception, anger, bitterness, and fear. When we do we choose a path we
choose between right and wrong, good and evil. These are decisions of the greatest
magnitude and define who we are. If I start to make these choices for you, I stop you
from becoming what you were meant to be. Don't you understand that?"

Though Ryson and Holli became silent, Lief was not impressed and made his own
understanding known. "And how many times do I have to tell you? It's not just what we
do, it's what we don't do. We are asking you to act. You are using excuses to avoid such
action. That is not a reflection of us, it is a reflection of you. You talk to us as if we are
making some kind of unholy request. That is nonsense. We are asking you to do what you

are capable of doing and what should be done. When you do not act, there are
consequences. Look at this carcass on the floor." Lief paused just long enough to point to
the body of Edward Consprite. "This is the human that attempted to stand in our way
when we needed to destroy Ingar's sphere. Tell me wizard, how many lives would have
been saved if I killed this pathetic excuse of a human when I first met him as opposed to
now? How MANY?!"

The elf would not cease to allow for an answer. His own anger flushed his face and his
temple throbbed with a pulsating vein.

"Now let's turn to this sorceress. You don't wish to interfere in the choices of others
so you will let her simply go about her business in the desert. I can not take such a
position, not in good conscious. If I do nothing when I have the ability to act, then I am
just as responsible for the evil she commits because it could have been avoided if only I
did something to stop her. I don't wish to live with that. That is my choice!"

Lief was not yet done and now he turned to the delver.

"And what of you, Ryson? I call you friend, but you have not yet divulged your
decision. We've actually had this discussion before, and more than once. Only a few days
ago, you would not allow me to kill the river rogue. Do you remember? You believed all
life had value. Fine. I won't argue the point, I'll use it instead. We allowed Consprite to
live back before we left for Sanctum Mountain to retrieve the sphere. We could have
killed him right there, but you insist there's a value on life, even Consprite's. But what of
the lives that have been lost since? Have they no value? How many died because of
Consprite? How many from the Church of Godson suffered? How many were tortured by
a mad sorceress because he condemned them.

"And let's not forget about that sorceress. Are we not responsible for her? We are the
one's that brought her to Sanctum Mountain when we needed to destroy the sphere. As I
remember it, she didn't want to use the magic, isn't that what she said to us at Sanctum's
peak? But we convinced her it was necessary."

Ryson recalled the event clearly. He remembered how he implored Lauren, who had
become Tabris, to use the magic to help get the sphere out of Sanctum Mountain. Still, he
also remembered how important it was to get to the talisman and he said as much. "It was
necessary. Everyone would have died if the sphere was not destroyed. She used the magic
to save everyone."

"And now she uses magic to kill," Lief shot back. "The truth is we have to take
responsibility for what we've done. Who knows what would have happened if she
decided not to use the magic? Who is to say that we wouldn't have found some other way
to stop the sphere? Your friend here says we have to deal with choices. We had a choice
then, and we have a choice now. Do we face up to our responsibility that in some way we
created Tabris?"

Lief turned to Enin and fired off his final thought. "One other thing you should
consider, wizard. Maybe actions can be right and wrong, good and evil, as you like to
profess. But what about inaction? Where do you want to place the decision not to do
anything, to stand back and allow things to happen that should not happen? Where is the
good and evil in that?"

"What do you mean?" Enin asked.

"I mean that certain inaction can be as harmful as any action. It's not always enough
to say that I did not do anything unjust or evil, as you seem to like to put it. I've realized
that not doing anything can lead to just as much pain and suffering. How many suffered

because the elders of my camp did nothing when Petiole was in charge? And now you
hold to the same attitude. You are using an excuse of not interfering, but it is the same
thing. You point to what has happened here in Connel as justification for your inaction.
You want to point to everything good that occurred here and use it to defend how you did
nothing. In my mind, that is beyond cowardly. You wish to actually take credit for not
acting."

"I am not taking credit," Enin responded angrily. "I only said that my decision not to
interfere was the proper one."

"And I say to you it is an argument of convenience. It allows you to stand back and
remove yourself from what needs to be done. If that's what you want, very well, but there
are others that do not feel the same way."

Enin frowned, but said nothing further to the elf. He turned to the delver instead.
"What about you Ryson? Do you agree with him?"

Ryson heaved a heavy breath and replied with all the honesty his heart allowed. "I don't agree with everything Lief says. When I listen to him it sounds as if he wants to punish people for what they are capable of doing and not what they actually do. That's not right. But the truth is that's not what we're dealing with here. We know what Tabris has done. I don't know if I am responsible for it or not, but I do know we can't just pretend it never happened and just leave her in the desert. I wish you would see it that way, Enin. I really do think you are the one best suited to handle this, but if you won't, then I don't see any other choice. This may be our best opportunity to stop her." Ryson paused and looked to both Holli and Lief. "I'll go with you and do whatever we have to do."

Holli did not let any silence stand for long. Instead, she made one last attempt to make Enin understand. "Ryson is correct. There are times we simply must act. You taught me how to use the magic and I'm grateful, but I have to choose how to use it. Isn't that what you also have been trying to tell us? Based on what I've seen and heard, I choose to help them. I will take them to Tabris, and though it will use most of my energy to get them there. I will use what I have left and all the rest of my abilities to stop her and keep her from being a threat in the future. That is my choice."

"I see," the wizard said. "I will not stand in your way. You all must do what you think is right."

"I'm not sure if it will be enough," Holli admitted, "so before I go, I want you to consider something. You once said you were blessed with an understanding of your power. I truly wonder now if that's true. I for one can't accept some of the things you have told me. I understand the importance of balance in many things, but you're grasp of it escapes me. You say there is good and there is evil and in order to make sure that all choice is fair, the two must always even out. Based on this notion of balance, you want me to believe that you do not act because it means something evil will happen somewhere else. To me, that makes no sense at all. If everyone has a choice of whether to do right or wrong, good or evil, then it has to be possible that everyone could choose good. If that were the case, there would be no evil.

"I've never accepted your argument that we must know sadness in order to experience happiness, or that we must know pain in order to feel joy. Perhaps I am making things too simple, but I do not think seeking a balance between these things would be in anyone's

interest. It makes more sense to maximize the positive and minimize the negative, focus
on what is good and enhance it, deny what is bad and try to eliminate it. This is never
how you look at things. You constantly tell me that every good act can be evened out
with an act of evil. If that were true, perhaps we would have been better off if we let the
sphere destroy us all.

"Maybe because you are so powerful you have come up with this notion in order to
maintain your own reason. I can't say. I see how powerful you are I think you have
become obsessed with the idea of balance. There are other things, however, you must
consider as well. Choosing means taking risks and when you use balance as an excuse,
you insulate yourself from these risks. You are right in not wanting to interfere with
people's lives, but you are not right when you avoid using the gift you have been given
simply because you do not wish to take a risk."

Holli stopped for just a moment and placed a hand on Enin's cheek. "Thank you for
all you have taught me." She then turned to Lief and Ryson. "If we are to do this, haste is
our best ally. Are you ready?"

Both nodded.

"Then prepare yourselves for we shall be on Tabris' doorstep in a matter of moments."
She then concentrated on a point in the Lacobian Desert and brought her hands together.
A green octagon of pure energy encircled her around her shoulders. She brought Lief and
Ryson together with her in her mind and the emerald shape expanded to surround them as
well. As she focused on a path through space and time that would bring them to the
desert, the green magic shimmered and crackled and then the three were gone.

Enin looked upon the empty space where they stood only moments ago. He thought of
Lief and he was sorry his last words to him were ones of anger. He considered Ryson and
knew that he would survive somehow for his destiny was not done. Finally, his thoughts
turned to Holli.

He did not wish to dwell on their parting for too long as her words struck something
within. As much as he tried to push aside what she said, tried to convince himself she did
not truly understand, he could not deny the spark of doubt that was now growing inside.
Something she said nagged at him because it seemed to generate a tremor in the vast
magical energy within him. For an instant, he wished to close the door on that sensation,
bury it back down deep. He could not, however, bring himself to do so. There was more
than a spark of truth in what the elf guard said to him, and at this moment, Enin needed to
be honest with himself more than at any other time in his life.

He focused deep within his own being, searched the magical energies which gave him
so much greater understanding of this existence and the next. He struck down at the false
perceptions of his own creation and opened himself up to the simple basic truths. He
would not allow his own fears and his own doubts to raise barriers against that which he
must now truly understand. He recalled his own words that it was his choice on how to
deal with moments of destiny. Would he face this moment with courage and faith, or with
fear and deception of his own making?

In a moment of unparalleled awareness, he realized that he now faced his own
moment of destiny. He did indeed face choices on how to use his power. He had been
correct about Connel, it was not always his right to interfere with the decisions of others,

but not all choices involved the same consequences. He also realized he had been wrong
about a number of other things. In that realization, he understood there were times when
he would have to act, when he would have to fight for what he believed in, when he
would have to use his power to defeat evil, not for his own glory, but for the sake of what
was right. One such time was before him now, and it was time for him to use his power.

Chapter 24

During the last few moments of transport, Holli felt the waves of magical energy that
guided them over the land being ripped from her control. Just as she sensed the path
becoming distorted before they reached their destination, she found it more difficult to
maintain a link to her two companions. She doubled and redoubled her efforts to maintain
a path of travel and to keep Ryson and Lief enveloped in her spell. Despite her focus, the
disruption increased in intensity as they closed in on Tabris' oasis. The pain was
agonizing and before they hit the sandy rock ground of the desert, she felt her own spell
rupture.

Holli hit the ground heavily, her legs absorbing a great force as if she fell from the
heights of a tall tree. She bit back a scream of pain as she crumpled to her knees. She had
reached her target, the very edge of Tabris' oasis, but Lief and Ryson were not at her
side. She quickly felt her legs for breaks and was greatly relieved to find both were
sound. When she tried to rise up, she felt only slight pain in her left knee, but a wave of
exhaustion kept her from standing. She looked to her left and immediately spied Ryson a
short distance away. She peered deeper into the dark desert night and realized that Lief
was much further off in that same direction.

Ryson ran at top speed to Holli's side. He bent his head low to get a look in her face.
"Are you alright?"

"I don't know what happened. I lost control of the spell at the very end. I don't think
I'm injured, but I feel weak, empty."

Ryson explained his own experience. "I could feel your presence when you cast the
spell and the energy surrounded us. I could actually feel you carrying me and pressing me
over Dark Spruce and the rocky hills at the edge of the desert. In that last moment,
though, I felt something else, something that was pulling me away from you. Eventually,
both forces just stopped and I landed on the ground."

An angry, bitter voice called from beyond the cold, dry air of the desert. It came from
within the oasis and it chilled Ryson much more than the pressing emptiness of the
Lacobian. "Is that Ryson Acumen? Is this the one I see? It is! The delver that brought me
to Sanctum now tries to invade my home with this pathetic elf witch as his guide. How
fitting! If you and your little witch are wondering what happened, let me make it clear. I
am what happened. The elf witch came here once before without my permission, did you
think I would allow that to happen again without taking precautions?"

Tabris halted her words after remembering the last time she saw Holli it was at the
side of Enin. A great moment of apprehension concerned her being as she spotted another
figure off to the side. She worried that Enin had somehow past her notice, that he
shrouded his great magical energy in order to catch her unaware. That concern ended
when she saw the shadowy figure raise a bow and fire an arrow at her with deadly
intentions. Enin would never have to resort to such a wretched attempt on her life. He had
the power to obliterate her with the wave of his hand. This new invader was almost not
worth her notice.

Lief had dashed further off into the darkness when he heard the voice of the sorceress.
He took a curved path to the very edge of the oasis away from Ryson and Holli in hopes
of being overlooked. When he raised his bow, he believed he had the chance to end this

conflict before it truly began. As he fired his arrow, he realized Tabris was now aware of
his presence, but he believed it was too late for her. She did not have the time to cast a
defensive spell in the instant it would take for the arrow to find its mark. To his
astonishment, the arrow flew off its intended path and disappeared into the night air.

"Did you also think I would place myself out in the open without taking a few
precautions?" Tabris scoffed toward Lief. "I cast a wind gust shield to deal with your
projectiles before you arrived. Anything you send toward me will be redirected
harmlessly away. You may fire all the arrows you wish at me, but unless you are standing
right in front of me, don't expect them to hit their target."

"Then I will stand right before you," Lief shouted. He leapt forward, and though he
could never match the speed of the delver, his elf legs carried him with nimble quickness.
Not knowing if the sorceress might cast a spell, he darted to his left and right as he
endeavored to make himself a difficult target. He found it more than unusual that Tabris
made no attempt to raise her hands to cast a spell of any kind, until his body ran hard into
a powerful barrier he could not see. His own speed forward was matched by a nearly
identical force pressing outward from the oasis. The impact nearly hammered him into
unconsciousness. It certainly succeeded in knocking him off his feet as he fought back
the sting of pain that sucked away his breath.

"I recognize that voice as well," Tabris hummed in amusement. "Isn't that Lief
Woodson? This is too grand for me to believe. I have before me the delver and the two
elves that joined me in Sanctum Mountain. And just so you know, there is one more that
is with us tonight. He too was at Sanctum, though he did not enter the mountain."

Lifting her arms in an arc above her head, Tabris focused her power into a crisp
diamond of crackling violet energy. She pressed her hands outward and a swirling wave
of wind danced through the plants and trees of her oasis. For a brief moment, no one
could see the target of her spell until the cradle of wind returned back to Tabris carrying
the body of a one-legged man. The spell evaporated just off to the sorceress' right side
and the man dropped to the ground in an unbalanced shambles.

Ryson knew immediately that the form on the ground was that of the Reader Matthew.
He watched as the reader grappled with the hard rock to turn over on one side. When
Matthew finally raised himself on his lone knee and steadied himself with two hands flat
on the ground, the delver called out in concern.

"Matthew, it's me, Ryson! Are you alright?"

"I've been better," the reader muttered with a weak cough.

"His health will not be a concern in a matter of moments. I can sense through my own spells that Sazar's forces have been greatly reduced, almost completely eliminated. I imagine you have something to do with that, don't you delver?"

"We've taken Connel back from the serp," Ryson answered sharply. "You won't be getting anymore helpless victims to practice on, if that's what you're worried about."

"Shame," Tabris sighed. "But if that's the case, then I also no longer need to keep this reader alive. I did so only so he might witness what I have become. I do not think he is happy about it. I don't know if I'm happy about it either, but I know who is to blame. The truth is you are all responsible for what I am. Thus, you should all share in the understanding of what that means."

It was Lief who answered, and he did so with a raging fury from the center of his being. "It is you that will understand that I will not allow you to continue."

Tabris almost laughed, but she found anger as she looked to Lief. "You have no say at all in what will be allowed. Have you learned nothing by being knocked to the ground? Be aware that my wind gust shield that is so effective against your arrows was not the only spell I prepared in advance. There is a storm barrier that protects my oasis. None of you can enter, but my power can reach out to you."

Lief jumped to his feet and then twirled about with his bow in hand. He pulled another arrow and fired it at the sorceress. Again, though the arrow pierced the storm barrier, it was easily blown wide of its target by the wind gust.

"You don't learn, do you?" Tabris asked in slight amazement. "The arrow can enter the oasis because of its very narrow form. It may be able to penetrate the storm barrier, but that same shape allows it to be easily redirected by the power of the wind. As I said, you can not reach me."

"I can not reach you now sorceress, but I have patience. Your energy is not limitless. Even now I can tell these two spells draw on your magical essence. You can not keep these shields up indefinitely. They will eventually fall, and when they do, so shall you."

"As I said before, you can not get to me but I can reach out to you," Tabris growled. "My energy does not need to be limitless. It only needs to last as long as it takes me to dispose of you. As you are nothing but an insignificant insect, believe me I have far more energy than I need for these shields to last."

Lief said nothing. He leapt back several paces and then darted to his left. He grasped another arrow and let it fly. Again, the projectile was pressed harmlessly away from Tabris. The failure did not seem to frustrate him at all.

"I have dozens of arrows," Lief finally shouted. "Each one that I fire weakens you slightly. Each moment that passes drains you even more. I will remain here as long as it takes. Your energy will fade and you will die."

Tabris scowled. "You only have as long as I wish you to have!" She pressed her hands together in front of her chest and mouthed several words. She then flung her hands forward toward the elf and a bolt of deep purple lightning flew from her body. The streak of deadly energy crackled as it knifed toward Lief. As the bolt made contact with the ground, a dazzling explosion of violet light lit up the desert darkness and a boom of thunder rattled the rocks nearby. Sandy debris clouded the area where Lief stood as the sorceress pulled her arms back to the sides of her body.

A mere instant after the echo of the thunder clap subsided, another arrow streaked

toward Tabris. This one came several paces to the right of where Lief had previously
stood. As the dust settled, Lief's outline became more apparent in the darkness.

"That will only hasten the time it takes for you to run out of energy," the elf baited the
sorceress. "Keep it up, do not stop. You said you can reach us from where you stand, but
I am beginning to doubt it. With each spell you cast, you grow weaker. Your time is
running out."

"Imbecile!" Tabris shrieked. "You have no idea of the extent of my power. I can cast
thousands of bolts of that power before I weaken. You can't dodge forever. You are not
faster than the lightning."

Lief shook his head with obvious scorn toward the sorceress. "I do not have to be
faster than the lightning. I only have to be faster than you."

"Let us see if that's true."

Tabris pressed her hands together once more. Indiscernible words crossed her lips that were snarled in anger. As a violet diamond formed at her pressed palms, her body shook and trembled. The magical shape glowed brighter with each passing moment. When she flung her arms toward Lief, the purple diamond exploded from her hands not in one bolt, but in four. The streaks of energy cut across the dry air and pulsated with even more radiance. As they struck the ground, they exploded into much larger blasts of power. These separate fields of crackling energy joined with thin streams of electric arcs creating a wide field of interlaced magical force. Once the streams surged the four fields together, the entire area exploded in one massive burst.

At first, Ryson could see nothing, his vision spotted from the after effects of the blast. As the flashes died away and his sight quickly cleared, he peered into the enormous smoldering crater that resulted from the explosion. Very little remained beyond Lief's charred and broken bow, a few shattered arrows scattered among the rocks, and tatters of a burnt and shredded cloak. There was no doubt in Ryson's mind that Lief's body had been obliterated by the blast.

"Lief!" Ryson shouted out in agony. He wanted to run to the center of the crater, but his legs would not move. Sorrow kept him frozen as his mind reeled against the loss of a friend.

Tabris smiled with brief satisfaction. She turned her attention away from the smoking rock and watched in glee at Ryson's torment.

"I guess I was faster then him after all," she taunted those that could hear.

The joy in her voice left Ryson beyond angry. His emotions boiled and he nearly shook with rage. He stepped away from Holli to create a clear path between him and the sorceress. He knew he could not reach Tabris at the moment, not while the storm barrier between them still stood, but he also knew that Lief was right. The sorceress could not maintain the energy shields forever. He would only have to wait for the moment they fell, and he knew he could avoid her blasts indefinitely, no matter how large she made them.

"You're not faster than me," he growled.

Tabris eyed the delver with caution and quickly placed her hands together. "Careful, delver. Do not do anything rash. No, I am not faster than you, but then again I don't have to be. At the moment, you can't reach me, and I will not waste time or energy on trying to strike you. I am aware of your speed. I am also, however, aware of the other elf's condition. She has many powers, it's true, but right now she has exhausted her energy. She is no match for me. And then, of course, there is this pathetic human by me. He is also your friend. How easy would it be for me to extinguish his life? How long can you stand there, delver? At what moment will you make a mistake and miscalculate what I might do. Eventually, I will strike you down, just as I struck down your friend."

Tabris paused for a moment as a devilish grin washed across her face. She took a quick glance at the reader on the ground in front of her and then toward Holli still on her knees. Her smile grew as she made an unholy offer.

"I make a deal with you, delver, one that I'm not going to give you much time to consider and no time to argue. I'm going to cast a single energy bolt spell at where you stand. You will be able to dodge it easily if you so desire, but that would leave us in the same position we are right now. If, however, you accept your fate, allow the bolt to strike you and end your life, I will spare your other elf friend. I will allow the female to walk

away. All you must do is surrender yourself to death. Do so and I will even let her escort
the reader out of the desert as well. Your life for theirs. It's a simple bargain."

Ryson tried to shout out, but Tabris would not listen. She made her offer clear. "There
is no argument. I am casting the spell now. You will not get a second chance. If you
dodge the bolt, I will kill them both. If you don't they will live."

Tabris pressed her palms together and began to whisper the words of the spell. She
watched Ryson intently, wondering if he would fight off the instincts to survive and
sacrifice himself, or if he would leap away and allow the next bolts she cast to strike
down his friends. The violet diamond returned to her hands as she prepared to finish the
spell.

With Tabris' attention so fixed upon the delver, Reader Matthew was able to struggle
up from his one knee. He kept his hands palm down against the cool grass-covered
ground of the oasis. He was already within the barrier that blocked Ryson from reaching
Tabris and so he had an unbounded path to the sorceress. With all his remaining strength,
he used his hands and his one leg to launch himself toward her. In that brief instant, he
caught her totally off guard as he wrapped his arms completely around her.

Tabris' hands were still locked together at her chest. With the reader's arms clamped
around her and his own body pressed against hers, she could not release her arms. She
had just finished reciting the spell but found herself completely unable to release the
magical energy that continued to swell between their two bodies.

"Release me you fool!" she screeched.

Matthew's arms only pulled tighter around her. "Not today. I told you faith was
stronger than magic and I guess I finally have the faith to defeat you."

Tabris struggled to free her hands, but she could not break the hold of the reader. The
glow of the violet diamond doubled then tripled. It began to swirl and soon it encased
both Tabris and Matthew. In one climactic burst, the energy imploded on them both.
Tabris' body was torn apart by the internal blast and the force threw Matthew heavily
against a large boulder.

With Tabris dead, the wind barrier collapsed and nothing stood between the oasis and
the delver. Ryson sprinted to the side of the reader and dropped to his knees so he could
lift his head from the ground. Something felt very wrong with Matthew's body, as if it
was much too yielding and offering almost no resistance to Ryson's grasp.

"Matthew? Can you hear me?" Ryson asked wondering if the reader could even
answer.

Matthew's eyelids flickered, but his sight seemed out of focus. His eyes rolled about
in all directions as if searching for a moving target behind a shifting screen. "Ryson?"

Ryson knew in that moment there was nothing that could save the reader, yet still he
wanted to help his friend. "Is there anything I can do for you?"

"Actually there is," Matthew offered in a hollow, raspy voice. "Tell Consprite that
faith is no fairy tale."

Ryson bit down on his lip, but managed to tell the truth. "I'm sorry. I can't tell him.
He's dead."

"Then I guess he already knows."

"I'm sure he does," Ryson replied through a hard swallow.

Matthew's eyes stopped rolling about. They fixed on a position in the sky and for one
last moment there was pure clarity in his vision. "Do you see it? Within the stars, not all
of them… but some of them are more."

Ryson turned his head skyward and looked into the twinkling mass of light overhead.
In this darkness, many of the stars seemed to almost mesh together into one mist-like
cloud that sparkled with purity. One point of light, however, appeared to separate itself
from the rest. It grew brighter, its intensity magnified. It looked almost as if the star was
floating down from the sky, gently lowered by a cool desert breeze.

Matthew's last gaze fixed upon this star and the moment before he died he recognized
the face of an old friend imbedded in this light. He could clearly see the features of the
interpreter that had died on Sanctum Mountain.

"Stephen?" Matthew questioned as a smile folded across his lips. "It is you! I am
ready."

Reader Matthew died with those words.

As if Matthew's death was a cue for his entrance, Enin appeared out of the darkness
and placed a hand upon Ryson's shoulder.

"His faith was strong as will be his reward," the wizard said.

Ryson wanted to cast off the wizard's hand, but instead he held to Matthew. He
managed to speak what he was feeling. "You could have prevented this, all of this."

"No, I couldn't. It was his time, as it was Lief's time. I've known that for many days
now. There is nothing I could have done to prevent it. The important thing is that they
met their fates in a way we could all only hope to—with courage, with determination, and
with faith. If you wish to be angry with me, you have the right, but don't diminish how
these two chose to meet their own end."

"I don't understand any of this," Ryson admitted in an angry response.

He could not continue. The sadness in his being was suddenly overwhelmed by a
familiar feeling, a feeling that was much larger in intensity than it had ever been in the
past. The dryness he had felt many time before washed over him in waves. It dove into
his core just as it flushed him of every emotion. This time, the sensation did not just
vanish. It stayed with the delver and it pointed out a being of great power that was now
laughing with hysteria.

Enin did not even have to ask. His own link to the magic allowed him insight into
what Ryson was sensing. The wizard's own spirit grew cold at that which was unfolding
before him. He had now realized that while he had indeed been using balance as an

excuse, that didn't mean the concept didn't exist. He knew the equilibrium had just
shifted.

"Baannat," Enin whispered. He quickly moved toward Holli and placed a hand upon
her forehead. He concentrated on opening a connection with the elf and let a fraction of
his own energy flow into her. It was enough to restore her.

"You should be able to walk now," Enin stated.

"What's going on?" Holli questioned.

"I'm not completely sure, but I would venture to guess that the magical energy that
once was Tabris now belongs to Baannat. Magical energy is never extinguished. It is cast
out in spells and then it is absorbed once more. He must have known what was going on
here and waited for Tabris' end. When she died, all of the energy that was hers became

his. I'm afraid he has used this cataclysmic event not only to steal her energy but to
expand his own capabilities. If I'm correct, he is now much more powerful than before."

"Is this Baannat the one that's basically your equal in power?" Ryson asked as he
slowly walked over to the two.

"Yes," Enin answered solemnly. "Unfortunately, this leads to a greater problem. A
problem I have been doing all I can to avoid, but I'm not going to avoid it any further."

"What is it you are going to do?" Holli asked.

"What must be done. In truth, I had already made my decision before I came here to
you. You were right, Holli. While balance is important, it must never be used as an
excuse, or as something to hide behind. And that is certainly what I have been doing. A
greater threat now exists, and it's a threat that must be dealt with."

"You just said he is much more powerful than before," Holli noted. "Is he now more
powerful than you?"

"If I am correct about what happened here, then yes, I would bet he is."

"Can you defeat him?"

"It is not my destiny to defeat him," Enin stated firmly. He took a moment to look into
Ryson's being and simply nodded his head. "But I believe I can weaken him, and I must
at least make that attempt. If I don't try, I would not be able to live with myself. I have
been fearful for too long."

"Hold on here," Ryson demanded. "What are you talking about? Now all of a sudden
you want to act? You're almost sounding like Lief and that's about as far an opposite as
you can get from what you have been saying all along."

Enin frowned. "The truth is we were both wrong. Lief would go too far, and I would
not go far enough. The best solution is as it always is, somewhere in the middle. Balance.
The very concept I've been using as an excuse not to act, it the very thing I now
understand."

"So you're going to fight another wizard because you think he is evil?" Ryson
pressed. "That doesn't sound like balance."

Enin sighed. "I have made many mistakes. I guess that proves I'm still human, and
that in itself is a bit of relief to me. I suppose I had to go through this. I was given a gift
of so much power, but I still have all the failings I had before. It's still possible for me to
lose my courage, even my faith. The important thing to remember is that even something
that is lost can be found. Mistakes are made. It's how we learn. Anyway, the truth is I
now see things clearer. You came here to stop Tabris because she was ultimately

responsible for what happened in Connel. That is only partially true. She certainly shared
in the responsibility, but now I can sense there was another hand shaping events."

"Baannat?" Holli wondered aloud.

Enin nodded.

"So he is responsible," the elf stated with no true surprise.

"I don't know how he hid it from me, but it is clear to me now."

"If you know you can't defeat him, then why will you do this?" Holli demanded.

"For the very reasons you came here," Enin responded. "I will have no regrets about
what I must do this night. I understand things better now. I hope you can also understand.
Destiny can't be stopped, but it can be slowed or sped up. We will turn things faster
today, so to speak. I think we already have. Things that might have waited, no longer
can." He paused only for a moment, wondering if he should say what he wanted to. In the

end, he decided to speak freely about what he was about to do and let the events play out
without deception or denial. He looked toward both Ryson and Holli. "What I do, I have
decided to do. What Linda does, is up to Linda. What you do, is up to you. Destiny and
choice, they can indeed go hand in hand."

With this, Ryson found concern exploding in his chest. "What do you mean Linda?
What does she have to do with this?"

"She must decide that for herself." It was all Enin said before he disappeared.

Chapter 25

Enin appeared outside the door of the Borderline Inn. He stepped quickly inside and moved to the bar that Linda was tending. It was very late, near closing and only a few patrons sat scattered about the room. It was a slow night anyway with most of the guard out of Burbon and involved in the attack on Connel. Linda was just about to begin closing up the bar when Enin called for her attention.

"You and I have to speak in private, we must do it quickly," he said with a graveness Linda was not used to.

Without hesitating, she directed him back behind the bar and to a small storage room filled with mugs, plates, and other assorted items used during the inn's daily activities. With a look into the wizard's face, Linda quickly assumed something terrible had happened, and she imagined the worst.

"What is it? Is Ryson alright, did something happen to him?'

"Ryson is fine," Enin began, "but he is the reason for my coming to you. The truth of the matter is that so much has already happened this evening. Eventually, you will come to learn all the details, but there isn't enough time for that now. What you need to know is that Connel has been freed and Tabris is no longer a threat. In fact, she is no longer alive. Your Ryson and Holli are alive and well in the Lacobian Desert, but I am afraid two of Ryson's close friends have also past. Lief and the Reader Matthew from Connel died in the battle with Tabris."

Linda found herself very torn at this moment and her head swam with the confusion of opposing emotions. She could not understand how Ryson became involved in a battle with Tabris in the Lacobian Desert. She knew this night was critical for many that called Burbon home, and the last six days moved at a snail's pace for her and everyone else that had a loved one in the town guard. Still, she only believed Ryson would be working to evacuate the people trapped in Connel. The thought of him fighting Tabris left her near breathless. While she felt great relief to hear that he had survived the confrontation, she also realized how the loss of his close friends must be affecting him at this very moment. She also wondered what else he might be suffering from for fighting magic was not something she could easily comprehend.

"You fought with Tabris?" she questioned after finally finding her voice. "I thought they were going to Connel, not the desert. How did Ryson end up in the desert? Why did he fight Tabris?"

"There will be time for greater explanations later," Enin stated flatly.

"But I don't understand…"

"I know you don't, but this is not the time for that."

"Can't you bring Holli and Ryson back here now?" she asked as she realized Enin was
not about to explain much of what happened. She hoped if Ryson was here he could
explain and she in turn could try to comfort the delver during his time of loss.

"I can, but we don't have the time for that either," Enin admitted. "There is something
of great importance I must ask of you and it's going to be hard to explain. It's not
something you're going to want to hear, but you must. You have a decision to make and
you need to know everything."

"What's going on?" Linda pleaded growing more frustrated with Enin.

Enin for his part leapt right to the area of his focus. He did not even attempt to guide Linda slowly into what needed to be said. He breached the subject with all the subtlety of a mountain shag at a sheep farm. "You once asked me what Ryson's destiny was, what it was I saw that allowed me to know that he would not fall at the hands of Tabris. I didn't tell you then, but I will tell you now. There is a magic caster, a dark creature—very powerful. At this moment, he is now even more powerful than me. It is Ryson's destiny to face this creature."

This news immediately and completely obliterated any relief Linda felt only moments ago. "What are you talking about? Is this going to happen now?"

Enin frowned but did his best to explain. "I hope it will happen soon, but this is beyond my control. This is more of a choice Ryson has to make. I can set the stage to a degree, but how it plays out and when, I can not say."

Linda now became visibly angry with the wizard's answers and made as much clear to him. "If it's his choice, why does he have to face this creature?! And it sounds like you're trying to manipulate something. What is it you're not telling me?!"

"I'm trying to tell you everything. It's important that I hold nothing back from you, but you're really not giving me a chance."

"Give you a chance? A chance for what? Ryson can't face something like that! That's insane! This is exactly what I told you couldn't happen, exactly why I asked you to tell Tabris to stay away from him. Tabris is dead and you come to me and tell me that something even more powerful than you is going to face Ryson. You can't do this to me!"

"It is not my doing, it is destiny."

"Don't hand me that, you just said he had a choice. If he has a choice, then it doesn't have to happen. You have to stop this!"

"Linda, calm yourself. I can't stop it, but I intend to help him, and I am here to give you the opportunity to help him as well, but you have to listen to me!"

"We…I can help him?" At that moment, Linda found the strength to calm her fears. She took a deep breath as she waited for the wizard to finally offer some form of explanation.

Enin took the opportunity to spell out the situation to the best of his abilities. "Yes, I am sure you can help him, but only if you listen to me. The problem is you will not like what you are going to hear. Baannat is the name of the magic caster. He is very evil. He has manipulated many things in the past few days, of that I am now certain. He has done this to grow powerful in magic and it looks like he has succeeded. For a while now, I

have known of his existence, and though I thought I was keeping him in check, I have
failed to do that. I have been hesitant to confront him, but I can no longer avoid that. I am
going to face him now and do everything in my power to weaken him. If I go alone, I
believe there is no way I can win. If you go with me, there is a great chance we can
succeed. That is the key, for it will give Ryson the ability to survive what he must face."

    "You want me to face this Baannat?" Linda asked with near amazement.

    "Not exactly, I will battle Baannat, but you will serve as the shield. As we have talked
about this before and you showed great reluctance to admit it, you are immune to magic.
If I bring you to Baannat, I can use you as an anchor, a reference point for me to actually
cast spells to defeat him. Because the magic does not affect you in anyway, you will
allow me to be present in Baannat's realm without really allowing myself to be

vulnerable to his attacks. It will seem to you as if I'm there, but I will not be in a physical
sense that would allow Baannat to use his magic on me. He will, however, be vulnerable
to what I can do."

Linda found herself torn once more, this time between the opportunity to help Ryson
and the situation she would have to face. "So we're going to go to this Baannat and I'm
going to be some sort barrier between you two? He won't be able to get to you through
me, but you'll be able to get to him?"

"That describes it fairly well. You will be the focal point between us. As long as you
remain conscious, he will not be able to get to me."

"Conscious? I thought you said I was immune to the magic. Why is there a chance I
might become unconscious?"

Enin looked directly into Linda's eyes and did his very best to make her aware of this
certainty. "This is very important and you must believe it to be true. Baannat will be
unable to hurt you physically in any way. He has created a realm for himself that consists
entirely of magic. You, however, are totally immune to magic. Everything he hurls at
you, you will cast aside. That one thing you must never forget. There is no way he can
cause you true harm. Because you will be in a place that is made of pure magic, he can't
even attack you indirectly. But that does not mean you can let down your guard or not be
strong. He will undoubtedly recognize your immunity very quickly. At that point, your
true struggle will begin.

"He might have been able to deceive me, and for that I'm truly sorry, but I still know
him. There is only one thing he can do that will affect you, but it will not be real. Just like
me, he is strong in all facets of magic, which includes illusion. He can create things that
look real, sound real, even feel real, but they are not. No matter what you believe is
happening, you must not accept it. Everything your mind sees will be of his creation. It
will be fake, it will be a lie, but I don't wish to lie to you, too. I believe he can create very
dark things and though they are not real, they might appear very real."

"But you're sure he can't harm me?"

"Only if you let him. If your mind begins to believe the attacks are real, you will end
up descending into the darkness of your own fears. You will lose consciousness and then
he will be able to attack me. At that point, I would be in danger. Rest assured if that does
happen, I will make sure you are returned here, but I will not be so lucky."

Linda grew silent and she turned away from the wizard to contemplate what was just
said to her. Enin offered a final explanation of why it was necessary.

"I want you to understand why I am here asking you to do this. There are two reasons. You have a unique power, extremely unique. You are not simply resistant to magic, it is much beyond that. You deflect it completely from your being. As long as you understand that, then I am not putting you in any danger. With you there, I believe I can critically weaken Baannat beyond his ability to mend himself. It is not my destiny to eliminate him completely. As I said before, Ryson must face him. That is your delver's destiny. For me, I need to this. I need to move beyond the excuses I have made in the past and I have to do what is right.

"The second reason is one that is much more personal to you. It is what I see and why I feel obligated to make this offer to you. Your destiny is hard to define. You are meant to be with Ryson and he is meant to be with you. It doesn't take a wizard to see that. It is, however, my plight to know that Ryson's fate is to face this being. And that is where we

come to you. I can not see a destiny in you. Perhaps it's because you have none at this
point, or maybe because you deflect the magic I simply can't see it. When we last talked
of this, you said your destiny was to help Ryson. I also see, however, that you feel in
many ways unable to help him on your own. I believe you will know in your heart what
you are supposed to do. As it is my choice to face Baannat, I believe you deserve the
same opportunity to do what it is you believe is your own fate.

"It's not going to be easy, and you must be sure of yourself or you will accomplish
nothing. But if you do believe this is what you must do, keep your strength and you mind
on your purpose, you will win. Of that, I have no doubt. You will also, however, carry
memories of what you will face for a very long time. They will not be pleasant. In the
end, it's up to you, your choice."

Linda turned and asked the one question she was afraid to hear the answer. "What if I
say no?"

"Then I will go alone. As I said, facing Baannat is now something I have to do. I have
been very good at coming up with reasons for why I shouldn't act, why I shouldn't help
others even when they are in great need. For the most part, they were excuses because I
was afraid. I really don't wish to interfere in people's lives, but I can't use that anymore
to keep from doing what I should do. This creature is evil and he is very powerful, more
powerful now because I was so easily deceived and so willing not to take any action.
Many people have been hurt because of him, and many more are now in danger. All the
reasons I used to talk about for not getting involved now seem small in comparison. I
need to do this for myself, to makeup for what I have done. Maybe I will get lucky.
Maybe I can weaken him enough and still escape. If I do that, I will succeed in giving
Ryson a better chance."

"If you can't weaken him at all, can Ryson defeat this creature?"

"I can not say. The delver has a unique inner power and has already done much of
what I would have guessed impossible. But in all honesty, I don't like his chances."

"And if I do go with you and you accomplish what we set out to do, how do you know
Ryson will be able to defeat him?"

"Again, I don't know for sure, but I know he will have a much better chance. We will
probably find out very shortly because I believe he will arrive in Baannat's realm shortly
after we do."

Here Linda became more than just concerned. A look of terror washed across her face

as she erupted back at Enin. "Ryson? You're bringing him? You just said you didn't
know when Ryson would have to face Baannat!"

"I don't, but I believe I know him well enough to know what will happen. Before I left
him in the desert, I said you had a choice to make and nothing more. He is a delver. His
feelings for you and his own curiosity will force him to find out what I meant. I left him
with Holli. She knows where I am at all times and she will undoubtedly reveal as much to
Ryson. He will follow my trail here. If you decide not to go, his journey will end and he
will face Baannat at some point in the future. If you go with me, he will follow. Holli has
the ability to send him forward to where we will be. I made sure of that many days ago."

"So if I go, then Ryson will end up right where I don't want him, facing this Baannat
creature."

"That is true, but if you think by saying no he will avoid that confrontation, you are
only fooling yourself. He will still have to face him eventually. If this happens now, he

will face Baannat with your help and mine. If he does it in the future, he will most
certainly do it alone."

Linda pressed with one more question, a question that would determine her own final
answer. "I'm going to ask you one question that I want a simple and honest answer to. Is
there anyway for Ryson to avoid facing this Baannat?"

"No."

Linda wished to be certain of this. "I need you to swear on all that you believe in that
that's the truth."

"I swear on everything I hold dear, Ryson will have to face Baannat. There is
absolutely no way to avoid it. I know it just as I knew Holli would come to me and ask to
be my guard. I know it just as I knew that Lief would die this day. I honestly don't know
how I know these things, and part of me wishes I didn't, but I do."

Linda no longer hesitated in her decision. "Then my choice is that I will go with you
and I pray that you are right."

Enin actually felt a wave of relief for he knew if he faced Baannat alone at this
moment, he would certainly die. With Linda, he had a chance. He was beyond grateful
for this, but he felt a greater need than ever before to alert her for what she would face.
"Before we go I must prepare you for what to expect. While Baannat has done his best to
hide his true being to me, there are things I do know for certain about him. Baannat is not
a creature natural to this land, nor is he a being of pure shadow. He is something
between, or perhaps a mix of both. He has substance, but not the kind you and I are
familiar with. He is not made up of simple flesh and bone, but he does exist in our
physical plain and thus can be attacked as well as destroyed. He is very powerful, even
more so as a result of Tabris' death. He has most certainly absorbed all of the energy she
once controlled. Just remember, no matter how much power and energy he now controls,
he can not physically harm you."

"I'll remember," Linda said while trying to focus on that very thought. "So what do we
do now?"

"We go together to face him. I will cast a spell and you will find yourself in a place
that will appear to be shrouded in a white mist. You will eventually see Baannat. Ignore
everything else you see or hear from that point on. Simply concentrate on the fact that
you are immune to his power. We should not wait. If you are ready, we should go right
now."

Linda nodded. "Let's get this over with."

#

Ryson felt two large gaping holes in his soul—one for the loss of Lief and one at the
death of the Reader Matthew. He did not wish to ignore their deaths, but the words of the
wizard left him unable to focus on little beyond his concern for Linda.

"What's going on? What did he mean by saying Linda has a choice? Do you know?"
Ryson demanded of Holli.

Holli did not hesitate in answering. "I do not know for certain. There is nothing he has
spoken of which I can rely on to give you a complete answer."

Ryson looked hard at the elf guard. "But you have spoken about Linda with Enin
before, haven't you?"

"Yes."

"About what?"

"She is immune to magic. It can not touch her in anyway. I've known of this since I
first met her. Enin also knows of this."

Ryson took a few moments to consider this. "Enin said he had to deal with Baannat
before he left here. Enin said Baannat is now stronger with the magic, but you and Enin
have talked about how Linda is immune to it." He stopped after that thought and looked
back toward Holli with dismay. "Do you know where Enin is now?"

Holli nodded. "He is at the Borderline Inn."

"Godson! How fast can you get us there?"

"I can get us there as I brought us here, but I can not move as fast as he does. Enin
returned most of my energy, so I have the power to get us there far faster than if you had
to travel on your own."

"Do it!"

                                    #

Linda found herself in a place that was nearly beyond her comprehension. Pure
magical energy surrounded her, yet her body could not be touched by it. In the simplest
of terms, she was hovering in a state of tactile suspension. She simply floated in this
existence, but the sensation went well beyond any similarities to floating in water or even
in air. It was more like wafting in the merest sliver of space between the flame and
smoke, never feeling the heat but knowing it was there. The moment she was placed in
Baannat's realm she lost all physical contact with everything around her. The feeling was
unnerving to her and she wrapped her arms around herself as if to confirm that her body
still existed.

She didn't understand how she could move in such an environment for there was
nothing for her to stand upon or press a hand against. Still, she was able to turn about in
all directions and move forward and backward with steps that fell upon this all
encompassing emptiness. She somehow knew she was no longer in the same type of
existence as back home in Uton. Her body was here, but she was not dependent on the
same needs. She wondered if she could feel hot or cold, wet or dry, because at the
moment she felt nothing about her at all.

The sensation of touch seemed to be the only sense that was deprived of her. She
could see into the white haze as she made out two figures in the mist with her, and she
believed she could smell a strange, almost electric scent as if she stood in a smoldering
depression where lightning had just struck. She could hear as well, and she recoiled at the
sound of a bellowing, insane voice, the voice she knew to belong to Baannat.

Baannat spoke between vicious giggles of uncontrollable laughter, but his attention
was focused on the wizard who was also now present in this misty place. "Hello, Brother.
I was wondering if you were going to come here right away, or if you were going to wait
until I actually committed some act you viewed to be worthy of your attention. Since
you've shown up so fast, I imagine you've figured out that I now possess all of the
energy that used to belong to that pathetic tart of a witch from the desert. This can't make
you happy."

Enin gave a quick glance over to Linda to ensure her condition before responding. "I
am very aware that you have taken the power of Tabris. I am aware of many things now,
and so there was no need to wait."

Baannat actually howled with delight. "And in being so newly aware, do you realize
what has truly been happening? Are you admitting how foolish you have been? I must

tell you, brother, I have been so amused by your antics. You kept coming here looking for some kind of obvious clue, as if I was stupid enough to leave a clear trail for you to follow. It was beyond entertaining to watch you looking for a direct link between me and Tabris, or me and Sazar. How pathetic. Do you really think I would be that obvious? You don't always have to use magic directly to get someone to do what you want. Sometimes all you have to do is set the stage for them, and they do it all on their own."

"I realize you have been interfering all this time, and yes I admit my mistake," Enin replied without shame.

Baannat, however, wished to relish the point. "Do you know how easy it was to make one of Sazar's goblins walk through one of your stupid Pinesway web spells? And then you kept talking to me about how your prized delver could sense me. I allowed that. It was necessary to keep him focused on what I wanted him focused on. When you knew Sazar was attacking Pinesway, I wanted the delver interested in this as well. I wanted him to spoil the serp's plans, which is exactly what he did. I even placed a river rogue in the town long before all of that happened to entice that elf friend of his to show up just at the right time. With Sazar defeated by the delver, it was simplicity to direct him to Tabris. Sazar was destined to grow in power. You're not the only one that can see fate, brother. I just know how to use it."

"And that will be your undoing," Enin said firmly. "Destiny is for the purpose of the individual that it belongs to. It is for him or her to experience, to learn, to grow. It is not for you to exploit."

"And yet I did anyway," Baannat countered. "Do you still not understand? I needed Tabris to choose a path opposed to you so that her energy could also grow in opposition. I needed her to join with Sazar so that she could be the source of his new power. Once he became a sufficient threat, it was clear he would bring other forces down against him and his ultimate defeat. But I knew it would not end there. Those that fought Sazar would then focus on Tabris and ultimately she would fall as well. When she did, I was waiting to grab everything she had. All of that loose energy just there for the taking. I have it now, just like I wanted."

"It was not Tabris' destiny to become evil," Enin shot back. "That was her choice. You may have benefited by it, but you were simply lucky. Remember, luck can be changed."

"So you do not wish to give me proper credit?" Baannat asked.

"Credit? For Tabris' ill-advised decision? No, you earn no credit there. She made that
choice of her own will and she has faced the consequences of that act."

"And now are you here to tell me of the consequences I face?" Baannat chided the
wizard.

"No, I am here because of my own choice, of my own decision. Your action did not
bring me here on its own. In the end, I realized I would no longer try to hide from what I
am, just as you hide in the shadows of your mist."

"You think I hide from you?" Baannat seethed with hate. "I used the mist to cover
myself only so that it would continue to confuse you. It was part of the game and nothing
more. The game is coming to an end, so I will indulge you and let you see me for what I
am."

Baannat's figure seemed to almost solidify out of the misty white shadows that
covered him. His full features came into focus just as his angry growls turned once more

into a maniacal laugh. The long thing fangs that jutted from his cat-like muzzle glistened
in the clearing mist. He stood on hind legs that were curved deeply and bent on two
separate joints, but his arms were long and straight. His hands were like the thick heavy
paws of a tiger with thin razor claws. His eyes glowed green with deep black irises, and
bent whiskers drooped from the balloon like cheeks that extended his muzzle. His body,
however, did not match the cat-like appearance of the rest of him. A dark brown cloak
covered a twisted, shifting mass. There appeared to be no solidity to his center, as if his
shoulders, chest, back, and pelvis were made of nothing more than melting taffy. His core
trembled with waves from each cackle, like the surface of a pond disturbed by the
churning oars of several boats.

"Is this supposed to frighten me?" Enin asked without a hint of surprise. "I've
suspected all along that you were nothing more than a slink ghoul. You could shadow
your form, but you could never truly hide your basic instincts. Each time we talked I
sensed more of what you were. I have enough of an understanding of the dark realm to
know the kind of creatures that are spawned there."

"Congratulations," Baannat answered sarcastically. "You should also know that my
physical prowess exceeds yours. You can not match me in magic and now you can be
assured you can not match me in physical battle."

"If it's that simple, why don't you just get rid of me once and for all?" Enin dared the
dark creature. "Use your new found magical advantage to obliterate me, or show me the
strength in your arms and the sharpness of your claws and kill me with one quick strike."

"If I wanted to, rest assured you would be dead already," Baannat answered with a
twisted grin that wrinkled his whiskers even further. "You've always amused me and I
like being amused."

"The time for your entertainment is coming to an end. I have come here so that one
way or another, this will be our last encounter."

"But once again you did not come alone." Baannat took a quick glimpse over at Linda.
He did not recognize her, and that bothered him greatly. Still, he sensed no great magical
energy in this woman and he scoffed at her presence. "I am surprised, however, that you
bring this human with you. I expected the elf you've been training. I would have bet you
might have thought the elf's assistance might have leveled out the imbalance that now
exists between us. You would have been wrong, but that was my guess."

"It does not matter who I bring," Enin responded hoping to keep Baannat's attention on him and away from Linda. "I am the one that will bring you to an end."

"You? I thought it was the delver that was supposed to take care of me? What happened to his destiny?"

Enin did not wish to discuss Ryson, especially in front of Linda, and he turned the conversation back at his nemesis. "You were the one that scoffed at that destiny. You even came out and told me I would have to face you eventually. As it turns out, you were right. I do have to face you. It seems you know my fate better than I."

"It is not your fate to just to face me," Baannat giggled. "It is your fate to die by my hands."

"I do not think so, Baannat. Although I am not gifted enough to see my own destiny, I do not feel that it is yet my time. If anything, I feel more alive then I have in a very long time. For too long I have constrained myself, not daring to truly test my powers."

"This will be no test," Baannat growled with bitter hate. "No simple game this time as we have played in the past."

"Indeed, all the games are over, even the one I've played with myself," Enin admitted freely. "I've lived much too carefully and not taken my own advice. I have a choice just like the others in this existence. I choose not simply to be a bystander. I will not allow you to get away with what you have done. Many have suffered needlessly just so you could obtain the power you craved. I choose not to be afraid. The power that has been gifted to me is great and I have been hesitant to use it. I've worried about becoming too involved and excused my inaction by convincing myself it would only be interference in the lives of others. I know now that was only weakness on my part. Most of all, I choose to use my gift to help others. Right now I can think of nothing I could do more to help this land than to rid it of you."

Baannat was about to laugh, but he turned his head and snuck another glance toward Linda. "You seem almost confident you can beat me. At the same time, you know I am now more powerful than you. Why is that?"

"The elf that I am training once told me that the battle doesn't always go to the strongest," Enin replied.

"That is true." Baannat admitted while continuing to glare at Linda's form in the swirling mist. "Some times it goes to the better prepared. How have you prepared for me in such a short time, and what does this woman have to do with it?"

"I'm sure you'll figure that out eventually," Enin offered without giving further details. "Until then there are some spells of my own that I've always wanted to try. I wouldn't dare back at my home as I might obliterate the town I live in. But I'm not really too concerned if that happens here, so I guess I'm free to give them a try."

Baannat heard Enin's words but his attention was now fully on Linda. Enin took advantage of the opportunity. He placed his hands far apart, extending both arms across their full width. He mouthed a few words and two snow white rings appeared near his hands, one at each palm. He quickly threw his arms together, clapping his hands and the rings together with great force directly in front of him. The white magic exploded into thousands of tiny jagged stars all about the size of a fingernail. They shot toward Baannat with great velocity, so fast in fact, they appeared like small lightning bolts darting through the space between them.

Baannat did not have time to cast a counter spell and the vast majority of the shrapnel

imbedded itself into his body. He growled in pain, but then shouted a spell of his own.
Two white hot circles dropped about his body and began to swirl around him. The jagged
pieces of magic shards began to melt into his body. He quickly turned his own hands
toward Enin. The circles of magic then rode down his extended arms and unfurled into
two long spears. The pulsating javelins flew toward the wizard but they made no impact.
They passed right through him as if he was not there. Baannat understood almost
immediately.

    "You are a coward and a fool!" Baannat screamed. "You chose to split your being and
hide behind this woman in the walkway of existence as she exposes herself. But you can
only use her to reach me as long as she lives, and that ends now."

    Baannat cast another spell and the two white circles that encircled his arms erupted
into cascading flames that burst over Linda's entire body. He let the flames roar into an
inferno until Linda's body was no longer visible through the white plasma that now

surrounded her. When he ended the spell, this time Baannat could not fathom what he
saw.

"She lives? What games are you playing, brother? Are you wasting your energy
shielding her against my power? You could not hope to continue such folly for long."

Throwing his arms in the air, Baannat called for another spell and this time a wave of
energy exploded from over his head. It rushed toward Linda like a tidal wave of immense
proportions. It flooded his intended target with such fury that the very mist that made up
this realm shook with violence. Once more, Baannat was left gaping in disbelief at what
he saw.

Enin took advantage of Baannat's dismay and hurled his own magical spell at the
demon. He waved a single hand in a ring over his head and a large circular blade
appeared with hundreds of razor sharp teeth at its edges. It spun with near unfathomable
speed and Enin hurled it at the slink ghoul with all his power. The blade sunk deep into
Baannat and exploded at his core just as the ghoul roared with anger and frustration.

"This can not be!" Baannat screamed. "You should not have the energy to defend this
woman and still attack me with such power. Unless…"

Baannat waved his hands and called for a force barrier to protect him from further
onslaughts from Enin. He then turned to Linda and whispered a simple spell of light. A
small beam of yellow broke through the misty fog, but it would not shine upon Linda.

Baannat started to laugh again which quickly turned to an angry bellow. "You found
one that is immune! That explains it all. She has agreed to assist you and so you can use
her as both a shield and an anchor."

"Now I suppose you are deserving of congratulations," Enin mocked the dark spell
caster.

"And how long do you think I would allow this to continue?" Baannat challenged. "I
can not harm her with magic, but I do not need magic to kill her. She is a human and easy
prey for me. Once she is gone, you will have to face me on your own."

Linda felt more than a twinge of fear as she saw Baannat's eyes focus on her with evil
intent. As he crouched down with spit cascading through angry snarls, she felt more
vulnerable than she ever had before. Even when she saw the magic flame or the tidal
wave rush toward her, instinctively she knew it could not harm her. Now, however, she
was no longer certain if she was truly safe.

The claws sprung out of Baannat's fingertips as he leapt toward Linda and she braced

herself for searing hot pain. It never came. When Baannat got within reach of her, a burst
of energy exploded between him and Linda and flung him backward like a rag doll tossed
from a baby's crib.

"Did you think I would actually take the chance of sending her here without physical
protection?" Enin asked. "I told you I knew what you were. Of course I also knew it was
only a matter of time before you tried that. She is well shielded against physical attacks."

Baannat roared with anger. "You have not the power to shield her and attack me as
you have! What trickery is this?!"

"Come now, Baannat," Enin ridiculed his nemesis. "Think about it. Do I have to really
spell it out for you? The shield does not require more than a fraction of energy. I only
have to use enough of my magic to protect her from you physically, not magically. She is
her own protection against magic. The truth of the matter is you are doomed."

Flailing his arms in swinging motions at his sides, the wizard sent a spell of a windspin toward his opponent. A small tornado of fierce power struck at the ghoul, but it disintegrated in a blaze of cackling energy.

Spitting toward the wizard now, Baannat made his own proclamation of the situation. "You are still weaker than I am. Even if I can't harm the woman, I can protect myself from your attacks. The shield I now wear will cancel any spell you cast and I can wait until she tires. She can not stay like this forever. Eventually she will need rest. I only need patience now."

"Patience would work if I allowed you the time," Enin countered. Utilizing his greatest effort, the wizard placed all of his focus on a spell of pure power. He threw his hands outward as he whispered words of a higher level of consciousness. He embraced the borders between existence, between light and dark, life and death, good and evil. He allowed the thin layer of separation between these concepts to grow into a greater magnitude of enlightenment. Black magic was that energy fueled of change and it could become a spell of ultimate power. Spinning his palms outward, he centered this bolt of pure force directly at Baannat's being.

A thick shadow engulfed the ghoul and though it could not touch him through the slink ghoul's own shield, it battered the very essence of his energy. Baannat could feel the very fabric of his power being decimated by the endless turmoil inherent in Enin's spell. Such was the strength of this one spell that the demon quickly realized his own existence might actually be in peril.

"You insane fool!" the ghoul cried out. "I can deflect your spell, but not indefinitely. The cataclysm of our two powers absorbing each other will deteriorate us both."

"Is this supposed to stop me?" Enin demanded. "I came here to weaken you, and I will succeed, even if it costs all that I am."

"I will not allow this!"

"You have little choice. You can't attack me as long as I remain out of your reach. I, however, can assault you as long as I use my friend as the conduit she has now become. She serves now as both a shield and the sword against you."

"Then I will remove her at all costs!"

#

After what felt like an eternity to Ryson, he and Holli finally appeared at the front of the Borderline Inn. The streets were dark and empty, but a few lights burned within the tavern. He raced through the door hoping to find Linda behind the bar. He saw no one. No customers, no Enin, no Linda.

"Linda?!" the delver called out as he raced through the back rooms and kitchen.
Again, he found no one.

"The door wasn't locked, but no one's here," he said more to himself then to Holli
who had now entered the main room of the establishment. "She usually locks up, so she
should still be here."

Holli took a long moment to make her own assessment of the room and realizing the
inevitable, she reached out with her feelings to locate the wizard.

"She is gone. We are too late."

Ryson turned with both dread and fury toward the elf. "What do you mean?!"

"Enin is no longer here, no longer in this plane of existence. He is with Baannat but
not completely. He is somewhere between the two realms, but his consciousness is

certainly focused on the evil creature, of that I'm sure. There's only one way he could
accomplish that. He would need an anchor point. Someone would have to be in Baannat's
realm that is allowing him to make contact with the creature. It has to be Linda. She is
immune to the magic, so Baannat must be unable to attack her."

"You have to stop this!" Ryson demanded. "If you know where he is, you can tell him
to send Linda out of there!"

"I don't believe I could get that message to him," Holli revealed.

"Try!"

Holli nodded as she closed her eyes. She focused on her link with Enin and made
every possible effort to create a line of communication. With every ounce of her
consciousness, she tried to force her thoughts through space and time to reach the wizard.
Nothing.

"I can not reach him."

"This is insane! Linda can't survive this. We have to do something."

"What can we do? It is not like they are just outside this inn. They are beyond us."

This one comment leapt out at Ryson and gave him hope. "Are they? Are they beyond
us, Holli?"

"What do you mean?"

"You can reach them, can't you? You can cast a spell that would bring us to Baannat's
realm. You know how to get there."

"I would be putting you in great danger. This is not like fighting a shag or an army of
goblins. This creature is immensely powerful."

"I can't just let Linda be in there alone."

"She is immune to the magic, you are not."

"I don't care. I have to be there."

Holli hesitated for only a moment and then through the line of communication she had
tried to forge only moments ago, she got her response from Enin.

Send him! Alone!

                    #

Keeping his own magical shield intact to fend off Enin's attack, Baannat garnered the
remainder of his energy to focus on Linda. The white circles of power rotated over his
head as he whispered words of ancient evil. The white magic turned gray and though it
could not touch Linda it began to swirl around her.

Shadows grew in the pale misty fog. They spun in all directions and the twisting spin
of gray made Linda even more unsteady in her surroundings. Slowly, the gloomy chaos
around her began to take actual shape and form. More color became prevalent as Linda
witnessed the insipid haze dissipate into clear horizons. Three very different
environments came into focus—one of a barren desert, one of a mountain top, and one of
a lush forest. The three scenes continued to sway around her, shifting and changing their

location relative to her own position. With each moment that past, the detail of each place
grew more vibrant and very soon each came alive with moving nightmares of terror.

In the desert scene that flashed before her, she saw an army of mutated insects
swarming toward her. The bright sun highlighted their sickening features as they skittered
over gritty, dry rock. The swarm included insects she thought she knew and horrid
creatures she could not describe. They flew, they crawled, they leapt, and they slithered
forward in a sickening motion of unorganized chaos. Almost immediately, they were

upon her, and just as she could actually feel the hot sun baking her skin, she experienced
the painful bite of misshapen ants and piercing sting of scorpions. Her flesh felt as if it
was going to disintegrate away in this agonizing attack.

Just at nearly every insect had reached her body, the desert scene washed away into
the background and she found herself upon the side of the mountain with its peak at the
forefront of her vision. The ground was steep and rugged. There were no trees, only rocks
of varying size. At the start, all was peaceful and she felt a wave relief from the removal
of the insects. Her relief would not last as the peace and tranquility were immediately
shattered by a thunderous explosion. The ground beneath her split and it seemed as if her
body fell into a wide fissure.

She did not sink below the surface. Linda's arms, chest and head remained above the
ground, but her legs and hips were below the surface and she could not pull herself free.
The echo of the blast faded in her ears, but the thunder returned in a rolling, swelling tide
that grew louder with each passing moment. She looked up to the peak of the mountain
and saw a swirling cloud of brown dust coming right for her.

At first her cheeks were stung by the impact of small pointy rocks and pebbles. The
dust seemed to swallow her entire body and she coughed at the taste of dirt and debris in
her mouth. Soon the sting on her face turned to much harder collisions of hand-sized
stones that bounced down from the mountain and struck her arms and chest. She felt as if
she was being beaten to death by a thousand angry fists that struck all about her upper
body.

Soon after, she felt pressure increase on her legs and waist. She looked down into the
fissure and realized it was filling quickly with dust and dirt. Now, she felt the bottom half
of her body being crushed but she could not pull herself free. The rocks and dirt began to
accumulate around her middle. The pile of debris continued to rise up her chest. Soon her
arms were completely buried just as the top of the mound reached her chin. She tried to
scream but could only cough out a cry. The dust began to fill her mouth as she was
drowning in dirt.

Once more, the scenes shifted. The mountain faded away into a forest of lush green.
Linda's body fell limp as she felt the pressure of the dirt freed from her body. The
overwhelming swing of sensations, however, left her grasping for breath. Terror gripped
her mind as she peered into the trees around her and wondered what waited for her here.
She would not have to wait long for an answer.

The trees themselves bent down over her. Thick, wooden branches wrapped around
her arms and legs and pulled her high into the air. In the blink of an eye, she went from
the forest floor to a point well above the surrounding treetops as several tree limbs
stretched high into a deep blue sky. She looked down in sheer terror, realizing a fall from
the distance would leave her body crushed and broken.

The tree limbs that held her aloft began to swing and sway in an uneven pitch. As the
horizon appeared to roll back and forth all about her, Linda began to feel queasy in her
stomach. The fact that she had no control over her own motion and that all of this
movement occurred apparently high above everything else did little to calm the sickness
growing within her. She tried to shut her eyes to the tumultuous scene, but every time she
did, she heard the crackling snap of branches below her. Her growing fear of falling
forced her to reopen her eyes to ensure the branches that held her remained intact.

Enin continued to press his spell upon Baannat, but he stole a glance toward Linda and realized her mind was under the assault of an illusion. He could see the torture painted on her face as tears streamed down her cheeks. He watched as she opened her mouth over and over again to scream only to clamp her jaw shut before she could make a sound.

"Linda!" Enin shouted out. "What you see is not real! It is an illusion in the space around you. He can't hurt you physically, but he can alter the appearance of your surroundings. Whatever you think is happening to you is only in your mind. Magic can not touch you, but that doesn't mean you can't see it. But whatever surrounds you is only a shadow of a false image."

Linda could hear Enin's words, but only barely. The limbs had dropped her and she was falling through the air at tremendous speed. First, she broke through the top branches of the surrounding trees and the leaves and thin branches split and ripped as her body plummeted past them. She then passed into the thicker limbs and these would not bend or break. Her body bounced off of these with heavy thuds. Back and forth, left and right, she tumbled through the thick branches like a ball being swatted by a thousand paddles. Very quickly, she could no longer focus on which direction was up or down. She believed the ground was close and she wondered how long it would take before she met the bone crushing impact and how it would feel.

With that thought and with Enin's words ringing in her mind, she grabbed on to a substantial realization. Although she believed she could feel the crack of the limbs against her body just as she felt the sting of the insects that attacked her or the impact of the rocks battering her body, it no longer made sense. Had she truly fallen from that height and struck so many tree limbs, she would have already been torn apart and unconscious. Her arms and legs would be broken and paralyzed and yet she could still wave them within this downward fall.

"I haven't hit anything!" she screamed. "I'm not even falling."

She shut her eyes again and this time kept them closed despite what she thought she heard. She focused on a spot of inky blackness and let it expand across her mind. She blocked out all other sensations, she even hummed to herself to help drown out the sounds of the illusion. Slowly, the sensation of falling faded away and she found herself rooted in the same suspended position she was in when she was first brought to this place.

"That's it!" Enin shouted again. "Take hold of your reality. He can not hurt you! Keep telling yourself that."

At that very moment, Ryson appeared in the same misty paleness of this place. With his first appearance, he found himself overwhelmed with the environment. He could see, but only three figures. Everything else was nothing more than a misty fog. He could hear, but the sounds he was so used to were absent. There were no voices in the background, no insects buzzing or animal calls off in the distance, no rushing sound of the wind or running water of a far away river or stream. He could smell but again the ever present scents of Uton were gone. They were replaced with the unequivocal smell of the magical energy. He could move, but without anything around him to act as a marker, he could not judge how fast he was moving.

The senses of a delver were all much more receptive than a human or even an elf. In this place, Ryson's senses were completely awash with the extraordinary. Just as Linda had to block out the illusions that assaulted her to regain her sense of reality, Ryson now

had to readjust his own senses so that they might cope with the complete strangeness of
these surroundings. As he focused on what he could see, he placed all of his attention on
Linda and in her he found an anchor for his own consciousness.

"Linda, are you alright?" the delver called out.

Linda heard his voice and at first wondered if it might be another mind attack by
Baannat. Still, she could not resist and opened her eyes. The three scenes of shadowy
illusion still swayed all about her. She focused all of her energy on brushing these images
aside and peering into what was really there.

"Ryson?" Linda replied. "Where are you?"

"I'm over here."

She focused on the sound of his voice and slowly his body came into view. She felt at
first a wave of relief to see him, but then it turned to a shiver of fear as a new scene
appeared around the delver. It included monsters and dark creatures beyond her ability to
describe and they stalked her love with hateful intentions.

Enin realized at once that the true moment of fate for all of them had now arrived.
None of them could afford to be weak.

"Not now!" the wizard demanded. "The two of you must face your foe! Linda clear
your mind and remember what you see is not real. Ryson, if you wish to save Linda you
must defeat Baannat. Otherwise, we all die here now!"

Ryson saw the look of terror on Linda's face but also sensed an immediate danger
behind him. Regardless of that danger, he wished to run toward Linda and help her, and
an overwhelming instinct brought his hand to the hilt of the Sword of Decree. As he
pulled the blade free, an understanding of what he faced in this place came across him
with unerring force. The blade did not glow, for in this place there was no natural light of
the sun or the stars. Still, the weapon remained a magical talisman and it held the power
to reveal an all encompassing knowledge of a certain time or event. The sword gifted
Ryson with the understanding that Baannat was causing Linda's terror and the dark
magic-caster was the true threat to them all.

Swirling about and facing the slink ghoul, Ryson growled with authority. "Leave her
alone!"

Enin continued to focus on his spell that was draining the magical power from both
him and Baannat. His own energy was pouring into the power of the attack just as the
ghoul's magical energy was being drained by the defensive shield. Even with that, he
knew his own level of power remained very high and thus Baannat's would be even
greater still. He allowed himself a moment to yell a warning to the delver.

"He is still very powerful and very dangerous, Ryson! Be careful!"

Baannat seethed with hate and scorn. "So this is the precious delver that is so special. Tell me, brother, what should I do with him? Should I blast him into a thousand pieces or burn him into a cinder?"

Ryson said nothing, he only steadied himself for an attack. He bounced evenly on the balls of his feet as he did everything in his power to attune himself to the strange realm he now stood. He held the sword in front of him with both hands just below the hilt and he prepared to move in any and all directions.

"Neither of you answer?" Baannat screamed. "Then I will decide myself."

Baannat mouthed a few words strange to Ryson's ears and then threw his arms toward the delver. Two pure white rings of power erupted from the ghoul's fingertips and shot

out toward Ryson like shock waves from some massive explosion. The force blast moved
with such speed it created its own rumble of thunder.

Even being prepared for any attack, Ryson was surprised with the speed of the assault.
He leapt as high as he could at the very last possible instant and avoided the blast by the
thinnest of hairs. The concussion of the explosion nearly sent him tumbling head over
heels as he landed, but he caught his balance and danced away to Baannat's side.

Enin found this more than unsettling. That strike was simply too close and he knew
that Baannat had great reserves of power. Ryson would not be able to dodge each spell
for long. It would only take a matter of time before Baannat figured out how to offset the
delver's speed. If he managed to strike Ryson with a spell, the results would be beyond
cataclysmic. Linda would see Ryson fall and she herself would spiral into the chaos of
Baannat's illusions. Everything they had gained to this moment would be lost. He had to
do something more to help the delver survive.

As if blessed by divine inspiration, Enin immediately thought of a way to assist the
delver without tipping his strategy to the dark ghoul.

"Ryson, do you remember how to fly?" Enin yelled out quickly.

Ryson kept his focus on Baannat but shouted back his own reply. "How to what?
What are you talking about?"

"To fly! Do you remember how to fly?" Enin insisted.

And in that moment, Ryson understood. "Yes!"

Enin restrained his assaulting spell just long enough to cast a new spell toward the
delver. He focused on the exact spell he had cast back in Dark Spruce Forest that allowed
Ryson to enjoy the sensation of flying, but this time he would make the spell last
indefinitely. Just as two rings of white magical energy spun about his wrists, he threw his
arms forward directly at the delver, and the two circles of power twisted outward.

Ryson saw the spell coming toward him, and unlike his reaction to Baannat's spell, he
raced toward this one. He allowed the energy to strike him at his center. As Enin's energy
hit the delver, the air shimmered about him and everything in this realm slowed to a
snail's pace to the delver's perception. Ryson spun about and watched as the slink ghoul
moved as if encased in molasses. Each turn of Baannat's hand, every thrust of his arm
appeared as if caught in a dream of slow motion.

Disregarding Enin's spell, Baannat could not understand what had happened, and he
did not care. He focused the fury of his power on the delver, knowing that if he could
defeat him he could finally turn the battle in his own favor. He cast spell after spell, firing

flames and bolts of sheer energy in nearly every direction. The ghoul held little back and
plastered the entire area with spells of devastation. His realm shook with the ferocity of
his attack as he showered every inch of space with spells of vicious intent.

Ryson, however, moved with uncanny speed, quickness well beyond that of even a
full-bred delver. And it was not just speed with which he moved. He leapt and danced
away from danger as if he knew ahead of time where a spell would explode. With his
augmented perception, he watched the very fabric of Baannat's spells unfold as if
restrained by an unseen hand. Even as each spell exploded around him, Ryson maintained
an awareness that far surpassed anything that the dark ghoul might possibly anticipate.
For the delver, dodging these blasts of power was nothing more than dodging feathers
being cast at him by a slow breeze.

For his part, Enin returned his focus to his own spell. The constant discharge of the
black facet of magic, the power of change, began to diminish his own vast reserves. He
actually began to feel empty as the energy within him began to decline. Although
Baannat now exceeded him in power, the ghoul was also expending much more magical
energy. Both of them would soon reach a point where they would actually face the
prospect of exhausting themselves.

Baannat, however, appeared unfazed by the sheer volume of energy he was
expending. Instead, he seemed bent on destroying the delver and infuriated with each
failure. Frustration was growing within him and this simply spurred on the use of even
more of his power. He continued to cast spell after spell as if he could not believe the
delver could possibly survive another instant. When the ghoul watched in disbelief as
Ryson simply dodged every assault, he raged on with even more spells.

Even as this pale realm of pure magic erupted with raging assaults, no one within it
was touched by any of Baannat's wrath. The delver outmaneuvered every spell, Linda
was immune to the magic, and Enin simply was not physically there. The fury of the
ghoul washed over empty space and the cast magic began to spread out into the
emptiness of this place.

Realizing that vast amounts of loose magical energy was now expanding the borders
of Baannat's creation, Enin made one last gamble to end the threat of the evil magic
caster. The wizard ended his own spell of attack and turned his attention to the
dimensional properties of this environment. He called on his understanding of existence
and cast a new spell that would open a rift in this place. A gateway to a dark plane
opened at the very heart of this realm and the pale mist began to gravitate to the fissure. It
seemed almost as if the very essence of Baannat's sanctuary was now being consumed.

Enin called out one last time to Ryson. "Do not let him escape through the rift. He can
not transport himself away without taking all of us with him. This place we are in is
bound to him. He can, however, escape through the gateway."

"Then why did you open it?!" Ryson shot back angrily.

"You will see," was Enin's only reply.

Almost as if on cue, a wave of dark creatures beyond Ryson's imagination bounded
through the hole that Enin had opened. Monsters of every size swarmed into the pale
space. They ignored Ryson, Linda, and Enin, but they set upon Baannat with ravenous
hunger. The tore at the ghoul—bit and clawed at every opening. With each swipe, with

each bite, they stole more and more of Baannat's power.

"No!" the ghoul screamed. The dark wizard attempted to make a path to the rift. He
pushed aside those monsters that continued to crowd over him. With one massive burst of
energy, he cast them aside and raced through an open path to his one hope of escape.

Ryson would not allow it. He covered the space between them in less than a heartbeat
and stood defiantly between the ghoul and the gateway. He held his sword in front of him
to block any attack.

Sneering and spitting, the ghoul's eyes narrowed on the delver with hatred. "You will
let me pass. I will kill you all. I will kill you, the woman, and finally the wizard."

Ryson responded with a swing of the Sword of Decree. The enchanted weapon sliced
through the air and then through Baannat's malleable midsection. The ghoul was cleaved
in half.

The dark creatures that had entered this realm fell upon the remains further tearing the ghoul into shreds and feeding on the torn pieces. When there was nothing left, they leapt back into the rift and out of sight.

Staring into the fissure, Ryson viewed a land beyond description. For the first time in his life, he witnessed something completely foreign and felt no desire whatsoever to explore. He turned away as fast as he could.

With the realm they stood in now shuttering as if ready to break apart, Enin cast two spells. One quickly closed the rift and the second spirited them all away. The three of them were instantaneously brought to the Borderline Inn where Holli awaited.

Ryson ran to Linda who had fallen to the ground in exhaustion. He held up her head and called for her attention.

Linda appeared dazed as if looking far off into the distance. Her eyes were unfocused and her body mostly limp. Ryson shook her lightly and she finally came to. She looked about the room with a dazed expression and then into the face of the delver.

"Ryson? You're alright?"

"Yes, I'm fine. What about you?"

"Tired."

"Are you hurt?"

"No, I just need a moment."

Enin stepped slowly, almost painfully, over to them both. "She will be fine. Give her a few moments and she should even be able to stand."

"Enin…" Ryson began angrily, but then stopped to take a deep breath. When he continued, his tone remained bitter. "I don't know if I can ever forgive you for this, for bringing her there, for putting her in danger."

"She has a gift that would protect her."

"Protect her?" Ryson questioned, his anger growing once more. He wanted to stand and face the wizard, but he would not take his attention away from Linda. "I saw for myself, she was in pain. You're as responsible for that as Baannat was."

"No, he wasn't," Linda intervened. "I was. It was all an illusion and for a while I didn't understand that. The pain I felt was inside of me all the time."

"It was still pain, and it was still dangerous. He shouldn't have put you in that position."

Linda shook her head slowly and finally focused squarely into Ryson's eyes with a resolve of her own. "You have to forgive him because if you don't then I won't be able to forgive you. He gave me something I needed very much, something you have always been either unable or unwilling to give me—a chance to help you. Since I've known you, you have helped so many—saved so many. You've never stopped thinking about other

people first. Because of that, and because of what you are, it's almost impossible to be
able to help you. This was my chance to do that, maybe the only chance I'll ever have. I
can live with that now because I know that when you needed me the most, I was here for
you. Enin gave me that and I will always be grateful to him for it. If you don't forgive
him, it means you don't understand what that means to me."

"It was her choice," Enin added. "I also believe it was her destiny, though on that I
can only guess. She believed it was her duty to be there for you, her responsibility. She
did not want to leave you to face Baannat on your own. I did nothing to force her and
very little to convince her. Her decision was based entirely on her concern for you. You

can blame me if you like, but it would be a dishonor to her if you did not give her the
credit she deserves."

Ryson did not need Linda to take these kinds of risks to help him. He never expected
it of her. It wasn't necessary. It was enough that she accepted him for what he was and
was willing to share his life with him. That was enough to ask of anyone. Still, he could
not deny the courage it took to do what she did, and he could not deny the look he saw in
her eyes as she hoped he would grasp what this meant to her. If this was something she
needed to do, something that would bring them closer, he found it impossible to argue
further. Ryson could say nothing. He held onto Linda and allowed the anger to flee from
his soul.

Holli placed a hand on Enin's shoulder. "What about you?"

"I will be fine," Enin answered with a tired smile. "Baannat is gone and I am still what
I was, but perhaps a bit less afraid. I just need to go home and rest for a while."

"With me?" Holli asked somewhat hesitantly.

Enin's answer erased her concerns. "Yes, certainly with you, and the dogs of course."

Epilogue

Several days after his army was annihilated by the dwarves of Dunop, Sazar skulked
through a dark tunnel under Burbon with one thing on his mind, revenge. The delver had
defeated his plans on more than one occasion and the serp was now tired of losing to this
Ryson Acumen. It was the delver that helped save Dunop and brought a premature end to
Sazar's raid of the underground dwarf city, and it was Ryson Acumen that had thwarted
the serp at Pinesway. Losing Connel, however, was the last straw. He knew Ryson was
the first to enter the caverns under the city. Sazar saw what the rock beetles saw before
the dwarves killed them off. He knew Ryson led the way, and when the dwarves followed
the delver into Connel, Sazar's dreams of conquering the eastern lands died as well.

The more he considered what he lost, the angrier Sazar became. He had taken Connel
without losing a single minion. He removed the most trained soldiers and had the humans
ready to knuckle under to his will. The human Consprite was taking care of supplying
Tabris with test subjects for her spells. He had everything under control until that delver
appeared in the caves below Connel.

The serp could only guess what happened to Consprite and the vampire that protected
him, but for some reason he knew that Tabris was dead. He felt the power she gave him
being ripped away, and when it was gone, he somehow knew the sorceress had ceased to
exist. There was no point in returning to the desert to reaffirm his bargain with the witch.
At the moment, there was very little point in anything.

He no longer commanded an army. The horde of goblins he controlled was decimated
by the dwarves, the hook hawks shot out of the sky by the human cavalry. Only the one
giant shag that served as his body guard remained under his will, that and a small number
of razor crows. His riches were gone, his supplies hastily left behind in Connel. His
augmented power to control creatures at far distances died with the sorceress. Everything
he had obtained since coming to this cursed land was lost, and he placed the blame for
that squarely on Ryson Acumen.

There was little point in returning to what he was, a meager raider of outposts
scratching for survival. What point was there to gain control over a half dozen goblins
when he tasted the power of controlling a horde? Everything before him appeared
tarnished and this too fueled his hate for the delver.

With little incentive to do anything else, Sazar focused on this hate and vowed to gain

his revenge. He knew which town the delver called home—Burbon. When the dwarves
attacked Burbon back at the onset of the dormant season, they created several tunnels
under this town. He had discovered one that he hoped would prove useful one day.
Today, he decided upon a purpose for it. He walked within this tunnel now with a focus
on obtaining his vengeance.

Sazar used those few remaining razor crows under his power to scout out the streets of
Burbon and find where Ryson lived. He now knew of that location, and once they
reached the proper point, the shag would dig to the surface very close to that spot.

The shag could dig quickly, that was the only thing that saved Sazar in Connel. When
the dwarves flooded the interior of the city, the serp knew all was lost. His self-
preservation remained strong and he took to the dark streets with his large shag guard.
The rock beetles gave him a great understanding of the tunnels below the city before they

fell to the might of the dwarves. With that understanding, he ordered the shag to dig.
They reached the caves before the dwarves or the humans could find them and Sazar
escaped down a southern access tunnel.

Escape, however, was no longer on his mind. This time Sazar would use the shag to
reach the delver and then kill him. He didn't care how fast the delver was or how nimble.
The shag would catch Acumen in his home where he lived with his mate. Sazar would
use the human female to distract the delver and in the close confines of the house, the
delver would die. It would be a painful death. Sazar almost smiled at this thought, but any
delight ended there.

"I've been waiting for you," Sy said as he stepped out into the center of the dark
passage. He lit a torch so that they could all see equally well. "I'm sure you remember
me. I'm the captain of the guard here. You once threatened this town with destruction if
we didn't give you what you wanted. Do you remember that?"

Sazar hissed but said nothing.

"That always left me with a bad taste in my mouth," Sy continued. "You went on to
plunder a great deal of treasure from the dwarves because I didn't want to risk stopping
you. I guess I have my chance now."

Before Sazar could answer, another figure stepped into the new light of the torch.

"Hello Sazar," Ryson offered with no true emotion beyond disgust for the creature.
"What is it you're planning now?"

Sazar's eyes burned red with hate as they fell upon the delver. He found his voice
quickly this time. "I plan to have you killed! So nice of you to accommodate me by
showing up here. You will not be able to outmaneuver my shag in such close quarters."

"Are you sure your shag can defeat all three of us?" Ryson asked.

"Three?" the serp stammered aloud.

A third member of Burbon's protectors moved out of the shadows behind Sy and
Ryson. Sazar recognized her as the elf guard.

"I can see you know me as well," Holli offered, "but did you know that I am no longer
an elf guard? I now protect another and I do not leave his presence often. I am usually
wherever he is and that includes now."

Sazar was not given even a moment to fully understand what that meant. The true
meaning was spelled out to him immediately as the fourth and final member of the group
stepped forward.

Enin walked past the other three directly up to Sazar. "You are an evil creature," the
wizard said with both contempt and sadness. "You are responsible for much suffering and

that ends tonight. Did you really think I would be so naïve to leave this tunnel
unguarded? We knew you were here the moment you entered."

Even standing beside the great shag, Sazar now feared for his life. He understood the
power of this wizard and even the shag's physical strength was no match for that kind of
magical force. What Sazar did not notice was the shag showed no sign of agitation
whatsoever. It stood there with an empty stare simply waiting for the serp to order him
onward.

While Sazar seemed oblivious to this, Enin decided to make him more aware of the
situation. "Instead of worrying what I might do to you, you should be wondering why
your large friend hasn't shown any alarm to our presence. Take a look at him. The truth is

he doesn't know we are here. I am blinding him to us. He can't see, hear, or smell us. The only one he thinks is here is you."

Enin paused for a moment to allow the serp to take a good long look at his protector.

"Go ahead, order him to attack us," the wizard finally continued. "You'll just confuse him. There's nothing you can do that would remove the block I have on his meager mind. You might send him into a rage, but who knows what he might do. In his mind, there's no one here for him to attack, no one accept you. In fact, I would start to worry about that if I were you."

With that, Sazar suddenly found a new fear tearing at his twisted soul. "What do you mean?"

Enin found no true pleasure in this moment, but he wanted to make the situation clear.

"The shag can not see, smell or hear anyone else here but you. We are in a very narrow tunnel with no real path of escape. What do you think this shag would do right now if you suddenly lost the ability to control him? He looks hungry to me and I think serp is a meal he would accept."

"You would not…" Sazar began but fear ended his sentence.

"I would and I will. I will, however, give you a very small chance. You have a few moments to get out of this tunnel before I convince this shag he no longer has to listen to you."

Sazar did not waste any time arguing or begging for mercy. He turned and attempted to move off back toward the tunnel exit. Serps, however, are not agile creatures. His run was more of a shuffle and he made little progress.

Enin gave him more time than he first intended. As the serp moved beyond his sight down the sloping tunnel, Enin waved his hands in front of the shag. Two pure white circles appeared at the wizard's fingertips and then dissolved in front of the monster's face.

At first, the shag appeared dazed, as if waking from a long sleep. It peered about the tunnel trying to get its bearings. Finally, it sniffed the air. It caught a scent and turned about. Without delay, it bounded after the serp.

Enin watched the departing monster with a heavy sigh. This signified the true end for everything that had happened. All those that had played a part in the attack on Connel would face the consequences of their actions. It seemed almost as if each and every matter of importance had found a suitable conclusion—from Baannat's destruction to the dwarves restoring of their own honor. Everything appeared to be as it should, until he

thought of the delver and Ryson's own deliberations regarding what was right and what
was wrong. Ryson always seemed to have such a definitive measure of things and the
wizard wondered what the delver was thinking at this very moment. Enin turned to his
friend and asked the question outright.

"I need to ask you this, Ryson. Do you think I just did the right thing?"

Ryson looked down the tunnel. He knew the shag would catch Sazar, knew that the
serp would die. He then looked down at the ground and thought of Lief. He believed the
elf would have approved without hesitation, but the question was did he approve.

"Sazar came here on his own," Ryson offered. "He brought the shag with him. He put
himself in this situation, and I think we can all agree he didn't come here planning to do
anyone any favors. No one twisted his arm. All you did was remove Sazar's control of
the shag. You once told me that you can't keep people from their fate. I'm not entirely

sure about destiny and all that, at least not the way you talk about it, but I do understand
that you can't always escape responsibility. Eventually, it catches up to you. And in truth,
I think that's the way it should be. Sazar pushed the limits, and tonight it caught up with
him. The only one that gets blamed for that is him. I don't think it's a matter of approving
or disapproving of what happened here. I just accept it."

With that, Ryson thought of Lief again. He also thought of Reader Matthew, the old
man in Pinesway, and even Edward Consprite. None of them asked for the situation they
were placed in. Lief didn't want to be banished from his camp. Reader Matthew certainly
didn't ask to be sent to the Lacobian desert. The old man in Pinesway didn't want goblins
to attack what was once his home. Even Edward Consprite didn't ask for the events that
led to his removal as mayor—the return of magic to the land.

These were events beyond their control, but their actions to deal with these events
were not dictated to them. Each and every one of them made choices. Lief turned his
anger outward to the land and on to its inhabitants. He died fighting valiantly against an
evil sorceress, but Ryson wondered how much Lief had lost of himself before his own
end. Matthew courageously gave his life to save Ryson, and in the process reforged his
faith. The old man in Pinesway might be dead or alive, Ryson had no idea. He was living
in a dangerous place and that was his decision, but it was a decision based as much on
honoring his deceased wife as it was an unwillingness to accept other alternatives, other
paths to travel. Finally, there was Edward Consprite. He died when Lief's arrow pierced
his heart, but there was little left to save by that point. He had moved beyond a bitter and
angry man and became a deviant dealing death for those he blamed for his misfortune.
Ryson always found it difficult to believe that any creature deserved to die, but it was just
as difficult for him to believe Consprite didn't deserve his fate.

In the end, Ryson found it impossible to judge any of them. It was not his place.
Everyone can't determine the circumstances they face. To Ryson, most of it always
seemed like nothing more than blind chance. He never understood why one person was
forced to face so much adversity while another simply could glide through life without
having to face a single challenge. That never made any sense. He knew good people that
faced constant misfortune and people of lesser character that somehow found wealth
wherever they looked. It didn't seem fair and that always bothered him, it always would.

He then considered what Enin tried to tell them all, how everyone had a choice.
Maybe they couldn't determine the fortune of their circumstances, but they could decide
how to deal with it. He thought of his very own words and how often things came down
to simple matters of responsibility and acceptance. He told Enin he would just accept
what happened here this night and that is what he was determined to do.

11384693R00265

Printed in Germany
by Amazon Distribution
GmbH, Leipzig